"I never pegged you for a New-Ager."

Diana stifled a shriek and whirled, dropping the book. "You startled me," she said to the man standing there. Despite her shock, she noted his height (tall), his brown eyes (twinkling with humor), and his face (chiseled and incredibly handsome). The moisture evaporated from her mouth and sprang to her palms.

"I can see that." He had bent down to retrieve the book. "Hmm...*The Tarot Explained*." He straightened and offered it back to her. "Your aunt would be astonished."

Diana didn't take the book. Instead, she stared at him. Had they met? At the funeral, maybe? But then suddenly his voice and easy smile connected with her memory. "Oh, it's *you*," she said, at once recognizing Ethan Tannock. She couldn't help that her tone was unenthusiastic.

And what else would he expect, having walked into her house uninvited *twice*?

He had shaved and cut his hair, and although it added years to her estimate of his age—he was definitely mid-thirties—it did wonders for his looks. His shorn face was very attractive, with high cheekbones and a firm, square jaw. It made his eyes look bigger and darker, and his lips, which had settled into a sort of smirk, were no longer hidden by mustache overgrowth.

She swallowed hard, feeling suddenly at a loss in the presence of this tall, attractive stranger—who'd been in her house twice. Somehow now, especially in this small, crowded space, he seemed more intense, with more presence and confidence.

Other Titles by Colleen Gleason

THE GARDELLA VAMPIRE CHRONICLES
Victoria
The Rest Falls Away
Rises the Night
The Bleeding Dusk
When Twilight Burns
As Shadows Fade

Macey/Max Denton
Roaring Midnight
Raging Dawn
Roaring Shadows
Raging Winter
Roaring Dawn (2016)

THE DRACULIA VAMPIRE
The Vampire Voss
The Vampire Dimitri
The Vampire Narcise

THE MEDIEVAL HERB GARDEN SERIES
Lavender Vows
Sanctuary of Roses
A Whisper of Rosemary
A Lily on the Heath

CONTEMPORARY GOTHIC ROMANCE
The Shop of Shades and Secrets
The Cards of Life and Death
The Gems of Vice and Greed (2016)

STOKER & HOLMES BOOKS
(for ages 12-adult)
The Clockwork Scarab
The Spiritglass Charade
The Chess Queen Enigma

THE MARINA ALEXANDER ADVENTURE NOVELS
(written as C. M. Gleason)
Siberian Treasure
Amazon Roulette

THE CARDS
OF LIFE
AND DEATH

COLLEEN GLEASON

AVID PRESS

PROLOGUE

Damariscotta, Maine

H E CREPT SILENTLY INTO THE HOUSE, aided by the light of the full moon. It streamed though the windows like a beacon, casting everything with a film of blue-gray.

There wasn't a sound but the distant lapping of water against the lakeshore and the barest rustle of breeze through the trees.

Such a remote area.

So convenient.

He smiled to himself as he passed through the kitchen. Only hours before, the old lady had pressed tea and cookies and a delicious chicken salad sandwich upon him at that very table.

She'd been delighted to see him—and he'd actually enjoyed their visit quite a bit. Belinda Lawry was an interesting and amusing old woman, if not a little batty. People actually believed she could tell the future by looking at a deck of Tarot cards. Absurd, but entertaining nonetheless.

He'd humored her, of course. He knew how to charm old ladies. Especially when he needed something from them.

It was too bad things had to go this way, but a man had to do what a man had to do. His jaw tightened with determination and his fingers curled into their palms. Soon, his troubles would all be over.

A complacent smile on his face, he continued silently down the hall. When he caught sight of a shadow slinking from beneath a table, he crouched immediately to greet the cat in case it had the tendency to yowl at night-time visitors.

He'd made friends with it and its companion, and tonight he'd come prepared with tuna sandwiches in order to distract them.

Nothing could go wrong, for this was his one and only chance to set things in motion.

Crouching in the hall, he offered a sandwich to the cat. No sooner had he opened it from its plastic wrap than the second feline appeared, also interested in the delicious-smelling food.

He left them there, delicately eating their treat, and slipped into the old woman's bedroom.

Her soft snores told him she was dead to the world (he grinned silently at this appropriate metaphor) thanks in part to the doctor, who'd considerately prescribed a strong sleep aid. Not only was she deeply asleep, but her face was upright, and her arms safely beneath the blankets.

It was almost as if she were making it easy for him.

He moved quickly and with efficiency, snatching up an extra pillow next to her on the bed and shoving it over her face.

Belinda jolted beneath the onslaught, but he was kneeling over the blankets, pinning her in place as he pressed the goosedown pillow onto her nose and mouth...holding it, holding it... pressing harder, harder, *harder*.

Come on, come on, he thought silently, as the old biddy struggled and jolted beneath him like a fish out of water.

Then suddenly, she was still.

Breathing heavily, he held the pillow over her face a few more minutes just to be sure.

Then he slid off the bed, checked her pulse (none), replaced the pillow, and stood back to look down at her.

"Thanks in advance, Belinda."

His smile was cold and pleased as he strode from the room.

He paused only to scoop up the remains of the tuna sandwich bribes and dab the floor where they'd been with a damp paper towel. Then he walked out of the house without a second glance.

Though his hands were shaking a trifle, he was still smiling.

ONE

Boston, Massachusetts

DIANA IVERSON STRODE into her sleek office suite carrying a fresh, large coffee and her laptop case while thumbing through emails on her smartphone. Despite being exhausted, she had a confident stride that matched her jubilant mood.

"You did it! You won the case!" Corey, her receptionist, came around from behind the desk and gave Diana a hug.

"Thanks," she said, unable to hold back her own smile as she read an email over her receptionist's shoulder. "Dr. Merkovitz is just as pleased."

Extricating herself from Corey's exuberant hug, she set her computer case on the table and sank into one of the leather chairs in the reception area, sipping from her scalding coffee, scrolling through the emails on her phone.

"Merkovitz is a douche," said her outspoken assistant Mickey Luciano—and also the best paralegal with whom she'd ever worked—as she emerged from the depths of the suite. Perching on the edge of the table next to her boss, she crossed her arms over her middle as Diana set her phone aside. "He probably didn't show his appreciation at all, did he? Dickwad probably figured it was his due."

Diana ran a hand through her thick, bouncy curls and immediately regretted it, knowing how messy and out of control they would make her look. "He might be a jerk," she said, slipping off her heels, "but he's an influential jerk, and winning his malpractice case is going to go a long way toward building up this firm's reputation."

But even as she said the words, she felt a niggle of discomfort.

Yes, she—a young woman who owned a small, relatively new law firm—had won the high-profile case.

Yes, Roger Merkovitz could make or break her in the medical malpractice community of Boston because he was the executive medical director for MassGeneral, the largest, most reputable hospital in Boston. But he *was* an unpleasant man and difficult to work with.

And...Diana had never felt completely comfortable about the case in which a young man had expired during routine orthopedic surgery on a fractured tibia. There was something about it that bothered her.

Regardless, she'd done her job: defended her client to the best of her ability, and subsequently won the case. And she'd been brilliant, if she did say so herself.

Now it was done, making Merkovitz her most valued client. Jonathan would be so pleased. And maybe even her mother would find something nice to say for once.

It had been a long, grueling week, and even though it was Friday, she had more to do before she could relax. Jonathan was at a convention in Atlantic City this weekend, so he wouldn't be around. She could pull out the Desai and Morbuti case files and start reviewing them. And—

Diana realized with a start that Mickey was speaking to her. "What?"

"I was *saying*...was it worth 60 hours a week for the last six months, not to mention your other cases? Was it worth sitting in the same room as Merkovitz, letting that snake snap and yell at you at the same time as he was looking down your blouse?"

"He wasn't looking down my blouse," Diana said, seizing on the lowest-hanging fruit of her assistant's tirade. "He's Jonathan's colleague. He wouldn't do that."

Mickey snorted violently. "Yeah, right."

"Well, anyway, the hours might be long, but they're necessary if I want to build up this firm," Diana told her. "It benefits all of us," she added, looking around at her two staff members. Yes, that was it: two full-time staff members, although she had a slew of consulting attorneys and paralegals she could call on as needed. Her reputation was solid and professional, built on her own blood, sweat and tears.

"I suppose it's a necessary evil, working with him. Let's just hope we don't have to do it again any time soon. So why don't you go down to Atlantic City and meet up with Jonathan?" Mickey said. "Take a breather this weekend? Play a little blackjack or something fun. Do you even remember what fun is, Diana?"

"Jonathan doesn't gamble," Diana replied, imagining her serious fiancé sitting in his hotel room. He'd be working on the speech he was giving to a group of cardiologists at their annual convention. "Although he's probably golfing right now. But…I suppose I could bring my files with me," she murmured, flipping through her mental to-do list.

"You should celebrate," Mickey said. "Dom is taking me out for dinner tonight since we won the case. You should do the same. Or better yet, stay in town and just do something for yourself."

"By the way, here are your messages," Corey said, handing Diana a stack of pink notes.

Diana took another gulp, and then began to flip through the slips as she pulled up her schedule on the smartphone. Corey had taken several phone calls from physicians from MassGen—that was good, word of mouth from the Merkovitz case already—and…hmm. Joe Tettmueller? From the Damariscotta Police Department? She sat up straight and looked at Corey. "Joe Tettmueller? What did he say?"

Corey shrugged. "He called three times while you were in court. He didn't say why."

"Damariscotta, Maine. That's where Aunt Belinda lives," Diana said slowly.

She hadn't seen her great-aunt for more than fifteen years due to an estrangement between Belinda and Diana's mother. A wave of memories—of the big clapboard house, the bright, sunny kitchen, the walks in the woods, the smell of the lake on a summer day—assaulted her. "I wonder what he wants."

The phone rang, its low, tasteful bleep breaking into her thoughts. Corey looked down at the phone, then at Diana. "Caller ID says it's from Maine. It's probably him again."

She took the phone, a sudden surge of trepidation replacing the nostalgia.

She had to get up to visit Aunt Belinda in the next few months. She *had* to. Before it was too late.

"Hello. This is Diana Iverson," she said into the phone.

"Ms. Iverson," said a man in a very slow, comfortable drawl. "This is Captain Joe Tettmueller from the Damariscotta Police Department. Are you related to Belinda Lawry?"

"Yes, she's my great-aunt," Diana replied, her heart beginning to pound. *No.* She already knew what he was going to say.

"I'm afraid I have some bad news for you. Your Aunt Belinda is dead."

—⁂—

Three weeks later
Damariscotta, Maine

Diana found the cards wrapped in black silk, nestled in a plain mahogany box.

She fanned the deck in her hands, recognizing the swords and cups of the Tarot. Tracing the soft, rounded corners, she noticed how dull the gloss had become, as if the cards had often been fingered and shuffled.

An intricate design of royal blue, black, and dark red in a snakeskin pattern decorated the backs of the cards, and on the front were kings and queens, cups, wands, pentacles, and swords— all in painstaking detail and bright colors.

As Diana held the oversized cards in her hands, the vaguest, faintest whisper of a memory—like a dream—settled over her.

Then it was plucked away like a veil being drawn from her head. In the wake of the wispy thought, some awareness skittered over the nape of her neck, raising the fine hair there and causing prickles to run down her spine.

She gave a short, sad laugh, then rewrapped the cards and set them back in the box. Aunt Belinda, she thought, shaking her head. *I waited too long.*

Diana's eyes moistened and the back of her throat burned. The first summer she visited Damariscotta had been twenty years ago, but she remembered it vividly. She'd been ten, tall and gangly with teeth that needed orthodontic attention—a serious city girl with wild, bushy hair and a penchant for reading instead of the outdoors. But a summer with Aunt Bee had begun to change that.

A real tear stung her eye and Diana brushed it away. *Later.* She'd grieve later. She had work to do now. Her law practice to run. And a fiancé…maybe…to return to.

At the thought of Jonathan, a crushing pain settled over her chest. Despite the sad news, this visit to Damariscotta—to Aunt Belinda's house—couldn't have come at a better time.

Diana drew in a deep breath and closed her mind to the hurt. *Later.*

The shrill *brrring* of an old-fashioned phone jolted in the silence. Relieved from the heaviness of emotions she'd tried to ignore, she reached for the shiny black monstrosity, complete with dial and heavy handset. "Yes?"

"Hey, it's Mickey. News on the home front—don't know whether you'll be happy about it or not," said her assistant in a tone that indicated she already knew the answer. "I tried your cell first, but the call didn't go through."

"So, what is it?"

"Merkovitz called. I told him you were out of town on a family emergency."

Diana had come up for Belinda's funeral the week after Captain Tettmueller had called, but returned to Boston the same day.

Since then, she'd worked from home and avoided Jonathan as much as possible for the next two weeks, trying to figure out what to do. How to handle the rift between them.

So when the probate had been settled early this week and she had gained access to Belinda's property, Diana took the opportunity to leave Boston and put some space between her and her fiancé.

Former fiancé.

Maybe.

Her heart squeezed whenever she thought of breaking things off permanently. For good. She could already hear her mother's voice: *I knew you'd never be able to keep a man like him.*

"Merkovitz has been named in another suit," Mickey was saying.

Diana squeezed her eyes shut as a churning began in her stomach. "Already?"

"Merry Christmas in July," Mickey said dryly.

"Let me find something to write with." Diana pulled Aunt Bee's box of Tarot cards back out of the bedside stand, setting it on top, and looked in the empty drawer. There wasn't anything to write with inside. "I'm not on a cordless phone, so hold on while I go grab one."

"Do you have wi-fi? I can email you the info."

Diana gave a short, strained laugh and shoved a hand into her short, thick hair. "In Damariscotta? Don't make me laugh. This place is in the middle of the forest, practically in a small mountain range. I can hardly get my cell phone to work, which is making me climb the walls. But the cable guy is supposed to come tomorrow, so I should be online by then," she added, rising abruptly to head briskly to the kitchen.

Once there, she picked up the extension—another wired plastic monstrosity—and rummaged through a drawer to find a pen and paper. "Why don't you give me an overview and send the details by email," she told Mickey. "It'll be several weeks before the deposition."

"And you'll be back in Boston by then, won't you?"

"I'll be back in a *week*." Even as Diana made her vehement comment, she felt a twinge of discomfort.

She couldn't afford to be away from her practice for very long, but at the same time, all of a sudden, she had an inheritance to deal with—Aunt Belinda's house, as well as all of her personal effects and a substantial sum of money that had made Diana's eyes widen and her knees give out when the estate lawyer called with the information.

And aside from that, she didn't mind the excuse to put some distance between her and Jonathan.

It'll be okay. He loves you.

But did he really?

Her mother's admonishments suddenly filled her thoughts: *You're so gawky with those long legs and clumsy hands, Diana. I keep expecting you to drop anything you get near. And stop playing with your hair. It looks terrible, all bushy and messy when you do that.*

She closed her eyes and took a deep breath, pushing her mother and her criticisms away. *I am a successful businesswoman. I have a thriving practice. I've got a successful, handsome fiancé who loves me.*

Her stomach ground tightly. *He* does *love me.*

"All right, I'll talk to you tomorrow," she said abruptly, looking at the list of notes she'd just made.

Her assistant disconnected and Diana returned to the bedroom, distracted by the faint drum of pain starting at the back of her head. She hadn't had a migraine in years, but this felt like the beginning of one.

Or maybe it was just tension, thinking of Roger Merkovitz. Of having to start the process all over again with him and a new case. Another half-year of 80-hour workweeks.

The receiver of the bedside phone dangled from the table, a testament to her hasty departure to find a writing implement. And although she didn't remember doing it, the box of cards had been knocked off, and the deck lay scattered all over the wool carpet.

Hanging up the bleeping receiver, Diana crouched to gather up the cards. She noticed they'd all landed face down except for one. Reaching for the swatch of black silk, she replaced it in the mahogany box, then picked up the single face-up card.

The artistic rendering was exquisite, she thought, looking at its bold red and blue design. *The Fool*, she reflected, dimly remembering Aunt Belinda's explanation of this first card of the Major Arcana—the backbone, so to speak, of the Tarot.

What had Aunt Belinda told her about the Fool?

Diana stared at it for a moment, looking at the out-flung arms of the young, carefree man as he danced down a slight incline. The Fool looked like he hadn't a care in the world. He was handsome and smiling—which was more than Diana could say for herself. She couldn't remember the last time she'd felt carefree or relaxed... especially now, when the thumping in her temples was beginning to nauseate her.

She needed to take something to catch it before it got worse, but she wasn't going to leave a mess. Diana placed The Fool at the top of the deck and set the cards in their mahogany enclosure, swathing them with the ends of the black cloth. Just as she put the box back in the drawer, the irritating *brrring* of the phone broke the stillness.

This time, she answered the phone in the kitchen, deciding that if her smartphone was going to refuse to work she needed to get a cordless phone. Tomorrow.

"Hi sweetie." It was Jonathan.

Diana drew in a deep breath. That was the thing about these old phones—no Caller ID.

"How are you?" he said in his soft, empathetic voice. "How are things up there? I miss you."

She gave herself a mental shake. *I need to forgive him and forget.* "I'm doing all right," she said, making her voice sound livelier than she felt.

"I tried your cell, but it just went to voice mail without ringing. I guess you are in the middle of nowhere." He gave a little chuckle that sounded strained—which was only right, she reminded herself. *He'd* been the one who strayed; *he* was the one who'd put the chink in their relationship.

If only she *hadn't* gone down to surprise him in Atlantic City after winning the Merkovitz case.

But then she'd never have known. She drew in a deep breath and tried to calm her churning stomach.

"Yes, it's a little rustic up here. How are you?" Diana pulled the refrigerator door open. She found a six-pack of beer—*Aunt Bee drank beer?*—a bag of prewashed carrots, a half gallon of milk long past its expiration date, and three-quarters of a stick of butter. *Guess it's going to be the Grille for dinner tonight.*

She realized Jonathan had paused in a stream of complaints about the other partners in his practice and seemed to be waiting for a response from her. Normally, she followed his explanations closely, but all she could think about this time was whether she was one of the new partners.

Valerie Somebody.

Doctor Valerie Somebody: Young, Sexy Cardiologist—who'd been sharing a hotel room with Diana's fiancé in Atlantic City.

Her fingers tightened on the phone as she swallowed a ball of nausea. A dull pain began to thud in her temples. "I'm sorry, Jonathan, what were you saying? The line's a little fuzzy."

"I asked if you wanted me to bring anything when I come up this weekend."

She bit her lip, wishing there was a way to keep him from coming. She wasn't certain she was ready to see him yet.

But when she'd confronted him about Valerie Whoever, he'd apologized—even cried when he told her it had been a one-time thing and that he'd made a mistake, and that he didn't want to lose her.

I love you, Diana. I was just a little scared—things have happened so quickly between us—and I made a mistake. I felt terrible the whole time. I knew it was wrong. I'm sorry I hurt you.

"Well?" he asked, a tinge of impatience in his voice.

"Um, I really can't think of anything I need right now," she replied—then forced herself to joke, "other than a cell tower in the yard here, but I don't think even you can make that happen."

He chuckled at the compliment. "Well, then, that's it. My flight gets in Friday night—can I text you the details? How far of a drive is it up there to your aunt's?"

"It's a bit more than an hour from the airport. You can try to text. I'm pretty sure I can get service in town," she told him, and briefly closed her eyes when a telltale flicker of white light skittered across her vision. This migraine was coming on fast.

Just then, a knock sounded on the front door—the old, heavy brass knocker thunked twice, then paused, then twice again.

"Belindaaaa," a masculine voice called as Diana heard the door open. "Belinda, it's me!"

Diana started for the foyer before remembering she was restricted by the ugly black phone cord. "Jonathan, I've got to run. Someone's at the door."

"Belindaaa!" The door closed and footsteps thudded across the wood floor.

Diana hung up the phone and started for the foyer.

"Hey, Belinda! I'm just here to pick up my be—" The man stopped as Diana swung around the corner from the kitchen. "Oh! I'm sorry, I just stopped in to see Belinda."

"Excuse me, but who are you?" A pang of apprehension at the sight of a a very tall, unshaven and unkempt young man standing in her foyer made her voice high and tight.

Diana came halfway across the high-ceilinged foyer and folded her arms across her chest. Obviously he knew her aunt— or, at least, she *hoped* he knew her aunt.

"I'm Ethan, a friend of Belinda's. Who are you?" his voice was polite, but the dark gaze that examined her was bold and thorough.

He was young and fit, probably mid-twenties, and looked like a hippie. He had a wild-looking goatee and moustache that needed trimming, long sideburns, and a dark ponytail that rode low upon his neck. She wasn't really frightened—mostly irritated, and a little confused. Maybe he did the lawns or was a delivery boy.

But still—he'd just walked in without even knocking.

"I'm Diana Iverson, Belinda's niece," she told him coolly.

"*You're* Diana?" To her surprise, he smiled, and the crinkles that fanned from the corners of his eyes required her to adjust her estimate of his age upward a notch. Thirty, maybe. "I'm so glad to meet you. She's spoken often of you. So you were finally able to make it up here for a visit? I'll bet she's thrilled."

"Mr.—uh—"

"Actually, it's Doctor—Tannock. Ethan Tannock," he said as if surprised that she didn't know his name. Now his eyes became wary, focused steadily on her.

Diana hid her surprise at the title. "Dr. Tannock, I'm not sure what you're doing, barging into my aunt's house like this—"

"I'm sorry if I startled you. I just stopped in to get the beer she owes me." The smile returned and she noticed a deep crease on the left side of his face that ended at the unruly goatee.

Diana frowned and the headache pain radiated from over her left ear. The flashes of light were becoming stronger, nearly blinding her.

She knew the migraine would rapidly become unbearable, and she wanted to get him out of her house as quickly as possible. "Dr. Tannock, I don't know when you spoke to my aunt last—"

"A few weeks ago, when I learned I'd won a little bet we had—"

"—but I have some bad news for you," she continued to speak over his congenial explanation while trying to ignore the agony that was beginning to seep toward the front of her temples. "She—I buried her more than two weeks ago."

"*What?*" Shock replaced confidence and charm.

"My great-aunt passed away three weeks ago last Thursday," she told him. "Heart failure—in her sleep." Nausea settled in her stomach and she swallowed hard, blinking against the string of lights that hovered at the edge of her vision. The dull throb radiated in her temple and she closed her eyes briefly. *Go away before I lose it and vomit right here.*

"My God." Tannock skimmed his hand over the hair pulled smoothly back into its tail. "I had no idea—I'm sorry." He stepped toward her then seemed to think better of it. "What happened? She was fine when I talked to her. She sounded *fine*." His eyes were a sharp, hard beer-bottle brown as they looked closely at her. Almost as if he didn't believe her…

The migraine was becoming more insistent and she had to resist the urge to push her fingertips into the sides of her forehead. "She died in her sleep, Dr. Tannock, and the funeral was the Wednesday following. Two weeks ago yesterday. Now, if you'll excuse me, I really have quite a bit to do."

"Of course." His voice was clipped and Diana felt the weight of his intent stare as he persisted. "Uh…are you all right?"

"Yes. I'm fine, I just didn't expect visitors at this time." She forced herself to say the words as politely and calmly as possible. The last thing she needed was a young know-it-all intern telling her how to treat her migraines when she'd already tried everything under the sun. A large black spot leapt before her eyes and she blinked rapidly, and in vain, to make it disappear.

"Well, I apologize for barging in on you like this," Tannock said, backing toward the door while he continued to study her with a frown. "Your aunt was a good friend of mine. If there's anything I can do to help you out, please let me know."

"I'll do that," she said, purposely neglecting to ask how to contact him. "Thank you for stopping by."

She barely closed the door behind her unwanted visitor when a moan escaped from the back of her throat. Fighting the black spots and flashes of light that accompanied the debilitating pain, Diana hurried to find the bag where she'd left her medication.

Moments later, she was curled up on the bed, hands fisted over her closed eyes, fighting the agony.

—⁂—

Ethan strolled down the lane from Belinda Lawry's house and cut across the Hornbergers' yard to his own, two houses down a twisting, narrow tire-track lane that ended at his small log cabin.

He was shocked and saddened, even devastated, to learn that Belinda had died that night after last talking with him.

He was even more disturbed that he'd been down in Princeton and missed the funeral. What the hell was up with that? Joe should have known he'd want to know. Of course, he hadn't been in town much since returning late last night. Damn.

Not only that, but he was beyond irritated by the cold brush-off given him by Belinda's bitchy niece. He'd heard enough about Diana Iverson over the last year to know that the woman was a self-centered, career-focused ballbuster who had no time for family or anyone but herself.

But the worst of it was that Belinda was *gone*. *Damn, Bee. I'm going to miss the hell out of you.*

And not just because of his work. Belinda was a fascinating subject, and the center of his latest study—but she'd also become a friend and mentor to him. Especially after the divorce.

To his surprise, a wayward tear stung one eye as he yanked open the door to his cabin. Cady bounded across the room to meet him, leaving a telltale imprint on the couch from which she was supposedly banned.

"Hey, girl." Ethan knelt to ruffle her thick fur, pulling the black lab's face close to his. "Belinda's dead. Can you believe it? I sure can't. I just can't believe it. I didn't even know about the funeral. I'm going to have to have words with Joe Cap about that." A big pink tongue slathered his face, carefully avoiding the bristly goatee, as Ethan sank to the floor.

It was some time later, when the sun had dipped behind the fringe of trees at the edge of the lake, that Ethan hoisted himself to his feet. His face was damp from Cady's attentions as well as a narrow rivulet of tears that had settled in his beard.

I could go for a beer just now. He peered into the refrigerator, but the six-pack of New Castle Ale was still sitting in Belinda's fridge—at least, as far as he knew.

When she'd called him down at Princeton almost a month ago to tell him he could pick up his winnings the next time he came up, she'd cackled gleefully and told him she had it in the fridge, getting cold for him. He told her he'd be up as soon as the semester was over, and here he was, as promised.

But she was gone.

Ethan pushed the fridge door closed with more force than necessary, sorrow welling inside him again. *In her sleep*, the niece had said.

Diana. Diana Iverson. His brows tightened—Belinda had always called her something else, something fanciful like Avalina... Lianella? .... No, wait—Andiana. Andiana Maria.

Andiana Maria?

He shook his head, pulling a TV dinner from his freezer. He'd never met anyone who looked less like such a frou-frou name. Stress and tension had emanated from her as she confronted him in the hallway. Apparently, she was a malpractice lawyer down in Boston, and was obviously used to working long hours for massive fees in prim suits and sensible heels. No wonder she went by the shorter version of her name.

"Not that she's not good-looking," he told Cady pleasantly as he crushed the cardboard box and put it in the trash compactor. "She's actually pretty hot, despite the fact that she's an ice-queen and dresses for the country club even up here in Damariscotta." Her short hair was thick and dark and curled around her face and jaw, making her look as if she'd just rolled out of bed...or, better yet, been tumbled into it.

Cady flopped in a heap on the floor and groaned.

"So sorry if I'm boring you." Ethan grinned down at his best friend and lifted the lid from a glass jar on the counter that held dog biscuits. Instantly, Cady scrambled back to her feet, ears perked up in anticipation. He lightly tossed his pet a treat and replaced the jar.

Diana Iverson, he thought again, with a short laugh that turned bitter. His first reaction on meeting her had been surprise and pleasure on behalf of Belinda, delighted that the niece had finally come to visit—until he'd learned why. The busy, ass-kissing lawyer who couldn't bother to visit her great-aunt in twenty years finally made the trip just in time to collect her substantial inheritance.

Aside from that, she'd looked at him like he was some sort of furry, crawly bug when he'd corrected her to say "doctor."

Just then, he caught sight of himself in the mirrored microwave door—spotless, thanks to his cleaning lady—and grimaced. Oy. He'd forgotten about that god-awful beard. He looked like a mountain man. He kept it during the year because it did the trick to keep the young things away from him on campus. No wonder Diana Iverson been so wary, and so intent upon getting rid of him.

Fiona had been giving him shit about the beard too, for months, and he supposed he'd better get rid of it before her wedding. Now that he was home for the summer and away from campus, he'd take care of it. Maybe he'd even get the ponytail cut and look a little more respectable. It would be cooler, at any rate.

The microwave beeped that his well-preserved dinner was ready to eat, and he gingerly slid the plastic tray onto a plate. Moments later, he was settled in a heavy cedar lounge chair on the screened porch that overlooked Lake Damariscotta.

Ah. July in Maine.

Though the sun had set and the sky held only a glow near the horizon, there was still plenty to see. Lights winked along the shoreline in homes that were inhabited year-round. The tops of tall pines swayed with a faint breeze, brushing against each other high in the sky. A bold streak of pink in the western sky echoed the fading sunlight. There were the sounds of whippoorwills and crickets, the rustling of various wildlife in the forest that surrounded the lake, and, occasionally, the hoot of a lonely owl.

It was peaceful.

Ethan looked through the trees along the lake and picked out Belinda's home. One faint light shone through a window in the old clapboard structure. Sadness washed over him.

Abruptly, he decided he wasn't hungry for cardboard food and set the TV dinner tray on the floor for Cady, thinking, still, about Diana Iverson.

—ᗰ—

Diana dragged herself awake into darkness, blind fear crushing lungs that dug deep for air. Struggling to push the weight of terror from her chest, she grappled with the tentacle-like sheets and pulled herself upright in the bed.

Moonlight streamed into the room as she sat there, gasping, shaking, trying to push away the remnants of the black nightmare that twined around her, engulfing her with its heaviness. She saw the pale oval of her face reflected in the mirror on Belinda's bureau drawer and shrank away from the vision made by the dark holes of her eyes and the stark terror on her face.

She'd never had a dream so completely consuming, so mind-numbingly frightening—yet she didn't know what it was about. There had been only blackness descending upon her, smothering her, pressing her down into some dark, horrifying state.

Diana dragged her shaking limbs out of bed, glad she'd never had such an experience while with Jonathan. Glancing at the tussled bedclothes, she realized she didn't trust herself to go back to sleep without falling into the dark pit again.

Still reminding herself that she was awake, out of the dream, she pulled on a light silk robe as she stumbled out of the room, banging her elbow on the corner of the door as she left. She'd curl up on the settee in the den and sleep with Aunt Belinda's two cats—if they would have her, and if she could find sleep again.

TWO

DIANA AWOKE TO SUNSHINE. It glared from a crack between the heavy velvet curtains and the windowpane, making a crooked line over the floor of the den. She pulled herself up, stretching her aching back, and blinked a few times to clear her vision. Last evening's migraine was gone, as was the terrible dream, and she felt relatively well rested, though a bit hollow.

She caught sight of the digital clock on the desk—an anomaly in the lacy, Victorian room—and started. *Nine o'clock?* Could that be right?

Diana rolled quickly off the velvet-upholstered settee, her feet landing on the rug with a profound thump. She couldn't remember the last time she'd slept past seven. Even on vacation, she and Jonathan rose early to golf.

A little dazed that her internal alarm clock had failed her, Diana stumbled down the short hallway to the bathroom. Moments later, under a tepid shower, she planned her day as she poured Aunt Belinda's cheap, strawberry-scented shampoo in her hair.

By the time she was tousling her short hair into a damp cap, wishing that it wasn't quite so unruly, Diana knew exactly what she had to get done—including a run to the grocery store for something fresh. It was odd not being able to check her cell phone every few minutes—but she couldn't unless she was in town. And Mickey was handling things back at the office.

Wrapped in a towel, she padded down the hall to Belinda's bedroom, and, to her chagrin, felt her heart begin to pound as she pushed open the door. After a moment of hesitation, she forced herself to stride purposefully into the room despite the uneasiness curling in her stomach. The bed was a disaster of sheets, pillows, and the matelassé coverlet—very much unlike she normally left her sleeping abode. In fact, Jonathan often teased her that if it weren't for him, their bed would never look as though it had been slept in.

That brought back unpleasant thoughts about whether Valerie the Slut messed up her sheets (of course she did) and Diana distracted herself by quickly making up the bed here. Only when that was finished and the pillows neatly arranged was she able to turn her attention to dressing.

Just as she was pulling on a blue polo over pleated khaki shorts, she heard the heavy doorknocker at the front of the house. Diana started out of the bedroom but paused when her attention fell on the mahogany box. It was out of place, sitting on the bedside table with its lid sitting next to it. She'd neglected to put it away yesterday because of the onset of her migraine. For one absurd moment, she wondered if that was the reason for her wrenching dream.

The Fool sat on top of the deck, and suddenly Diana had a flash of memory. The vision was so abrupt and so strong, she curled her fingers around the bedpost to steady herself.

He—the Fool—figured widely in the mental image that presented itself in the front of her mind, cavorting throughout and mingling with obscure images of Aunt Belinda and Jonathan, as well as a dark-haired man she didn't know and a scrap of newspaper that kept reappearing. It was almost as if she were dreaming, right here in the middle of wakefulness.

The Fool is the Number Zero, and is the beginning of the Major Arcana, she could almost hear Aunt Belinda say. *He is also as we are at the beginning of any journey—gay, innocent, inexperienced, artless, and open-minded.*

How could she know this? And remember such detail? She hadn't seen Aunt Belinda since she was thirteen. And after that, her mother had done everything she could to wipe away any memories that might have persisted, completely destroying the relationship between Diana and her great-aunt.

Another series of metallic thuds at the front door brought her attention from the card, back to the present. "I'm coming," she muttered, rushing from the room.

At the large oaken door, she peered through the frosted, stained glass sidelights. It was the FedEx man with a package of contracts and documents from Mickey. As she closed the door, Diana turned just in time to see a streak of white dash across the hall.

"Motto," she exclaimed, crouching in the hall in hopes of luring the cat back out. "It's about time you came out of hiding, kitty. Where's Arty? You two must be missing Aunt Bee."

She'd seen neither hide nor hair of the cats since she arrived, although they'd eaten the food she left out for them every night. Aunt Belinda's description, through their phone conversations and the letters she sent regularly, hadn't included the fact that the cats were extremely anti-social. In fact, if they hadn't eaten the food Diana left out for them, she would have thought they were the figment of an old lady's imagination.

Diana pulled to her feet and spoke in the general direction of the felines. "I guess you'll come out when you're ready, won't you? I'm going to run into town. Don't party too hard while I'm gone." She started into Belinda's bedroom to get her purse and car keys.

She stopped short in the doorway. The mahogany box had been upended off the bedside table, and its contents spilled all over the floor. How odd.

"I could have sworn...." Her voice trailed off as she remembered how she'd left the room in haste to answer the door. "What a klutz." She stooped to gather the Tarot cards.

They were oversized and awkward for her to straighten into a neat stack. And when she pulled them all together and was just tapping the deck into place, somehow a card slipped out. It flipped onto the floor and landed face-up.

Diana meant to simply replace the card on top of the deck, but something compelled her to look at it...really look at it. *The*

High Priestess, the caption read. A Roman numeral two identified it as the second numeric card of the Major Arcana.

The High Priestess was crowned and seated on a throne behind which were pomegranates and palms. She held a scroll in the lap of her blue gown, and seemed to be tucking it under her cloak. On the left of the throne was a black column labeled **B**, and on the right was a second column—white—labeled **J**. A crescent sat on the floor in the trailing pool of her gown.

Diana studied the card for a long moment, her breath turning shallow as she fought back an unaccountable sense of unease. What did it signify to one who believed in the Tarot? Not that she bought into that malarkey, but her Aunt Belinda had. Much to her mother's disgust.

With a sudden *tsk* of irritation, she returned the card to its place in the stack and replaced it once again in the smooth wrapping of black silk and mellow mahogany. *This time, I'll put you away,* she thought, pulling open the drawer of Aunt Belinda's beside table.

But something happened as she did so, and the drawer, always a little unsteady, came completely out of its slot with the force of her yank, thumping onto the floor and just missing her bare foot. When Diana tried to fit it back into place, she banged the back of her hand on the corner of drawer. And the old, sticky wood refused to slide home, thus she was left with a drawer that wouldn't fit in its hole and a painful mark on the back of her hand that was already bruising.

Fine, Diana thought, pulling herself to her feet and retrieving the mahogany box from the recalcitrant drawer. She set the box of cards on the kitchen counter and, after one last (ignored) invitation to the cats to join her, Diana headed to the grocery store.

—❦—

An hour later, Diana stumbled back into the house, arms hooked through plastic bags filled with groceries and hands filled with mail from the post office. She dumped the whole pile on the kitchen counter with a sigh of relief and went back out to make another trip.

As soon as she walked back in, Motto and Arty decided to make an appearance directly underfoot, and she nearly landed on her face trying to avoid a fluffy tail.

As soon as she dropped the bags onto the counter, she crouched, calling for them to reappear. "Come out, come out, wherever you are," she sang in a falsetto, remembering the Good Witch of the North's entreaty to the Munchkins. And then she looked around in embarrassment, as if someone might hear her. Good thing there wasn't anyone around. "I brought you some treats, kitty-kitties. Do you like catnip? How about Fresh Feline Fancies?"

Of course they didn't come.

Diana gave up and turned back to the bags of groceries sprawled on the counter. It was then that she noticed the note.

Note?

Diana snatched it off the counter, eyebrows furrowing. *"Just dropped by to pick up a book I loaned Belinda, and my beer,"* the bold, black letters read. *"Hope you don't mind I let myself in. Sorry to have missed you—since we're neighbors, maybe we'll run into each other on the lake. Call me if I can be of any help. (Dr.) Ethan Tannock."*

A little shiver raced down her back. He'd been in the house again! But her twinge of discomfort was abruptly replaced by a wave of irritation. *Hope you don't mind I let myself in,* indeed!

Of course she minded.

People didn't just let themselves into other peoples' houses. Not where she came from, anyway. Especially when they didn't *know* the person living there. And if she weren't so irritated, she might be more than a little freaked out about it.

And what if he'd still been there when she got home and was singing and talking like that to the cats? Her cheeks burned at the very thought.

She crumpled up the note and flung it into the garbage, then turned and yanked the telephone book from the drawer under the phone. Flipping through the pages, she quickly located the Ls—laundry, lawn services, liquor stores, *locksmiths.*

"I'll fix him," she muttered as she dialed the number.

After she arranged for a locksmith to come and change all the locks later that afternoon, Diana strolled through the house just to make sure Ethan Tannock hadn't disturbed anything.

The living room seemed as empty and formal as she remembered it being, furnished as it was with heavy, dark antiques and hundreds of knickknacks in several cabinets. Long, heavy curtains brushed the floor, covering tall windows that overlooked the front yard of the big clapboard home. Diana noticed some thick white cat fur on one of the upholstered chairs and paused to brush it off.

That room seemed undisturbed, so Diana moved on down the hall to Aunt Belinda's den. This was a room that she hadn't even begun to go through and organize because it was so cluttered.

A heavy, oaken desk dominated one corner of the dimly lit room, and stacks of magazines, papers, and books littered its top. Diana flicked on the light. Even if Ethan had rummaged through the contents of the room, she wouldn't be able to tell. Messy piles of periodicals from all over the country lined one wall, more books filled shelves from ceiling to floor on an opposite wall, and three battered filing cabinets edged a third wall. Their drawers gapped open and files hung haphazardly out, but the mess didn't alarm Diana. That was the way it had been when she first arrived at the house, and although she itched to get in there and begin to clean things up, she had work to do first, and she'd already wasted half the day.

Belinda's bedroom was next. The sense of discomfort Diana had felt earlier still hung in the air, as though a fine fog hovered, but it wasn't compelling enough to keep her from walking in. This room also seemed undisturbed, but she almost tripped over the empty drawer that she'd left in the middle of the floor.

Diana picked it up, determined to wedge it back into the bedside table if she had to slam it into place. To her surprise, it slid back so quickly and easily that she smashed her fingertip. *What in the world?* She glared, sucking on the end of her finger—which happened to be on the same hand she'd bruised earlier. *I must just have been in a hurry.*

She would have gone upstairs to look through the other five bedrooms, but the telephone rang. Too late, she remembered that she hadn't hooked up the cordless phone yet, and she rushed into the kitchen to answer it.

It was Mickey, doing her daily check-in call. "Hey, boss, how's it going?" she asked.

"Things are fine. I got your overnights this morning, but haven't had a chance to look at them yet. Any new developments?"

"No," Mickey replied, "except that Merkovitz agreed to Skype with you tomorrow at two—he says he's not available until then. And then he gave me shit about making certain I send an agenda to him and plan of action by the end of the day today—but he's the one who's got the information, and how can you have a plan of action if you haven't gotten the details from him yet? How's it going up there all by yourself anyway?"

"Fine, but I have a lot to get done before the house goes on the market," Diana told her, neglecting to mention her need to put some space between her and Jonathan.

She hadn't told Mickey anything of what had happened when she went down to Atlantic City. Her gaze fell on the mahogany box that she'd left on the counter, and she idly opened it to finger the black silk.

"You're going to sell it?" Mickey sounded surprised. "Why don't you just keep it for a weekend getaway? It's not that far from Boston."

Diana raised her eyebrows at the suggestion. "Well, I guess I didn't think seriously about doing that. It might be nice to have a place to get to once in awhile." Then, she frowned, "Nah—you know Jonathan and I never have a free weekend anyway. We're either working or going somewhere."

"Yeah...maybe you ought to change that," Mickey said tartly. "You're just a little uptight."

Diana rolled her eyes, but didn't comment. She was used to her assistant's blunt commentary on her life—not that Mickey, who was the same age as Diana and had been married since she was seventeen, had had any simpler a life.

She spent the next fifteen minutes jotting notes on her laptop and answering questions about other issues at the office. As they were finishing, Diana's attention was drawn again to the mahogany box.

As Mickey was giving her some more personal updates about the office—namely that there was a cute guy who'd just started working in the architectural office across the hall with whom Corey had become immediately smitten—Diana pulled out the deck of Tarot cards from the box and smoothed them into a facedown pile. Idly, she picked one from the center and turned it over. *The High Priestess.*

Again? Huh.

Diana stuffed it back into the center of the mass of cards and mixed them up by pushing them around the kitchen counter. "So, do you know anything about Tarot cards?" she asked her assistant.

"Tarot cards?" Mickey sounded as if her boss had just announced she was joining a cult. "I've had my cards read a few times—just for fun," she added hastily.

"I think it's a lot of baloney, but my aunt used to play around with them. When I was going through her things, I found her set. I was just looking through them, wondering what some of the cards mean." She pulled one from the mess of cards on the counter.

The High Priestess.

A shiver zipped up her back. *Weird.*

Diana held the phone between her neck and shoulder as she gathered the cards into a tidy pile. Her insides were doing funny things, but she was determined to prove that there was nothing to this.

"I never told my mother," Mickey said, "because she'd freak out. But, you know, the times I had my cards read, the psychic was pretty on-target about some things."

"Right. She just picked up signals from you and deduced things. It was probably so general that it could have applied to anyone."

"Maybe." Mickey didn't sound convinced. "She did tell me she saw me driving a red car—and at the time, I had that old white Honda Civic. Then three weeks later, it got totaled and I bought a red Grand Am."

"You probably remembered what she said and that's why you bought the red car." Diana smoothed the cards around on the counter some more.

"Well, I had picked out a white one on the lot—I was going to lease it—and then the day I went to pick it up, they told me there'd been a mistake and the white car was already sold. So, they gave me fifty bucks off the monthly lease payment if I took the red car."

"Really? You never told me that." She picked up the cards and tapped them into a neat pile.

"Yep. Oh, there's the other line. I'd better take that."

"All right. Talk to you tomorrow." Diana hung up and looked down at the stack of cards. She felt little butterflies in her stomach as she reached for the deck and pulled off the top card. She turned it over.

The High Priestess.

—⁓—

Ethan twisted off the cap of a New Castle Ale, popping the small piece of metal into the trash. "To Belinda." He toasted her memory, her ghost, her presence—whatever it was that seemed to hover around him. The full-bodied beer slid down his throat, cool and smooth, and the nutty, rich flavor settled on the back of his tongue. "Thank you, Belinda!"

He'd felt strange, entering Belinda's house, now that she was dead. She'd always told him he could come and go as he pleased. Since he took care of her yard work when he was in Maine during the summer in return for her assistance in his work, he was over there quite a bit. Now, he supposed, that would change.

Ethan had knocked on both the front and back doors for a good five minutes before retrieving the key hidden in the birdhouse. He'd been sure he'd seen someone moving around inside the house, even though there was no car in the drive or the garage. After calling and knocking, he finally went in, leaving Cady sitting on the porch.

"Ms. Iverson," he'd called, stopping in the foyer and listening for her response. Silence. He hurried down the hall to the kitchen, feeling like an intruder—which, of course, he was—and opened the refrigerator door to retrieve his six-pack.

Cady began barking outside, running around the house and stopping at several windows. Ethan glanced outside and didn't see any evidence of a rabbit, squirrel, chipmunk, or bird—the usual suspects in a Cady bark-a-thon.

"Cady, chill," he yelled out the back door, then turned in search of paper and a pen.

He saw the mahogany box on the counter by the telephone and recognized it. Belinda's cards. A twinge of melancholy prompted him to remove the lid and open the silk wrappings. He wondered what Diana Iverson was doing with them—if anything.

Diana doesn't believe in anything unless it's in black and white and been proven beyond a shadow of a doubt, thanks to her mother Victoria. He could almost hear Belinda's indignant voice. *And even then if she sees it in black and white, she's gotta question it and question it. A good lawyer, she is, but a very poor psychic. She's got the Gift, all right, but she won't pay any attention to it.*

He opened the black silk wrapping, looking down at the diamond-shaped blue, red, and black pattern of the back of the deck. He picked up the top card and flipped it over. *The Lovers.*

Ethan knew what it implied—not necessarily the obvious. Relationships, sexuality, yes, of course, but the card also could mean the joining of any two entities—whether it be people, ideas or thoughts.

If she were there, Belinda would tell him to meditate on the card for the day, to open his mind and let the image dig into his unconscious, unlocking answers to questions in his life. She said that the cards unleashed her psychic abilities by opening doors in the back of her mind.

He stared down at The Lovers. He'd been working with Belinda for three years to learn the extent of her ESP, testing it and dissecting it with and without the use of the Tarot cards to see if her abilities were related to their use. So far, his work had been inconclusive, much to his frustration and that of his colleagues at Princeton. One thing was certain, however: Belinda Lawry was one of the best examples of true precognition ability that the team at Princeton Engineering Anomalies Research—PEAR—Lab had ever studied.

And another thing was certain: he'd never be able to finish the study now that Bee was gone.

Cady began barking again. *What is with her?* He replaced the card, wrapping the deck and slipping the cover back onto the box. Then he found paper and a pen and scrawled a note to Diana.

He would have hurried out of the house to quiet Cady, but as he passed the bedroom that belonged to Belinda, he found himself turning into it. Ethan stopped just inside the doorway and looked around the room.

The bed was made, and a half dozen lacy, Victorian pillows had been organized in a neat pile at its head. The drawer to the bedside table lay on the floor, and the rag-rug that covered the wooden floor had a corner flipped up as if someone had left in haste—the only thing out of place in the room. Had he interrupted someone?

Ethan paused and waited, listening...then shook his head. No, he didn't sense the presence of anyone else nearby.

Yet, for some reason, he was compelled to walk further into the room, curiosity overtaking him. The scent of something pleasant—floral and feminine—hung in the air. The open suitcase on a trunk at the end of the bed indicated that this was the room

Diana Iverson was using...and Ethan found himself wondering about her once more.

A hairbrush and comb sat neatly on Belinda's dressing table, along with various other toiletries and an open travel case of jewelry. He stepped closer, wondering what kind of baubles the uptight businesswoman he'd met yesterday would wear.

Pearls: that's what she'd wear. Simple, elegant, and luminescent, they coiled in a neat pool on the dressing table, the necklace embracing a set of matching studs.

Ethan thought back. Yes, they would look lustrous against her thick, dark hair and fair skin.

Abruptly, he stilled. *Dude, what the hell are you doing?*

He left the house after that, ashamed that he'd been tempted to snoop. Despite his chagrin, however, he hadn't forgotten the six-pack. And even now, as he relaxed in his leather armchair with a cold one in hand, Ethan felt an unpleasant tightening in his middle. Whatever had possessed him to be so nosy?

He took another swig of beer, mollifying himself with the thought that everything had been out in plain view, *and* he had been checking to make sure no one was in there.

It wasn't as if he'd gone digging through her underwear drawer.

Ethan smirked in spite of himself, wondering whether the straight-laced lady lawyer wore black lace thongs to court...or no-nonsense hip huggers and plain white bras from the Sears catalog.

He didn't have a problem picturing her in either one.

THREE

DIANA HAD ANOTHER DEBILITATING migraine that evening and went to bed at seven o'clock, snuggling under the quilt in Aunt Belinda's bed.

Some time later, she woke, sweating and shaking, trying to throw off the heavy blackness of another nightmare. Bedraggled and drained, she stumbled down the hall into the den and crashed onto the sofa, where she was able to find a more peaceful rest.

When she finally peeled her eyes open to bright sunlight, it was nearly ten o'clock—but today, she wasn't surprised that she'd overslept. Time and place seemed different up here in Damariscotta. And aside from that, Diana realized with clinical detachment that she was surely suffering from a bit of depression, thanks to Jonathan's betrayal and Aunt Belinda's death.

When Diana came back to the bedroom after her shower, wrapped in a scratchy, threadbare towel from Aunt Belinda's aged collection, trepidation skittered up her spine.

There was something about this room that made her feel as if the nightmares lingered, heavy and dark and hot.

Yes, Aunt Bee had died here, but there was nothing more natural than an elderly lady easing into death while in repose. Practical Diana had no qualms about that. Still, she hesitated before stepping into the room, as if afraid the nightmares might come back even in broad morning light—but upon seeing the white cat, Motto, sprawled in the middle of the bed, she forgot her disquiet.

"Hi kitty," she crooned, moving carefully toward the beady-green-eyed feline. The cat had burrowed right into the center of the maelstrom of sheets and was busily licking the inside of her back leg until the interruption of a mere human.

Diana was surprised but pleased when she was able to get close enough to scoop Motto into her arms. She nuzzled the thick white fur of the feline's head. "I'm so glad you decided to come out of hiding, sweet-thing," she said in a silly voice. "Now if only Arty would be as brave."

The annoyance plain on her face—most likely at Diana's undignified tone—Motto struggled out of her captor's arms and plopped lightly to the floor. Tail swishing in a last gesture of disdain, the cat ducked her head and disappeared under the bed.

"Well, fine, then. See if I bring you anymore catnip toys," Diana told her. But, she realized, the cat's presence and warm, furry body had done much to alleviate her discomfort with the bedroom.

After dressing in a pair of khaki capris and a red button-down shirt, she went to the kitchen. She eyed the mahogany box by the phone, but was absolutely *not* going to give in to the urge to open it.

She wasn't going to take the chance of pulling out The High Priestess again. The four instances of it showing up were random, of course, but still it was creepy.

Today, she had to go down to the post office, which had a FedEx drop box and send some signed documents back to Mickey. She had to get them out before the early truck came at eleven.

The locksmith had come the day before, and now that all the locks were changed, Diana felt much more secure about leaving the house...not that there was much of value here. All of Belinda's considerable wealth was in securities and a few real estate investments—and was not at all evident in her manner of living, Diana thought with a wry smile at the memory of the threadbare bath towels and off-brand shampoo.

There's not much here of any value except a few antiques—unless someone wants a deck of old Tarot cards. At the thought, queasiness started in her stomach and she swallowed hard, forcing herself to take another sip of tea.

Diana grimaced, adding another stop at the market to her list of things to do. She'd forgotten to buy coffee yesterday, and the only brew available in Aunt Belinda's house was her choice of herbal tea: peppermint, chamomile, and blends of rose hips, lemon verbena, all of the mints, and comfrey. Curiously, she'd also found a box of dog biscuits when foraging for coffee, and wondered if the cats liked canine treats. But when she offered, neither of them bothered to even show and turn up their pink noses at the cookies, and so Diana left to go on her errands.

Damariscotta had one main street lined with tourist shops, bed-and-breakfasts, small cafes and restaurants. The practical buildings—post office, library, hardware store, supermarket—were at one end of the street, and that was where Diana chose to park. It didn't look much different from how she remembered it as a child, but the details were wavy in her mind until she actually got out of the car and stood on the sidewalk, looking down the street.

As she swung her purse over her shoulder, she heard a masculine voice hailing her. Turning, Diana saw the neat figure of Dr. Marc Reardon standing at the edge of the parking lot. "Good morning," she called, waving briefly to her aunt's physician.

She had met him along with several other townspeople at Aunt Belinda's funeral, and he had been a model of sympathy and conscientiousness. Now, he strode across the street to meet her.

"How odd," he said, with a smile that squinted into the sun, "I had just been wondering how you were doing up in that big old house by yourself and then I saw you pull into the parking lot." He gestured to a quaint cottage-like house across the side street. "My office is right there."

The house was robin's egg blue with white shutters and a white picket fence that kept a border of wildflowers from spilling onto the sidewalk. "How charming," she said, noting the sign in its front yard that stated Marc Reardon, *M.D. ~ General Practice.*

Diana turned back to him, looking up at his tall, handsome figure. His hair was sandy brown, and would have been perfectly combed if a swift breeze from the lake hadn't been ruffling it. His choice of attire included a tie, and was a bit formal for the small town of Damariscotta. But Diana couldn't fault him for his taste in a starched shirt with monogrammed cuffs and well-creased trousers above buffed leather shoes. He wore a lab coat over his crisp shirt, and *Dr.* Reardon was monogrammed on the pocket.

He shifted so the sun wasn't glaring in his eyes and tried futilely to smooth his hair. "How *are* you managing in that big old house by yourself?" he asked with a warm smile that showed perfect teeth.

Diana closed the door of her car and looked up at him through the filter of dark sunglasses. "There's a lot to do, but I'm taking it bit by bit. The hardest part is going through Aunt Belinda's personal things, of course."

"If you think of anything I can do to help, please let me know." He smiled, hesitating, and slid his hands into the lab coat pockets. "I'm glad I ran into you, as I wanted to invite you to a barbeque I'm having on Tuesday."

Diana raised her eyebrows, about to refuse—there really was no reason to get social; she'd be leaving the area soon—but before she could reply, he added, "The ladies from Belinda's quilting group will be there, and I know they'd love to see you. And there will be several other people from Damariscotta that I'm sure you'd enjoy meeting."

Belinda had talked quite a bit about the quilters, and with a pang of conscience Diana changed her mind. "It sounds like fun—I'll plan to make it," she replied, aware that it was another excuse not to return to Boston right away.

The physician smiled in return. "We'll all be looking forward to it."

She took her leave then, citing her errands, and began to walk up a slight incline to Main Street. It was early on Thursday morning, and although it was still early June, summer tourists were already filling the town.

After turning in her parcels at the post office, she made a beeline for a small cafe, whose painted sign proclaimed the availability of lattés and cappuccinos and espressos. *Real coffee!* Maybe this was a more civilized little town than she realized. Diana ordered a double cap to go and continued down the street, sipping the heavenly drink with relief.

It felt odd not to have to go anywhere or be on a schedule. And although there was work waiting for her back at Aunt Bee's—both professional and personal—the quaint town lulled her into allowing herself a reprieve, and Diana strolled beyond the post office and past a small camera shop. Next, there was a small structure set back from the sidewalk with a tiny yard and an open, narrow doorway. *Used Books*, its sign read. Before Diana knew it, her feet had propelled her down the cracked and shifting sidewalk, up the single step, and into a musty bookshop.

An oscillating fan blew in the direction of the shop's proprietor, who sat at a table laden with books and was surrounded by even more stacks and shelves of tomes upon tomes. The woman looked up, frowning slightly at Diana's large paper cup, and said, "Hello. Let me know if I can help you find anything. The shelves go all the way into the back and up those stairs there." Then, with a smile, she returned to her work.

"Thank you." Diana walked past her, careful not to jostle a particularly tall stack of books, not exactly sure what she was looking for. She didn't want to be rude and turn around before at least skimming through some of the shelves, so she pressed on to the back of the shop, noting the faded, curling handwritten labels on the shelves: *Fiction, Mystery, Science Fiction, Romance, History, Business, Biography, Religion,* and, finally, a newer tag that read *New Age.*

Catching a glimpse of some of the books, which had titles like *Find the Angels in Your Life,* and *Out of Body Experiences for Everyone*, Diana rolled her eyes. Aunt Belinda would have a field day in this section. *Runes*, read another one, *Palmistry Made Easy,* and *The Tarot Explained* were lined up along with them.

Before she knew what she was doing, Diana reached for the last title. Setting her cup down on a half-empty shelf, she flipped through the yellowed pages of the book. They were brittle and stained with what looked like coffee, and several of the corners were torn off. She paused at a chapter entitled "The Major (or Greater) Arcana."

She ignored the fact that her heart thumped wildly as she turned the fragile pages, and refused to consider why her fingers trembled. *The Fool, Number Zero. The Magician, Number One. The High Priestess, Number Two.*

"I never pegged you for a New-Ager," drawled a voice from behind her.

Diana stifled a shriek and whirled, dropping the book. "You— you startled me," she said to the man standing there. Despite her shock, she noted his height (tall), his brown eyes (twinkling with humor), and his face (chiseled and incredibly handsome). The moisture evaporated from her mouth and sprang to her palms.

"I can see that." He had bent down to retrieve the book. "Hmm...*The Tarot Explained.*" He straightened and offered it back to her. "Your aunt would be astonished."

Diana didn't take the book. Instead, she stared at him. Had they met? At the funeral, maybe? But then suddenly his voice and easy smile connected with her memory. "Oh, it's *you*," she said, at once recognizing Ethan Tannock. She couldn't help that her tone was unenthusiastic.

And what else would he expect, having walked into her house uninvited *twice*?

He had shaved and cut his hair, and although it added years to her estimate of his age—he was definitely mid-thirties—it did wonders for his looks. His shorn face was very attractive, with high cheekbones and a firm, square jaw. It made his eyes look bigger and darker, and his lips, which had settled into a sort of smirk, were no longer hidden by mustache overgrowth.

She swallowed hard, feeling suddenly at a loss in the presence of this tall, attractive stranger—who'd been in her house twice. Somehow now, especially in this small, crowded space, he seemed more intense, with more presence and confidence. Irritated with herself, she turned to pick up the cup of cappuccino.

A hand smoothed over that clean jaw line, then dropped to sling loosely on his hip. "I forgot you haven't seen me shorn." He continued to lean against the shelf, holding the book, and grinning down at her. "I didn't mean to startle you."

"Forget it," she told him coolly. "I was just—deep in thought."

He glanced down at the book. "From everything your aunt has told me, I'm sure you aren't really interested in the Tarot."

The certainty and hint of accusation in his voice caused her to bristle and she pulled an invisible cloak of haughtiness around her for protection. "Although I can't imagine why my aunt should be discussing me with you, I admit you're right. I don't believe in this foolishness." Just how well *had* he known her aunt?

"Okay," he shrugged. "Would you like me to put this back, or were you going to buy it?"

"*No,*" she said sharply, too quickly. "No." She softened her tone, ignoring the throb that was just beginning to tom-tom at the back of her temples. *Not again. Not here. Not in front of him—* again. "I wasn't going to buy it. As I told you, I haven't any use for it."

"I'll just put it away, then." Ethan turned, sliding the book onto the shelf in an approximation of where it had been. "Hmm. Palmistry. My sister might like this," he mused, pulling out the book next to it. Not that Fiona needed a book to tell her how to read palms—she was quite gifted in that regard, just like their mother. He, Ethan, was the one who didn't possess any real sensitivity. Maybe it was a gender thing.

Holding the book, he glanced up at the woman in front of him and noticed that her face had seemed to tighten with pain. Clearly physical pain. "Are you feeling all right?" he asked, shoving the book back onto the shelf.

"Yes," she told him, obviously lying. Then, she looked up at him for the first time with honest eyes. Misery and pain showed in them. "No, actually, I'm not. I get these debilitating migraines, and—"

"What can I do for you?" he asked, taking her slim arm and urging her to sink into a well-worn armchair. She looked as if she were going to keel over, or else be violently ill. Or both.

"A glass of water," she said in a thready voice. "I have medication in my bag." Her brows furrowed and her mouth tightened with pain.

Ethan hurried to the front of the shop where Maggie sat going through her books. "Hey, Mag, I need a glass of water for Belinda's niece—she's got to take some medicine." He slipped past her nod, into the private bathroom, and filled a small cup with water.

When he returned to Diana, she was reclining in the armchair, eyes closed. Her features were ashen and sharp. He pressed the water into her hand and she half sat up, drinking greedily. "Thanks. I'll be better in a few minutes." She sank back into the chair and closed her eyes.

He wondered what she had been doing, perusing a book on the Tarot when she professed non-belief, and he reflected on the combatant look in her eyes when she denied her interest in the cards. Had she come to recognize her Gift, or was she just interested in the cards because of her aunt? Or—the thought made him shudder—could she be considering selling Belinda's cards or books?

He stood next to her, looking down at her lidded eyes fringed with thick dark lashes. The hardness had melted from her face, leaving only the starkness of pain over her classic, Grace Kelly features, and he was surprised by sudden raw attraction.

It wasn't mere objective, appreciation of her beauty. The sizzle of attraction was strong enough to supersede the anger and irritation he felt toward someone who would ignore an old lady for years. Most of all, however, the surprise and inappropriateness of his reaction to her pissed him off.

Her eyelids fluttered and she opened them fully. "I'm sorry," she said in a soft sort of groan that didn't help his surge of awareness, "that one came on fast." She looked a bit sleepy and bewildered, but as he offered her his hand, the glaze cleared from her eyes.

"Listen, Diana, why don't you let me drive you home, hmm?" he heard himself say as a thought—a really clever, rather brilliant idea—popped into his head. He could tell she was about to refuse, which, he was later to reflect, might have been for the best.

But then she surprised him and said, "That would be great. Really great." Her smile was forced, but her gratitude seemed genuine.

He assisted her to her feet, but when he tried to support her by holding her arm, she slid out of his grasp and tottered toward the front of the bookstore. Ethan followed, mulling over the brilliant thought that had just lodged in his scientist's brain.

One of his current research projects had originated from a conversation with Bee. She'd always asserted that her niece had psychic abilities, but, of course, denied them. And Ethan had been studying families where psychic aptitudes seemed to be more prevalent than the average—related either to genetics or a more open-minded philosophy. Recently, he had begun to focus on the psychological aspects of hereditary ESP and how it affected different people within a family.

Diana Iverson, with her black and white, logical ways and, according to Belinda, the suppression of her gift, would be a perfect subject to round out the study. He already had enough data on Belinda to compare the two of them. Or—his interest spiked higher—she could be a candidate for a different project, about how the suppression of precognitive abilities manifests itself physically.

The dimness had edged from her eyes by the time they came outside into the mellow Maine sunlight. Diana took a deep breath and Ethan's gaze dropped automatically to the rising swell of her breasts outlined by the red shirt she wore. "I'm feeling better already," she told him, and he drew his attention back to her wan face.

"I'll drive you home anyway," he told her firmly, holding out his hand for the keys. "Where are you parked?"

He thought a flicker of relief flitted across her face. She jerked her head to the right. "In the lot behind the drugstore. But what about you? How will you get home?"

He started across the street, forcing her to follow him. "I can walk home from your house and pick up my car later. Don't worry about me."

She was quiet in the car until he turned onto the narrow dirt road that led to their respective homes. "I really appreciate this," she said.

He glanced at her, but she'd tilted her head back and had her eyes closed. "It's no big deal. I'm glad I was there to help."

At the large clapboard house, Diana alighted from the car before he was able to come around and help her out, reinforcing his initial impression of her as prickly and stiff. She started up the porch steps, clutching her straw bag, then turned toward him. "I'll need the keys, please," she said, holding out her hand.

He dropped them into her palm and watched as she turned to fit one into the lock. She stopped, shook her head, and looked down at the keys, sifting through them one by one. "Oh...*no* ...." she said, her voice low and frustrated.

"What's wrong?"

She sighed and looked up at him, sheepishness poorly hidden in her features. "I forgot to take the house keys when I left. I haven't added them to my car keys yet. I guess I'm locked out."

"I can fix that," Ethan explained easily. "Belinda always kept an extra in the birdhouse." He turned to stride off the porch.

"Uh...wait," she called. "Never mind, it won't work."

"What do you mean, it won't work?" he grunted, reaching up into the birdhouse. "It's right here." He pulled the key from its hiding place, holding it up for her to see.

"I—uh—" She looked embarrassed.

Ethan came back on the porch and brushed in front of her to fit the key in the lock. He stopped, noticing how shiny and new the deadbolt was. He didn't even have to try the key to know it wouldn't fit. Understanding dawned and he stepped back as she said, "I changed the locks."

"I see that." He looked out off the porch, suddenly darkly furious. "I'm sorry if I imposed upon you in any way. I'll—if you like," he flashed a stony glance at her, and was gratified to see a dark red flush on her face, "I'll open a window and help you get back in, then I'll just be on my way."

Diana felt miserably ashamed as Tannock stalked off the porch, striding purposefully around the corner of the house toward the kitchen. She followed slowly, wondering why she cared that she'd offended him, and wishing the heat in her cheeks would dissolve. Even facing the dreaded, male chauvinistic Judge Fernwitz never set her off-balance as much as Ethan Tannock seemed to do.

But then again, she'd never been confident or comfortable around men—especially ones as devastatingly handsome as this one. Though she'd worked hard to get past the insecurities, her mother's sly, sharp criticisms always seemed to lodge in the back of her mind. And when she was in court, she was wholly prepared with what to say. Around men in a casual situation...not so much.

That was why she'd been so stunned by the fact that Jonathan had been the one doing the pursuing, with a single-mindedness that took her breath away. When she would have discouraged him, or allowed her insecurities to keep him at arms' length, he was persistent and charming, wooing her, sweeping her off her feet just last summer.

And now...what had she expected? That he'd be content with her?

The ugly thought made her feel nauseated again and she ruthlessly closed her mind to it as she hurried after Tannock.

As she came around the back of the house, she found him struggling with one of the basement windows. It's painted shut," he grunted, trying to lever it open with a stout stick. "I think I can get it, though."

"Dr. Tannock, I'm really sorry—"

"Just call me Ethan," he said over his shoulder, voice tinged with annoyance. "And don't worry about it."

Diana had just stepped closer when he succeeded in forcing the window open. He tossed the stick aside, kicking the windowpane so that it opened wider. "I'll climb in and come around and unlock the door."

"You really don't have to …. " she began, but her voice trailed off as he ignored her and clambered awkwardly through the small space. She heard a dull thud as he landed on the floor inside, and, biting her lip in consternation, she turned to go meet him at the kitchen door.

When he came out, brushing the dust off his jeans, Ethan was brusque but polite. "Well, there you go. Now, don't forget to add the new key to your keychain." With a smile barely touching his chiseled lips, he started to walk off the back porch.

"Ethan, wait." She didn't know what to say, and why she felt she needed to repair the awkwardness between them. Perhaps in respect for her aunt's memory she should at least properly thank the man who obviously knew Belinda well enough to know where the house key was hidden.

How *did* he know where the house key was? And just how good of friends were they? Suspicions as to why an attractive young man would befriend an old, odd lady like Aunt Belinda suddenly blossomed in her mind and her thoughts turned considering. Just what had he gained from the friendship?

Or expected to gain?

He paused at the top step, and turned. His eyes were unreadable, shadowed, as he stood half in sun, and half in shade.

"Why don't you come in for a minute?" she asked suddenly.

"What about your headache?" he temporized.

"I'm fine now," she told him. "Come on in, won't you?"

He hesitated for a moment, then, giving a more genuine, but still restrained smile, he acquiesced.

In the big, bright kitchen, Diana bustled about, trying to keep busy while she decided how to eliminate the awkwardness between them, and at the same time, wondering why she'd done something so foolish. She should have just let him leave. It wasn't as if she was going to see him more than once or twice ever again. But, yet, she found herself saying, "I'm going to have a bite to eat—could I interest you in some lunch?"

Ethan leaned against the counter near the phone, propping a hip against it and folding tanned arms over his chest. He seemed hesitant for a moment, then the lines on his face relaxed. "I could eat. I can *always* eat," he added. "Thanks." He smiled at her, then, as though to indicate all was forgiven.

A little sizzle zipped through her belly. He was *so* damned attractive, and probably well-used to having his way around women...particularly ones who stammered and stuttered and didn't know how to act around men because they knew they couldn't begin to have the least bit of interest in them.

"How about some iced tea to start?"

"Wonderful. Thanks." Crinkles formed at the corners of smiling brown eyes as he grinned again.

Diana gave him a considering glance. He looked as though he could charm the Christmas presents from a toddler. She wondered again what he had charmed—or tried to charm—from her susceptible and wealthy Aunt Belinda...and just what he expected now that she was dead.

Then guilt washed over her. She of all people should not cast stones. She hadn't made the time to visit since learning a year ago that Belinda wasn't dead—as her mother had led her to believe for more than a decade. So many years wasted, and now she'd never have them back. Thanks to Victoria.

Pushing the uncomfortable thoughts away, she poured two tall glasses of iced tea and garnished them with lemon wedges. Just as she was pulling cheese and grapes from the refrigerator, the phone rang. Diana turned from her task, arms laden with food, in time to see Ethan reach for the black phone. He stopped suddenly, snatching his hand back as if burned.

"That's okay, go ahead," she said, and unloaded the food onto the counter, her cheeks warming again.

He caught it on the next ring. "Belinda Lawry's," he said in a smooth voice that felt like velvet over her skin. Then, after a pause, he said, "Just one moment. She'll be right with you."

Diana took the proffered phone. "Hello?"

"Who was that?" It was Jonathan.

"Oh, just a friend of Aunt Belinda's. Are you still getting in tonight?"

"I tried your cell, but you didn't pick up." His voice was tight. "Diana, is this—are you—what's he doing there with you? Who is that man? Is that why you aren't answering your cell?"

Diana felt a spark of annoyance, followed by a bit of a thrill that Jonathan might be worried about her fidelity, about whether he could trust her. He did love her, and he wanted things to work out—just as she did. "Jonathan, you have nothing to worry about," she said in a firm voice, wholly aware of Ethan standing there listening without appearing to listen. "I told you—the cell phone service up here isn't very good. There are tons of trees, and I haven't seen one tower nearby."

"Are you sure?" he insisted, his voice dropping to that mellow, empathetic tone he normally used. "I can't wait to see you. That's why I was calling—to let you know I've gotten tied up. I'm not going to be able to make the flight tonight and I won't be able to fly in until tomorrow morning. Eleven a.m."

A sudden, ugly feeling lodged in her belly. He wasn't flying in tonight, but tomorrow morning instead? So he could spend the night with Valerie the Wonder Surgeon? "That's fine," she forced herself to say lightly. She realized her fingers were a little unsteady as she unwrapped a chunk of Gouda. "Are you still on United?"

"Yes, of course," he said, irritation in his tone. "Flight 439. I'll text it to you."

"I'd better write it down in case the text doesn't come through." Diana turned to get paper out of the drawer near Ethan and became flustered when she noticed he had opened the mahogany box, and that he stood between her and the drawer.

She hesitated, then reached past Ethan, brushing across his warm midriff to pull the drawer open. He stepped back, allowing her access to the pen and paper she sought, taking the box with him.

Irritated and disconcerted that she'd been forced to touch him, even as lightly as she had, and distracted by the mahogany box in Ethan's hands, Diana had to ask Jonathan to repeat his flight number twice more before she got it written correctly.

"Okay, then," she said hurriedly, watching as her guest pulled a chair from the kitchen table and sank into it, mahogany box in hand. "I'll see you tomorrow morning."

"All right darling," Jonathan replied. "Diana, remember: I love you. I only love you."

"Mm, love you, too," she managed to reply, acutely aware of her guest and the fact that she felt forced to respond that way. Of course she still loved Jonathan—she was just hurt and shocked by his actions, and it was going to take some time for her to feel comfortable again.

But he was such a successful professional, quite handsome, and he'd pursued her with intelligence and charm. He was the type of man she'd always dreamed of marrying, but that she'd never believed she could have.

Even Victoria approved.

Diana hung up the phone and turned back in time to see Ethan pull the deck of cards from its black silk swaddling. She couldn't turn her eyes away.

"Husband?" he asked casually, seemingly unaware of her attention on the cards.

"No," she told him, and further explanation stuck in her throat. "What are you doing?"

Ethan looked up at her, innocence written all over his face. "These are Belinda's cards, aren't they? I just wanted to see them. I know that you're not supposed to use anyone else's deck, but...no one's using them now." His face sobered and she felt a fresh stab of pain for Belinda's loss shoot through her. "You don't have any use for them, do you?"

"No." Diana turned defiantly away, ignoring a jab of nausea in her stomach. "But I don't know if you should be...playing with them."

Why did it bother her so much? She forced herself to ignore him, washing grapes and strawberries, cutting thick slices of bread, and preparing green salads for each of them. She wanted to ask him questions about his relationship with Belinda, but her thoughts were scattered and her nerves surprisingly on-edge as she heard him shuffling the cards behind her.

When she returned her attention to Ethan, she saw that he'd cut the deck into three sections, facedown, and was just re-stacking them. He seemed absorbed and thoughtful. Just as he finished piling them up and reached to pick up the top card, she made an involuntary noise.

Ethan looked up in surprise, still holding the card he'd picked up. He hadn't looked at it yet. "What's wrong?"

"Nothing. Nothing." She shook her head as if to clear the cobwebs, trying to still the churning in her belly. It couldn't be The High Priestess, she told herself. That would be crazy. Then, in spite of herself, she forced out the question. "What is it?"

Ethan glanced at it, then up at her. "The Death card," he told her solemnly.

"Oh." Diana felt the tension drain from her body. "Would you like some Dijon mustard with your bread and cheese?"

He looked at her, cocking his head to one side as if unsure what to make of her. "Most people would be freaked out if the Death card turned up," he said, still watching her.

Diana shrugged. "It doesn't bother me—I don't believe in that stuff."

"Thanks," he said as she placed the food in front of him. "This looks much better than the peanut butter and jelly sandwich I would have made." He set down the card he'd been holding, resting it face-up.

The High Priestess.

Diana dropped her plate, allowing it to clatter onto the table. She felt the blood drain from her face and her pulse throb heavily in her throat.

"What's wrong?" He got to his feet, looking as if he were ready to rush to her side.

"I thought you said it was the Death card," she whispered, sinking onto a chair, trying to control the trembling in her fingers. *Don't be ridiculous.*

"I was just joking," he told her. His gaze was concerned. "Diana, why don't you tell me what's going on here."

"That—*card*," her voice was thready, although she made a bold effort to keep it from shaking, "*only* that card, keeps showing up. Four—no, five times now—five times in a *row*. It's too weird!"

He sat down in a chair across from her, linking his powerful hands loosely together and studying her carefully. He didn't seem to be looking at her as if she needed to be admitted. He was... interested. "Do you know what that card means?"

Diana shook her head.

Ethan stood back up. "I'll get Belinda's book. Sit there, I know where she keeps it. I'll be right back." He started to go, then stopped to brush her cheek with a forefinger. She was too confused to jerk away from the unexpected intimacy, and allowed herself to be held by his safe gaze. "There's nothing to be upset about, Diana. Tarot cards don't have psychic abilities: people do."

And with that cryptic statement, he left the room. Diana stared at the card while he was gone, wondering what it signified. The woman—the priestess—seemed to be pushing a scroll under her cloak, as if to hide it. She sat in front of a backdrop of pomegranates and palm trees. Diana pressed two shaking fingers to her temple as she stared and stared at the card.

Approaching footsteps drew her attention to Ethan, coming back down the hall. He had an old, tattered book in his hands— one that was in similar condition to the one at the bookshop— and he had already marked a page with a forefinger.

With a brief smile, he took his seat, opened the book, and began to read. "'The High Priestess, Number Two. She is meant to represent the Guardian of the Unconsciousness. Her throne rests between our conscious mind and the innermost thoughts and knowledge of our *un*conscious mind.'" Ethan looked up at Diana. "She's telling you to look beyond the obvious, to allow your intuition and inner voice to guide you. Let your imagination and dreams abound, open your mind to the unknown, seek that which is concealed."

The nausea that had been lingering in the pit of her stomach lessened. "I don't believe in this stuff," she repeated, shaking her head. "It's a bunch of bunk. *You* don't believe it, do you?"

"Believe what? Believe that Tarot cards can tell the future? No, no, I don't believe that …." He leaned forward, his eyes serious and his face sober. "But I know that there are people—many people— in this world who have abilities beyond our understanding...and I know that our unconscious minds have capabilities of which we've hardly scratched the surface. Your aunt was one of those people...and she believed you are too."

"What a load of *crap*." Diana stood and folded her arms across her chest as if to hold in her fiercely pounding heart. "You're talking nonsense. I know Aunt Belinda thought she had some crazy powers, and she liked to tell people's fortunes using Tarot cards, but you're talking about her as if you took her seriously. That's ridiculous!"

Ethan remained seated, tenting his fingers together, staring at them as if trying to decide what to say. "Your aunt had ESP— actually, to be more specific, she had precognitive capabilities. It's a fact, Diana. She had a gift." He looked up at her as if to gauge her reaction. "I know. I tested her."

"What do you mean, you tested her?" Diana shot back, ignoring the odd, sinking sensation that was tumbling in her middle. *Who is this guy?*

"I've been working in the field of parapsychology for over ten years, and your aunt was one of my best, most conclusive examples of precognitive ESP."

"What do you mean—you're a ghost buster?" Diana couldn't hold back an incredulous laugh. "I can't believe I'm having this conversation with a straight face. You actually study ghosts and UFOs and someone *pays* you to do it? Who would do that—some association for clairvoyants?"

And then like the dawn, it all became clear to her—why Ethan should have befriended an old, *wealthy* woman like Belinda. And why he should be here now, with her. Fury lanced through her, replacing the shattering reality of their conversation, and she turned on him. "*That's* what you were after, then, wasn't it? Trying to fleece an old, gullible, *loaded* woman like my aunt!"

He blanched as she pulled to her feet and stood nearly nose-to-nose with him. She forgot her bewilderment and confusion, pushed aside her timidity and insecurity with a guy who had everything she didn't and channeled all of her suppressed emotions into the accusations. "How much did you get from her? How much did you con her into giving you?" Despite the harsh words, she didn't lose control. Instead, she used the same firm, cool persona she engaged when cross-examining a witness—and forgot that he was a dangerously attractive man around whom she should be intimidated.

Even when that heart-stopping face darkened with an anger that matched her own, Diana did not back down. He rose, too, forcing her to step back from his chair, eyes flashing. "How dare you accuse me—"

"No," she shot back, "how dare *you* come into this house uninvited—twice!—and how dare you pretend to be a great friend of my aunt's when I suspect all you really were after is money. What was your plan now that she's dead—to con her mousy, timid little niece into giving you more? By wooing and flirting and pretending to care?" That, she realized, was the worst of it—her old insecurities bubbling to the surface.

Ethan's lips were drawn together so tightly they nearly disappeared and the tic of a muscle wavered slowly, deliberately in his jaw. "You are a fool, Ms. Iverson, and don't deserve the least bit of the pride and affection your aunt showed you—not to mention the money. Good day."

He spun and walked heavily, angrily out of the house.

FOUR

Ethan's irritation with Diana Iverson still simmered a day later, that Saturday evening. He replayed their conversation over and over—wondering what it was that had caused her to go from a confused and bewildered woman he was consoling to a harpy, firing unfounded accusations at him. He'd never been so insulted in his life.

Tamping back a renewed sense of irritation, he pushed open the door of the Green Oaks Grille and ambled across its worn, warped hardwood floor. He gave the proprietress a smile as he slid onto one of the barstools at the end of the long, thickly shellacked bar.

"What can I get for you tonight, honey?" asked Mirabella.

"How about a tall Blue Moon?" He settled into his seat as she bustled over to three levers that dispensed the beers of choice at the Green Oaks. "I like that new shade of red on your hair, Bella," he called down to her. "You look like Flo from that old TV show *Alice*."

"Why thank you, honey," she patted the bouffant hairdo that sparkled like a ruby even in the dim light. The amount of hairspray she used to hold each swirl and curl in place was approximately as thick as the shellac on her bar. "My Tommy likes it too—even better than that Dusty Gold color I was wearing a few months back." She placed a tall glass of beer in front of him. "You eatin' here tonight, too, honey? Tommy made a good soup today—chicken barley—and we got a special with broiled cod and rice.

There's always a hamburg or fried clams, if you're wantin', and I got some potato salad and co' slaw if you want that too."

He sipped his beer. "How about a Reuben, with some cole slaw on the side," he suggested. "And a cup of that soup." Ethan craned his head around, looking out over the half-filled restaurant. "The girls coming in for their regular Saturday night meeting?"

Mirabella shrugged as she wiped off the counter. "I don't know for sure. Everyone's been pretty upset since Bee passed."

There was a holler from the back room and Bella rolled her eyes, making her penciled brows jump. "That Tommy. I wonder what he needs now. I'll be right back with your soup."

Despite the peremptory yell, Mirabella took her time making her way back into the kitchen. Her lime green dress splashed with daisies and thick white lapels hugged Rubenesque curves and the generous bottom that had the same saucy wiggle that 'her' Tommy had fallen in love with twenty years ago...or so she'd boasted to Ethan many times.

He smiled, thinking how great it was that those two had lived and worked and run this restaurant together for more than twenty years...and she still loved Tommy as much as she did from the first. She'd do anything for him, or so she'd told Ethan and anyone else who'd listen, time and again.

Ethan's amusement faded. The desire for single-minded devotion and commitment had been yanked right out of his life at about the same time he signed his name to the divorce papers.

It was pretty much not gonna happen—opening himself up to trusting a woman, or even casual dating—now that he'd been well and thoroughly screwed by Jenny, his ex-wife. Not to mention Lexie, one of his female students who'd wanted to get in his pants badly enough to lie about it. Oh, and Bruce—one of his friends who, as it turned out, had been boinking his wife for more than a year. It had been hell, that whole mess—and it was Belinda who'd listened to him blather about it over more than one six-pack. An unlikely pair they'd made, the two of them—along with Cady—sitting on the porch, talking for hours. Sometimes coherently, sometimes not so coherently.

Using one long forefinger, Ethan systematically wiped the condensation off his glass, his lips flattening with disgust. Women were either conniving, sneaky bitches like Jenny and Lexie, or cold, haughty ones like Belinda's niece, and he figured he was safest staying far away from any of them except for a good, hard lay when the urge struck. And even then...he'd had a moratorium on that for well over two years now.

He just hadn't been interested. In anyone.

A burst of raucous laughter erupted as a group of ladies swarmed through the front door. Five of them, varying in age from thirty to eighty, and in size from four to sixteen, flowed toward a large, circular table in the far corner of the room. They were chattering and laughing, carrying handbags of all assorted shapes and sizes.

"Well, I guess that answers your question, there, honey." Mirabella set a steaming bowl of soup in front of Ethan, jerking her head toward the quilting ladies. "Eat up, and let me know if you want more."

When he finished his dinner, Ethan pushed back from the bar and slid off his seat. "Good evening, ladies," he said as he strolled over to them.

"Ethan!" crowed a blue-haired, bespectacled lady. "Why, I didn't see you sitting over there."

"You can't see nothing past your own old nose, Martha," grumbled Helen Galliday, who wasn't far behind her in age but still possessed eagle eyes and super-bionic hearing. "He's been sittin' over at the bar, eatin' his dinner the whole time we been here. Have a seat, young man." She pointed a wrinkled, hook-like finger to an empty chair next to her. "And tell us how you're doin'. You missin' Bee like the rest of us?"

He sat. "I sure am," he admitted. "I didn't know what happened until Wednesday, when I stopped by her house and ran into her niece."

"Pity, pity," Martha of the blue hair shook her head. "And she was so young to just go like that. She wadn't no more than sixty-seven."

"And she had the best doctor in town," added a younger member of the group. Rose Bettinger, who was somewhere over fifty, had had the distinction of being the most junior member of the quilters until Betsy Farr, aged thirty-three, joined last year.

"If Doctor Reardon couldn't get her healthy, then, well, you know, I don't think anyone could." Betsy had a dreamy look in her eyes.

Ethan sat silently, watching the ladies in amusement as the banter jumped across and around the table with alacrity. "How's your Crazy Quilt coming?" he asked when there was a pause in the conversation.

"We might be finished by next year if Pauline and Martha would get their blocks done," grumbled Helen as she bit into a piece of bread, showering crumbs in her lap. She brushed them onto the floor with impatience and sour humor. "But Pauline's so blamed worried that she'll miss seein' Doug Horner one time she won't sit at the meetin' long enough to piece one block, ain't that right, Pauline? And Martha—her eyesight ain't much good no more anyway so that we have to do all the sashin' for her blocks. Good thing we got a system worked out for the ones we actually sell, or we'd be in more trouble'n a puffball in a tornado." She snapped another bite of bread with teeth that were too perfectly straight and white to be real ones.

"Helen, don't you be yammering about my personal life to this young man here," Pauline admonished, pointing a coral-tipped fingernail at her friend. "And I can't say you've been exactly timely with your last two blocks either." She plumped heavily in her seat—a daring move for a woman whose generous size threatened the stability of the chair—as her perfectly manicured nails fluttered with indignation. "The only one of us who's been on schedule has been Bee, and she isn't gonna be here to see it completed."

Pauline's point seemed to sober the group, and even Helen had nothing to add.

"I've seen your other work at the craft shows," Ethan said after a moment, "and I'd certainly like to see this Crazy Quilt of yours someday."

"Well, you know we ain't plannin' on selling it, young man," Helen snapped. "It's just a way for us to use up some old cloths we had layin' around. Truth to tell, I don't know it'll ever get done, 'cause we keep addin' to it, you see." Her eyes took on a special gleam. "But if you're lookin' for somethin' for your own place, why we have a real nice double wedding ring quilt pieced in dark blue and burgundy and sashed with cream that would fit real nice in your house."

Ethan hid a smile. Helen was most definitely both the brains and the brawn of the group when it came to the business end of retailing their work. She'd never even seen his cedar-sided cabin, much less have a clue how it was decorated. Not that you could call what he'd done to it 'decorated,' he thought ruefully.

"Now, Mrs. Galliday, you're making me nervous here with talk of wedding rings. You know I don't go in for that stuff." He allowed his grin to show now as he leaned over to pat her wrinkly, veined hand. "But my sister Fiona is getting married, and maybe I should get one for her. She'd like something bright and fun, I think."

Betsy Farr tittered at his comment, peering shyly at him from behind her coffee cup. She was young and single and just about as mousy as they came—and she'd never even said 'boo!' to him in the year he'd known her. "We have other patterns too, like a shoo fly and a couple monkey wrench ones. You could get one for your sister *and* one for you," she offered boldly, then hid behind her mug again.

He nodded. "If that's so, I certainly will stop by for a look. It gets mighty cold up there by the lake some nights."

"Doctor Reardon just bought a bright yellow and blue and green churn dash to display in his office," offered Rose Bettinger, reaching for a dinner roll. "We've sold several to tourists who stopped in his office since then. It's been a great bit of free advertising."

The door to the restaurant opened just then and Ethan looked up. "Well, speak of the devil," he muttered, recognizing the trio who'd just entered: Marc Reardon, along with Diana Iverson. Their companion, he suspected, was the man she'd been talking to on the phone yesterday, assuring him he had nothing to worry about with Ethan at her house.

Anger roiled inside him at the memory of her subsequent nasty accusations, and he figured he'd better split before Helen called them over. Then, he reconsidered. There was no reason for that narrow-minded, arrogant lawyer to make him feel uncomfortable. He'd done nothing wrong, and hadn't he already learned the lesson with Lexie? Avoidance wasn't the way to go when one was falsely accused.

"There he is!" whispered Betsy, staring over her shoulder. "I wonder who's that lady with him?"

"That's Diana," Helen snapped, peering through narrowed eyes. "Don't you remember her from the funeral? And that must be her young man with her. Jonathan Whose-its. He's a big shot doctor down to Boston."

"Oh, right." Betsy seemed relieved and turned back around to sip her coffee.

Helen stood and waved her arm vigorously, its loose skin flapping with the effort. "Diana! Doctor! Over here!" Her greeting was more of a command than a hello, and they responded to her hail.

"Good evening, Mrs. Galliday." Marc Reardon's smile oozed gentility as he offered an abbreviated bow. "Ladies," his gaze swept the group as his smiled warmed them. "And Dr. Tannock."

"Reardon." Ethan's response was drowned by the enthusiastic greetings of the quilters. "Hello again, Diana," he added coolly as she noticed him for the first time. Somehow she managed to look down her nose at him, even though he'd stood and now towered over her, and then she turned away to greet the quilting group with hardly an acknowledgment to him.

Suppressing irritation at her rudeness, he swept her figure with a chill gaze, deciding instantly—reluctantly—that purple was a great color for her. It made her thick, curling hair look almost black and her grayish eyes a deep blue. The cut of the dress didn't hurt either, he thought, allowing his attention to wander over her curves while she was involved in greeting the ladies. Why deny himself the pleasure of looking just because he wasn't interested in jumping into the deep end?

When he finished his leisurely perusal and turned his gaze to her companion, his eyes locked with those of Diana's boyfriend. *Oops. Caught with the hand in the cookie jar.* He smiled as if he didn't see the glare in the man's eyes and, offering his hand, returned to his seat. "I'm Ethan Tannock. Glad to meet you."

"Doctor Jonathan Wertinger," the man replied coolly, shaking his hand with a firm grip.

Ethan stopped a wider smile that would have turned deprecating. Wertinger was even more formally and expensively dressed than Reardon, and bristling from some stick up his ass. Ethan wondered if he got more out of Diana than the icy, suppressed anger she'd unleashed on him yesterday. From the looks of the man, the answer would be *no*.

Wertinger had sharp, intelligent eyes, however, and enough bravado to eye Ethan with the same cool interest he was showing.

"Thinking about joining the quilters, Tannock?" Marc Reardon was asking. "You'll have to be pretty talented with a needle to keep up with this bunch." He patted Betsy Farr's hand, and Ethan watched her eyelids flutter in ecstasy. "I bought a quilt from these ladies not three weeks ago, and already I've had five offers for it."

"I don't think they'd take me in," Ethan replied with a good-natured laugh. "I don't know a shoo fly from a monkey wrench, whatever that means, and I sure as hell can't thread a needle." He glanced at Diana and suggested with more than a bit of malice, "Why don't you see if Bee's niece might want to join while she's here?"

"What a *wonderful* idea!" gushed Rose Bettinger, jowls jiggling with enthusiasm. "Would you like to work with us in your aunt's place, Diana?"

The woman in question shot Ethan a nasty glare before turning a sweet smile toward the group of ladies. "Oh, I'm absolutely no good with a needle and thread, and I really don't have a lot of time up here. It wouldn't make sense for me to get in the group and then have to leave in a week or two."

"A week or two?" repeated Jonathan Wertinger, looking decidedly displeased, echoing Ethan's own dismayed thoughts.

That wasn't nearly enough time to observe Diana for his study, particularly since he didn't dare tell her his intentions—which he wouldn't be doing if they couldn't have a civil conversation.

"You're only staying for that long? We thought you'd be here for the summer like the rest of those blasted tourists," Helen Galliday groused.

"I love it up here, but I really can't take that long from my practice back in Boston," Diana tried to explain.

"Well, you'll be back to visit, won't you?" Pauline Whitten pressed.

Diana looked at Ethan as if she'd like to murder him for bringing this up, her blue-gray stare cutting him into little pieces. Then she seemed to collect herself and returned her attention to Helen Galliday, absently tucking one short tress behind an ear to reveal a large pearl stud. The dark lock curled under, peeking out beneath the earlobe and just brushing the pearl. Even in the dim light of the restaurant, the luminescence of the jewel and the shiny embrace of her hair were a combination of classic beauty and elegance. The rest of her walnut-colored mop, rising in soft waves from her forehead and brushing her bare nape, was tousled and full...almost messy, as if she'd just had sex. It left the long expanse of her neck bare to the potential caress of a finger...or a pair of lips.

Doing a mental double take, he reapplied his attention back to the conversation at hand. Wholly annoyed with himself, and that part of his anatomy that traditionally led him into troublesome situations, he shifted in his seat and firmly directed his thoughts elsewhere.

"You aren't going to sell Bee's house are you?" Helen Galliday was demanding.

Diana smoothed the skirt of her sundress, relieved when she felt the weight of Ethan's gaze move away. She was incredulous that he would just sit there, as calmly and innocently as if nothing had transpired between them and she hadn't uncovered his ulterior motives. Didn't the man have any sense of shame?

"Well, Mrs. Galliday," she equivocated, "I really haven't decided what I'm going to do with the house yet. I have a lot of paperwork to go through before I can make a final decision anyway."

"Bella, she's gonna sell the house!" Helen announced as Mirabella walked up with a pot of coffee.

"Oh *my*. I can't imagine what Tommy will say 'bout that!" She stood with a hand planted on her generous hip and looked questioningly at Diana.

"Who's Tommy? And why would he care?" Diana asked, feeling more uncomfortable now with all eyes on her.

"Why he's your great-uncle's cousin's son—didn't you know that?—and my husband for forty years. Your Aunt Bee used to have him come over and plow her out in the winter time."

Diana stared at her. "I'm sorry. I had no idea we were related." Anger swept through her—how many other relatives had her mother kept from her? "We'll have to get together some time and catch up on things." She would not let this opportunity to spend time with her family get away from her, as it had with Aunt Bee.

"Well, now, honey, that would be right nice. It's not as though you're close cousins or anything, but blood is blood is blood. I'll tell Tommy, an' I'm sure he'll be tickled pink! Now, he will be a mite disappointed if you do sell the house—"

"I'm sure Ms. Iverson will make the best decision she can." Marc Reardon entered the fray with a smile at Diana. "But we can't expect her to make it so soon, now, can we?"

Diana nodded gratefully as Jonathan leaned closer to her so that his shoulder pushed against hers. She shifted away, suddenly claustrophobic, and felt Ethan's attention return to her. An amused smile twitched his mouth and humor twinkled in his eyes, crinkling their corners. It seemed as though he was enjoying a joke at her expense and she bristled at the patronizing look. If she weren't so tactful—and fully aware of the ramifications of libel—she'd bring the whole subject up again, right here, and see what he had to say about it then. And who could know, perhaps he'd been working on one of the other old ladies. Why else would he be having dinner with them on a Saturday night?

At that moment, Ethan stood, taking Helen Galliday's hand in his. "It's always a pleasure to see you ladies."

As he said his goodbyes to the quilters, Diana noticed the easy smile that warmed his face again and again, and the way he spoke to each of the women. Charm and casual flirtation came so easily to him, she thought, watching as he made Betsy Farr giggle and Rose Bettinger blush with an off-hand, but seemingly sincere, compliment.

When he finally turned that smile and those warm, crinkling eyes toward her, for a moment she, too, was almost disarmed by them. Then, as if realizing on whom he was wasting his charm, Ethan shuttered his face into a polite mask. Diana cooled her faint smile to an urbane one and accepted his hand for a business-like shake. "It was nice to see you again," she told him, ignoring the fact that his grip was firm and warm and made her uncomfortably aware of the heat of his touch.

He moved away to shake Jonathan's hand, and then Marc's, and then, with one last quick wave, he left the group.

—◊—

Diana battled herself awake, clawing her way out of the dream.

Heavy darkness suffocated her and a sob jerked deep inside as she struggled to bring herself back to the present. Her hair was plastered to cheeks damp with sweat, her skin clammy with fear, and her breath caught and rasped in the dead silence.

She was curled up on the settee in Belinda's den, a crocheted afghan tossed over her in protection against the chill Maine night.

The Tiffany lamp by which she'd been reading still burned on the table next to her, creating a small circle of light in an otherwise dark, shadowed room.

The dream ebbed, but the fear, the visions and the sense of terror did not. She finally understood what it was: the heavy, claustrophobic sense of being smothered, of heavy softness pressing down over and into her nose and mouth as her arms and legs fought helplessly, unable to pull it away, unable to free herself from the dull, hot staleness of stunted air.

Before she fully shook herself from the nightmare's grip, a remnant of the dream crystallized in her mind. The clarity was so perfect, so sudden and perfect, it was as though she was looking at a film before her eyes—only it was in her head, not on any screen anywhere.

It was Belinda. No, *she* was Belinda—Belinda struggling against a heavy force that pressed against her face, filled her nostrils, silenced her gaping, gasping mouth...then Belinda, slowing, succumbing to the inevitable end, sagging into stillness.

Diana froze. Her whole world stopped, her mind and body going deathly, silently still. Even the murmur of her heart, the shallowness of her breathing, the trembling of her nerves paused... and an incredible certainty flooded her. Then she *knew*.

She knew.

A movement in the doorway caused her to shriek, clapping her hand to her heart. "Jonathan!" The lurching of her stomach calmed and she regained the ability to speak. "You scared the hell out of me."

"I thought you were coming to bed," he said, his tone faintly accusing. "It's after two."

"I'm sorry. I fell asleep reading." She could hardly form the words from lips that felt frozen in place. Her body was numb while nausea roiled in her belly and the trembling began in earnest. Hiding her shaking hands in the afghan, she looked toward Jonathan, wanting to rush into his arms—someone's arms—for comfort...but something held her back.

Diana forced a smile as he approached. She couldn't move to stand for fear her knees would buckle, and Jonathan's sudden intrusion into her...whatever it was...left her feeling unfinished and disoriented. She blinked hard, gave her head a little shake, and shrugged off the remnants of the dream—or most of it, anyway.

He was dressed only in a pair of cotton boxers, and his half-nude body slanted toward her, lean and pale in the dim light. His sandy brown hair was mussed, tufting from his temples in soft fluffs, and the lids of his eyes drooped partly closed. He'd fallen asleep in bed while she straightened up, washed her face, brushed her teeth, fed the cats, locked the doors—did her normal nightly routine.

She couldn't help but wonder if he was tired because he'd been up late—or even all night—the night before. With Valerie, the Vixen Surgeon.

Biting her lip, Diana silently chastised herself. *I've got to let this go. He's a good man. He loves me. He wants to marry me. I'm thirty-three, and I'm ready to get married. I may never have another chance.*

"Diana, I haven't seen you all week," he reminded her coaxingly, pulling the afghan from her lap and tossing it on an ottoman. Taking her hand, he eased her to her feet, and the book she'd been reading thumped onto the floor.

When she would have reached for it, he gathered her to his bare chest, wrapping arms warm from sleep around her. "I've missed you, darling," he murmured into her hair. "So much."

Diana slid her arms around his waist and dropped her head onto his shoulder, willing herself to stay in the moment, to *be* with him. But she couldn't relax, she couldn't give in to the affection and emotion she'd once had. She felt nothing.

Bitter tears filled her eyes and she blinked them back, furious once again with him for breaking her trust, and with herself for this empty, bland feeling...and still uncomfortably aware of the horror of being asphyxiated in her dream.

Of Belinda being asphyxiated.

She felt the shift beneath his boxers as his arousal swelled, nudging against her. He dropped a kiss into her hair, then tilted his head back to kiss her on the mouth. Closed lips, warm and dry, the kiss was a formality, a prelude to what would follow. His hands slid to cup her bottom, pulling her closer to his erection.

She'd never been a particularly eager lover—sex was messy, and she worried about how she looked naked, along with a variety of other things—but now she felt a complete absence of interest. She felt nothing. Not even aversion.

Just...nothing.

"Why don't you come to bed now," he suggested in her ear, his mouth slipping to kiss a tender spot on her neck.

She wanted to *want* to go with him. She wanted things to be all right. She didn't want this blank feeling rising between them. And she suddenly dreaded the thought of following him back into the bedroom where such a horrific thing had happened to Aunt Belinda in that room. In that bed.

"I ...." She pulled away, turned to pick up the book. "Not tonight, Jonathan."

"What do you mean, not tonight?" He sounded shocked and irritated, and he had sleep-breath tinged with wine. "I came all the way up here to see you. I have to go back tomorrow."

She folded the quilt deliberately, straightened the pillows, and replaced the book on its shelf. "I'm too tired," she lied, not willing to go into the reasons. Not yet, not now. She'd get over this distance from him soon enough, but she needed time. "And you must be too, you fell asleep so quickly."

"But now I'm awake," he said, the hint of a whine in his doctor's voice. "And so are you. Diana, you're not still upset about...what happened, are you?"

She had to bite her tongue not to snap back at him, *No, I'm not at all upset that I showed up to surprise you at your conference hotel and found another woman sharing your room. Why should I be? We've only been together a year, we've only been planning to get married this fall. Why should something like that bother me for more than, oh, say, a minute or two?*

But instead of saying what she really wanted to, she put on the bland mask her mother had taught her to wear and said, "I'm just tired, Jonathan. And I'm still grieving for Aunt Bee. But I am ready to go to sleep."

At least, she'd give him that. And maybe, just maybe, in the morning she'd wake up next to him and feel better.

—⁂—

Sunday mornings were lazy ones at the Tannock household. Ethan rolled out of bed—to Cady's immense relief—at ten o'clock, and staggered sleepily to the door to let the whining dog out to do her business.

He stood in the doorway, arms folded over his bare chest and enjoyed the feel of the morning breeze over his naked body. Ethan yawned, stretching one arm straight into the air, and let it drop to scratch his head, then to his rump, then to adjust his balls. It was heaven living in a place where you could walk in your back yard naked.

Cady finished her business and decided she wanted to play, and Ethan, starting to become fully awake, stepped off the porch onto the lawn. His yard was a half-acre of clipped grass, studded with a few trees and surrounded by sky-scraping pines and heavy woods—and was less comfortable in the evenings than the morning because of the flies and mosquitoes. The lake glittered blue just down a small incline, between pines and maples and cottonwoods.

"Come on, Cady, let's go swimming." He grabbed a pair of shorts that hung over a chair on the deck.

At the suggestion, the lab dropped the stick she'd been prancing about with and tore down the incline, splashing gleefully into the water. Ethan yanked on the shorts, then followed Cady down a cedar chip path and dove quickly from his dock into the lake.

He surfaced, whooping from the refreshing eye-opener, and whipped his hair back. Cady paddled up next to him, thumping against him with her paws (and occasionally, with a claw), then headed back toward the shore where she could chase a goose.

Ethan swam out from the tree-lined, shady shore and turned to look back.

His gaze went immediately to the white clapboard house just a half-mile down from his. It sat on a bigger hill than his cabin's, and had a larger yard cleared of trees. Ethan could even see Diana's pale gold Lexus sitting in the drive.

He floated on his back, narrowing his eyes against the sun. He tried to stop the mental image—but there it was: the ice-queen and her cardiologist, messing up those lacy pillows and embroidered sheets on that high Victorian bed.

Disgust roiled inside him once again—anger for Belinda, and annoyance for himself. Although Diana's accusations had infuriated him at the time, he'd since come to realize that he didn't give a rat's behind what she thought about him …. And he actually felt more than a bit smug, knowing that she thought the worst of him while he *knew* the worst of her.

Ethan allowed himself to sink under the lake's surface, then rise back up and let the water plaster his hair back. Cady was paddling back out to him, her nose just above the water, whuffling and snuffling. "Wanna go back?" he asked, then did a shallow dive, resurfacing several feet away.

They stumbled to shore at the same time, Cady shaking herself from head to tail as Ethan tossed his hair back and wiped the water from his eyes. They hurried back to the house, refreshed and hungry.

Just as they stepped onto the screened-in porch, Ethan heard the phone ringing. He grabbed a towel slung over a chair, pointed a finger at a dripping Cady and ordered, "Park it." He grabbed the cordless just as the answering machine began to whir into action. "Tannock."

"Hey, buddy, get off your ass and let's go catch us some walleye."

"Hey, man, what's up?"

"I just told you. I'll be over in fifteen with the worms and sandwiches if you supply the boat and the poles." Joe Tettmueller's voice had such a drawl to it that even when he was furious, the end of the sentence didn't catch up to the beginning until the next day.

"Sure sounds better than what I had planned. Make sure you bring some of Lucy's corned beef for me. A big thick one."

True to his word—for he drove faster than he spoke—Joe Cap, as he was commonly called—pealed down the gravel drive in his shiny, nick-free, black F10 pickup minutes later.

Taking the tackle box and four fishing poles, along with a net and a six-pack, Ethan commented, "You're not on today, I guess?" He gestured to the beer.

"Naw. We had enough excitement down the station the last month what with Bella and Tommy's till bein' broken into, and Bee Lawry bein' found, and a fender-bender down over on 213 with some drunk tourists, that I decided to give myself the day off." Joe Tettmueller was the chief of the two-member police force in Damariscotta.

The two men trudged down the incline, carrying a large cooler suspended between them, Cady tramping through the brush in a zigzag toward the lake. "Yeah," Ethan said as he tossed the tackle box into the small dinghy. "That's too bad about Belinda. I wish't you'd have called me."

"Sorry, buddy. You're right. I shoulda done that. I just figured when you're down to Princeton, you don't want to be bothered with what's going on up here."

"Not true," Ethan told his friend. "I'm more interested in what's up here than what's down there."

"So you seen her niece here in town?" Joe smirked as he yanked a baseball cap down on the top of his buzzed head. "She's pretty hot, and now she's loaded, too."

Irritation flitted through Ethan as he turned to step into the softly rocking boat. "Maybe hot looking, but an ice-cold ballbuster underneath. Besides, I don't think Penny would take too kindly to hearing her husband talk that way."

Joe actually looked a bit frightened at the thought, then his face shifted into a grin that matched his drawl as he stepped into the boat. "Naw, Ethan, I'm not looking for me—I'm looking for you. How long's it been since you and Jenny split up? Two years? You've had that—what'd ya call it?—moratorium thing going on for long enough. You got t'be mighty lonely in that big old cabin."

"Don't be an ass, Cap. My cabin's not that big, and yes, I'm still staying far away from any females. Especially that viper Diana Iverson. Cady and I are just fine all by ourselves." Without waiting for his friend to sit, Ethan shoved the boat away from the dock with enough force to set it rocking. "Besides, she's got a boyfriend."

Cap glanced at him from under his brim as he sat down abruptly. "Sounds like you had a bit of a run-in with the lady lawyer. What happened? She didn't seem that bad to me."

Ethan chose a pole and unlatched the hook from its moor through one of the rings. Digging into a Styrofoam carton of rich black soil, he pulled out a squirming worm and wove it onto the hook. Then, setting it down, he gave the oars two powerful strokes before replying. "When did you have occasion to meet her?"

"At the funeral."

"You went?"

"Yeah—I found ol' Bee, and it didn't seem right not to go." He baited his own hook as he added as hastily as he ever did, "Not that I wouldn't've not gone anyway, yannow."

"I didn't know what happened until I showed up at Belinda's house the other night, and surprised the hell out of Diana." His mouth quirked at the memory of her prune lips. The humor vanished and, after giving one more long, sweeping row, Ethan folded the oars back into the boat and looked out over the sparkling lake as they slowed to a mere drift.

Joe Cap slipped the anchor into the water with a minor splash and, with a quick flick of his wrist, sent a long, smooth cast over the lake. The fishing line glinted like a cobweb in the sunlight, then settled over and into the depths of blue.

"So you found her, huh?" Ethan's line soared in a different direction, and was followed by a third and fourth cast...then all was peaceful.

"Yeah. She didn't show for a doctor appointment, and Reardon got worried and called the station. I went down and got into the house and found her. Poor old woman—die alone like that."

It was a shame Belinda died by herself, and a damn good thing Joe Cap'd found her so quickly. "She died in her sleep is what Diana told me."

"Yep, so it appeared."

"At least she didn't go through any pain."

"Nope. Hope not." Joe's attention was not fixed on the two fishing lines he owned, nor was it on the cooler through which Ethan had begun to rummage.

His statements sounded even less solid than usual, and Ethan noticed. "Everything all right, Cap?"

"Mm." He thought about it for a moment, staring out at the lake. "She had a heart problem—documented in her medical records. There was no sign of struggle, of forced entry, of robbery... but something don't seem right about it. It's been bothering me...but I dunno what it is." He sighed, then abruptly jerked to attention when one of the silvery lines shivered. "Got one!"

Quick as a flash, he grabbed the pole and began to manipulate the reel—in and out, in and out...pull'em in...slowly let it out—in a natural rhythm that echoed the lapping of waves against the boat.

Ethan's line twanged, and he snatched the pole just as a third line began to bob in the water. Over shouts of glee and good-natured cursing, they worked the lines in the familiar pattern well into the afternoon.

—⚊—

The wind rushed through the Lexus's moon roof, tossing Diana's hair with the same abandon as her mind zipped through her thoughts. She was cruising at a speedy seventy miles per hour along Route 1, north from Portland, after dropping Jonathan off to catch his late afternoon flight.

As she maneuvered the car around smooth curves and up and down slight inclines, Diana considered the other question that had been brooding in her mind all day: *Was* it possible? Had Belinda been murdered in her own bed?

And could it have been Ethan Tannock?

Keeping her lawyer hat on, and refusing to allow her dislike of the man to color her thoughts, Diana considered the situation. First of all, she was basing this on a dream. A mere dream.

Yes, a terrifyingly real one. One that she'd had every night since she arrived in Aunt Bee's house, even though she hadn't recognized it for what it was. And she'd awakened with a certainty that even she couldn't shake, using her logical, science-based mind.

If it were true, then...who could have done it? And why?

Obviously, Ethan knew her well—well enough to walk into her house uninvited for a visit...unless, if he *had* killed her and he knew she was dead, he walked into the house intending for Diana to *think* he had that kind of freedom.

But he knew where the house key was hidden—so obviously Belinda had trusted him. Tapping her finger against the steering wheel, Diana frowned. Poor Aunt Bee...so gullible and trusting to be taken in by a pretty face.

But then...now that she was dead, Tannock's source of money would also be gone, for Diana knew he hadn't been named in the will. She, Diana, and the local animal shelter, were the only beneficiaries. So what motive was there for someone to kill Aunt Belinda if they weren't going to inherit any of her money?

Ethan had been friendly to Diana—but not overly so, as if he were trying to inveigle his way into her good graces in order to keep the flow of money going.

She grimaced. If he had meant to cozy up to her, he'd definitely blundered that part of it, for it seemed he only knew how to rub her the wrong way. And aside from that, he had an almost accusatory hint in his eyes at times when he looked at her, as if he found something about her as distasteful as she did about him.

But, then...the way he'd been studying her at the Grille last night had caused her fingers to become clumsy and her heart to pump just a little faster. When he didn't think she noticed, when she was busy trying to dig herself out from the hole he'd dug for her with the quilting group, she'd caught a look on his face. It was as far from distasteful as one could get. It was...thoughtful... heavy...*avid*.

Her heart fumbled a beat at the memory. That was a dangerous look, coming from a dangerous man.

So caught up was she in her train of thought that she almost missed the turn-off for Route 213. Slowing the car, she made the turn and forced her thoughts onto a different track. As she tooled along the two-lane road, Diana looked to her right and was able to see glimpses of the dark blue of the Damariscotta River, which widened into Damariscotta Lake further north, where Aunt Belinda's house was. The sun was low in the sky, and dropping nearly as quickly as she was driving. Soon, she wouldn't be able to see the water at all.

The forest was so dense along the lake that the houses were completely private—you couldn't even see the lights of a neighbor's house at night. Diana didn't mind the isolation, but as she turned onto the dirt lane that led to the house, she realized just how far away from civilization she was.

Ethan Tannock lived on the lake too, and from their brief conversation on the day he'd driven her home, she knew that he lived very close by. He took the same dirt lane that she did, but when it made a triple fork near the lake, she turned right and he turned left. Nevertheless, there was no more than a half-mile between their houses.

Somehow, the thought that Ethan Tannock lived so near by both relieved and unsettled her.

The Lexus's headlights cut beams through sudden, enveloping darkness as the car bumped down the road through the forest. The intermittent winks of fireflies broke the solid black, and twice she saw reflections of the eyes of some critter crouched by the side of the road. Of necessity, she drove slowly—between the potholes, the curves of the road, and the possible intrusion of deer, she had no choice but to do so. Bugs collected, thick and angry, in the lights, and as a result splashed onto the windshield like raindrops. *So much for late-night swimming*, Diana mused, shuddering at the thought of moths, mosquitoes, and deer flies swarming around her.

It was nearly pitch-black by now, and Diana was thankful that she'd left a porch light on, as well as two lights in the house.

When she came to the fork in the lane, she tossed a glance toward the darkness where Ethan's house would be and was surprised and, to be honest, relieved to see the faint glimmer of light through the forest. He was closer than she'd realized.

Now, she turned onto the tire-track lane that led to Aunt Belinda's house. Driving required her full attention, as tree limbs brushed into the car's path and the ruts were enough to jounce the car like a rough boat ride, even when the vehicle crept along at five miles per hour. At last, she pulled up a slight incline into the clearing. The white clapboard house, with its three gables and large wrap-around porch, sat in the center of an open area surrounded by trees. *In darkness.*

Diana pulled the car up next to the dark house and stared, her heart lodged in her throat. She was certain she'd left the lights on—on the porch, and in the den and kitchen. Hesitantly, she turned off the ignition and sat in the car for a moment, unease pattering along her spine and kneading her stomach.

Why was she so creeped out?

Steeling herself, telling her odd nervousness to go away, she slowly opened the car door. Perhaps she'd meant to turn on the lights, and had forgotten. But, no, she distinctly remembered going into the den to turn on the lamp just before she walked out the door to take Jonathan to the airport.

The power could be out. She wasn't sure if that was a relief or not.

Diana grasped the door handle and pulled the latch to open it, stepping hesitantly into the night air. There hadn't been a storm, but perhaps there was another reason for a power outage.

The darkness of the forest hovered at the far edges of the open yard, and she glanced up to see the glittering display of stars. The

Milky Way and a quarter-moon lit the clearing nearly as well as a porch light would, increasing her flagging courage. She muddled through her key ring and located the key to the front door, then grabbed her bag and stepped lightly up the porch steps.

It was a bit of a struggle to fit the key into the lock, shadowed as it was, and once the key slid into place, she had to rotate it one way, then the other, and back again before the knob would turn.

Finally, the door caved open into the dark house and Diana stepped in gingerly, her heart still doing odd things in her chest. She felt along the wall for a nearby light switch, and just as she turned to flick it on, she caught a movement out of the corner of her eye.

Whirling, she gasped and screamed at the sight of the murky silhouette, which froze. Then it was a flurry of movement, rushing toward her. A powerful shove sent her slamming full-force into the wall and the impact knocked all of the breath from her body. Diana slid to the floor, bracing for another blow as she blindly grasped for something to use as a weapon. But the intruder dashed past her—out the open door, stomping across the wooden porch and thudding down the steps.

Shaking, nauseated and terrified, Diana managed to struggle to her feet in time to rush to the door and see a figure dashing into the woods...into the woods toward Ethan Tannock's house.

FIVE

A FULL, FIERCE ANGER swept over Diana, and all of her nervousness slid away. *That jerk!*

Without a second thought, she picked up the keys, turned on the foyer light, and slammed out the front door. Not even bothering to lock it behind her, she ran down the steps, gripping the key chain, her lips tight and her eyebrows puckered so firmly that her head started to ache.

This was going to stop.

She yanked the car door shut behind her to punctuate her fury and determination, and cranked the key so far that the engine ground for a split-second before it caught. The tires spewed gravel from the drive into the air, raining onto the porch as she turned the Lexus around and started down the winding lane.

Driving much faster than she had on her arrival, Diana had little care for the scrapes and nicks her beloved gold car would get from the tree branches. She was that incensed. And as furious as she was, she remembered to feel alongside her seat for the can of pepper spray that she always carried with her—just in case.

Although she had never been to Ethan Tannock's home, she knew where it was and turned down the curving drive that could only lead to his doorstep. When her car rounded a sharp corner to face a closed garage entrance, she slammed on the brakes and turned off the ignition, leaving the keys in the car, and jumped out.

Blind fury drove her as she stalked around the side of the house, the can of pepper spray at the ready, into the small clearing...and stopped short.

Two men had turned to gape at her. They stood near a smoking grill. A floodlight illuminating the yard clearly indicated that they were in the midst of preparing to eat. The luscious scent of grilled steak permeated her anger, as did the casual demeanor of the men and the fact that neither of them were breathing heavily from a dead-heat run. Nor were they dressed in black.

"Well, now, Ethan, you didn't tell me we were gonna have company for supper," drawled one of them in a voice that she vaguely recognized. "Who is that?"

Wishing that the earth would open up and swallow her, Diana forced herself to start forward nonchalantly, crossing her arms over her chest to obscure the pepper spray.

When she stepped into the illumination, she heard Ethan's soft exclamation. "Well, well. Diana Iverson, what are you doing here?" He started toward her slowly, looking at her with an expression that indicated total shock and wariness.

Not the most welcoming of greetings, she thought wryly, focusing on anything but how incredibly stupid she felt. But under the circumstances, it was not unexpected. "I—uh ...."

Words failed her, and stuck even further in her throat when she actually looked at him. Her gaze became trapped, fixed on a shirtless, muscled, darkly-haired torso that looked like it belonged to someone like David Beckham. Diana swallowed, jerking her attention away so that it bounced down over his swim trunks, to legs that matched his abdomen in physical perfection, and finally up to a stony, set face.

"Is there something I can help you with?" His voice was calm, but irritation glinted his eyes. "Unless you normally go speeding up someone's driveway like the hounds of hell were after you, on your way to a neighborly visit."

The man didn't have to like her, but he didn't have to be so rude either, Diana thought desperately—conveniently dismissing her own previous rudeness. Hoping for assistance, she glanced at

Ethan's companion for the first time, and suddenly recognized him with a flood of relief. "Captain Tettmueller, I'm so glad you're here!"

He stood, unfolding a tall, lanky body topped by a worn baseball cap. Spiky, straw-colored hair stuck out from around the hat in endearing little curls, giving the grown man a boyish look. "What can I do you for, Ms. Iverson? Is ever' thing all right?"

Suddenly, the impact of what she'd experienced rushed over her and, as her surge of angry adrenaline dissipated, weakness flooded her body. What a stupid thing to do, she thought numbly.

Ethan must have seen something change in her demeanor, for he snagged a lawn chair and swung it to a place right in front of her. "Sit down, Diana. Do you want something to drink? Obviously something's wrong," he added, glancing at his friend.

"Yes, yes." She began to babble—something she knew she was doing, that she hated herself for, but she couldn't help it under the circumstances, and poured out the whole story.

Ethan thrust a cold bottle into her hand and she took a gulp of unexpectedly heavy, stout beer—then had to swallow the awful stuff. She handed the bottle back to him and finished her explanation, "So I got in the car and—" She stopped, realizing what she had been about to say.

Ethan wasn't slow. He knew exactly why she clamped her mouth shut. The woman had done it again—thought the worst of him—and nearly accused him to his face of breaking into her house. Attempting to hide his growing pissed-offness, he brought the bottle to his own lips, and, as he sipped, realized that her full, sexy mouth had just covered the very same opening. Damn.

It wasn't just the beer that made a warm trail snake down to his belly. He drank again, checking her out from beneath lowered lids while Joe Cap slid into police officer mode and began to question the damsel in distress.

Man, she'd come roaring up the drive like a maniac. Lucky she hadn't hit anything on the way or spun into a tree. She wouldn't have surprised them like that if Cady hadn't gotten herself sprayed by a skunk—a regular happening in the summer that they were both used to—and was locked away in the laundry room while the tomato juice bath did its work.

Then, with a snort of disgust that caused Cap to glance at him in confusion, Ethan placed the bottle on the ground with a dull thump. What the hell was wrong with him? The poor woman had come home to find an intruder in her house, had been pushed around by him, and all Ethan could think about was his own pride...and those full, sexy lips and flustered, tousled hair.

"Are you hurt?"

His question caused the others to look at him as though surprised he even existed. She turned to him, her dark blue eyes large and showing more vulnerability than he'd yet to see, and something twisted deep inside him. *Not good.*

"Nothing more than a bang on the temple and a bruise on the hip," she replied. Then, turning back to Cap, she resumed the conversation between them. "So I'll need to file a report tomorrow?"

"Yep. Got any idear why someone might have wanted in the house? Was anything disturbed?"

Diana shook her head. "I didn't stick around long enough to see. I had...the crazy idea that I might be able to catch...the guy."

Ethan snorted. This time the derision was aimed at her, even though he knew she'd assumed he was the intruder, and he folded his arms over his bare chest. "*That* was a smart thing to do."

Temper flared in her expression, bringing a sparkle back to her eyes and a slight flush to her cheeks. "I had *this*." She shoved a can into his face, just under his nose. "Want me to try it out?"

He blinked, looking down awkwardly at the spray nozzle that was aimed right at his mouth. At least her finger wasn't on the trigger. "No thanks. I guess you were prepared."

And then, just because he couldn't resist and because she really did need to be taken down a notch, he made a quick movement—fluid and sharp—and suddenly the can was in his hands and she was slamming into his chest, one arm folded back behind her.

Heat flooded Ethan the instant she connected with his body, shocking him so that he nearly released her as quickly as he'd grabbed her. Thanks to his post-divorce moratorium, he hadn't had female curves plastered against him for two years.

Diana's face tilted up in surprise of her own, eyes flaring wide and lips parting in a startled gasp. Her breasts rose with quick, shallow breaths, pressing against his chest, and one knee was cocked into his thigh. He could smell that floral, feminine scent from her hair, and felt the fragility of the narrow wrist he'd captured behind her back. For a moment, it was just the two of them caught in an awkward, titillating pose. Then suddenly, with a short laugh to cover his chagrin, he released her.

"It was a foolish thing to do," he said mildly, handing her back the can of pepper spray—his point having been made quite clearly. Still, his heart did leaps and dives even as she retrieved the can with those pruny lips and turned away.

Cap spoke up then and offered to see her home and to check out the house to be certain nothing else was amiss. Ethan considered going along, but one frigid look from the lady lawyer gave him cause to rethink that option.

He didn't want to go anyway.

—⚄—

Belinda's house loomed dark and forbidding in the center of the clearing. Diana had left in such haste that she hadn't turned on any lights. But somehow returning in the company of a police officer did wonders for her courage.

Captain Tettmueller led the way inside, and she followed, dogging his footsteps silently as he went from room to room, thoroughly checking them. Nothing seemed out of place at first glance and when they finally returned to the kitchen, Diana felt more comfortable, knowing that there was no one in the house.

"You've got sturdy locks and there's no easy entry," he commented in his snail's pace drawl. "Looks like he forced his way in through the back door. He won't come back tonight. You caught him in the act, he knows you're home...and since he didn't—er—attack you, violence is not his intent. I'll send the patrol car down here a coupla times the rest of the night, though, and notify the Lincoln County sheriff about the break-in as well. But are you sure you want to stay here by yourself?"

She didn't hesitate. Somehow she knew there was nothing more to fear tonight. "I'll be fine. Tomorrow I'll come down and file a report, and get the locks changed again, but—"

"Again?"

She felt the slight flush of embarrassment creep over her face. "I just had them changed a few days ago."

"Has the house been broken into before?" Intensity replaced the golly-gee look on his face as he waited for her answer.

She might as well tell him, for the record. Just because she had been wrong about Ethan tonight didn't mean he was innocent of everything else. "Ethan Tannock was in here the other day when I was in town."

The dawn crept over his face. "Ahhhh. So that's why—" He changed the route of his words and asked, "How do you know that?"

"He...left a note." As she said it, she felt even more foolish. Who would leave a note advertising a break-in?

The expression on his face echoed these thoughts, but manners obviously won out and he didn't say anything about that. Joe Cap just looked at her very seriously and said, "Now, Miss Iverson, I know you're new to these parts, but Ethan Tannock is the last person you'd ever have to worry about in that way."

She shot him a disbelieving look. "You're right, I am new to these parts. But I don't trust him as far as I can throw him. You may all be part of the good-old-boys' club, and if I hadn't seen him hanging out so casually tonight with my own two eyes, I would still suspect he was the one who was here this evening. He was taking advantage of my aunt, and her eccentric beliefs, and when I find the proof, I'm going to nail him."

Captain Tettmueller made a strange noise that sounded like a choking laugh, but when she turned to look at him, his face was deadpan serious. "Right, miss. Well, I sure hope for the professor's sake you don't take too long to...uh...nail him."

Having the suspicion he was laughing at her, Diana drew her lips together. But something else he'd said had caught her attention. "The professor?"

"Yeah, that's Tannock. He's some bigwig down to Princeton in the labs where they study ESP and psychics—though when he's up here, he's just a reg'lar guy who likes to fish and drink beer. Nasty divorce a coupla years ago, and—"

"Princeton?" she repeated, frowning, and a tiny snake of uncertainty zapped her. Then, she regrouped. If that's what he was telling people, including Belinda, that was easy enough to check on. She'd do that first thing in the morning, before going down to the police station. "Well, thank you very much, Captain Tettmueller. I'm sorry if I interrupted your dinner, but I do appreciate your checking things out down here."

"No prob, miss." He touched his fingers to the brim of his cap. "Gotta get home to the wife, anyway. She's probably chewed a hole through her lip, wondering where I am."

After he left, when the house became silent again, Diana retreated to the kitchen. It was late—nearly midnight—but she was wide-awake and her veins were zipping with energy. By all rights, she should be a bundle of nerves, here, alone, in this house where she'd come to believe her aunt was murdered and she had just tonight surprised an intruder.

But she wasn't. It was odd...it was as though she *knew*. Knew things were safe now.

Just as she'd felt nervous arriving home tonight, for no apparent reason. She'd known something was wrong then.

She remembered a pitcher of tea that was chilling in the refrigerator. Aunt Bee's herbal tea is starting to grow on me, she thought with a sudden nostalgic smile. Little had she known that one day she'd sit at her aunt's table and willingly sip peppermint tea...without her.

"Aunt Bee, if you can hear me, I just want you to know how badly I feel about not seeing you for so long. I'll find out what happened to you—the truth—and make whoever it was pay." She said the words aloud, fervently...and then felt horribly foolish for doing so.

But just as she turned to pull a glass from the cupboard above, Diana felt the air stir, and she smelled something soft and floral. A sense of comfort swept over her as if someone put an arm around her shoulders. The sensation was warm and familiar—as if Aunt Belinda was right there in the room. Of course she wasn't, Diana knew, but she did feel the essence of her aunt, the sense of her, here in the kitchen that held many memories of those three summers she'd spent here.

Oh, how many times she'd sat at that table during those summer visits while her aunt baked peach cobbler or patiently taught her how to cross-stitch, or showed her how to roll out a pie crust. She remembered the long walks they'd take through the cemetery—and the stories Aunt Belinda would make up about the people whose graves littered the fenced-in plot. There were exciting moments in the little dinghy she used for fishing, and the one time a walleye almost won the battle for its life by pulling Diana into Damariscotta Lake.

She felt better now, warm from the memories and maybe a bit less guilty about not seeing Aunt Belinda before she died. Taking her iced tea, she wandered from the kitchen down the hall to the den—the room in the house that seemed the most comforting to her. She sank onto the settee and sighed, thinking about all the work she would need to do to clear out this room before she could sell the house.

Then, she noticed the mahogany box of cards on the floor next to her foot.

She didn't remember moving them there.

A strange prickle crawled up her spine, slowly, as she looked down at the small chest. She'd pushed them away, but now some of Ethan's words from the other day came floating back to her. *Cards don't have psychic abilities...people do. Your Aunt Belinda had the ability, and she believed you did too.*

Tightness banded her chest and she reached for the box before she realized what she was doing. Here, too, were memories—long suppressed ones, she now realized, but memories. Vague images, just out of reach of her consciousness, hinted of Aunt Belinda taking the cards, showing them to her one by one, talking about them, encouraging her to look at them and think about them.

Then, the wisp of memories evolved into angry words from her mother and a horrible argument with Aunt Belinda...and then there were no more memories of Aunt Belinda. The summer visits stopped abruptly the year she turned fourteen.

With a shake of her head, Diana tried to clear her thoughts. Wow, she thought, that was odd. *It was almost as if I were reliving those times...times that I don't ever remember having.*

Perhaps there was some validity to those faint images—for after that last summer, Diana's mother steered her toward more scientific pursuits: chemistry, mathematics, logic, even piano lessons, and Aunt Belinda's name was never mentioned again until Diana was older, in her late teens, and asked about her. She was told that her aunt had moved away and didn't want to see any family anymore. And then just after college, when Diana pressed Victoria for her aunt's contact information, her mother told her that Aunt Bee had died.

How could she ever forgive her mother for that lie? She'd long forgiven her for the years of criticism and sly remarks, even though she still had to fight the insecurities. But this—such a blatant lie. Why would her mother do such a thing?

Pressing her lips tightly together to keep tears from coming, Diana forced her attention away from the Tarot cards. She gazed around the room, taking in the haphazard stacks of magazines and newspapers, the messy shelves of books, and dust-covered trinkets and statuettes that littered tables and cubbyholes. But her gaze was irrevocably drawn back to the mahogany box that shined russet in the soft light.

It beckoned to her, and this time she didn't resist.

A tingling started in her fingertips when Diana lifted the lid and opened the smooth, cool silk wrappings to expose the cards. She stared down at the red, blue, and black pattern on the reverse of the deck. *Now, how do I begin?*

Concentrate. Breathe slowly, open your mind.
Think of the problem you wish to resolve.

The advice came from the depths of her memory, long buried.

She reached for the deck, ready to make the cut. Drawing a deep breath, she closed her eyes and concentrated.

Brrrring!

The jarring ring of the old telephone startled her and her hand jerked, sending the cards slipping onto the floor.

Diana scrambled to her feet, heart pounding wildly in her chest, feeling disoriented, as if she'd just awakened from a deep sleep. She rushed for the phone, desperate to stop the shrill, discordant sound.

Brrrring!

"Hello."

Silence.

"Hello?" she said again, more firmly. "Hello?"

Again, there was nothing.

Diana slammed the receiver back down onto its cradle, her heart lodged in her throat. She darted a glance around the room, then rushed to the windows, staying out of sight of anyone who might be lurking in the darkness, but peering out into the moonlit night.

Her nose brushed up against the heavy velvet curtain, and her breath rasped loudly in the silence.

There was nothing to see out there, of course, but that didn't make her feel any better. She slid back from the window, wondering if Aunt Bee had kept any of Uncle Tracer's hunting rifles. Even if they weren't loaded, she'd feel better with one in her hands.

Slipping away from the wall, she bolted out of the room, taking care to stay out of view of the windows, and went upstairs to the cabinet where the guns used to be stored. The cabinet wasn't locked, and she found three rifles within, selecting the one that looked the most manageable.

After loading it with some old Winchester bullets she located in a faded cardboard box in the bottom of the cabinet, she hurried back downstairs. It was unlikely she would get any sleep tonight, but she could at least curl up on the settee with the gun.

But then, at the bottom of the stairs, she remembered the cards, remembered what she'd been about to do...and she stopped cold.

What was I thinking? What was I doing?

Her jitters from the phone call lessened to be replaced by clammy palms and a sharp twinge in her stomach. The phone call could have been anything—a wrong number, a bad connection...but the *cards*...she swallowed, nervousness creating pain in her temples. They had spilled all over the floor when she leapt to answer the phone.

What if the High Priestess shows up again?

Diana shuddered. Then, the nausea came, starting like a lull in the base of her belly, easy, soft, subtle. It was followed by a distant throb in her temples and one sharp pain behind her left eye.

I've got to stop this. I'm making myself sick. They're just cards.

She forced herself to return to the den. Shouldering the rifle like a militiaman, she took a step then another, and another, reluctantly moving toward the room.

If she wasn't afraid of an intruder, she told herself, why was she so frightened of a deck of cards? If it didn't bother her to stay in the house where her aunt had likely—possibly—been murdered, why couldn't she walk in to look at a pile of cards?

Pausing in the doorway, Diana peered warily at the ottoman and the shine of the cards scattered all over the floor. Her stomach twisted and the tom-tom in her temples became stronger.

She walked closer, staring at the pile, certain that if she saw The High Priestess from far enough away, she could change her mind and walk out of the room. As she drew nearer, Diana saw that only two cards had landed face-up. And neither of them were The High Priestess.

The clutch of dread that had hold of her middle eased as she picked her way gingerly among the cards. She checked the safety on the gun, leaned it against the settee, then stooped to gather up the pile.

She pulled all but the face-up cards into a neat deck, then reached for those last two. Neither of them were familiar to her: *Wheel of Fortune*, one was labeled. The other had no title, but bore the Roman numeral two at the top.

Diana looked at them for a moment, her curiosity getting the better of her, and noticed that the pounding in her forehead had begun to ease.

Wheel of Fortune was labeled with the Roman numeral ten, indicating that it was the tenth card of the Major Arcana. The Wheel itself hung suspended in what appeared to be the heavens, for it was surrounded by clouds and all types of creatures. Each creature seemed to be reading a book.

Diana looked more closely at the picture of the Wheel. There were two concentric circles drawn on it, and lines cut the two innermost circles into six pie-shaped pieces. Symbols that she thought might be those of astrological signs ringed the outermost portion of the Wheel.

Placing it on the ottoman, she turned her attention to the second card. A blindfolded figure sat on a beach, holding two swords crossed over his or her chest. The swords were long, creating a v-shape and bisecting the drawing at the horizon line between water and sky. *Two of Swords*, she thought. A very simple image. Yes, it was a picture with little detail, but the impression it gave her was a powerful one. The person on the beach, blind to anyone approaching, held the swords in such a way that seemed to ward off any encroachment upon the ocean with those two sturdy weapons.

She returned her attention to Wheel of Fortune as she rested Two of Swords next to it on the ottoman.

I wonder what they mean.

The thought came from nowhere...and just as suddenly as it popped into her head, Diana pushed it out again. She pulled herself to her feet, determined not to indulge the fantasy any longer.

"Enough of this nonsense. I'm going to bed," she said aloud, now unwilling to stay in this room which had early offered a bastion of comfort. With one last look down at the two lone cards on the ottoman, she grabbed the gun and walked quickly from the room—refusing to look back or to even handle the deck again.

What if she turned up The High Priestess again?

She'd put them away tomorrow.

Drained, she didn't think twice about slipping between the covers of Belinda's bed. The rifle was within easy reach, leaning against the wall. The headache that had threatened was gone, as was the nausea. A shiver wavered across her shoulders. Both maladies had hovered at her physical consciousness until she began to examine the cards...and then, coincidentally, they disappeared.

Absurd. Psychosomatic symptoms.

She rolled to the side and closed her eyes.

Wheel of Fortune.

Two of Swords.

———

Diana woke the next morning to the sound of a motor rumbling very near her bedroom window. It came closer, then backed away; closer, then away. It sounded like someone was mowing the lawn.

She sat up in bed, and her gaze went automatically to the digital clock. Nine-thirty. She spewed out a long breath. Her sleep habits had really gotten screwed up in just a few days. She was getting lazy.

Her heels made little annoyed thumps as she strode down the hall to the front door. As she passed by the den, Diana couldn't control a glance toward the ottoman. The two cards were still there, just as she had left them, looking innocent and unimportant. *I'll deal with that later.*

By now, she'd reached the front door. She whipped the chain lock open and snapped the deadbolt back, then turned the knob and pulled the door open.

Heedless of the fact that she wore nothing but a modest nightshirt and no shoes, Diana walked out onto the porch and followed it around the back, where the sound of the mower was louder.

As she came around the corner, she stopped. Her breath caught, and she just stared for a moment. *Aunt Belinda sure had good taste in gardeners.*

From behind the man pushing the mower, all Diana could see was a broad-shouldered back, well-toned with muscle and glazed with a light sheen of sweat. It narrowed to a slim-hipped waist, covered with a loose pair of shorts that looked like chopped off sweatpants. Regardless of the fact that they were loose, they covered a very pleasing, well-defined rear end. His legs were long, lean, and muscled from thigh to calf.

Wow. Maybe I won't lodge a complaint after all.

He turned a corner then, and was suddenly facing her. Somehow, although a jolt of awareness shot through her, Diana wasn't really surprised that it was Ethan Tannock. He looked just as good from the front, she thought wryly as she started across the grass toward him.

He looked up and gave an obvious start at seeing her. His face settled into a remote expression as he released the mower, and it puttered into silence. "Good morning." He slung his hands at his hips, turning toward her with a hint of defiance.

"Good morning. What are you doing?" Diana allowed irritation into her voice. As she came closer, she felt his gaze sweep over her lightly clad figure. Self-conscious, she tried to be inconspicuous as she tugged the hem of her nightshirt down, stretching it to mid-thigh. *Shorts and a tank top are more revealing than my nightshirt. And my hair must look like a disaster.*

"Mowing the lawn," Ethan replied, taking a leisurely look. It had taken her long enough to wake up. He'd been working for two hours, trimming and clipping.

When she pulled the nightshirt down, it did nothing but tighten over her chest. Moratorium or no, he wasn't about to deny himself the pleasure of looking at the lovely apple-sized breasts she was conveniently displaying. "Did I wake you?" He smirked at her consternation and irritation, then used his forefinger to wipe a trickle of sweat from his forehead. Served her right.

"As a matter of fact, you did," she replied. She must have realized that drawing the edge of the t-shirt down did nothing to preserve her modesty because she let go of the hem.

"I'm sorry," he told her with just the faintest sincerity in his voice. After all, he was doing this for Belinda—and to further the cause of science. He didn't have to like the woman, although it sure as hell wasn't a hardship to look at her, dressed as she was, all rumpled and heavy-lidded from sleep. His fingers itched to touch those thick, full curls that danced in a riot about her head, leaving her long, slender neck bare.

"I thought you'd be an early riser, " he added, but with more sincerity this time. He couldn't help a small grin as she glared at him. "I'm upholding my end of the bargain your aunt and I have had for years—and I'll do so until you can make other arrangements for having the yard work done."

"Bargain?"

"Yeah. She never would accept any payment from me for all the time I spent working with her, so we had an agreement that I would take care of her lawn work in the summer, and make sure the plowing was done in the winter."

"Work you did with her? You paid *her*?" The consternation on her face would have been more gratifying if he hadn't seen the wheels turning in her mind—considering whether she should believe him or not. *She really does think I'm a shyster.*

Despite the anger rising in him, he kept his voice even and well modulated. "Yes, I compensated her—or tried to, anyway— for the para-psychological experiments she participated in for over five years. You see, Diana, regardless of what your lawyerly, ambulance-chasing brain might think, I don't need her money. I get paid very well by Princeton University to do my 'ghost busting', as you call it. Go ahead—check me out. It'll be easy enough. I'm on their website." He flashed her an arrogant smile, one that was sugarcoated with niceness, but had the underlying steel of his outrage at her accusations. "Under *Staff*. Picture and all—although they haven't updated it since I shaved."

"I certainly will check it out." Her voice was frosty, although he saw the waver of uncertainty in her eyes.

He wondered if she'd apologize when she found out how wrong she'd been. Unlikely, he thought, taking in the cool facade of her beautiful but stony face and defiant stance. Why would someone like her bother to eat crow?

Diana took a step backward, obviously trying to find a way to excuse herself politely. "Well I do appreciate your taking the time to come over here and do this. I have to run into town, so I may be gone when you get finished. But—uh—could I get you something to drink before I go?"

Ethan could feel her discomfort, and although he'd have liked to continue teasing her, he decided against it. If he wanted to spend enough time observing her to make it worthwhile—and to eventually get her permission to be a full-fledged participant, he couldn't afford to have her too angry with him. Perhaps it was time to call a truce. "I don't mind doing it because I know you probably have your hands full. I probably won't be much more than another hour—I have to run the mulcher over it. Then, if you don't care, I'll jump in the lake to cool off."

"No, that's not a problem," Diana told him. "If you'd like to stop in for something cold to drink before you leave, that would be fine. Just holler when you come in if I'm still here."

He felt one eyebrow lift. She was inviting him to just walk in the house?

"Thanks. That'd be great. I'll take you up on it." *And now, you little rumpled sleepyhead, you'd better get in the house and get some clothes on before I forget I don't like you.*

But the problem was...he was beginning to wish he did.

—⊶⊷—

As it turned out, Diana didn't make it into town before Ethan finished the lawn. She was on the phone with Mickey when she heard Ethan's "helloooo!" reverberate through the house.

"Who's that?" her sharp-eared assistant asked.

"Just one of the neighbors. He just finished mowing the lawn," Diana explained. Then, cupping her hand over the receiver, she called, "Come on in—I'm in the kitchen."

"Is he a young neighbor or an old neighbor?" Mickey asked with a sly tone in her voice.

"Young," Diana whispered as she heard Ethan walking down the hall. "Take off your shoes, please," she called to him.

"Already did," he said as he came into the kitchen.

He'd put a t-shirt on, but the swim he'd obviously taken caused it to cling to his shoulders and the front of his chest, and his hair dripped onto its collar. She noticed bare, tanned biceps rounding smoothly from under the cuffs of the sleeves. Somehow, the shirt made him look even less decent than when he was bare-chested outside.

Diana realized Mickey was talking to her. "I'm sorry, what did you say? The phone lines are kind of staticky up here."

Ethan tossed her a grin. "I've never had any trouble with my phone," he told her, turning one of the chairs around and straddling it backwards. The teasing look in his eyes held a second layer of some other emotion.

Heat.

Diana's mouth went dry and she turned her back on him, her heart suddenly thudding in her chest. "No other issues regarding the Merkovitz case?" she asked Mickey, fervently hoping that there weren't.

"I don't think you want to hear about them."

"Oh no." Diana leaned both elbows on the counter. That niggle of discomfort exploded into full-blown anxiety. "What happened?"

"DUI. Last week, Merkovitz got picked up on a DUI."

Diana said a very unladylike word and heard a faint chuckle from behind her. She turned her face downward, cupping her hands lightly around the phone in an effort to keep prying ears from hearing things they shouldn't. DUI. Her insides shivered as she remembered her concerns about the previous case. There'd been something *off* about it. "Well, that'll help his case," she said, unwilling to put her fears into words, even for Mickey. "He gets sued for malpractice and now he's going to have a drunk driving record. Great. Let's just hope this case goes to court before his DUI becomes public knowledge."

She raked a hand through her thick hair and closed her eyes. She should dump this case...just walk away. But Jonathan had reminded her how important it was to be representing one of the most reputable orthopedic surgeons in the Boston area, and how her career—as well as his own—could be over in a snap if Dr. Merkovitz should become dissatisfied.

Not for the first time, she wondered why Merkovitz had chosen a small firm like hers rather than one of the big powerhouses with a string of partner names across the stationery's masthead. "Is there anything else I should know?"

"Not yet. I'll keep you posted." Then a teasing note crept into Mickey's voice. "How young is young?"

"Never mind." Diana was brisk and she felt heat gather at the base of her neck, even though she knew Ethan wasn't able to hear the other side of the conversation. "It doesn't matter anyway, Mick. Listen, if anything else comes up, I should be around—give me a call, or I'll call you tomorrow."

Diana hung up the phone and turned around to find Ethan looking at her with flagrant attraction in his eyes. Then, as their gazes caught, the interest drained away to be replaced by nothing more than friendliness. He'd propped his chin on hands that rested on the back of the chair.

"How about some iced tea?" Diana asked, her stomach filled with butterflies. What the heck was wrong with her?

"That would be great." Ethan lifted his chin and let his arms drop so they hung over the back of the chair. "So...did you check the Princeton website?"

Diana's shoulder jerked, and an instant flush warmed her face. "As a matter of fact, since my wi-fi is finally working, yes I was able to." She kept her acute embarrassment hidden as she continued with sincerity, "I owe you a big apology. I'm sorry that I jumped to conclusions and made assumptions. Quite truly, that's very unlike me. I usually require much more...evidence before making judgments."

He seemed just as surprised as she was sincere. "Thank you for apologizing. I have to admit, I didn't think you would, and especially with such grace." He smiled the most genuine smile she'd seen since the first time they'd met. "Thanks."

Diana drew back, offended and chastised at the same time. "I don't have any issue with admitting when I'm wrong. And if everyone else did, there'd be a lot less strife in the world."

Nodding in agreement, he took the tall glass of iced tea that she handed him. "Very true." As their fingers brushed, he commented, "As your aunt used to say, you have to see it in black and white before you believe anything."

She stared at him, an uneasy feeling rising inside. "Aunt Bee used to talk about me?"

"All the time." Bitterness tinged his words and that smile faded. "She would have loved to have seen you—she talked about you as though you were her own daughter."

Shame and deep sadness crested over her, and she had to blink back a sudden welling of tears. With an impatient hand, she brushed them away before Ethan noticed and tried to quell her guilt. "I hadn't seen her since the summer I was thirteen. My mother didn't even let me know about my Uncle Tracer's funeral when he died."

"Yes, Belinda mentioned that she and your mother had had a falling out, and that was why you didn't spend the summers up here anymore."

Diana felt even more uncomfortable. This man seemed to know her whole life story. "I don't know what they argued about, but I do know my mother always disliked Aunt Bee. She was my father's aunt, but I had to have somewhere to go in the summers when I was younger, so I got to come here for three years. Mother refuses to talk about what happened to change that. And we're... not close."

"But surely you could have visited your aunt when you got older—if you'd wanted to." He looked at her with steady brown eyes, pinning her there under his microscope.

"Believe me, had I known Aunt Bee was interested in seeing me, and was still alive, I would have." She couldn't keep the enmity from her voice so she turned to pour her own glass of tea. "Mother told me outright that Aunt Belinda died, I guess so I would stop asking about her."

Ethan was looking at her contemplatively, and for the first time, that faint hint of accusation was gone. Instead, she thought she saw sympathy and understanding in his eyes. "Then I owe you an apology as well," he said. "For thinking that you'd ignored Belinda for years, and only came back into her life for the money."

Diana opened her mouth to say something sharp...and then closed it. "Apology accepted. Thank you for admitting that."

He gave her a brief smile and settled back in his chair. "My mother never married my father—or my half-sister's father, either, for that matter—and she kept us from meeting them or knowing much about them until we were older and could do it on our own." He picked up his glass and gestured with it, making the ice tinkle. "So I can empathize just a little. And I'm sorry you didn't get to know your aunt as an adult. I think you would really have enjoyed her. I know I did. She was a mother figure as well as a really good friend of mine, as odd as that might seem. She helped me through a very rough time."

Diana nodded and sipped from her iced tea, more relaxed around Ethan than she'd ever been. This was good. They were actually conversing, and she hadn't said anything lame or rude. Making casual conversation was so much different from arguing a case, when she knew exactly what to say and how to say it. "Your mother...er, she sounds like an unusual woman." Well, crap. There she went, stepping into it with that comment. She looked quickly at him to gauge his reaction.

But he didn't seem to take offense. "She's a modern day Flower Child, and Fiona and I were raised in a commune in Western Pennsylvania abounding with Free Love, marijuana plots, a nude beach, and lots of other earthy things." He flashed her a brief smile that sent a little zip of heat down to her core.

"Free love, huh?" she repeated, wondering why she fixated on *that* aspect of his speech.

He raised a brow, creating more squiggly stirrings in her belly. "Yes, indeed—free love." His voice had dropped to a low rumble and Diana found herself unwilling to look at him. "And nude beaches."

She stood abruptly and walked over to refill their glasses. "What sort of rough time?" she asked, hoping to turn the conversation to something less...intense. At least for her.

He stilled, then began to move his glass in small circles on the counter. "My wife and I split up a little more than two years ago."

"Oh," she said, surprised that he'd been married, and at the dark, pained expression that settled on his face. "I'm sorry to hear that. Really sorry."

"She was sleeping with one of my friends. But the divorce was my fault." Bitterness flattened his tone.

"Because...she was sleeping with one of your friends?" Diana repeated, allowing full irony into her voice. "That sounds logical." Now she regretted bringing it up, for it clearly bothered him. And aside from that, it was a situation too close to home for her comfort.

"Yeah. Well, as it turned out, Jenny figured she'd get out of our marriage since I was screwing around with one of my students, even though *she'd* been sleeping with my friend for months. Maybe even before we got married. I don't know for certain. So it was my fault. Except that I wasn't screwing around with Lexie, even though Lexie, my student—are you following this?—made everyone *think* that's what was going on."

"Nice," Diana said. "How did she do that? Lexie, I mean. The student."

"Yeah, my life was like a soap opera around that time." He flashed a brief, wry grin. "Lexie was very smart. She set it up and I walked into it like a complete idiot. She'd been trying to get my attention for awhile, taking all my classes that she could, stopping by at the end of every office hour session so she could walk with me to wherever I was going next. It was the perception, you see. Like I said, she was smart. Anyway, I wasn't having any of it—not only was I married, but she was a student—*and* ten years younger than me, and I just wasn't into that. So she got desperate, I guess, and made sure her car broke down one night outside a place she knew I'd be. She got me to give her a ride home—with witnesses, of course—and then when we got there, she tried her best to get me to come in." He looked up sharply at Diana, as if expecting her to accuse. "I didn't. Not even to see her safely inside. I didn't even step onto the porch."

She was staring, listening in disbelief. "That does sound like a soap opera. I take it your wife heard about it and didn't believe you when you told her what happened."

He shrugged, his mouth a hard, flat line. "It wasn't only my wife who heard about it—it was the whole damn department and half the campus. You know what they say about a woman scorned, and Lexie considered herself scorned. It was a very difficult time, and instead of defending and supporting me, like you'd expect a partner to do, Jenny used it as an excuse to end the marriage."

"She sounds like a real winner."

"Yeah. I really know how to pick 'em." He gave another one of those wry smiles, and she could see hurt lingering in his beer-bottle brown gaze. "So...when I walked by the den just now, I noticed you were playing with those Tarot cards again."

Nothing like changing the subject, turning the spotlight back on her.

"I dropped them on the floor last night," Diana replied casually. But her insides tightened and the ease she'd felt with him dissipated.

Ethan cocked the eyebrow that let her know he didn't believe her. It arched like an inverted black vee, the point edging into his hair. "And you just left them there, did you?" He gave a little laugh, adjusting his position on the chair. "You aren't going to give even a little, are you?"

"I have no idea what you're talking about," she said firmly. "The cards are nothing to me."

He shook his head, folding his arms across his chest. His biceps shifted smoothly, round and sleek. "Diana, we all have instincts and gut feelings. Some people have honed those skills to become even more than just intuition. If you have that ability, it's a gift. If you want to talk about what's been going on with those cards you 'dropped' on the floor, I'll listen."

"There's nothing going on with them." She felt the force of the denial like a Biblical Peter, and pushed it away. "I just had a few odd coincidences and it unsettled me a little."

"You aren't ready to believe me, or to talk about it. That's okay," he held up his hand to fend off her intended fiery retort. "Just think about it, Diana, think about it. A card—The High Priestess—that has shown up randomly *five* times signifies that one should look beyond the obvious and listen to your inner voice. Isn't that a bit hard to swallow as a mere coincidence?"

He unstraddled the chair and stood, looming down over her. "Well, like I said—when you're ready to talk, I'll be happy to listen." Then the laughter disappeared from his face and intensity replaced the humor. "I guess I'd better get going. Sounds like you have a lot of work to do." He opened the refrigerator and pulled the pitcher of tea out again. "I really appreciate this." he gave a little gesture with his glass after he drained it for the third time.

"I appreciate the work you did in the yard." What else could she say?

"No problem." He gave her one last easy smile that sent a long, slow curling through her stomach, and started toward the front door. She resisted the urge to follow him, and paused at the entrance.

"By the way," he said, leaning his head against the doorjamb and giving her a calm look, "I don't study ghosts or UFOs. Just people."

SIX

HOW IN THE WORLD had he managed it? Diana frowned at the ugly black phone, still baffled even though she'd hung up with Ethan twenty minutes ago. She had half a mind to call him back and tell him she'd changed her mind about riding with him to Marc Reardon's barbeque that evening, but for some reason, she couldn't bring herself to do so.

With a last, perplexed glare at the phone, she pushed it from her mind and continued on her way to the den, where she'd been headed when his call interrupted her plan to work on clearing out the room.

The first thing she saw when she walked in were the two cards, lying where she'd left them on the ottoman two nights ago.

"Maybe if I start to straighten up this room I'll get those cards off my mind," Diana said aloud, sliding into the chair behind Aunt Belinda's desk. *And Ethan as well.*

At the desk, which was a heavy, old walnut clunker, Diana looked through the single neat stack of items: bills that were due to be paid that month. A little calendar hung on the wall behind the desk—a promotional item from Dr. Douglas Horner, DVM, Damariscotta Veterinary Hospital & Shelter—and each of the bills' due dates was clearly marked. She noticed that this Thursday was the date for Motto and Arty's annual shots.

Diana glared around the den at large, knowing that the aloof cats were lurking about somewhere. "I guess I'll have to keep that appointment for you two. Heaven knows why I should, since you've been nothing but inhospitable since I arrived." Despite the accusation, her voice was light and chirpy in case the cats were actually listening and would deign to make an appearance.

They didn't, of course.

Once she cleared off the desk, leaving only the stack of bills to be paid after she obtained access to Aunt Belinda's checking account, Diana moved to the nearest pile of newspapers. It would have made sense, she thought wryly, if her aunt had stacked each periodical in one place. Instead, *Oregon Posts* were piled among *San Francisco Chronicles* and *Chicago Tribunes* and *Detroit Newses* and *New York Timeses*.

As she flipped through them, wondering why on earth Aunt Belinda had saved a decade's worth of newspapers, Diana noticed that an article in the *Chicago Tribune*, May 30, 1995, had been circled in green ink. She stopped to read its headline. *"Blackout on Miracle Mile Caused by Train Derailment."*

The article was of little interest, simply explaining that an Amtrak train had derailed while backing into its station, knocking over a power line. No one had been injured and it had little effect on the city except that many of the shops and businesses were forced to close for part of a day.

Diana set that paper aside and looked through the next one. Now that she was looking more closely, she saw that another article had been circled in a different paper...and another in the next paper, and then another, and so on. Each paper that Belinda saved had something circled—most often, items of little interest. Many times, it was the score of a sporting event or an obituary.

By the time she had waded through the first pile of papers, it was almost six. Her stomach growled, reminding her that lunch had been forgotten. She'd have to wait for the barbeque, for Ethan would be there in less than an hour to pick her up.

Her stomach tingled at the thought, and Diana frowned at herself. It wasn't as if it were a date.

Of course it wasn't a date. She was engaged to Jonathan. Wasn't she?

With a start, she realized it was the first time she'd thought of him all day, and then in the next moment, realized that she and

Ethan shared a similar experience—that of an unfaithful mate. She wondered if Ethan had had the choice whether he would have forgiven his wife and stayed married after finding out about her affair.

And whether she would ever be able to move on from her own experience.

Despite the fact that she shouldn't be concerned about how she dressed, after her shower, it took much too long to decide what to wear. Finally, she chose a simple maxi-dress from a hanger. It was sea foam green with a halter tie that left her back bare. The skirt was long, just skimming the ground, but the dress flowed and fitted enough to more than hint at what it covered.

She'd barely finished dressing when she heard the front door open. "Hey, anyone in there? It's me," called a familiar voice.

Would the man ever learn to knock? But she felt only mild irritation at his presumption, along with a tingle of anticipation that she had no business feeling. "I'm coming," she called.

When she started down the hall, she didn't see him anywhere, and it wasn't until she came upon the den that she realized he'd walked in there to look at the two cards sitting on the ottoman.

"I'm ready to go." Her voice was cool, but it trailed off when he looked up at her. In fact, her whole insides turned inside out. *He sure cleans up well.*

A boxy maroon-and-cream woven shirt clung to his chest and shoulders, unbuttoned just enough to show a hint of dark hair under it. His face was tanned from working outside, and his hair was damp and combed into some casual disarray. And that mouth...it tipped up in a faint smile, echoed by the crinkles at the corners of his eyes.

Ethan stepped away from the ottoman, looking less guilty than satisfied—like the Cheshire cat, she thought suddenly. "I had a thought," he said, taking the sweater she held.

"About...?"

"Let's go by water instead of by land." He closed the front door behind them and waited as she locked it. "Reardon just lives a little way south along the lakeshore. My canoe is down at your dock." He grinned. "What do you think?"

"Canoe?" Diana stopped. "Oh, I don't think so—what if we tip over? I don't want to get wet."

"We won't tip over if you don't stand up. I'm an expert at this." His eyes danced as he said, "It'll be relaxing to just paddle down the lake, don't you think? And it's a more direct route."

"That does sound nice," she said, smiling back at him. "All right."

His smile turned warmer, and for a moment she wished she hadn't agreed. It suddenly sounded much too romantic to be paddling down the lake with a man who wasn't her fiancé. But, geesh, it was just a boat ride.

—◊◊◊—

"What a beautiful place you have," Diana said as Reardon greeted them at his dock.

Ethan couldn't argue that. The house and grounds were very welcoming—the perfect place for an outdoor party. The patio stretched a good twenty by twenty feet, and was graced along its edges by large terracotta planters overflowing with bright red flowers (he had no idea what they were called). Several benches were built into the sides of the patio, providing a comfortable place to sit and watch the sun set.

"How long have you lived here? Did you put the patio in yourself?" Ethan's ears found Diana's voice unconsciously—even over the screeching greeting of Helen Galliday, who came hobbling up to him with such speed that he feared she'd bowl over mousy Betsy Farr with her cane. Martha Woden trailed along at a much slower pace in the wake of her co-quilter, squinting behind her glasses and carefully placing her own walking stick firmly in the dead center of each tile.

"Good evening ladies." Ethan gave a little bow and his best charming smile, listening with half an ear to Reardon's cultured voice. The man had a slight accent, probably from the northwest, but combined with his precise speech it made him sound like a nasally snob.

Or so Ethan thought, listening as the physician explained, "I've been here for three years, and the patio was the first thing I did when I moved in. It seemed a shame to waste such a beautiful view of the lake on a mere deck off the house."

They were skirting along the edge of the patio, and soon they were out of earshot. Ethan, unaccountably irritated that Diana had allowed herself to be led off without a word to him, decided to put her out of his mind and enjoy the evening.

"...so glad you could make it," Helen Galliday was trumpeting. She curled her claw-like fingers around Ethan's wrist and started to lead him across the patio. "You must say hi to Doug Horner *and* his *niece*, who's here on vacation and helping out at his office for a few weeks."

Ethan paused and offered his other arm to the near-sighted Martha, who took it gratefully. Thus, he was able to slow Helen's freight-train pace and save a few people from having their toes smashed by her helter-skelter cane. Summer was a particularly precarious time to be in the way of Helen's cane, since sandals and bare feet abounded.

At one end of the patio, Pauline Whitten had settled her generous self in a wrought-iron chair facing Doc Horner, who was effectively blocked into a corner by her. He shot Ethan a look of gratitude as Helen stormed up with her charges.

"Ethan, great to see you again," Horner said. "How's that black lab of yours?" He stood, a short, stout man with a bristling moustache and a shock of straight white hair. Ethan thought that if Albert Einstein had been caught in the rain and his famous bushy hair gone flat, he'd have looked just like Doc Horner.

"Cady's just fine—swimming in the lake, chasing her tennis balls every day, barking at the squirrels and chipmunks. You know, the usual." He turned to take Pauline Whitten's soft, pudgy hand tipped with pearl-colored nails. "How are you tonight, Mrs. Whitten?"

"Just fine, Ethan, just fine. What a lovely sunset it's going to be."

"Why don't you sit yourself down right here." Helen fairly pushed Ethan into a chair she'd wrangled over to their corner, cane and all. "I'll go fetch Mindy so's you can meet her."

Doug Horner gave Ethan a helpless glance and sank back into his chair while Helen stomped off. With a shrug and a good-natured smile, Ethan, too, sat, knowing that his fate—for the time being anyway—had been sealed.

—m—

Marc insisted upon giving Diana a complete tour of his large, brick home, and encouraged her to call him by his first name. They finished in the kitchen, where he offered her something to drink.

"White wine would be wonderful," she accepted, turning toward the four large windows that overlooked the patio. There were about fifteen people out there, many of whom she recognized from the other evening at the restaurant.

"How are you coming with the work at your aunt's house?" Marc asked, handing her a glass of clear white wine. "I'm sure that den of hers is a project in itself." He poured his own glass and sipped, then swished it about before swallowing. Pleasure lit his handsome face. "Ah, wonderful. Mantigua, Sonoma Valley, 2003. Beautiful."

Diana took an experimental drink and silently agreed that it was a good vintage. She stepped toward the windows, automatically seeking Ethan. At first, she couldn't pick him out, but then she found him sitting in a group of people. His dark head rose above the others clustered in the corner and, through the open window, she heard his laugh carried in on the wind. He seemed comfortable and at ease in the crowd from an older generation. In fact, he always seemed at ease around everyone.

"What were you saying?" she asked politely, turning back to Marc.

"I was merely commenting that your aunt's den in itself would be quite a project to organize. The last time I was there," he added, "it was quite...er ...."

"A mess?" Diana laughed. "It still is, although I have started to tackle it. I can't imagine why she kept all those papers and magazines for so long. I've half a mind to just toss it all in a recycling bin."

Marc relaxed, leaning back against his counter. "That's probably a good idea—what's worth something to one person isn't necessarily a gold mine to the next. Besides, I suppose the fire marshal might have a few concerns if he were to see the condition of that den." He rolled the stem of his glass between two fingers. "Now, my dear, tell me if I'm being too forward, but what exactly is the situation between you and Dr. Wertinger? Have I even the slightest chance of capturing your attention, or has it all been gobbled up by your cardiologist?"

Diana thought she detected the slightest sneer in his voice at the mention of Jonathan's profession, but she was more surprised by his forthright question. She'd never imagined someone as handsome and distinguished as Marc Reardon might have any interest in her. "Jonathan and I are engaged," she told him, ignoring the pang of uncertainty that came with the thought. They were going to get past this bump in the road. Weren't they? "Although I'm flattered by your interest."

"Is that so? I thought I detected a bit of...tension between the two of you when we were together on Saturday." He gave her a warm smile that produced two long creases, one in each cheek, and only slightly warmed his blue eyes. "Perhaps there's a chance for me after all, no?"

Diana looked away. "You flatter me," she said evasively, trying not to consider whether he was right or not. Her attention slid to the patio, landing once again on Ethan's dark head. *Silly.*

"I'll wager I'm not the only one who'll be disappointed in the news that you're attached." He took another sip of his wine, his eyes holding hers over the rim of the glass, a spark of humor lighting them. "Helen Galliday has it in her head that it's her civic duty to match-make the two of us. So consider yourself forewarned."

Diana smiled. "I'll try to let her down easily."

Marc gave a genteel laugh. "That, my dear, is an impossibility—Helen Galliday does not allow herself to be let down. Well, let us rejoin the others, as it's time to see that the steaks aren't going to be overcooked. You do like your steak cooked in a civilized manner, and not burned into a hockey puck, I hope?"

Diana couldn't help another smile. "The bloodier the better," she agreed. "As long as it doesn't walk off the plate, I'm fine with it."

"I was hoping you'd say that." He took her arm to lead her out, but she slipped away.

"I'm going to dash into the powder room before I come out," she explained, somehow uncomfortable with the idea of re-entering the party on his arm. For some reason, she felt as though he was trying to brand her as his personal guest.

"Of course, my dear. Help yourself to another glass of wine if you like. And why don't you choose some music to play—the music system is over there."

Diana chose Frank Sinatra then joined the party, making her way toward Ethan and the group of people with whom he was chatting. As she drew nearer, he looked up at her, then away and back to the young woman sitting next to him.

As Diana approached the group, Helen pulled herself to her feet, obviously preparing to do the appropriate introductions.

"Come on over here, dear," she ordered, then turned to look over her shoulder at Ethan. "Get her a chair, young man, so she won't have to stand during Pauline's long-winded stories. I declare, a body don't have the energy to wait while she rambles on at the mouth." Her claw hand gestured toward Diana, while the other grasped her walking stick. "Sit yourself right here, honey, and let me introduce you to Doc Horner and his niece Mindy."

Mindy was the young woman sitting next to Ethan, and seemed to be looking at him as if she wanted to eat him. Not that Diana could blame the girl. Objectively speaking.

"Now, Doug, say hello to Belinda's niece," ordered Helen as she fairly pushed Diana into the chair.

"Glad to meet you finally." Doug Horner smiled beneath his bristling moustache. "Belindy used to talk about you all the time, and your own law practice down in Boston, and how you'd visit every summer when you was a little girl. She always said her cats would just love to see you—they'd probably want you to take'em home with you to live in Boston." He gave a wheezy chuckle and his basketball belly shifted.

"Love me?" Diana laughed. "Those cats haven't come out of hiding for more than ten minutes since I arrived last week. In fact, I don't know how I'm going to get them to your office Thursday morning for their shots."

Doug looked at her with a gleam of humor in his gray eyes. "You just tell them you want to take them for a ride. They'll come quick enough."

"You said you have a law practice in Boston?" The mellow voice came from the young woman who sat between Ethan and Doc Horner. "What type of law do you practice?"

Diana looked at her, noticing how her long, sleek hair brushed against Ethan's arm as she leaned forward in interest. And how Ethan didn't seem to mind. "Medical malpractice, defense," she replied, trying not to think about how messy her own hair looked. She barely refrained from trying to smooth it with her hand, a nervous habit that stemmed from years of sly comments from her mother—and one that did absolutely no good.

"You defend doctors?" Helen Galliday cried in an accusing voice. "I don't go to no doctors—they're all a bunch of charlatans. Belinda told me all about'em. Except for Dr. Reardon, and it took two years before I'd go to see him."

"I haven't run into too many physicians that I'd be uncomfortable defending." She pushed away the thought of Roger Merkovitz, reminding herself that just because he had the personality of a hyena with a stomachache didn't mean that he wasn't a good surgeon. When he was sober, she thought sickly. *What am I going to do about his case?*

Feeling everyone's attention on her, Diana continued in what she hoped was a low, modulated voice and not a babbling one. "A lot of lawsuits, unfortunately, are brought about by people wanting to make a quick buck. And many patients don't understand that everyone's body is different—even inside. The best planning or the most experienced physician can't guarantee that something unexpected won't happen." She glanced at Ethan, who seemed unaccountably interested. "Even though medicine is a science, it has its unknowns—even in routine procedures. So just because something goes wrong, or something unexpected happens, doesn't mean it's the fault of the surgeon."

"Bravo!" A sharp clapping behind drew Diana's attention to see Marc. "At last, someone who understands the plight of physicians." His eyes were shrewd as they looked at her with an intensity belied by the smile on his face. "And how long have you been defending those of us who practice the humble art of healing?"

Diana craned her head to look up at him. "I've been in practice for seven years, four of which have been solely medical malpractice defense."

"Why so curious, Marc? Are you in need of Diana's services?" Ethan's drawling comment drew her attention toward him.

"No, of course not," the doctor laughed heartily. "Do you think these ladies here would let me get away with anything untoward?" He winked at Helen Galliday, then turned to glance across the patio. "I see I'd better check on Robert and make sure he's not burning those steaks." He turned his wrist to look at the Rolex there. "I'd say another ten minutes, and the food will be done. Until then, please excuse me."

Diana heard a burst of low laughter next to her and turned.

"I think you're probably right," Mindy was saying as she looked up at Ethan with bright eyes. Surprised to feel a funny twist in her stomach, she turned at a sharp pain in her shoulder.

"Aren't you listening to me, young lady?" The pain in Diana's shoulder was from Helen Galliday's iron fingernail. "I said we'd like it if you'd stop by the shop next time you're in town to see what we're working on."

It was clearly *not* a request.

"That would be lovely," Diana gushed, studiously ignoring the low-voiced conversation between Ethan and Mindy—but trying to listen at the same time. "I have to bring Motto and Arty in to see Doc Horner on Thursday—are you ladies in on Thursdays?"

"We'll make sure we are," Pauline Whitten promised before Helen could speak. "I can reschedule my Scrabble game so I can be there. I don't generally like to miss my games on Thursdays—I have a 1500 ranking, you know—but I'd make an exception for you, dearie. Either way, I'd sure like you to do a couple stitches on Bee's block, if you could spare the time. She spoke often of you, and it would be nice if you could lend a hand in her memory."

Diana nodded. "I'll do that. But, remember," she said, raising her eyebrows at Helen, "I can't promise any expertise with the needle."

"Don't you worry none about that," she grumbled, "it's not as if the rest of them know what they're doin' anyway."

And on that note, the chime of a gong reverberated, calling them to dinner.

—⟋⟍—

Some time later, Ethan gathered up Diana's purse and the sweater she'd left by the group of quilters. The sun was low and the sky had become a dark, rich blue. Reardon had lit outside lanterns along with citronella candles, and the loud voices of the party had begun to wind down.

Diana had been sitting by Marc and another couple since the food was served. Ethan told himself he wasn't the least bit irritated that she'd barely spoken to him all evening, but it was time to leave. Cady needed to be let out—or at least, that was the excuse he'd use. The lab had an iron bladder and could go for ten hours if necessary.

His so-called date craned her head back to look up at him as he approached. "Oh," she said, rising immediately, "I was just thinking about you."

He looked into her eyes, dark now in the low light. "Were you?" He didn't mean for his voice to rumble low and be filled with meaningful interest, but there it was. And her response—eyes widening in surprise and a little confusion—was just fine with him. There was something about Diana that made him want to set her off balance whenever possible. Shake up that stiff lawyerly attitude and give her something to think about other than the boring cardiologist. "Want to give me the details?"

"I meant I was thinking about getting back," she said. "Thank you for a wonderful dinner," she told Reardon.

The doctor rose and extended his hand to Ethan. His grip was smooth and his palm dry as a bone. "I hope you enjoyed yourself." He turned to Diana, a smile crossing his lips. "I'm glad you were able to make it, my dear."

Reardon made a point of settling Diana in the canoe, facing the rear and Ethan climbed in the back. "Good night," he called, pushing them away from the dock.

"Good night." Their host's voice carried easily across the widening expanse of water as they drifted out into the silent, black lake. Even the wave-runners and motorboats had gone in for the night.

For a moment, there was only the fading sound of the last of Reardon's guests, and the light shining down from his patio. Then, the soft plop of the paddle into the water and a quiet dripping as Ethan changed sides with the oar. The light from shore grew fainter, leaving only the moon and stars and the disappearing sun to light the darkness.

Tall trees made a dark, forbidding fringe along the shoreline, and there were occasional splashes of light from houses or docks. But most of the illumination came from the quickly darkening western horizon. A streak of bright red glazed the sky where the sun had just dropped behind the forest, and then it, too, faded.

A loon called out, sending a shiver of familiarity down Ethan's spine, and its cry was joined by a whippoorwill and chirping crickets: the sounds of Maine in the summer.

They moved silently through the water, the oar cutting into its blackness with clean, smooth strokes. After awhile, he drew the paddle from the water and rested it across his thighs, letting the canoe drift. He was, he realized, in no hurry to get back.

Diana's silhouette only hinted at her features in the dim light, but he could picture the wide, full curve of her mouth with no trouble at all. The moonlight gleamed over her ivory shoulders, and earlier, he'd admired the slender line of her back bared by the halter dress as she walked away with Reardon. Now she sat on the canoe bench, facing him with her knees drawn up and her feet resting on one of the boat's struts. He could see the soft ripples the breeze made, playing with her skirt and that thick, sexy hair.

She'd surprised him yesterday with her integrity, apologizing for thinking the worst of him—perhaps even restoring a bit of his faith in the female gender. Watching her tonight talking passionately and intelligently about her work, and the way she kindly yet firmly managed the abrasive Helen Galliday had further eased his misgivings about her. And the exchange in her kitchen yesterday, when they were talking about his divorce...there'd been something there.

Something he hadn't felt for a woman in a long time. Ethan drew in a long, deep breath.

When he shifted in his seat, the boat rocked slightly, making a soft little splash. He hadn't felt this depth of attraction for a woman since he first met Jenny, and the knowledge that Diana was with another man was the only thing that kept him from making a move. Moratorium or no.

Rerouting his thoughts, he reminded himself that he was spending time with her only to further his research. "Would you like your sweater?" he asked, breaking the silence as he donned his scientist's hat.

Diana turned from her contemplation of the stars, bringing her classic profile into a full-faced view. Now he could make out the dark recesses of her eyes and a hint of chin and lips. "I am a little chilly, thanks."

She didn't ask him why he'd stopped paddling, nor did she seem to mind that they simply drifted—odd for a woman so hesitant about taking the canoe in the first place. Not that he minded in the least. She was a lot more approachable now that she'd mellowed out a bit.

"Did you enjoy yourself tonight?" Ethan asked as he picked up the sweater and leaned toward the center of the boat to hand it to her.

She shifted in a delicate shrug. "The food was good, the atmosphere was beautiful, and Marc was an interesting host." She draped the sweater over her shoulders, Jackie O-style, and clasped her hands in her lap.

"He's more uptight than a robot. I've never seen the man unbend." Ethan laughed quietly, but the sound still carried over the water.

Diana's smile gleamed in the darkness. "I think that's an understatement. For someone who's making a pass at you to sound as though they're chatting with the queen over tea is pretty bad."

"Reardon made a pass at you?"

She giggled—an unlikely sound coming from the Diana he'd come to know—and he was charmed. Maybe that glass of wine she'd been holding had loosened her up a bit. "I guess you'd call it that. It was pretty formal to be called a come-on. I think it went sort of like, 'if all of your affections haven't been spoken for, may I have the opportunity to try for some?' or something pompous like that." She drew the sweater closer about her throat. "I can't say I've ever been hit on so politely before."

"You shut him down ruthlessly, I'm sure," he teased.

She turned so that the wind caught her full in the face, allowing the breeze to lift and toss her thick hair. "I told him that I was with Jonathan."

He zeroed in on the odd note in her voice. "Aren't you?"

"Yes. Of course. That's why I said that."

But that strange tone was still there. Ethan couldn't help but recall that he'd noticed some remoteness between Diana and her companion at the Grille on Saturday night. At the time, he'd chalked it up to her general aloof demeanor, but now he wondered. And he wondered how to broach the subject without sounding predatory or accusing.

Silence reigned between them for a moment. Again, there was only the cry of the loon and the occasional plop of the oar sliding into the water as he adjusted their path. He would have been lulled by the peacefulness if he weren't so damned *aware* of her.

At last he spoke. "Have you looked up the meaning of those two cards you have lying out in the den?"

Diana's shoulders drew up and he felt the tension emanating from across the boat. "Of course not. I told you, I don't pay any attention to those things."

"Would you like to know what they mean?"

Diana didn't respond. Ethan continued to paddle, debating with himself. Was he pushing her too hard? He'd looked up the two cards when he got home after mowing the lawn yesterday. They'd still been sitting out in the den today when he picked her up for the barbeque, and he knew although she wouldn't admit it, she'd been messing around with them.

"The Wheel of Fortune indicates a turning point in one's life," he spoke quietly, suddenly realizing that he very possibly *was* broaching the subject of her relationship with Wertinger. It gave him the determination to gently persist. "It suggests that one is experiencing a change—such as in a relationship—or becoming aware of a larger picture...or even learning one's true role or purpose in life."

When Diana didn't speak, he continued, trying to keep his tone conversational. "The interesting thing is that the Two of Swords is an opposing card—it's very odd that you should pull those two up together."

"I didn't pull them up." Her words were defensive, but he detected a note of uncertainty in them. Her body language confirmed it, as her shoulders rounded and her hands fidgeted, drawing the sweater closer about her.

"The Two of Swords alludes to someone being at a stalemate, or having blocked emotions and denying one's true feelings. It can even mean that someone is avoiding the truth." He let those words sink in for a few moments, struck again at how oddly appropriate those two cards could be for her now. A little zip of excitement skittered down his spine. There could actually be something *to* this. Were the cards actually *guiding* her without her conscious participation? "What were you concentrating on when you drew those cards, Diana? Think about it."

She bent forward, resting her head on her raised knees. "I didn't draw them, Ethan." Her voice wavered, muffled in her skirt. "I didn't!"

He noticed with a shock that her shoulders were quaking. "Diana, are you all right?" he asked, setting the oar aside and moving toward the other end of the canoe. He balanced himself with one foot on either side of the gunwale, holding onto the sides of the canoe. Crouching, he took careful steps until he reached her. "I'm so sorry. I didn't mean to make you cry."

Any other words he may have uttered froze in his throat as he became wholly, startlingly aware of her—her nearness, her scent, the soft brush of her skirt against his legs. Ethan tentatively touched her head, his fingers sinking into the depths of her hair and sliding down the back of her skull. "Diana, I'm sorry."

She raised her face, inches from him, and he could see tears glittering in her eyes. He was shocked that the cool facade had been stripped from her face, and naked emotion—fear, pain, confusion—shone in her moonlit features.

"My head hurts," she managed to say, agony lacing her voice. "It's pounding...so badly...and I think I may be going to get sick."

Guilt surged through him. All the time he'd been badgering her, the migraine had been working its way to the surface. Why hadn't she said anything? "Honey, I'm sorry," he said again, taking another excuse to touch her. "Can I get your meds out of your purse? Can you take them without water?"

She shook her head, huddling back into her lap. "No." Her voice was muffled with pain.

Ethan turned quickly, gingerly, and hurried back to the end of the canoe as the boat rocked with his haste. But he was careful—the last thing she needed was to get dumped in the lake. He picked up the paddle and began to make clean, strong strokes. The boat surged through the water.

Fortunately, they weren't far from Belinda's dock and only moments later, he was helping her out of the tipsy canoe. "This way," he said, putting an arm around her warm, bare shoulders.

Through a haze of pain, Diana made her feet move in the requisite direction, and she stumbled as they started up the gravel path. Before she could protest, Ethan swept her up, gathering her against a solid chest. As his strong arms encircled her, she allowed her head to drop onto the front of his shoulder. His steps were sure and smooth, and she closed her eyes, trying to relax against the pain.

She felt the bob and sway of their progress up the path, the easy ebb and flow that jolted her close to him then lifted her away. Her cheek rested on the nubby material of his shirt, and when she drew in a deep breath centered on diffusing the pain from her temples, she caught his scent—that deep, masculine essence that seemed comforting and invigorating all at once. She was huddled in his arms, one arm around the back of his neck and the other flat on his chest, and she felt his stride changing as they neared the top of the incline.

"Almost there." His voice was quiet and steady in her ear, unencumbered by labored breaths, and whispering over the sensitive skin of her cheek. Diana shivered as a sensation zipped down her spine, causing him to ask, "Are you all right?"

"Yes," was all she could say. Her mouth almost brushed the warmth of his neck, and she turned slightly away, acutely aware that beneath her overriding misery was a strong flare of attraction toward him.

"I'm going to have to set you down," he said, stepping onto the porch. "Do you know where your keys are?" His voice was more gentle than she'd ever heard it, and he set her carefully, as if she were made of the most fragile glass, on the porch swing. "Are they in your bag?"

Diana had managed to unzip the small leather pouch and pulled the jangling mass of keys from its depths. Ethan took them as she continued to rummage in the bag, searching for the bottle of medication that she always carried with her. By the time he had the door open, she'd found it and pulled herself to her feet.

Diana tottered into the house, the nausea welling more strongly now that she was ambulatory. Ethan brushed past her on his way to the kitchen. "Sit down," he ordered. "I'll get you something to drink."

She turned gratefully into the nearest room—the den—and stumbled over to the settee. She pressed her hand to her mouth to keep from gagging as nausea surged and roiled. By the time she'd settled herself on the sofa, Ethan was there, fitting a glass of water into her palm.

She gulped two capsules and the water and allowed Ethan to take the glass from her limp fingers. Resting her head back against the couch, she closed her eyes as she heard him turn on the lamp with a soft click. "Thank you."

Without speaking, Ethan sat next to her, jolting the small sofa. She became aware of his hand resting lightly on top of hers, and the warm, solid weight was surprisingly comforting.

There was silence for a long while, and if he hadn't been sitting next to her, Diana would have thought he'd left. When the pain eased and she opened her eyes, she found him watching her steadily from his end of the settee.

"Better now?"

Diana nodded, suddenly very aware of his nearness and the blatant heat in his eyes. In the low yellow glow of the lamp, he looked even more handsome than usual, his even features soft and sensual. She shifted in her seat to shake off the intense awareness, her heart thumping crazily, and looked away from him—anywhere but at those steady, deep brown eyes fringed by thick, curling lashes.

By some misfortune, her gaze landed on the two Tarot cards that remained in their places on the ottoman, and Ethan's attention obviously followed hers, for he said, "Those cards are very interesting."

"Coincidence," she said firmly, leaning forward to scoop them up despite the flashes of light still blurring her vision. She bent further to pick up the mahogany box on the floor and, flipping its lid off, slid the cards into the recesses of the small chest.

"How often do you have migraines like this?"

"Hardly ever anymore," she replied, relieved by the change of subject. "But I've been having them much more frequently in the last week. And they've been more intense, coming on more quickly than I can ever remember. Maybe there's something in the air up here," she added with a little laugh that choked off when she realized what she'd said.

Ethan gave her a significant look. "I was thinking the same thing."

But Diana was already violently rejecting the idea—whatever it was. "I'm under a lot of stress," she explained. "With work, and...other stuff."

"Diana...at the risk of infuriating you, I'd like to suggest something." He grinned crookedly, but his eyes became wary.

"Infuriating me?"

"Sometimes migraines are the result of an inability, or an unwillingness, to allow parts of the unconscious to surface to the conscious mind." His gaze searched hers as he continued, "It's possible you have migraines because you're suppressing something from your consciousness."

Diana drew herself up, a hum of disbelief starting to sing through her veins. "What are you saying?"

Ethan didn't mince words. "It's possible you're suppressing any precognitive abilities that you may have, and the result is your migraines. Wait, wait, *wait*." He held up a hand to ward off her heated reply. "Will you just listen to me for a minute? I've never met anyone so stubborn," he muttered to himself.

"Look," he continued, "you seem to be having them more often lately, and they're stronger. Now, take a look at what's changed in your life. Your aunt passed away, you've come to the country...and you're trying like hell to believe that what's happening with these Tarot cards means nothing." He leveled a steady look. "I believe it's more than likely these things are related, whether you want to concur or not."

"Your theory is absurd, *Doctor* Tannock—it has so many holes in it, I could use it to drain pasta," she said coolly. "There are many things happening in my professional and personal life right now that could cause an excess of stress and tension. It has nothing to do with those cards, or anything here. I've been having these migraines for years—long before I ever picked up the Tarot."

Just then, a shrill *brrrringg!* cut the silence, causing Diana to jolt. She eyed the ugly black phone, which was on the table next to Ethan.

It was either Jonathan...or it wasn't. But it was after eleven o'clock. Who else would be calling here? She remembered the phone call from last night, when there was no one there. It could be another prank call, or the caller could be Jonathan. Either way....

"Answer it. Will you?" she said in a rush, fully aware of what she was doing.

With an odd look of comprehension, Ethan picked up the phone. "Hello." There was a pause, then he said, "Yes, she's here. Who's calling?"

Diana didn't need Ethan to convey the message, for Jonathan's irate tones were audible. Her insides were jumping and twisting, for she knew she'd just crossed a chasm, making a leap from which she and Jonathan might never recover.

Wordlessly, she held out her hand for the receiver. "Hi Jonathan," she said.

"Who is that?" he demanded. "I've been calling you all night, and you haven't answered your cell phone either. What's a man doing at your house this late?"

"Definitely not the same thing Valerie the Voracious Vixen was doing in your hotel room in Atlantic City," Diana said much more calmly than she felt.

"*Diana*," he gasped, his shock reverberating over the wire. "When are you going to let that go? I told you, I made a mistake. Is this—is this some revenge play? So you can get even with me?" He heaved a deep, wounded sigh. "I guess I can understand it, Diana-baby. And if that's what it takes for you to get over this, then I guess I have no choice."

She avoided looking at Ethan as she replied, "Think what you like, Jonathan." Then she lapsed into silence—a powerful place to be. Waiting for him to speak.

"Diana," he said again, a little more strongly this time. "When are you coming home? I miss you," he added, his voice softening. "Please...I don't know how you think we can work this out with you gone like this."

"I don't think I'll be here for more than another week," she said.

"Another *week?*" His voice rose. "What's Merkovitz going to say about you ignoring him?"

"Merkovitz? I haven't been ignoring him," she retorted. Her insides tightened at the unpleasant reminder. "And what does Merkovitz have to do with us?"

"If he's not happy, then word gets around," Jonathan warned. "It could affect your reputation."

"Merkovitz's case is well in hand. Thank you for your concern," she told him. "Now, I'm tired and ready to go to sleep. Is there anything else?"

"No," he said flatly. Then, again, his voice softened, "I miss you, Diana. I *love* you. Come home soon to me. Please?"

"Good night, Jonathan," she said, and reached across Ethan to hang up the phone. Only after the receiver settled into place did she look at him.

"Valerie the Voracious Vixen?" he asked, raising his brows.

Diana couldn't contain a little smile. "That's one of the more polite things I've called her." She bit her lip and then, suddenly feeling utterly awkward and exposed, rose from the settee. "Thank you," she said. "For everything tonight."

Ethan stood, still watching her. She could fairly feel the curiosity and unspoken questions rolling off him, and appreciated it when he only said, "I guess I'll be heading home now."

She started out of the den, intent on walking him to the door and sending him on his way. But her palms felt damp and something alive seemed to be squiggling around in her stomach, not at all unpleasantly. In fact, it was warm and expectant, and it made her feel flushed and on-edge.

The cool air of summer night wafted in the front door, bringing the scent of lake and tiger lilies. She paused, waiting for him to walk past her and out so she could shut and lock it. But instead of walking through, he stopped next to her.

Diana's heart began to thump harder as she looked up at him, and it was all she could do to keep from backing away. His eyes were dark, glittering with some intense emotion. "Have a good night," she said nervously. "Thank you again."

"Don't you think we ought to make this mutually beneficial?" he asked, his voice low and tinged with irony. His gaze seemed to pin her there, against the wall in the narrow hallway.

"What do you mean?" she asked.

"I mean, if you're going to use me as a deterrent to your boyfriend, or a pawn in your game of revenge, I think it's only right," he said, reaching for her, "that I actually earn the reputation." He closed his hands around her elbows, tugging her so close that her skirt flowed around his legs. "Don't you, Diana?"

She couldn't move, even when she saw that his attention had fixed on her mouth—the mouth that she knew was parted slightly, moist from the tip of her nervous tongue...and waiting in anticipation for his to close over it. "I...I ...." she breathed, unable to find the words to silence him. Her heart was ramming hard and loud in her chest, and a flush of heat surged up through her body.

"That's what I thought," he murmured, his face moving closer, filling her vision.

His lips were soft and sensual, coaxing her to relax against him. They caressed her mouth lightly at first, teasing her, playing with the taste and texture of her lips.

Diana settled her hands against him, against his solid chest, feeling the warmth and firm shift of muscle beneath. That lively squiggling in her belly turned to heat and pleasure, rolling through her, spiraling down to her core. Embraced by firm, powerful arms, she turned her face up to receive his mouth fully, their lips and tongues tangling in a sleek, passionate dance. His hair felt soft and thick around her fingers, his shoulders spanned wide and muscular beneath her palm.

When he moved from her mouth, trailing his lips to the curve of her jaw, to whisper her name near her ear, Diana realized she was sagging weakly, her body plastered to him, the wall pressing into her spine. Shocked at the way she'd lost track of herself, she pushed against him, stepping out of the circle of his embrace.

Ethan looked down at her with hot eyes, his chest rising and falling, his lips full and damp from *her*. She pressed a hand to her own swollen mouth and tried to pull her emotions and thoughts back to where she was.

"Well, then," he murmured in a low, rough voice. "That was a good start." He started to reach for her again, but she slipped away.

"Do you feel better now?" she asked with a little bite in her voice.

"Not precisely," he replied, still looking at her with dark intensity, and she felt her stomach flip over at the desire in his gaze. It couldn't be meant for *you*, she heard a nasty little voice say. "But if that's what's going to happen when you use me to get back at your boyfriend, I'm not going to complain."

"I didn't—I wasn't …." Her voice trailed off. "I'm sorry."

"Don't be sorry for that," he said. His eyes slid over her, as sure and heavy as if he touched her with his hands. "I'm not."

"Ethan," she said, struggling to keep her composure. "I didn't mean—I mean, this doesn't *mean* anything. Jonathan is still—" She crossed her arms over her middle as a shield against him.

"Everything was innocent until...you ...." Her voice trailed off. Her lips were still throbbing, and there were other areas of her body that were pulsing as well. "I think you'd better go."

He gave her one last steady look, then a curt nod. "All right. Good night, Diana."

SEVEN

DIANA GLANCED AT THE shiny black phone as she stirred the pasta she was making for dinner. It had been silent all day—the first time, she realized, since she'd come to Damariscotta just over a week ago.

No, she hadn't expected Ethan to call. He wouldn't. He'd just come over, and walk right into the house.

Not that he had any reason to do so. She reached up to touch her lips more than once, remembering that long, hot kiss. No, he didn't have any reason to come here. Not while she was still tied up with Jonathan. And even if she wasn't.

It was a kiss. One, simple, *hot*, crazy kiss.

Jonathan hadn't called since Ethan answered the phone late last night...and she wasn't certain how she felt about that. She wasn't certain how she felt about anything regarding Jonathan anymore. Hard to believe that a month ago, she was deliriously happy that she'd found a man to marry her—something her mother had despaired of ever happening, something that Diana herself had wondered about. Which was why she'd thrown herself so firmly into building her practice.

But now, she realized, she was rather enjoying her life without Jonathan in it. She hadn't missed him at all.

After working on the Desai case in the morning, Diana tackled more of the den in the afternoon as a way to distract herself from... things. She found a stack of Aunt Belinda's private journals during her bout of cleaning—as well as some curious information.

She'd been going through the bills to find the most pressing ones and found several statements for medical services. The odd thing was that none of them were for visits to Marc Reardon—they were all with a general practice physician fifty miles away, in Portland.

Diana recognized the procedure codes as ones for office visits and some general testing—blood work, a stress test, cholesterol screening and a hearing exam. Upon closer examination, she saw that they were dated over the last six months. Then, she found two more statements for recent physician visits with Marc Reardon. It seemed as if Belinda was being treated by two different physicians, making the drive to one fifty miles away for the same tests and consults she was having with Reardon. Second opinions were normal, but generally those were with specialists, not a general practitioner like Reardon.

As she made dinner later that evening, Diana mulled over those medical statements as well as her time frame for returning to Boston. Despite what she'd told Jonathan last night, she hadn't made a decision about when she'd return.

She'd been telling herself she was preparing the house to be sold, but in the back of her mind, something bothered her about that plan. If she sold, she'd feel a little like she was betraying Aunt Belinda. But what in the world would she do with an old house in the middle of Maine?

A house on the lake and you wonder what to do with it? Her own thoughts surprised Diana and she stopped dead in the kitchen, holding her plate of pasta in one hand and a glass of wine in the other. She would never have thought it of herself, but the time away from the crazy stresses of her professional and social life back home was a welcome change. Despite the odd things that had been happening, she was actually enjoying the opportunity to relax and be carefree.

The thought struck her suddenly: *The Fool.*

Hadn't that been the first card she'd seen from the Tarot deck? And hadn't her first thought been that she couldn't remember the last time she'd felt as carefree as the Fool seemed?

A shiver ran across the back of her shoulders and the hair on the nape of her neck prickled. She placed her dinner on the table and contemplated the absurd, ludicrous, impossible thought that the card—which had fallen randomly from the deck—had a pointed meaning in her life.

The second, and most insistent "random" card had been *The High Priestess.*

"Look beyond the obvious," Ethan had said it meant. "Open your mind ...." And that card, Diana reminded herself as the queer feeling rumbling in her stomach became more insistent, had turned up *five* times.

Five times. For that to be mere coincidence stretched even the boundaries of Diana's pragmatic mind.

Don't sell the house, she thought suddenly. *It* would *make a nice retreat. It's not that far from Boston—only a few hours, and it would be nice to have a place to take the kids—*

Whoa! She tried to stop the thought, but it roared in from nowhere and would not be ignored.

She slid into her chair at the table and looked unseeingly at her plate of food. Two children, she thought—maybe three...and suddenly, a picture, as clear and tangible as a photograph, flashed into her mind: two small dark-haired boys and toddling little girl chasing a big, dark dog, and Diana herself laughing at them, joining the chase over an expanse of green grass....

She shook her head with violence, dismantling the vision and refocusing on her dinner...but the pain had already started to throb behind her eyes.

"No," she moaned, concentrating, concentrating so hard on wrapping fettuccine around her fork. But it was too late. Though she forced herself to eat some of her dinner, the migraine had settled in her head with a vengeance.

—m—

When Diana opened her eyes after the storm of pain, she found herself lying on the settee. Blinking, squeezing her eyes shut, then opening them again, she struggled to sit up.

It was dark outside and she could hear the chirping crickets and the faint cry of a loon. The house was in darkness, and there wasn't enough moon to shine through the windows.

Nervousness clutched her middle as she swung her feet off the couch and fumbled for the switch of the lamp on the piecrust table. It took a moment, but she found the chain and yanked, and a soft glow broke the darkness.

"Motto?" she called, suddenly wanting to know that she wasn't completely alone. "Arty? Here kitty!" This time, her falsetto wavered and cracked.

Silence hung over the house like a pall, and Diana stood, wondering why her mouth was so dry. She'd taken two steps toward the kitchen when the phone rang.

Her heart jumped into her throat at the sudden noise, and she hurried to answer the ugly black phone, just to hear another human's voice. "Hello?" She picked it up, interrupting the second shrill ring.

Silence.

"Hello?" she said again, hating that her voice sounded desperate.

More silence.

"Is anyone there?" she tried again.

Suddenly, the dial tone blared rudely into her ear.

Her fingers were shaking when she let the receiver drop onto its cradle, and Diana had to swallow back a moan of fear. She ran to the front door and checked the lock, which was bolted firmly. All the windows were locked, upstairs and down, and the back door as well.

Diana turned on lights as she went, wanting the house to be a bright talisman against the night and against the ugliness of the voice out there. The remains of her uneaten dinner sat innocently in the kitchen, but all vestiges of hunger had disappeared.

Looking at the phone, she debated calling Joe Cap to report the incident, but decided it could wait until morning when she took the cats to the vet. *It's just a prank call. Some kids fooling around.*

But someone broke into your house.

But they can't get in. I'm locked up tightly. And I have Uncle Tracer's gun.

Speaking of which...she went back to the den to get the rifle and turn off the lights. The sight of the settee reminded her of her earlier migraine. It had been the strongest one she could ever remember having, and it had obviously put her out of commission for hours.

A shiver jolted through her and queasiness started in her stomach. The image that flashed through her mind just before the onset of the headache—the vision of herself chasing three children and a big dog—flashed back. A big dog? She didn't even *like* dogs. And she was afraid of the big ones.

She reached to pull the chain and turn off the light, but her attention was caught by the mahogany box and the small collection of books she'd placed next to it: Aunt Belinda's journals.

Almost before she realized it, Diana had picked up one of the books and began to leaf through the pages from twenty years earlier. From when she'd been much younger, and so had Aunt Bee.

And she began to read.

Much later, Diana set the battered, leather-bound book down, her heart lodged painfully in her throat. She felt light-headed and queasy. The hair on her nape prickled, and blood hummed in her head. It can't be, she thought frantically. *This is too weird!*

For once, Motto seemed to have found her presence acceptable, and he was curled up into a corner of the settee. Diana reached blindly for the cat, picking up ten pounds of dead weight and burying her chin in the fur. She stared across the room, seeing but not really seeing the stacks of papers and books, ignoring Motto's low, throat-growls.

When the snobbish feline decided her presence was no longer necessary, she struggled out of Diana's arms. The warmth that had been the bundle of cat left Diana, and she felt chilly, and lonely. She picked up the journal again, forcing herself to read the entry that had stopped her world.

"July 23, 1989. Diana has the Gift! Praise God, it is true without a shadow of a doubt! Little James Bettinger and his mama Rose were over, and the two children were playing with blowing soap bubbles.

Diana scampered up to me, cute as could be, and said, "Aunt Belinda, I know when Uncle Tracer is going to die. I saw it in a bubble." I looked at her, surprised, and asked, "What did you see?" "I saw his gravestone and it said January 16, 1992."

Before I could say another word, she ran off to blow more bubbles! My heart did not stop pounding for hours after—to have such a Gift! It seemed effortless for her. And my poor Tracer...I cannot hope but that she is wrong, but for her to see it with such clarity....

Well, I cannot write of my grief for his loss before it should happen, but I thank God that I have had this moment of foresight. At least I will have the chance to make our next two and half years together as wonderful as they may be...and should Diana be wrong, well, then I'll be a relieved and happy woman on January 17, 1992. I shall write more on this later."

Diana closed the journal, keeping her forefinger as a bookmark. Tears welled in her eyes. Thanks to Victoria, she'd learned long after the fact that Uncle Tracer had succumbed to cancer's death grip on that date in 1992. But more importantly, she didn't remember telling her aunt what she had seen in a bubble years earlier, at the age of ten.

"I *couldn't* have known that," she said aloud to Arty, who was just poking his salmon-colored nose around the corner of the desk. "Could she have been mistaken? Could she have misunderstood me?" The cat shot across the room, pouncing on Motto, ignoring Diana's question.

She opened the journal again. Perhaps if she read further, she'd find an explanation for this unsettling entry.

The next few days' entries were mundane, mentioning the things Diana had done with Aunt Belinda during that first summer's visit—fishing, weeding the garden, swimming—as well as a few readings she had done using her Tarot cards. These last items were interesting enough—especially one entry which read:

"July 30, 1989. I had an odd vision today when I was doing a quick spread of cards. I saw a large explosion in my mind, near a big body of water. I had posed the question 'What will happen today?' as an experiment, and kept my mind blank.

After I laid out the cards, and I spent a moment concentrating, the explosion happened as if I were watching it on TV. It was a large building, perhaps a factory or a warehouse, and it was on a shoreline. There were other buildings next to it. I don't know what it meant, or where it was, or even if it really happened.

And then, the entry for the following day:

"July 31, 1989. I was reading the New York Times today and saw mention of a large warehouse having burned down yesterday. I immediately thought of my vision—could that have been what I saw during that spread? It was near the docks, so the article said. I'll never know for certain, I suppose, but it may be true.

There was little mention of Diana herself in the ensuing entries—little but passing references to what they had done on a given day—and certainly no further comment about her "Gift".

As Diana read on, she found that Aunt Belinda learned that when she did a Tarot spread to answer the question "What will happen today?" she would often see a vision or get the impression of something that had actually happened. Aunt Belinda learned to scour the newspaper, looking for reference to her vision—and when she didn't find an answer in the *New York Times* or the *Boston Globe*, she began to increase her subscriptions to periodicals from all over the country. There seemed to be no particular geographic location or type of event that figured in the spread of cards.

That explains the piles of newspapers, and the circled articles, Diana thought, glancing at the papers stacked against the far wall of the den.

She read on, covering several years, where Aunt Belinda's journal entries had become sparse.

At last, she came to another entry, this written in the angry scrawl of an unhappy person.

"August 14, 1991. Victoria is being ridiculous! After three years, I finally told her about Diana's Gift and she told me that it was

absurd and made me promise not to speak of it to her daughter again! She refused to listen to anything I had to say—she refused to even allow me to tell her about Diana's prediction of Tracer's death and about the car accident in Dublin.

'I want your promise that you won't show her those cards of yours anymore,' she said, 'and don't even speak of fortune telling in her presence! I don't want her to grow up like some kind of gypsy who thinks she can make a living reading crystal balls!' Fortune-telling! I have never been so insulted—and so hurt!—in all my life! Is that what Geoffrey's wife thinks of me? That I spend my time reading crystal balls in a dingy tent at county fairs? Or that I do séances in my office? I wish there was a way for her to understand that I did not ask for this Gift, nor did I even want it at first...but now I've come to respect it and have learned that I should thank the Lord for it.

"Tomorrow, Victoria is taking Diana home, and the last thing she said before she went up to bed, was, 'If you don't promise not to speak of this again, I'll not have her visit you again! I'll find someone else to take her during the summer!'"

So that was the reason Diana hadn't come back to visit Aunt Belinda the following summer, when she was fourteen. That would have been after Uncle Tracer died, after Diana's prediction had come true.

Impossible. I couldn't have known that.

She pulled abruptly to her feet, trying to shake off the unsettling feeling that her aunt was either delusional or that she, Diana, had at one time predicted her great-uncle's death. A violent shiver overtook her limbs, then coiled around and around to settle, sharp and hard, in her belly in the form of queasiness. She felt light-headed, as though a chill wind was bearing down on the nape of her neck.

It can't be true, she told herself over and over—repeating the mantra as she made her way from the den and its eeriness to her bedroom. *Even if at one time I did predict Uncle Tracer's death—it could have been a guess, or a coincidence even, but even if I did predict it, I don't have the ability any longer. I haven't seen any visions in bubbles, or puddles of water, or mirrors—or crystal balls, for that matter—since then. It must have been a fluke.*

Diana pulled on her nightshirt and walked into the bathroom to brush her teeth. She went through the motions automatically, in a fog, trying to banish the unsettling thoughts. How could it be?

As she returned to her room, still unable to escape her horrified thoughts, the answer came...and suddenly all of the tension drained out of her.

Aunt Belinda! It was *Aunt Belinda* who'd had the prediction of Uncle Tracer's death—and because it was so traumatic for her, she somehow projected it upon Diana.

A relieved smile curved her face as she once more crawled into bed. That explained everything—why Diana had never had a vision or image since then, and why she didn't remember telling her aunt about the prediction. That was because she'd never had it!

Diana drew in a deep breath and let it out in a welcome, soothing sigh. That explained it all. She wasn't crazy, there was nothing going on with her mind that she couldn't control—she wasn't making predictions about people dying.

It was all Aunt Belinda.

That night, her dreams took a different approach. Real and unsettling, but not the least bit frightening ....A scrap of newspaper appeared in every venue of her nocturnal images—first in what must have been Aunt Belinda's den, but was designed more like a Dr. Seuss world, with curving buildings reminiscent of Manet's "The Scream" painting and in bold, ugly colors...and then in her own office back in Boston, this one more realistic but still a bit warped...and finally, fluttering through a room crowded with people celebrating something: Aunt Belinda, Jonathan, Ethan, Pauline Whitten, Marc Reardon, Doc Horner and Mindy, his niece...and even the cats.

The cats.

Diana awoke, sitting upright with the dread realization: somehow, she had to get the aloof felines to the vet. Today. She collapsed back onto her pillow and closed her eyes. Ugh.

—◆—

Ethan tossed the tennis ball straight into the air so high that it sang through the topmost branches of a pine, then caught it when it came whistling back down. He threw the neon yellow ball up again, flickering a glance at an at-attention Cady, who was frozen, poised to take off after it should he pitch it horizontally.

"Ready?" he asked, excitement tingeing his voice. Cady's ears perked up and her eyes brightened even more, riveted on the ball. Ethan wound up and fired the ball over the lab's head, toward the lake.

Cady was after it like a shot, thrashing through the forest down to the water. Ethan stood, hands on his hips, watching her black tail spiral down the incline. It was only mid-morning, and he felt like he needed to do something worthwhile today... something worthwhile like seeing Diana Iverson.

Ethan looked up at the towering pines that enclosed the clearing that was his yard. He was more than a bit disgusted with himself and the wayward thoughts that continued to creep back to that night—only two nights ago—when he'd taken the perfect opportunity to kiss her. And since then, he'd been distracted from just about everything productive—including sleep.

Hot damn. What a kiss.

But beyond that delicious interlude, Ethan wasn't certain how he felt about being manipulated. Sort of, anyway. He *had* been closer to the phone. It was logical for him to answer it.

Still, he knew she'd made the decision deliberately.

Obviously he was correct that there were issues between her and Jonathan, and while part of him would relish it if Diana dumped the pinhead's ass, he didn't want to be party to it. Even though his presence with her that night had been completely innocent—well, on her part anyway—he didn't want to get involved.

But Ethan's tolerance for infidelity was nil, and clearly Jonathan Wertinger had already crossed that line. So the guy should get what he deserved.

But Ethan didn't want to be Jonathan Wertinger's leftovers, either. Regardless of how appetizing they were.

Cady came racing up the slope, dripping wet, ball clutched in the back of her jaws. She pranced proudly in front of Ethan, circled him four times, squatted to pee, then paused to shake the water from her short fur. Then she dropped the ball at his feet.

Ethan picked up the ball, firing it toward the woods in the general vicinity of Diana's house, and wondered what the chances were of throwing it the half-mile to her yard. Maybe he'd surprise her sunbathing or doing something equally as interesting.

Then, he remembered Diana mentioning something to Doc Horner about taking the cats in to see him today.

He grinned a slow, easy grin.

—⚹—

Diana struggled to pull Motto's carrier from the back of the Lexus. She was sprawled across the seat, her feet on the pavement, her arms and shoulders stretched to the middle of the car where the carrier had somehow become entangled with the seatbelt. "You vicious cat," she scolded Motto, certain that the recalcitrant feline had done it purposely.

"My, what a pretty sight," drawled a voice behind her. It was a very familiar voice, and it startled Diana so much that she jerked her head and hit the ceiling.

She struggled to pull out of the car, crawling her hands backward across the seat, and whipped around to face him. "Didn't your mother teach you it's not nice to sneak up on people?" she said, a warm flush exploding over her face.

"Do you need some help?" Ethan asked courteously, ignoring her glare and leaning into the back of the Lexus. Within moments, he'd extracted the carrier and placed it on the pavement next to Arty's cage.

"What are you doing here?"

"You mean besides helping damsels in distress?"

"Is that what you call sneaking up on me?"

"I had to bring Cady in to see Doc Horner. What are you doing here?"

Diana looked up at him, squinting in the sun that blazed over his shoulder. "Aunt Belinda's cats are due for their shots. Who's Cady?"

"My dog." He turned to point toward an old white pickup. Diana saw a gigantic, black dog with huge white teeth sitting in the cab of the truck. He—or she—looked terrifying.

Her heart thudding in her throat, she picked up the cat carriers. "Oh, well, great. I guess I'll see you later then." She hurried toward the door of Doc Horner's office, anxious to get away from the ferocious dog and its unsettling master.

She pushed open the doors of the veterinarian office with effort, attempting to keep the cat carriers upright and their cargo from hissing angrily.

"Good morning, Ms. Iverson."

Diana felt her stomach plunge when she saw who greeted her behind the receptionist desk. "Hello, Mindy." No wonder Ethan had decided to bring his dog to the vet. "How are you?"

"I'm fine. Have any trouble getting the cats ready to go?"

"No, not at all," Diana lied, plunking the cat carriers down on the floor. She wasn't about to admit that she'd tried, and failed, to bribe them with tuna, kitty toys, begging and pleading on her knees in the front hall before remembering Doc Horner's suggestion to announce they were going for a ride.

The door to the outside opened behind her, and she turned to see a huge black dog charging across the room, towing Ethan on the other end of the leash. Diana gasped and, grabbing the carriers, scooted behind the counter with Mindy.

"Well hello, you!" crooned Mindy, slipping out from the other side of the desk to greet the big dog. "Hi, Ethan! Good to see you again. Who's this?"

"This is Cady." Ethan tossed an amused look at Diana, who still cowered behind the desk and tried not to look as terrified as she felt.

Wrapping the lead around his fist, he said, "Cady, park it." Instantly, the lab's rump settled onto the floor, even though she was wriggling in delight at the attention from Mindy. When the beast stood again almost immediately, Ethan lowered his voice to a more menacing tone and reminded her, "Cady, I said park it."

The dog sat again and Diana watched from her safe haven as Mindy and Ethan petted the lummox of a dog, accepting kisses from her long pink tongue. "Ugh!" she muttered to herself, aware that her heart still pounded at the sight of that ferocious hound. *You won't get me close to a dog that big in this lifetime.*

Just then, Doc Horner emerged from one of the back rooms. "Well, Diana Iverson, I'm so glad to see you and those cats of Bee's! And Ethan. What are you doing here? Come along with Diana?"

"No," she told him firmly.

Ethan stood, shooting a look at her, and answered, "Naw, I need you to take a look at one of Cady's paws. I think she may have strained it."

"Chasing tennis balls again?" asked Doug Horner, crouching next to the dog-petting party.

Diana leaned against the counter, wondering how long she was going to be waiting for her appointment. Motto yowled as if she was wondering the same thing, but no one seemed to notice.

"Which leg is it?"

"Front left," Ethan told him, then stood to lean against the other side of the desk from Diana. "I hope she's okay," he said, watching the vet palpate Cady's leg.

"Seems fine to me. I don't feel anything, and she's not wincing at all. Walk her a bit, Min, and let's see if she's limping."

Mindy obliged, and Diana found herself watching Ethan study the pair as they paraded around the office. She wondered if he was admiring the dog, or the vet's niece, who was wearing brief shorts and a t-shirt cut off to show her navel.

Her navel. Diana shuddered. She couldn't imagine showing off her own navel in public. Especially at *work*, in a *professional* office.

"Well, she doesn't seem to be limping," Doc Horner pulled himself to his feet. Diana thought she might have seen him shoot a knowing glance at Ethan, but then he just smiled. "Well, now, if she seems to be having any problems, you just let me know. And now," he turned to Diana with a broader smile, "let's take a look at those cats of yours."

She followed him back into one of the examining rooms after a brief farewell glance at Ethan, who didn't seem to notice her exit at all.

Getting two cats inoculated wasn't as much of a trauma as she'd expected it to be. Doug Horner was calm and certain and he had them in and out of their carriers before she could say boo. In fact, he gave them their shots in less time than it had taken her to get them loaded into the carriers.

"There you go—all set."

Just then, Mindy poked her head around the door. "Uncle Doug, it's Pauline Whitten on the phone for you."

Doc Horner's already pale face seemed to drain of all color. "Can't you tell her I'm with a patient?" His calm demeanor disintegrated into one of nervous anxiety.

"Uncle Doug, you've been having me lie to her all day. You just come on out here and take this call—she's a sweet old lady. Totally harmless." Mindy took her uncle's arm firmly and steered him out of the room. "Excuse us, Ms. Iverson, but my uncle's fiancée needs to speak with him."

Diana heard his squeak of protest. "She's not my fiancée!" she heard him exclaim as he was propelled down the hall.

"Yes she is," she heard Mindy say reproachfully. "You just haven't gotten around to asking her yet. I sure hope you do it before the Harvest Ball."

Diana chuckled as she turned to pick up the cat carriers. Just then, the door to the examining room opened and Ethan came in, minus Cady. "Let me help you get those out to your car," he offered, taking Arty's carrier before she could say anything.

"Where's your dog?" Diana asked, looking around anxiously.

"In the truck."

"Ethan," she said suddenly. He paused in front of the door, and she spoke rapidly, "Listen, I wanted to apologize for the other night. I didn't mean to make you feel manipulated, or used. It was irresponsible and immat—"

"Hey," he said, looking down at her. "No sweat. I was closer to the phone. It *was* innocent. Until I made it otherwise," he added, his voice dropping so low it seemed to slide along her skin. He held her eyes for a moment, then added, "So maybe I ought to be the one apologizing."

Diana felt alive and hot all at once. He didn't look the least bit sorry, and, to tell the truth, she didn't feel it either. Holding Motto's carrier with two wrists crossed in front of her, she tried to ignore her thumping heart. "Apology accepted," she said, her own voice shamefully husky. "No big deal."

She started to brush past him, but he stood firm, forcing her to take a step backward or to be standing right on top of him. Oh God, was he going to kiss her again? Right here?

He looked down at her, his brown eyes warm and steady. "The quilting group is expecting you to stop by, don't forget. I'll walk over there with you if you don't mind—I need to pick out a quilt for Fiona's wedding."

Why had she never noticed how disgustingly long and thick his lashes were? "I can't leave the cats in the car …." she said.

He shrugged, and Arty's carrier shifted and rolled. "Doc Horner would let you leave them in the back—he has kennels for the animal shelter in that barn, you know. And he'd probably be tickled if you went to visit the ladies and got Pauline Whitten off his back for a minute." He grinned, and heat flooded Diana so that she forgot her hesitations. His smile was so devastating it sent all lucid thought scattering from her mind.

Then, she forced herself to get serious. "What about Mindy?" Diana asked coolly. Maybe he was trying to make the other woman jealous—not that he needed to, from the looks she'd been giving him.

Ethan shrugged again. "What about her? Come on, I'll help you put these in the back. You can't disappoint those ladies— Helen Galliday will never forgive you."

He took the other carrier from her with ease, and turned to walk toward the back of the veterinary hospital to a white steel barn. Diana had no choice but to follow him, and as they drew nearer, she heard the clamor of cats and dogs waiting to find new owners. She realized that the inheritance from Aunt Belinda would be going directly to help these particular animals and she smiled in satisfaction. That was good.

A short time later, Ethan pulled into the parking lot of a little shop off Route 213. Diana had barely stepped out of the truck when Helen Galliday was thumping out onto the small porch.

"Well it's about time you decided to show up, missy." The old lady began her lecture before Diana had even pulled her purse from the truck. "We were beginning to think you weren't going to come by and see our place! Now come on in, before all the bugs get in." She gestured with her cane at the front door she'd left gaping behind her.

"Now, Mrs. Galliday, it's only eleven o'clock," Ethan said soothingly as he followed them up the steps to the porch. "You know Diana wouldn't have missed this for the world, and you don't close for another three hours."

"She's *late*. She left Doug Horner's place over twenty minutes ago. And Pauline gave up her Scrabble game to be here." Helen frowned, and turned just inside the front door to grasp Diana's arm with her talons and pull her inside. "Come on in, young lady."

Diana flashed an amused glance at Ethan. "Hello, everyone," she smiled, stepping into the small shop.

It was just what one might expect of a small, country-crafts operation—blue geese adorned the shop in every possible medium: on stencils around the top of the wall, wooden ones hung on pegs scattered throughout the room, painted ones on heavy stoneware dishes, embroidered ones on finger towels, and even ones printed on linen and canvas cloths. And then there was the apple motif—hand-painted on cookie jars, appliquéd on napkins and placemats, woven into small area rugs. And, of course, there were quilts of all sizes, colors, and types on display everywhere.

"Diana, it's so nice to see you again." Martha Woden peered in her general vicinity from behind coke-bottle glasses.

"You can't see nothin'," Helen muttered, steering Diana further into the shop. "Come on back into the workshop and see our quilt."

"Oh, yes, do come back," Pauline Whitten hauled her bulk to her feet. Diana noticed that her nails had been changed to a blood-red color that matched the ruby on her right middle finger. Somehow, she managed to usurp Helen's position at Diana's elbow and murmur into her ear, "Douglas mentioned that he saw you and your young man up to his office today."

Diana stared at her, feeling her face heat up. "He's *not* my young man," she hissed into Pauline's ear.

"What did you say?" Helen pushed her way back to Diana's side. "What were you saying?" she demanded again.

"It wasn't nothing of any importance, Helen," Pauline turned her nose into the air. "Just a bit of misinformation." And she gave Diana a mysterious, arch smile.

"What about?" demanded the termagant.

Diana decided she'd had enough of this, and she stepped away from the bickering ladies into the back room of the shop. Just inside, she stopped, drawing in her breath. There were approximately a dozen quilts in several stages of creation, but the one that drew her attention was made of varying shades of cream and white, eggshell, pale beige and ivory. Detail stitching was done in sage green and beige, and the border of the quilt was made of a patterned fabric of pale green and cream.

"Beautiful," she exclaimed, stepping toward the quilt where it was hanging on the wall. She smoothed a hand over it. The materials varied from silk to flannel to brushed cotton and lace, and even shantung. "This is absolutely gorgeous."

Helen crowded up behind her. "It's yours dearie, if you like it so. And because you're Bee's niece, we'll give you a special price on it." She named the price and Diana flinched. "That's *twenty* percent off, young lady. You can afford it—you're one of them high-priced ambulance chasers, and here we are these old ladies, living on a fixed income, our fingers crippling from arthritis. And jus' look at ol' Martha over there—her eyesight's a-goin' after spending all these hours on those little bitty stitches."

Diana dashed a glance at Ethan, who was leaning against the wall, snickering at her. She frowned a look that said *Just wait—you'll be next.* "Um, well—" she was just about to reply when she saw Ethan's lips moving. It looked like he was saying, "Bargain with her."

She blinked. Of course. "Well, you know, Mrs. Galliday," she said slowly, with real regret in her voice, "business has been a bit slow. Those doctors just aren't messing up as much as they used to. I could probably afford it if it were, say, fifty percent off."

"*Fifty percent!*" Helen clutched her hand to her chest, her beady blue eyes widening in feigned shock. "Oh my heavens, why that's like giving away the store! Oh my, oh my, oh, I just don't think we could do more than...twenty-five percent off." Her eyes grew shrewd as she appraised Diana, waiting but seeming not to wait, for her response.

"Oh, dear. Well," Diana drew in a deep sigh and turned from the quilt. "I guess I'll just have to wait then. I might be able to swing it at forty percent …."

Helen gave up all pretenses. "Twenty-eight percent!"

"Thirty-seven."

"Thirty!"

"Thirty-five."

"Thirty-three!"

"Sold!"

Diana laughed and Helen manipulated her lips into what passed for a smile. "Well, now, Betsy, why don't you package up that wedding quilt there for Diana while we look at the Crazy quilt."

"Wedding quilt?"

"Of course—couldn't you tell, what with all the white? You put it in your trousseau for when you get married." Pauline winked at Diana and let her gaze slide to Ethan.

Deciding to get herself off the hot seat, Diana turned to Ethan, saying sweetly, "Ethan, weren't you saying you needed a quilt for your sister? And what about one for *your* house?"

That was all she needed to say—Helen was on him like a pit bull, leaving Pauline free to take Diana over to the Crazy Quilt.

It was the largest quilt she'd ever seen, measuring, she guessed, ten by ten feet unfinished.

"Each of us does a block whenever we have some leftover materials," Pauline was explaining. "This one I did with the pattern we used for a fund-raiser last year for a little boy who needed a liver transplant. See, I embroidered little hearts and rainbows around the edge of the block.

"And this one here Martha created using some of the material from her granddaughter's wedding dress, and the dresses from her bridesmaids.

"Look at this block—we did this one for Damariscotta's centennial celebration."

Diana was fascinated, and the other ladies crowded around, eager to share the stories behind each of the unique blocks. And though they were each of different patterns and colors and materials, somehow they fit together harmoniously—just like their creators.

Rose Bettinger, who had been quiet until now, eased her way through the small knot of people. "Diana, this was the last block your aunt was working on before she passed. I've been trying to finish it for her so we can add it to the quilt."

She turned from the main quilt to take the four-by-four-inch piece of quilting Rose offered. "Do you know what its story is?" she asked, looking at the square. It was different from the others in that it was composed of one large square of material with a narrow border of black and red patterned fabric. The center square had stars and moons appliquéd on it, along with two fish that looked like the symbol for Pisces.

"I don't know much about it—she'd been working on it only the last few days before she died, and she didn't give any description where or how she got the idea." Rose patted Diana's hand in her motherly fashion, "Now, dear, I wish't I could tell you more. Only other thing is she had some notes she was making about it somewhere's around here. But I don't know where they went off to. And there are other squares that she's done—look here at this one with the yellow and blue triangles and circles. She said that one reminded her of the pyramids of Egypt."

Diana glanced at the indicated block, then back at the one she held in her hands. She was compelled to stare at it, to try and figure out what theme, what meaning Aunt Belinda had been using when she composed the odd-looking piece. "What do you suppose this is?" she asked, pointing to a group of small black stitches in one corner.

"Let me see that." Helen snatched the scrap of fabric out of her hand, peering down at it. "Looks to me like a snake climbing a tree. Looks like ol' Bee got a little Biblical on us!" She cackled and handed the scrap of fabric back to Diana.

"Could be," Diana looked at it again, a niggling in the back of her head telling her that she should recognize it. *Stars and moons. Pisces. A snake in a tree.*

She was jolted from her thoughts by Ethan's approach. "Well, I've got to get some lunch, and we'd better go get your cats. It's almost one o'clock."

Diana nodded, and absently handed the block back to Rose. "Thank you for showing this to me. I'll be very anxious to see it when it's all completed."

"I don't think it'll ever get finished," Betsy Farr ventured. "We just keep adding on to it."

"I have your quilt—and mine as well," Ethan smiled at her. "They're already in the truck."

Helen led the way to the front of the shop. "Now, you stop by again," she admonished with a curved forefinger. "Quilts make great gifts for Christmas and weddings, you know."

Ethan and Diana agreed they would be back, but as they started down the steps, Diana heard him mutter, "If I buy many more of those, I'll be bankrupt."

She slid into her spot in the cab of the truck just as he opened his door. "Hungry?" he asked. "Want to grab some lunch?"

She shook her head. "No, thanks—I need to get back to the house. I've got a million things to do there."

He shrugged. "All right, then."

But when they returned to the back lot behind Doc Horner's office, a surprise awaited them.

Diana's Lexus sat on ribbons of slashed tires.

EIGHT

"THEY MUST HAVE DONE it while Doc Horner's office was closed for lunch," Ethan told Joe Cap as they sat in his office. "She had it parked in back by the animal shelter barn."

The lanky, straw-haired officer sat back in his chair, tilted so that he could look up at the ceiling, and folded his arms over his chest, listening as they told the story.

Diana's face was drawn so tight her cheekbones were almost skeletal in the fluorescent lighting of the station's office. "Last night I received a prank phone call, too. It was the second one."

Ethan swiveled in his chair. "You didn't mention that."

She ignored him, speaking only to Cap. "I didn't think much of it—I answered the phone and no one was there, both times. I figured it was some kids playing around. But now...I'm rethinking that." Her hands were curled in her lap, but other than that and the whiteness of her face, she showed no other sign of emotion. Something he'd come to expect from her.

"You didn't feel, after a break-in last weekend, that it was important enough to call the police?" Ethan said harshly. "He was probably checking to see if you were home. For whatever reason."

Again, she ignored him. "I planned to stop by today and let you know about it," she told Joe. Her hand shook delicately as she brushed a thick lock of hair behind her ear.

Joe's chair thumped as he allowed it to right itself. He looked across his desk at them and said, "There's something more to this." His pale eyes probed Diana seriously. "I don't think this is just some kids messing around," he said.

"You said the other day you thought something was odd," said Ethan.

Joe nodded and returned his attention to Diana. "I remember thinking that when I found your aunt's body, there was something odd about it. She was in her bed, and had died probably of heart failure in her sleep—which was substantiated by Marc Reardon, who was treating her heart condition. There were no signs of forced entry, no signs of struggle, no robbery...nothing. But ...." He drew in a long, deep breath and faded into silence. Of course with Joe and the way he talked, one couldn't be sure he wasn't just pausing between words.

"Smothered. She was smothered."

Ethan spun to look at Diana, who'd spoken abruptly. The words sounded as though they had been dragged from deep within her. "Smothered? What makes you think that?" he demanded, knowing he was on the verge of learning something important— about Diana, about her abilities, about Belinda.

"I...just...know it." Her voice was steady but barely discernable as she forced the words from her lips—lips that moved stiffly and were white around the edges.

"I dreamt it." She seemed to brace herself, as though in protection of any ridicule they might send her way, but she didn't retreat from her words. Her eyes sat, huge and sunken, in her delicate face—blue-gray irises ringed with black, dark lashes fringing the deep lids, accented by dark brows.

"The bed was just too neat," Joe Cap said. "I wondered later how anyone could have slept without even wrinkling the sheets."

"And no reason to do an autopsy, hmm?" Ethan mused. "An elderly woman with a documented heart condition dies in her sleep, and no one thinks twice about it."

"Yep." Joe Cap scratched his head, then flattened the ruffled hair into a smooth sheen. "Shoulda gone with my gut. There were some faint bruises on one wrist, but they coulda been there awhile. Marc checked her over too, and said it was a heart attack. Coulda assumed too much there."

"We're talking about murder here." Ethan spoke the words flatly, aloud, to make certain he could believe it.

"Yep. Murder."

—m—

Ethan insisted on buying Diana lunch at one of the outdoor seafood places in town before giving her a ride home. She'd agreed that Belinda should be exhumed for an autopsy to determine if their suspicions were correct. There'd been miles of paperwork to complete, so it was nearly two-thirty by the time they left the police station, and he was ravenous.

As they sat at a picnic table shaded by a green-and-white-striped umbrella, Ethan watched Diana stare into space. He wished there was something he could do or say to take that stone-like, taut expression from her features.

The only part of her that seemed to have life was her dark hair: the breeze played with it, toying with a curl here, tossing a wisp into her face there. He loved that it was so full and soft, but left her neck and shoulders bare. Once, a few strands caught at the corner of her full lips and he reached over without thinking to brush it away, sliding his fingers over her smooth, warm skin. She came out of her reverie to look at him in surprise, then with a faltering smile settled further back on her bench—away from him.

"You have such beautiful hair," he said. "I couldn't resist."

She clapped a hand to her head, pushing the tousled mass flat, and looked at him as if he were crazy. "It's always so out of control and messy. My mom used to say—well, I always think of it as my worst feature," she added with a wry laugh. "But thanks for saying that."

"It's definitely not your worst feature," he said. "I think it's one of your best features. That and your eyes. Every time I look at them, they seem to be a different color. From blue to gray and everything in between."

Diana looked supremely uncomfortable. "Thanks," she said.

He saw her throat convulse as she swallowed nervously and he admired the long line of her neck, thinking how much he'd like to slide his mouth along and nuzzle its warm, intimate curve. But of course, that was out of the question.

"And then there's the rest of you," he continued, wondering whether she was uncomfortable because of the compliments, or because it was *he* who was giving her the compliments. "Including your mouth. I think it's pretty fantastic too—including what comes out of it."

He was certain it wasn't the sun's heat that made her face pinken, and he settled back and admired the view. Why an intelligent, beautiful woman like her was so blown over by a few compliments he couldn't understand.

He heard their number called from the restaurant counter and stood to retrieve their food. But before he went, he looked down at her and said, "Do you want to know what your worst feature really is?"

Diana went still, and he could see even her breathing stop. "What?" she asked, sort of shrinking away. Her whole demeanor changed: walls went up, eyes went flat, body went stiff.

Wow. Hit a soft spot there. "As far as I'm concerned," he said, "your worst feature is Jonathan Wertinger." And he walked away to get the food.

When they returned to Diana's house, Ethan turned off the truck and gallantly got out to help her carry the cats inside. Ordering Cady to "park it," he hurried over to take both of the carriers from Diana.

She unlocked the door and stepped in, turning to take Motto's carrier. After letting the cats out of their cages, he followed her into the kitchen, where the distinct odor of tuna reached his nose. "What's that?"

Diana looked embarrassed as she noticed the open can of tuna on the counter. "A bribe for the cats—I guess I forgot about it because I was so relieved to get them ready to go. I'm going to put the mail in the den," she said, and left him in the kitchen.

Ethan leaned in his favorite spot against the counter, noticing that the Tarot cards were no longer in their regular spot under the phone. He wondered what she'd done with them, and was just about to ask when he heard a startled cry.

He bolted down the hall toward the den, and found Diana in its doorway, leaning against the wall. Her hand covered her mouth and she pointed, wordlessly, into the room.

It was trashed.

The stacks of magazines and periodicals had been thrown everywhere. Torn paper littered the floor, books had been flung and lay, binding-side-up, pages crushed, every which way. A penholder rested on its side, with pens, pencils, and markers in a jumble on the desk and onto the floor. Even the settee had been destroyed—cushions torn open and tossed around, and the back slit open.

Diana sank onto the floor, cross-legged, and stared silently into the room. "What is going on?" she whispered. "What are they after?"

From her place in the doorway, she looked up at him—her eyes wide, frightened and very blue, her thick dark hair in disarray, her features etched with confusion. He dropped his hand to touch her hair, gently massaging its warmth and softness, while at the same time fighting stunning, encompassing anger.

"I don't know," he breathed. "But we're going to find out."

It was after dusk by the time Ethan pulled into his driveway, Diana and her overnight bag in the front seat next to him.

He'd been unshakable in his insistence that she not stay in Belinda's house alone tonight. Joe Cap had agreed, and Diana, to her credit, didn't argue. Once Joe started using words like *unauthorized entry* and *murder*, her initial hesitation evaporated. Although, to be fair, Ethan suspected Diana's reluctance stemmed more from staying with him than from being evacuated from her house.

Cady leapt out of the kennel in the back of the truck as soon as Ethan flung the door open, shooting into her yard to sniff around and make sure nothing had invaded her domain. He didn't miss the fact that Diana eyed the dog with trepidation before hurrying toward the cabin while the lab was sniffing at the base of a pine tree on the far end of his yard.

"I take it you don't like dogs," he commented, feeling a bit crestfallen that it was so.

"No, not really," she replied, still eyeing Cady warily. She looked as if she expected the dog to come barreling over and attack her at any moment. "Especially big ones."

Ethan whistled for his pet, and she came trotting across the lawn, grinning happily that there was another human about to give her attention. Poor thing was bound to be disappointed.

"Come on in." He gestured Diana into his high-ceilinged living room. "Cady, snooze—right there," he said, pointing to a worn, Navajo rug in front of the fireplace. The lab looked at him with her big brown dog-eyes as if to say *What did I do?* He went over to give his best friend a pat on the head to let her know that he still loved her, then said to his guest, "Would you like something to drink? Beer, wine, soda, coffee, juice? Water?"

"Um..." she paused for a moment, looking up at him with eyes dulled by stress, "A glass of wine? Red if you have it."

He brought Diana a glass of garnet-colored wine and popped the cap of the beer he favored. Then he rummaged through the fridge and found some cheese, hummus, raw carrots and tomatoes. "Have a seat," he invited, gesturing to the long, sienna-colored leather sofa. "And here's something to nibble on. The tomatoes are from my garden."

"Thanks. I just realized how hungry I am," she said, reaching for a small plate and filling it up. As she ate, she found herself gazing around the cabin, noticing every little detail.

The room wasn't overly large, but the high ceiling gave it a spacious feel. All the floors and exterior walls were a deep, honey-colored wood, in keeping true to the sense of a log cabin. The bar from a galley kitchen separated cooking from living space, and there was only a small table and chairs for eating tucked into a corner.

A fieldstone fireplace dominated the wall opposite the sofa, with a large television placed strategically so that it could be viewed from most places in the room: from the sofa, from a well-worn armchair, from the small dining table. The floors were polished, and covered with a variety of rugs. Bookcases were built into the diagonal wall that hid a staircase leading to the second floor.

Diana was struck by the sense that the place was a home. Comfortable, welcoming, neat but not sterile. Something she wouldn't have expected from a bachelor. Certainly nothing like Jonathan's sleek, red and black condo—at least before she moved in and softened it up.

Four rectangular windows faced the direction of the lake, and as she watched, Ethan walked over to pull their blinds partway down.

She admired him and appreciated how his rugged good looks fit in this setting...the way his denim shorts hugged his rear and showed off tanned, muscular legs...the thick locks of hair that brushed the collar of his shirt and fell onto his forehead...his solid, toned arms and fine, chiseled mouth ….

And she realized she felt at ease, even in the presence of such masculinity. Not only did she feel at ease with him, but she found she didn't have to censor what she said. Like she did with Jonathan.

Diana sipped from her wine, watching Ethan in consideration over the rim of the glass. As he came back around by the couch and sat on the other end she asked, "Have you lived here long?"

"I've had the place for almost seven years, but I just finished remodeling it last summer. I spend most of my time in Princeton, you know, and only make it up here during the summers and for long weekends—more's the pity."

"Did you get it in the divorce?" she couldn't help but ask, wondering if it was Jenny who had made the place so welcoming, picking out the pillows on the sofa and the thick, bold-colored rug in front of the fire. She found the possibility unaccountably irritating.

His expression shuttered just a bit. "No. Jenny was never here for more than a couple weekends. This has always been my haven. I like to fish," he added. "She didn't like to be away from civilization. Or, now that I think about it, she was probably using the time I was up here to fuck my friend Bruce. And God knows who else." He took a long swig.

"I only asked because it's such a comfortable, homey place," Diana told him, wishing she'd kept her mouth shut. "It doesn't seem like Jenny the Jerkette's style." Then her eyes widened. "Did I say that out loud?" Where was her filtering censor when she needed it?

But he was chuckling now, his eyes dancing as he looked at her from the other end of the sofa. "You certainly did. Jenny the Jerkette? That's pretty lame. I've called her a lot worse."

"I can only imagine," she murmured, feeling a little uncomfortable that she'd said something so thoughtless—and silly. But he wasn't looking at her as if she were an idiot either, so maybe it was okay.

"Thanks anyway," he said. "I'm glad you like the place. I *was* going for homey, as a matter of fact." He shrugged, looking down at his beer, wiping off the condensation on the bottleneck. "I think it'd be a great place to raise a family. I was kind of hoping I'd already have one by now. But, well...in the end, it was a good thing we didn't have any children. Jenny the Jerkette and I." He flashed her a wry look. "That really is pretty bad, even with the alliteration."

Diana stifled a little laugh. "Well, give me time. I'll come up with something better." She took a drink of wine and realized her glass was nearly empty already.

"Although I'm not sure how anything could follow Valerie the...what did you call her?"

"Which time?" Diana retorted. "I generally refer to her as Valerie the Wonder Slut, but Jonathan didn't appreciate that."

Ethan sobered. "I'll just bet he didn't." He looked as if he were about to say something else, then abruptly lifted his beer to drink, effectively muzzling himself.

"He said it wasn't a dignified thing for me to say," she said. "I told him it wasn't very dignified of him to be playing fuck-buddy with a bimbo surgeon while wearing a surgical mask and gloves. He was, you know. When I found them in the hotel together."

He gave a short bark of laughter that had the big black dog sitting up and giving its own high-pitched yip. "'S okay, Cady," Ethan told the canine. "Relax." Then he looked at Diana, still laughing. "You said that? And...he *was?*"

"Yes, he was. And what's so funny about what I said?"

"It's just that it doesn't sound like you," he said. "Not that I know you all that well," he amended quickly. "But you're so... you're not ...."

"Yes, I know. I used the F-word. Which is reserved for use by men only. But I was mad. And it slipped out. And I'm not all that dignified, if you really want to know the truth." Diana clamped her mouth shut. Had he put something in the wine, to get her talking like this? Or was she just over-exhausted, over-stressed, and disturbed beyond discretion?

He gave her a long, slow smile that made her insides go all hot and squishy. "I kind of like you when you're undignified. You're a lot more interesting."

And then, before she could formulate anything to say that wasn't going to sound inane, he stood. "Would you like to see the rest of the house?" Ethan casually held out a hand, and after a brief hesitation, she offered her own and allowed him to pull her upright.

To her relief, he didn't try to keep hold of her fingers, releasing them from his large, warm ones as soon as she was upright. Glass in hand, she followed him into the kitchen to check out its layout, next to his small office and then the guest bedroom—where she'd be sleeping tonight—along with its bath.

"The master suite is upstairs," he said, his voice very nonchalant. "You have to see it if for no other reason than for its deck and the view. It's my favorite part of the house." He gestured, and Diana climbed the stairs ahead of him, fully aware of his presence behind her...and excruciatingly sensitive to the fact that they were going to be in his bedroom.

In keeping with the rest of the cabin's décor, the master suite was done in heavy furnishings with bold colors. Diana tried not to look at the king-sized bed, and tried to ignore the lingering scent of Ethan mixed with male grooming products—but whatever they were, they smelled good. Fresh, clean, and masculine.

Very aware of the intimacy of being in his bedroom, more than a little uncomfortable, Diana gave it only a cursory look before walking across the thick, wool rug to the large sliding glass door.

Outside, a cool night breeze caught her by surprise. "Wow, it got chilly," she said. Nevertheless, she stepped toward the rail and folded her arms at her waist, taking a moment to look out over the darkness as she breathed in the lake air.

Hints of the water were visible as glistening reflections of the stars that spangled in the sky. The tops of tall trees brushed the heavens, whispering among themselves in answer to the call of a loon.

"It's so beautiful here," she murmured. "And so peaceful. How do you ever go back?"

He was standing so close she felt him shrug behind her. "There are many days when I wish I didn't have to." His voice was low, sending shivers down her back. "I'd give an awful lot to be able to live here year around. In fact, I'm working on a project that may turn into a book. If so, I'll take a sabbatical for a couple years and live here while I'm finishing it. Then hopefully I'll find another way not to return to the city."

"I don't think I could live this far from civilization," Diana said firmly, trying to convince herself that Boston was the place for her. "It's too far away from everything."

"I guess it depends what you mean by everything."

Crickets chirped and something rustled in the forest below. Cady gave a short yelp from downstairs, but said nothing more.

She felt him draw near, felt his warm hands cover her bare shoulders, then slide down her arms. "What a beautiful night," he said near her ear, cupping her elbows. For a moment, a wild instant, she wanted to turn around and face him. To go into his arms and see if his kiss was as good as she remembered.

Diana closed her eyes, heart pounding, her insides swirling with indecision and anticipation, her senses heightened and pinpointed to where he touched her. She could turn around...it would be so easy. And they'd kiss. And ....

His hands moved up her arms again, then dropped as he stepped back. "You're cold, Diana. Let's go inside."

She opened her eyes, the moment gone, and went back inside. But when he lingered in the bedroom, she walked briskly past him and toward the stairs. "I think I need a refill," she said, gesturing with her empty glass, grateful that she hadn't done anything she'd regret.

"Sure." He thumped down the stairs behind her.

The kitchen's bright lights and the solidness of appliances and countertops dispelled Diana's discomfort. She perched on a bar stool and watched as he poured more wine, then took a second beer from the refrigerator.

He leaned forward, resting his elbows on the countertop across the bar from her, his expression sober. "So, did you suspect Jonathan was having an affair? I," he said, looking down at his beer bottle as he slowly turned it in his hands, "didn't have a clue. About Jenny."

Startled by his choice of topic, Diana was nevertheless willing to follow it. "I didn't suspect at all. I showed up to surprise him at a convention hotel—it was a weekend, and I'd just won a really big case—and when I stopped at the registration desk to find out his room, they gave me a key, calling me Mrs. Wertinger. That was my first clue, and let me tell you...that elevator ride to the fifth floor was the longest ride of my life. I kept hoping I was wrong... but you know, hotels don't give out keys unless they're told to. And so at that point, I knew he was expecting someone else. *Mrs. Wertinger.* Who didn't happen to be me."

"That would have sucked," he said, his face grim.

"It did. I puked in the bathroom." Her stomach roiled even now, thinking about how her world had collapsed when she walked in on that scene. "Let me clarify—I puked *after* I chased Valerie the Strumpet Surgeon out of the room."

His lips twitched. "You should have horked all over her."

Diana grinned and took a sip of cabernet. "Too bad I didn't think of that." Then her smile faded. "Jonathan wants to work things out, but I …."

Ethan was looking at her intently, his gaze warm and heavy. Then suddenly, he reached across the counter and lightly brushed a finger over her lower lip. Diana didn't move as tiny tingles exploded beneath his touch, heat rushing over her face.

"You had this," he said, lifting his finger to show a droplet of red wine. He looked at it then looked at her and all at once she was even more hot and trembly and her heart was racing. He gently traced the rim of his beer with the wine-dotted finger then lifted the bottle to drink.

She couldn't look away from his long, strong throat as he tipped his head back. Just watching him made her weak in the knees, fluttery in the belly. Jonathan had never made her feel that way. But then, as nice-looking as Jonathan was, he wasn't as darkly handsome as Ethan. Nor as…easy, she guessed was the word. Easy, casual, informal. And it was rubbing off on her.

"I think I'm ready to go to bed now," she said suddenly, sliding off the stool.

Ethan rested his beer on the counter and nodded. "I'm sure you're exhausted—I'm pretty wiped out myself. Let me run upstairs and grab some fresh towels for you. For the morning." He turned and dashed up the steps.

Diana stared after him and his seemingly easy capitulation. She'd expected him to at least try to make a pass at her—and she wasn't certain she'd be able to handle it.

I have to figure out how I feel about Jonathan before anything can happen with Ethan. And then all at once, she was irritated about the very thought. There wasn't any future here, with Ethan.

He lived in New Jersey, she lived in Boston. And surely he didn't intend for anything more than a summer fling. Why would he?

Ethan returned with a stack of towels. "I think there's a robe in the closet in the guest room, and there's an extra blanket in there too, in case you get cold."

"Thanks."

"Is there anything else you think you might need?" When she shook her head, he continued, "Well, then, good night. Sleep well, and sleep as late as you like. And if Cady barks in the night, don't worry—she just likes to let the squirrels know she's still holding the fort down."

"Okay. See you in the morning." She watched as he turned off the lights and darted up the stairs, leaving her at the door of her room, safe, sound, and solo.

Ethan lay in his bed, thankful that sunlight was at last streaming through the sliding glass door. It had been a long night.

He folded his hands over his chest and glanced at the clock. Seven-thirty, it read. The last time he'd looked at it, it had been four-thirty. And the time before that, it had been four-twenty-five.

He smiled wryly to himself and scratched the hair on his chest. Served him right, inviting her to stay and being determined to be the perfect gentleman, unwilling to take advantage of her when she was emotionally drained. He'd behaved, but at the cost of a good night's sleep.

Ethan rolled over onto his side so that he could look out at the sunny day. His thoughts wandered to the moment last night, out on that very deck with Diana. He'd been close enough to smell her hair, and when he'd touched her chilled arms, he'd felt her flinch against him. There had been a moment when he'd almost forgotten all of his scruples, and turned her about in his arms to kiss her. Fortunately, she'd been smart enough to leave his bedroom when they came inside.

He felt himself shift and harden, now, remembering the way she'd looked at him with heavy-lidded eyes. Ethan squeezed his eyes shut. He had to stop thinking about her. He wasn't ready to get involved with a woman again, especially one who was clearly not fling material. Lexie and Jenny had done a good number on him. And Diana lived in Boston, anyway. And she was clearly conflicted about Wertinger.

And he was really only supposed to be spending time with her for research purposes. He had to get *something* done this summer, or he might have to go back to teaching full-time.

This is not the time, and Diana's not the—

Before he could complete the thought, a bloodcurdling scream rent the air.

Diana had been sleeping soundly, curled up in one of the most comfortable beds she'd ever experienced. She'd rolled over, up against a warm body...*Ethan*, her sleep-fogged mind told her. The thought fluttered through her in a wave of heat, and she smiled lazily in her sleep. However he'd come to be here, the memories couldn't be bad, she thought...and opened her eyes. Then she screamed.

Diana stumbled out of the bed as Cady's head shot up and she looked at her with startled brown eyes. The sound of a heavy thud upstairs, then faster, staccato thumps down the stairs alerted her to the fact that Ethan had heard her.

The door to her room burst open and he flew in. "What is it?" he exclaimed.

Diana gawked. He was naked, and absolutely magnificent in his natural state. For a moment, she couldn't say a word—she was caught between embarrassment, shock, and admiration.

Cady hadn't moved from her place on the bed, and Ethan's gaze fell on her. Understanding dawned on his face at the same time as he realized his state of undress. A tinge of redness colored his cheeks and he slipped into the bathroom to grab a towel. "Sorry," he said as a smile tugged at his mouth. "Did Cady startle you? I should have warned you to keep the door closed if you didn't want her in here."

"It's—it's all right," Diana managed to stammer. Although she'd averted her eyes as soon as she saw his nakedness, she could still picture his broad, muscled chest and flat stomach...and the evidence that he didn't sunbathe in the nude. *Deep breaths, Diana, deep breaths.* "I hope I didn't wake you," she added weakly.

Ethan gestured and Cady jumped off the bed, then paused to stretch with her tail in the air. "I'm sorry about that," he said again, tightening the towel around his waist. "No, you didn't wake me—I was already up. Did you sleep all right?"

"I slept like a log," Diana replied. There was no need to let on that she'd thrashed about sleeplessly for hours after he'd left her to go upstairs.

"Glad to hear it. Well, I promised you breakfast—we can eat out on the deck."

By the time Diana got out of the shower, the smells of something delicious were wafting under the door of the guest room. Her hair was still wet, and she considered blowing it dry, but decided that there was no reason to put any effort into her appearance for Ethan. It didn't matter what she looked like to him, Diana told herself, even as she inspected herself without makeup and hesitated before holding firm with her decision not to primp. He thought her hair was pretty? Wait till he saw it completely out of control. He'd change his mind quickly enough.

Taking a deep breath, she opened the door to the bedroom and found Cady lying there across the threshold. The black lab sprang to her feet, tongue lolling in excitement, and Diana looked down at her distastefully. "Get away," she suggested, beckoning with her hand.

The dog didn't move, just looked up at her with mournful brown eyes, and stood expectantly, blocking the doorway. "Move," she tried again weakly.

Cady licked her chops, sending a shiver of warning up Diana's spine. "Um...nice doggie," she said, and was relieved when the dog let her tongue hang out again. *I'm not moving until you greet me in a proper manner,* she seemed to say.

"Oh, all right." Diana gave in and patted the top of her head clumsily. The fur, a shiny blue-black color, was surprisingly soft—not coarse as she'd expected. Cady still didn't move, so Diana tried again, this time petting the dog's forehead. "Watch out," she said, and finally pushed past the lump of fur.

When she came around the corner into the kitchen, Cady was at her heels. "Good morning, ladies," Ethan greeted them. He was now modestly attired in a pair of twill shorts and a dark red t-shirt, and stood at the stove. "Blueberry pancakes okay with you?" he asked, brandishing a spatula. "The berries are fresh from the market."

Diana sighed deeply, inhaling the aroma of fluffy pancakes. "Wow," she said, sliding onto a bar stool. "You can cook."

"Yeah. I know how to crack a couple eggs and stir up a mix," he said, gesturing to a box on the counter.

"That's good enough for me." She watched as he expertly flipped each flapjack, then added them to a growing pile on a plate in the oven. She'd never had a man make breakfast for her before. She'd never even had a man *cook* for her before. Jonathan's idea of cooking was calling for takeout and putting it on a plate.

All at once, it struck her, like a bucket of cold water. The calm realization that she wouldn't care if she never saw Jonathan again.

It was odd, the way her decision came—in such an unexpected way, at this moment over breakfast—and with such vehemence and clarity. And freedom. She came back to the present, to the smell of coffee and frying cakes, and settled back in her seat.

I'm going to break it off. Today.

She'd call Jonathan when she got back to the house—and that was when she remembered what she had been able to forget for several hours. A heavy weight settled over her shoulders, and the cheer of the day disintegrated. Aunt Belinda...murdered. Maybe. Diana's tires slashed. Her house broken into.

"I was thinking," Ethan said, gesturing for her to follow him to the patio, "if you want, I could put some safety locks on all of your ground-floor windows today...and maybe add some extra dead-bolts, if it might make you feel more comfortable."

Diana sat on one of the wrought-iron chairs and gave him a surprised, grateful smile. "That would be great. You don't mind taking a day from work to do that?"

"Not at all. My projects can wait. And I don't know about you, but I wouldn't feel comfortable sleeping in that house unless something was done to make it safer." He slopped syrup on a stack of pancakes as he settled into his own seat. "I'll run into town to the hardware store after I drop you off, and get the stuff."

"Thank you so much," she said, suddenly feeling as if she wasn't alone—that she didn't have to deal with this whole terrible mess on her own. She smiled at him, he smiled back, and Diana felt a little bubble of warmth burst in her middle.

After breakfast, she cleaned up while he showered. Diana tried not to think about how domestic it all felt. After all, this was a temporary situation.

Ethan's thudding steps down the stairs, punctuated by Cady's four-pawed-gallop, came just as she finished wiping the counters. His hair was damp, he was clean-shaven, and he carried a pair of athletic shoes. "I've got to throw the ball for Cady for a few minutes, then we can go."

Diana followed him outside and sat at the picnic table, watching as man and dog played together. She even clapped a few times when Cady caught the tennis ball neatly in her mouth, then pranced around happily. Once, the lab even brought the ball over to Diana and dropped it at her feet. Diana couldn't disappoint her expectant look, and reached to pick it up. She almost dropped it when she felt its sloppy dampness, but managed to ignore the wetness long enough to toss it toward the lake.

It didn't go as far as when Ethan threw it, but Cady chased after it gleefully. "Uh-oh, now you have a friend," he said when the lab brought it back and dropped it at Diana's feet again.

Diana acquiesced and threw the ball a few more times, then Ethan called Cady to go inside. "Let's hit it," he said, heading for the truck.

When they reached Diana's house, he insisted on taking the keys and opening the door. Leading the way inside, he started down the hall, looking in each room.

Nothing else had been disturbed overnight, and Diana felt a wash of relief. She'd been afraid to come back and find even more destruction.

Ethan took charge in the den and Diana gratefully followed his lead. He turned on the radio to a station which blasted '90s rock by The Spin Doctors, Sheryl Crowe and Nirvana, and they talked about the differences in their childhood—his growing up in a commune, hers in a staid suburb of Boston—from that decade as they worked in efficient tandem. His conversation made it easy for her to forget why they were there and what had caused the mess, and for that, she was supremely grateful.

When they'd bagged the last paper bag of periodicals and the den looked cleaner than it had probably been in years, Ethan loaded the garbage into the back of his truck. "All right, then, I'll drop this off at the recycle place and get the locks and come on back. I'm going to leave Cady here, with you—outside," he added when she felt her face freeze up. "You don't have to let her in, and she won't go anywhere, but if—well, anyway, she'll be here. Let me count the windows, and I'll be on my way."

After he left, Diana took a deep breath and dialed Jonathan's cell phone from the phone in the den. She wasn't sure if she wanted him to answer or not. It was Friday, and he didn't usually schedule surgery on that day when he could be on the golf course. But before she could get anymore nervous, he answered.

"Diana!" The relief in his voice came through the phone. "How...how are you?"

Her heart gave a little bump. This was the first time they'd talked since the other night, when Ethan had answered the phone. Jonathan sounded sincerely happy to hear from her. And unusually tentative. Her palms became damp and she closed her eyes, aware of an unpleasant surging in her belly.

"I'm fine," she told him. "Fine."

"Diana, I want—will you come home? Please? I miss you. I'm—sorry about the other night. I was...well, I was jealous. And I want us to work through this, and we can't work through this if you're way up there in the middle of nowhere."

"I'll be home by Sunday night," she said, gripping the phone tighter. Now was the time. She had to tell him. "To pack up my things. I'm moving out."

"What?" The soft, empathetic tone changed to one of shock and dismay. "Diana, you can't—"

"Jonathan," she interrupted him, forcing herself to speak. "I'm moving out. It's over." She was aware of the unsettled feeling sinking over her, the deepening twist of nausea. *What am I doing?*

"Diana," he said, his voice sharper now. Then he drew in an audible breath and she could tell he was trying to force himself into calmness. "Okay, okay, then, if you want to move out, take a little space, a little time to work things through, I can understand that. I can work with that," he said. "We can do that."

That little bump of nerves in her pulse grew stronger. Maybe that was the way she should approach it. Just move out for a little while, try to work things out. Not just close the door without trying again. "Okay," she said.

"Okay," he repeated. "Good. You'll be home Sunday."

"Yes. But I'm packing my things," she said—as much to remind him as to remind herself. Her palms were clammy and the phone felt heavy and hot against her cheek.

"Where are you going to stay?" he asked. "There's no rush, Diana."

"Don't worry about me. I have a place to stay," she said, figuring she'd find a place. A hotel, at least, until she could find somewhere more permanent. Or with Mickey and her husband Dominic, if she got desperate. Her assistant had never been fond of Jonathan and would welcome the news that Diana had dumped him.

"All right. Whatever you need to do. Diana. I love you," he said.

"All right. Jonathan, good-bye," she said, forcing the words from her suddenly dry throat. She replaced the phone in its cradle and sank onto the settee. Numbness crept over her. Numbness and emptiness and a little fear.

What have I done?

Her fingers were trembling, and Diana clenched them tightly as if that would stop them from doing so. *I did the right thing. I don't feel anything for him anymore. I don't know if I've felt anything for him for a while.*

That thought shocked her, like a blinding white light in a room of darkness illuminating some ugly truth. Had she just been going along with him, with his pressure to get married? The pressure to be in a relationship, because it was something she'd despaired of ever happening?

Her attention fell on the familiar mahogany box, still in its place on the piecrust table. It beckoned, and she reached for it, a little prickling lifting the hair along her arms. The wood was smooth and surprisingly warm, and she lifted the lid. Then slammed it back into place.

"What am I doing?" She spoke aloud this time. She shoved the box back onto the table, aghast at whatever had compelled her to even *think* about pulling out those cards.

But she wasn't paying attention, and somehow the box landed cattywonker on the table, then tumbled off and onto the settee. Cards spilled out, over the table, the sofa, and onto the floor in a slick, haphazard pile of red and blue diamond patterns.

All except for one card, which landed face-up. Right on the sofa next to her hand.

Death.

Diana went cold. Then hot. Her fingers trembled as she reached for it. The image was unmistakable: a skeleton wearing black armor, riding slowly on a dark horse. Death carried a flag with a rose depicted on it, and a man, woman, and child collapsed before him.

The Death card portends the end or cessation of something: a phase, a journey.

A relationship.

—⁕—

Ethan finished putting safety locks on all the first floor windows as well as deadbolts on the two doors by three o'clock. Diana thanked him profusely, but when he tried to talk her into joining him for dinner, she declined.

She needed some space...to think about the change in her life. She didn't need Ethan Tannock distracting her.

She wanted to be alone.

After he left, Diana paced around the house feeling out of sorts and off-kilter. Part of her felt guilty for not joining him for dinner after he'd done so much work for her. She had the sense that he was lonely and would have liked the company...but she couldn't do it. If she did, she'd tell him about Jonathan. And she wasn't really ready to talk about it yet.

It was still too new—this sense of freedom and apprehension. And she didn't want him to think that he'd had anything to do with her ending the relationship with Jonathan. A guy who looked like Ethan, with his ease and charm around women, could easily assume that.

"What you need," she told herself finally, staring at her reflection in the mirror of the bedroom, "is some shopping. A dinner out...and maybe a movie. Anything to keep from thinking about this mess."

The idea brightened her. If she left now, she could be in Portland by three-thirty—plenty of time to shop on a Friday night. Diana threw open her closet door and found a casual dress and a pair of sandals. She couldn't remember the last time she'd done something so carefree and unplanned. She and Jonathan rarely went to the movies...in fact, she had a sinking suspicion that the last time they'd gone had been when they'd first started dating. A year ago.

The realization that she was about to do something spontaneous reminded her of the Tarot cards, and of The Fool. And of Death.

Nervousness prickled down the back of her neck and upset her insides.

So far, she'd managed to ignore the fact that she'd actually *told* Joe Cap and Ethan that Belinda had been murdered. Ethan had broached the subject once today while they were cleaning the den, but she cut him off and changed the topic. She couldn't go there. Not yet.

How could she have known what happened to her aunt? It wasn't a random Tarot card spilling out of a box. It had been a dream. A real, horrifying dream.

Was she really right, or was it some figment of her imagination? Or, could it have been just an intuition, an impression that garnered credibility when Joe Cap began talking about his suspicions of Belinda's death? Or was it a product of imagination after these other things had happened?

Her head began to pound, and Diana shook away the thoughts before they turned into another migraine. She gathered up her handbag and car keys, ready to get away from the house. But as she started for the front door, she had an insistent niggling in the back of her mind.

Something compelled her, urging her into the den. She'd replaced the Tarot cards before Ethan returned with the locks, and they sat in their mahogany box right next to Aunt Bee's journal on the desk.

She picked up the box and the journal, and walked out of the den, realizing that her compulsion was to put them somewhere else. She didn't want to leave them sitting out.

The kitchen wouldn't do, Diana thought, hesitating as her hand hovered over the counter. Nor did she want to put them in her bedside table. She picked up her laptop case and unzipped it to add the slim mahogany box and the diary.

And, when she left the house for her shopping trip, she felt the need—the insistent, niggling need—to bring the laptop with her.

NINE

ETHAN FLIPPED THROUGH all two hundred of his satellite television channels for the third time in fifteen minutes. He yawned, muttering, "Can't believe there's nothing good on any of these."

The truth was, there probably was something good on one of them—after all, it was nearly nine, and it was Friday night—but nothing seemed to catch his interest. It was all the same—either sports, sit-com reruns, or bloody, violent movies. Normally, any one of those categories worked for him on a Friday night...but not this one.

He'd tried to work at the laptop, making notes and pulling the pieces of his research together, but he hadn't been able to concentrate. He'd even spent a few minutes writing notes on his observations of and conversations with Diana in the last few days.

The subject showed vehement disbelief when the topic of her relative's psychic ability was broached...It remains to be determined whether the migraines are a result of the suppressed workings of the unconscious...The subject will bear more observation and tactful interview.... The subject, adamant about disbelieving in such tools, looks askance upon the Tarot cards and denies having interacted with them.

In light of all this, Diana's revelation in Joe Cap's office about her aunt having been smothered was a shock—but not completely unexpected. While Ethan's scientist side needed to ask more questions and find out more of what had happened to prompt her to make that statement, the compassionate side knew he couldn't push her. She was fragile enough without him manhandling her on the way.

But either way, no matter what he did he couldn't stop thinking about her. Despite having been well and truly burned by not one but two women in his life, here he was, unable to distance himself from yet another. And this one was a lawyer—used to manipulating information and facts in order to do her job. God, he'd be putty in her hands if she put her mind to it.

He wasn't even certain what it was that attracted him so strongly. She could be frosty, emotionless, and condescending... but she had a softer, more relaxed side with an odd sense of humor. And when she looked at him with those blue eyes, so grateful for his simple offers of help, he couldn't account for how it made him feel inside. Protective, yes, but hot and needy too.

Except that she was still tied up with that dickwad Wertinger. And much as he hated to admit it, Ethan knew he didn't want her to give in to the raging attraction between them. Because if she did, that would make her no better than Jenny—or Wertinger himself, for that matter.

And that was one thing Ethan couldn't tolerate, wouldn't be party to.

So, much as he wanted to pursue getting to know her in a more intimate, less scientific way, he shut those thoughts *right* down. It was a good thing she'd opted to go to Portland tonight. That way he wouldn't be tempted to insist she stay the night again.

Cady whined for the millionth time in the last half hour, smearing her nose against one of the windows. Her hackles stood on end and she growled faintly, then turned and charged toward Ethan. She whined again, bumping her damp nose under his arm, trying to lift it off the armrest of the chair in which he'd reclined.

"Oh, all right," he muttered in exasperation, folding up the recliner and hauling himself to his feet. "You see a squirrel out there or something? Hope it's not another skunk," he added, opening the door for the lab to shoot out into the shadows.

Just then, he saw the faint bob of light coming up the narrow drive. Ethan frowned, squinting into the darkening night as he heard the rumble of a car. Who the he—

Diana.

Damn, but his heart gave a little lurch as her sleek, expensive car came around the corner more rapidly than was prudent considering the condition of the road and the low light. The vehicle crunched over the stones and then jerked to a stop. The engine had just turned off when Diana bolted out, her stricken face illuminated by the yard light.

"Ethan," she cried as he moved toward her, demanding, "What is it? What happened?"

Cady burst out of the trees, circling the vehicle and doing a whiney sort of bark, but Ethan ignored her as he went to Diana.

"He came back," she said, her words rapid and her hands clamping onto his arms. "And he left me a w-warning."

Hearing the wobble in her voice, Ethan dragged her into his arms and wrapped her up close. Anger and fear had him squeezing her probably a bit too tightly, but she made no protest. "What happened?" he asked again. "Did you see him? Did he hurt you?"

She shook her head vehemently against his chest, and thus assured, he kept her there. Right where he wanted her. Her words muffled by his shirt, she said, "I got home from Portland and when I got out of the car...I saw it. Spray paint, all over the f-front of the house, on the door and window. *Get out* was what it said. And—and *You're next.*"

"You didn't see anyone? You didn't go inside, did you?" he demanded sharply. "Diana, you didn't, did you?"

Again she shook her head against him, and he heard a faint sniffle. "No, I'm not that stupid," she said with a wry laugh. "And I'm too chicken anyway."

"Good thing," he said, grateful for that at least. "The bastard's probably long gone—damn coward—but there's no sense in taking any chances." He pulled away enough to sling his arm around her shoulders and ease her toward the house. Cady paced with them, giving a short, sharp bark, but she seemed less agitated than before. "I'm going to get my rifle."

"Why?" She stopped dead still in the middle of the yard and looked at him, her eyes wide with shock. "You don't think he'll come *here* do you?"

"Not a chance. A guy like that only terrorizes helpless women. Or, at least, women he *thinks* are helpless," he added quickly. "Plus, Cady wouldn't let him near us. Damn," he swore. "*That's* why she's been whining and climbing the walls all night! I should have let her out earlier."

"Then what do you need your rifle for?" she asked, and in the distance, he saw a flash of heat lightning.

"I'm going to go over there and see what the bastard was up to. See if he broke in or took anything, or if he left anything behind. And if the cats are all right."

"Ethan, no, please don't. What if he *is* there? And it's going to rain, and—and we can go back tomorrow. When it's daylight. We can call Joe Cap then. I don't want to go there tonight. And I don't want to be left alone." She gave a violent shiver. "Besides," she added, looking up at him, "those cats don't even show themselves to me. He probably doesn't even know they're there."

He paused, standing on the threshold of his cabin. He'd never seen her look or act so vulnerable in the short time he'd known her, and the pleading in her voice gave him pause. She'd been through so much in the last two weeks. She had the right to be shaken up.

"All right, but I think we ought to call Joe," he said, opening the door for her. Cady gave a last rally of barks into the darkness, then streaked in ahead of them. She'd be much calmer now that everyone was inside.

"It can wait till morning, can't it?" she said. "I just want to sit down and—and watch TV and not think about all of this. Aunt Belinda, and my tires...and everything else. Just for tonight."

"I'm going to call him," Ethan said firmly, "but I'll tell him you aren't going to make a report until tomorrow morning. All right? How about a glass of wine—or something stronger? And

I think I saw an old chick flick when I was flipping through the channels...does that sound good?"

She looked at him with those blue eyes, her lips full and soft with worry, and Ethan felt his scruples waver. "Thanks," she said, "I know I sound like one of those helpless females—"

"No, not really. You sound reasonably concerned—which anyone would be if they realized someone was trying to chase them away from the house in which a woman was murdered."

"Ethan," she said with a short little laugh, "you're not helping the situation." But she gave him a quick smile and slipped from beneath his arm. "I'm thinking something stronger than a glass of wine would be in order. And a mindless, funny movie. Definitely not a thriller."

He poured a small glass of Scotch and called Joe while Diana flipped through the channels and sipped her drink.

"I'm going to go over and check the place out," Joe Cap decided. "No, you don't need to come—you should stay with her." There was a sly tone in his drawl that had Ethan deciding not to pour *himself* a glass of whiskey.

"Okay, let me know what you find out. We'll be down to see you in the morning," he said, and hung up the phone. From where he stood in the kitchen, Ethan could hear Diana chuckling at something on the tube.

Her face, always classic in its beauty, was even more beautiful when she laughed because it wasn't so perfect. Her nose crinkled a bit, her eyes lit up, and when the smile faded, her lips drew back into a brief pout before relaxing. *Hoo boy.* He sure wanted to kiss her.

Instead, Ethan settled for a beer and the armchair, rather than the other end of the couch. This not only placed him near the long, open windows that allowed a strong, cool breeze to skim over him, but it also put her out of his direct gaze. The fewer the distractions, the better.

"Thanks for letting me stay here again tonight," Diana said when the movie was over. She stood, giving a little stretch that had Ethan's imagination going off in all sorts of sordid directions.

With her sleepy eyes, courtesy of a long day plus the Scotch, and her short mop of tousled hair, she looked as if she'd just rolled out of bed.

"Anytime," he said, his voice probably a little more suggestive than it should have been. Damn.

There was the flare of reaction in her face, but he wasn't sure what it meant. Her eyelids seemed to droop a bit more, and he swore she skipped her gaze over him in his loose (thank God) cut-off sweats and t-shirt, but he wasn't certain.

"Can you think of anything else you need?" he asked, then wanted to bite his tongue. *Get a grip, Tannock.*

"No," she replied after the slightest of hesitations that had him looking at her closely—but this was Diana Iverson. From what he could tell, she'd never flirted with a man in her life. So he was reading the heat in her gaze totally wrong. "I was shopping and bought some sleepwear."

"Okay, well, then I guess I'm going to head up," he said, wondering what a woman like Diana considered "sleepwear." A floor-length, high-necked nightgown, or at least something loose that reached to her knees. Definitely not the lacy red thing he'd instantly pictured.

Bummer.

A loud crack of thunder woke Diana in the middle of the night, pulling her from swirling dark dreams into a dim reality. She turned to look at the clock next to her bed and it was illuminated suddenly by a great flash of lightning. It was three-thirty.

She stared up at the ceiling, watching shadows come and go as lightning flickered in the distance, then closer as a boom of thunder shook the house. She tried to push away the dark thoughts that threatened to pull her back into the maelstrom of nightmares, forcing herself to concentrate on the storm, and on the events of the day.

Her evening in Portland had been relaxing and fruitful—in more ways than one. Diana found herself looking at clothing she never would have considered in the past—bright colors that weren't always suitable for an attorney, flowing Bohemian skirts and even a pair of low-slung jeans in the style she'd seen Mindy Horning wear at Marc's barbeque. Not that Diana would show her navel—and definitely not her butt crack—but at least she could wear something other than chinos or a pencil skirt.

She attributed this new perspective to the fact that she suddenly realized she didn't have to please Jonathan—or anyone. She could dress how she wanted, wear her hair how she wanted, even, possibly, use the bright blue nail polish she'd bought. That had been an impulsive purchase, but Diana couldn't stop thinking about how pretty it would look on her toes.

Perhaps The Fool had taken hold of her after all.

All at once, another crack of thunder shook the house and a gust of wind sent hard, sharp rain against the window. Suddenly Diana remembered the row of tall windows open in the living room, and she flipped the blanket back and hurried out of the room. Brilliant flashes of lightning helped her find her way, and just as she was getting to the windows, she heard a clumping coming down the stairs.

It sounded like an army, but it was really just six feet: Ethan and Cady.

"Oh, hi," he said, seeing her struggling to close the windows. The wind was blowing in through them and their panes were wet. "I'll get them."

She moved out of his way and walked toward the screened-in porch to see what the storm looked like. She and Cady slipped into the enclosure and peered out to see trees bending and swaying with the wind, and jagged white lines of lightning spearing into the forest and onto the lake. Another boom shook the house and Cady whined, pushing her damp nose into Diana's leg, which was bare under her short silky nightgown. The chill of it startled her, but she bent down to pat the dog on the head.

She heard a noise behind her. It was Ethan coming out onto the porch to join them.

"Looks pretty nasty," he said as he approached.

Diana nodded, folding her arms across her middle, and looked back out at the storm. It was cool but not uncomfortable on the porch, but Ethan's presence sent a shiver through her body. His hair was standing up in endearing tufts, and he hadn't bothered to put on a shirt.

"I love storms," she murmured, peering into the darkness as she tried to swallow in her suddenly-dry mouth. "Especially at night."

"Me too." She felt him step closer to her and she drew in a breath, holding it. Though she wasn't facing him, she could feel how close he was. She shivered again.

"Are you cold?" Ethan asked, resting his hands lightly, very lightly, on her bare upper arms.

Diana held her breath again. She could feel the imprint of each of his fingers around her arms, almost brushing the sides of her breasts. "A little," she managed to reply. She let her breath trickle out.

Just as he'd done on the deck off his bedroom, Ethan slid his hands down to her elbows and back up to her shoulders...once, twice, three times...and then they paused, cupping her elbows.

A crash of thunder made her start and Cady whine, but Ethan said nothing.

"It's beautiful in its power, isn't it?" she said in a low voice, trying not to move for fear he'd think she was moving away... or that she'd turn around in his arms and launch herself into something she wasn't quite sure of. "Nature always amazes me."

His hands moved again, up to her shoulders, and she felt his fingers brush the ends of her short hair, brush over the sides of her neck. Little shivers erupted over her skin and down her spine. His fingers skimmed her shoulders and then fell away. "I saw a tornado once." His voice was soft and husky in her ear. "It was one of the most incredible things I'd ever witnessed. I should have been in the cellar, but I had to see it...and I made it down there just in time. My mother was furious with me," he chuckled quietly.

"How old were you?"

She felt him shrug behind her. "Oh, twelve maybe. Thirteen."

"You were brave to be out in that weather, especially at that age."

His hands settled on the curve of her shoulders, as if unable to keep from touching her. "My sister Fiona said I was an idiot—but she was standing there peeking right around me the whole time too."

They both chuckled at that, the short, husky laughs winding around each other, and then another boom of thunder filled the air. "I guess I'd better head back to bed," Diana said. But she made no move to go.

"I'd like to join you."

His words, unexpected, soft and heavy with desire, speared her middle and caused her to draw in her breath. "Ethan," she began, and then suddenly she felt his lips on her bare shoulder. Sensation exploded through her body, hot and delicious, and she caught her breath, smothering a sigh.

His mouth was warm and light and as his lips moved tenderly up the side of her neck she felt her knees begin to weaken and her eyes sink closed. Goosebumps erupted everywhere, her nipples surged and hardened, and she gave a soft sigh.

Ethan stepped closer as he pulled her so that she leaned back against him. Now his mouth was near her ear, kissing a vulnerable spot just behind her lobe, still gentle, coaxing, erotic. His hands slid around to cover her breasts and she heard his intake of breath as he found her ready nipples where they jutted through the silk of her nightgown. She stiffened in surprise then eased as sharp, hot pleasure jolted through her.

"Diana...I want to make love to you," he whispered. "Let me make love to you."

She shivered against him and felt the warmth of his torso seeping through her nightgown. His strong arms surrounded her, pulling her back along his body, and his lips nibbled on her earlobe. He found his way beneath the vee of her neckline, feathering the tips of his fingers over her sensitive nipples as if coaxing her into submission.

She might have tried to turn and face him, to slide her hands up over those broad shoulders...but he didn't allow her to move. Instead, he gently bit into the tender spot on her neck, and, gasping at the intense pleasure-pain, she sagged back into him. The silk of her nightgown was clinging to her everywhere, and although the cool rain's breeze filtered through the windows, she was warm and liquid...and yet very much awake. Alive.

"Mm...yes," he murmured as she closed her eyes, resting her head back onto his shoulder, his mouth close to her ear. "Come with me, Diana," he said in a mellow voice, hot and velvet against her skin.

One of his hands eased down over the clinging silk to its hem, and the next thing she knew, his fingers were sliding up her bare thigh. Light and sure, his hand moved to the warm, moist center between her legs and Diana found herself sagging even more as he covered her most intimately. A dull, pleasurable throb reverberated through her body, swelling and pounding as his fingers went slickly to work, exploring and teasing her into a shivering mass.

Now, his fingers hiked up the hem of her nightgown over her bare thighs, and he lifted his face from her neck. Diana opened her eyes. In the window in front of her she could see their reflections: she, with her dark head flung back, exposing a stark white throat and white thighs, he with a shadowed face, staring into the reflection. His hands pinned her against his body in some erotic game, and as she watched, their eyes met in the mottled image.

Behind her, she felt his chest move with ragged breaths and he pulled a strap off her shoulder so that one white breast slipped out from the nightgown. Her nipple, full and tight, was dark in the center of her white skin beneath the long expanse of her throat. In that moment, instead of herself, Diana saw some exotic movie starlet, flush and lush with passion, captured in place by a pair of solid brown arms.

The image aroused her even more, and perhaps him as well, for all at once, two probing fingers slipped deep into her wet sheath.

He groaned from deep in his chest as she gasped and pulsed around him. "You are so ready," he muttered into her ear. "Come with me now, sweetheart. Come…with me." He slid his fingers in and out and around, massaging her own tiny, swollen erection, brushing over the plump, sensitive skin around it.

Diana felt herself gathering up, the heat rushing and surging through her as his rhythm never faltered. Her toes curled into the wood floor, her fingers closed around his arm as she bit her lip, trying to keep from crying out as she drew closer and closer…and then all at once, she went over the top, her world exploding like a bright flash of lightning.

She gave a cry of release, of triumph, as the pleasure undulated through her limbs. Her knees gave out and she clung to his arms as he chuckled softly, deeply into her damp neck.

"That's what I meant," he said, pleasure and delight evident in his voice. " Ah, Diana …." He turned her suddenly and wrapped his arms around her, pulling her up close as he bent to kiss her. His hand came to brush the hair from her cheek, and she could smell her own muskiness on his fingers.

Diana raised her face to meet him, to take his lips, and she felt his trembling from pent-up desire. His mouth was as sensual and his kiss as beautiful as she'd remembered, but grew hot and sleek as their bare skin connected. At last her hand could slide up his arms, over his broad, warm shoulders, her fingers tracing the curve of his collarbone, pressing her hips into his.

"Diana?" It was a question, breathless, low, a little desperate.

"Yes …." she sighed. Suddenly, she was in his arms as he turned to take her off the porch.

Ethan, intent and nearly blind with desire, stumbled over Cady, who'd collapsed on the floor behind him. But he was able to right himself before disaster, Diana giving a little huff of a laugh as she jolted in his arms. His veins thrummed with heat and he had one thing, only one thing, on his mind. With long strides, he carried his burden across the living room and up the stairs into his cool, dark bedroom.

He let her feet slide to the floor in front of the bed, and, pinning her there with his thighs, kissed her long and thoroughly as he yanked his shorts down with one hand. Then, he pulled away just long enough to whisk that soft, silky gown up and over her head.

"Ah." Ethan drew in his breath sharply at the sight of her nude body, pale in the dim light, warm under his palms. He thought again how beautiful she was, how perfect her breasts were with their small, tight nipples, how smooth and flowing the lines of her torso were. He filled his hands with her, touching, caressing, fondling as he bent to kiss her again. Ready. So ready... but thorough. He'd be thorough.

He tumbled them onto the bed, onto the wad of blankets and mussed sheets he'd left earlier, and settled against her. Hot damp skin to hot damp skin, curves pressed up against firm muscle and coarse hair. They fit together well, and she welcomed him as he eased her legs apart.

Lifting himself away just enough to reach into the drawer of his bedside table, he pulled a condom free from its depths. With one movement, he ripped the package open, then bent to take one of those perked-up nipples into his mouth. Diana gave a sexy little tremor as he closed his lips around her, sucking and teasing her with his tongue, getting her all worked up again so that she'd be sleek and ready for him.

She was mumbling things he couldn't understand, but they sounded good: breathy and desperate, and he made short work of slipping the condom in place. And then, shifting up to kiss her full and long and hard on her parted lips, he fit himself into place and at last...ah, yes.

She made a soft, erotic little sound that stoked him, grasping at his shoulders and lifting herself up to meet his thrust. And he began to move with long, slow strokes, trying to keep them easy and deep, she whimpered and shifted on the bed. In the back of his mind, he heard the boom of thunder, and was faintly aware of the flashes of lightening mingling with the soft sounds of pleasure she made beneath him. Her sudden cry, low and husky, nearly undid him, and but he kept his mind for a moment longer... just long enough to make it last. To listen to her rough, addled breathing and feel her orgasm shuddering around him.

And then he stopped thinking. He slipped into his own pleasure and let go. And when it came, the release rolled through his body in a sharp, hot wave.

He smiled with long-awaited contentment as he eased down next to her, the thunderstorm still raging beyond the windows as they edged into slumber.

—m—

Ethan opened his eyes to a damp, gray morning and an empty bed. There was still a warm spot from where Diana had been, and he could hear her running water in the bathroom.

Which was just as well, because it gave him time to pull his head back together. He felt *good*. More than good. Better than he had felt in a long time.

Except for the fact that he'd had amazing, toe-curling, explosive sex with a woman who'd done to her fiancé exactly what Jenny had done to Ethan.

The selfish part of him didn't give a shit—obviously, Jonathan Wertinger was a douchebag who'd already cheated on Diana and deserved whatever he got. Not to mention the fact that they didn't belong together—it was obvious to anyone with a brain that Wertinger wasn't the right man for her.

But.

It was the "but" that had Ethan's insides feeling hollow and scraped empty when he should have been figuring out how to coax her back between the sheets. Either Diana had used the opportunity last night for a sort of revenge against Jonathan, or she'd easily succumbed to her own form of betrayal.

Either way, that made her just the sort of woman he loathed: manipulative, opportunistic, and unfaithful.

The fact that Ethan had played the role of seducer in her infidelity didn't make him feel any better. It certainly did take two to tango, and he was just as culpable. Nor could he blame it on the fact that he'd had a long, empty dry spell when it came to women and sex.

Nope. He'd wanted Diana. Not just anyone. Diana. Only Diana.

The bathroom door opened, and there she was, wrapped in one of his robes, her thick, short mop of curls just as tousled as he'd imagined they'd be after a night of hot sex. Her face was damp, as if she'd just washed it.

"Good morning," she said. Hesitation hinged in her voice, making Ethan even more disconcerted.

So now she regretted it? Damn straight she should.

"Hey," was all he said. He knew his smile wasn't as warm or natural as it should have been, but he couldn't help the cold, sinking feeling sliding down his spine. He'd never been very good at deception.

"Hey...uh …." Her gaze skittered around the room, and her attention landed on the wad of blue silk that lay crumpled on the floor. "Oh," she said, and went to pick it up.

He hadn't noticed the color last night, and although it wasn't red—or lacy—it had certainly done the job. For a minute, his mind wandered back to the feel of that silk sliding over her curves, warm and clinging, and he felt a rise of desire again. No doubt about it, she pushed all his buttons, the very right way.

"We should probably talk about—uh—this," she said, clutching the blue silk to her chest. Her eyes, nearly the same shade of midnight as the lingerie, focused on him.

"Talk?" he said, forcing a casual little laugh. "What's there to talk about?" He patted the bed next to him and mustered up a warm grin and seductive look. "Aren't you cold standing there?"

"No," she said. "I'm fine. I—uh—Ethan," she said, her words coming out rapidly, as if she needed to push them through, "I don't know what happened to me last night. I mean, I don't normally do things like...that. I—I really—it was wonderful, really amazing, but I'm just coming out of a relationship and I don't think I'm ready for anything...new. So, um, could we just pretend...I mean, I'm good with just leaving it as one wonderful night, and—that's it. No, uh, expectations. Okay?"

"Yeah, sure," he said automatically. His mind was spinning as he tried to make sense of her rushed, tumbling words along with his own feelings about the situation. *Wonderful, amazing*—he caught that. That was good. *I don't do things like that.* Okay, he'd buy that, based on her obvious discomfort.

"Okay, good," she said in a rush, hurrying out of the room. She closed the door behind her.

Wait.

Just coming out of a relationship?

Ethan bolted upright and stared at the door. What the hell did that mean?

———m———

Diana rushed down the stairs, her face hot and her insides churning, but her dignity intact. *That went well.*

She felt like a complete idiot, yet she couldn't banish the memory of Ethan sprawled all over his bed, oh so naked and gorgeous. Dark and muscular, with a few tan lines and just the right amount of hair, he was magnificent with the muted light spilling over his long, lean body. She'd never been this close to such a perfect specimen of masculinity, let alone been intimate.

And yet she managed to say just what she'd practiced in the bathroom, in a relatively coherent manner, she thought. *No expectations.*

Even though those words made her insides twist and churn all the more, she figured it was the best way to approach the situation. She was going back to Boston, he was heading to Princeton, and aside from that, Diana was under no illusion that she was anything more than a summer fling for a guy like Ethan Tannock.

Just as in *When Harry Met Sally...*, it was better that she'd had the opportunity to say first that it was just a one night thing. And, based on the expression on his face when she came out of the bathroom, it had been the right thing to say. Despite the beauty of his tanned self among the rumpled sheets, the expression on his face had clearly been one of regret and discomfort.

Not that she hadn't had similar feelings. *Yesterday I was engaged to Jonathan. And today, here I am, rolling out of another man's bed. Now who's the Wonder Slut?*

As she reached the bottom of the stairs, she realized Cady was right behind her. The lab went to the door and whined. Clutching Ethan's robe more tightly around her, Diana let the dog out and then turned to go to her room and get dressed. She had to file a report with Joe Cap—another unpleasantness to deal with, although this one should be easier than telling a delicious hunk of a man that she was letting him off the hook for last night.

Maybe she should have gone for one more night before she walked—if for no other reason than to wipe away any lingering memory of Jonathan. Not that that had been hard to do, at least with Ethan.

Geesh. Even now, her knees weakened when she thought about what he'd done...how he'd touched her and teased her, brought her up and over the edge so easily. He was...amazing.

As she headed toward the guest room, she glanced into Ethan's office. The windows had been left wide open all night, and papers were blown all over the floor. Probably rain had come in too, for it had been a fierce storm.

She walked over to see if anything had gotten too wet, picking up the papers as she went, and as she set them on the desk, noticed they were typed notes, with dates on them. Unconsciously scanning them, she paused when she saw Belinda's name appear on the top of one page, and then her heart stopped. And she stared.

July 10: Diana Iverson.

The sight of her own name sent a queer shiver over her shoulders, and, although she knew she shouldn't, she did—she began to read, her attention darting around the page, catching phrases that caused her hands to go cold.

"The subject appears to be at least wary of Tarot cards, although she denies any belief in their ability to assist in precognitive—or other—abilities.... The subject, adamant about disbelieving in such tools, looks askance upon the cards and denies having interacted with them.... The subject insisted that the cards had dropped onto the floor, and became clearly uneasy when pressed for further information.... It remains to be determined whether the migraines are a result of the suppressed workings of the unconscious. The subject will bear more observation, and tactful interview, as the subject is unaware of this research."

Diana allowed the sheaf of papers to slide onto the desk, aware that her eyes had begun to burn.

The subject.

Emptiness seeped into her bones, numbing her mind, as she turned toward the door. How foolish she'd been to think that perhaps he'd been interested in her for herself. How preposterous to consider that she—awkward, shy Diana Iverson—could attract a man like Ethan Tannock.

In the sanctuary of her room, she dressed slowly, aware of the thumping footsteps when Ethan came down the stairs moments later, and the excited clatter of claws when he let Cady in from outside.

"Di?" There was a knock on her door that had her freezing. "Do you want something to eat?" His voice sounded low and mellow, and sent little remembering shivers up her spine.

Or at least, it would have if she weren't so angry with herself for being so damned stupid. No, wait, she was angry with *him* for using her.

But...had he really used her? Or had it been a mutual using?

Either way, she was *not* going to tell him what she'd seen in the office. She wasn't going to let him know how being labeled a "subject" had effectively deflated any feelings she might have begun to have for him. Better to let him think she'd always intended this to be a summer fling. Not that she'd intended *anything* with him anyway ....

She sank on the bed, rubbing her temples vigorously. *I need to get out of here. Go back to Boston, go back to my work, to my real life.*

"Diana?" he said, knocking again. "Are you all right?"

"I'll be out in a sec," she said, straightening up, putting on her game face.

She could do this. How the hell many times had she been torn apart by a judge's snide, Good-Ol'-Boys' comment? Or been slyly insulted by the opposing legal team? "I'm not all that hungry," she added. "Just coffee for me."

"That's too bad, because, you know, breakfast is my best meal," he teased through the door.

Yeah, I'm sure it is. After all those one-night-stands a guy like you has.

"I'll be out in a minute," she called.

By the time she finished dressing and brushing her teeth, a miracle occurred: Joe Cap had driven up into the yard and was waiting outside, chatting with Ethan as they waited for her and took turns throwing Cady's ball.

"I went over and checked things out last night," he drawled as she approached. "Did a real good number with that spray paint. Looks as if someone was inside, too—broke right through a window."

"Sonofabitch," Ethan muttered. "Guess the locks didn't do much good." He glanced at Diana, his expression a lot less regretful than it had been earlier. In fact, the intensity there made a warm flush rush over her face.

She hoped Joe Cap didn't notice.

"Ethan says how you were gone all afternoon, and night," he said, looking at her blandly. "You got back around nine?"

"It was just getting dark. Around nine-thirty, nine-forty-five. I didn't see anyone," she added before he could ask. "And I didn't even go in the house. As soon as I saw the paint, I came here."

"Someone must've known you were gonna be gone, because whatever they did happened before dark," said Joe. "That's more'n a bit ballsy if you ask me. Someone's getting a little desperate."

"Jesus, Joe, you sound like a bad cop show," Ethan said, clearly frustrated with the whole situation. "And you can lay the blame for spilling the beans on me. I was in the Grille for dinner yesterday and happened to mention that you'd gone to Portland for the evening." This last was directed at Diana, his face grim with disgust. "I was talking with Bella and Tommy, and then Helen Galliday came up."

"You need say no more," Joe said, shaking his head. "Durn busybody probably had to know every breath the both of you took all day yesterday. And from Helen's lips, it wouldn't have taken long for everyone in Damariscotta to know that Diana was going to be in Portland for a few hours."

"She did make a point of mentioning that there were plenty of shops here in town, and why did Diana have to go so far just to buy clothes," Ethan admitted.

"You think it's someone here in Damariscotta?" Diana asked, her head beginning to pound. *Great. This is the last thing I need.*

"I don't know who else it would be," said Joe. "Someone's got to be around here, watching your every move. And surely it's someone who knew Belinda."

Ethan glared at him as a shiver caught Diana. Neither of them liked the thought of her being watched all the time.

"How about we head over and you can check around and see if anything's missing, or been disturbed," suggested Joe. "And I can finalize the report."

"That's good. I can pack up then too," she said, and Ethan went still.

"Pack up?" he asked.

"I forgot to tell you...I'm heading back to Boston tonight. I need to get back to my practice, and...I've got other things to take care of. I'll go get my keys and stuff," she added, and started off to the cabin.

As she walked away, Joe gave his friend a long once-over. One eyebrow lifted and he shook his head. "Naw...you didn't."

Ethan's lips tightened but he declined to answer. What the hell was going on? She *forgot* to tell him she was leaving? *Today?*

No way that was true. No wonder she'd allowed him to seduce her last night. His mouth flattened grimly.

Was she broken up with Wertinger or not? And why did he feel as if Damariscotta, his favorite place in the world, was going to be much less interesting once she was gone?

"Damn, Tannock, you *did,* didn't you? You ended your dry spell and slept with Bee's niece. Jay-sus. What the hell happened?"

"I wish to hell I knew," he replied with an unaccountable surge of anger. He picked up the tennis ball and fired it into the forest with all his might. Cady tore after it as he struggled to keep his expression blank in front of the much-too-perceptive police chief.

"Well," said Joe as Diana came back out of the cabin. "At least if she's back home, no one's gonna be trying to chase her away from Damariscotta. Or worse."

Yeah. That made him feel *so* much better.

TEN

EVEN AFTER THE FIVE-HOUR DRIVE, Diana had to resist the urge to stop at her office—her haven, her lifeblood—before going to the townhouse she and Jonathan shared in the Back Bay, despite the fact that the office was *not* on the way to her house.

It was as though now she'd returned to Boston, her job had once again become the sum of her existence. Odd how being in Damariscotta had not given her the panicked feeling that she was missing something, unable to check in all the time and be on her computer constantly—as usually happened when she traveled or vacationed—but that she'd allowed her work to take a back seat.

The Fool.

She'd been acting the Fool—in more ways than one—and now she had to put those carefree days (if one could call having one's house broken into and tires slashed carefree) away and get back to work.

Especially now that she didn't have a wedding to plan.

Diana tightened her grip on the steering wheel. She'd had hours of solitude in which to think and mull—something that rarely happened in her busy life. And if she'd expected the return to Boston and her life there to make her second-guess her decision to end things with Jonathan, she would be disappointed. In fact, when she thought about her former fiancé, she felt weightless and relieved for some reason.

Maybe it was because she no longer had the burden of needing to learn how to trust him again. How to forgive him for his betrayal. Or maybe it was because she'd never really needed him in her life after all.

But it wasn't Jonathan who filled her thoughts much at all during the drive. It was Ethan, and the way he'd said goodbye to her...if one could call what he did a farewell.

Joe Cap had done his review of the house, taken her statement and that of Ethan's, and was putting his notebook away as the three of them stood on the porch at Aunt Bee's. "I'll be getting in touch with you with any information we get about the vandal. And the autopsy results on your aunt should be in in a coupla weeks." He shook his head at her surprised look. "This ain't New York or CSI or whatever shows you're watching. We'll be lucky to get word by middle of August."

And then, with a long, meaningful look at Ethan, he shook Diana's hand and trudged off to his vehicle.

"So you're hitting the road?" Ethan said as Diana turned to walk back into the house. He stood, blocking her way.

"I'm not going to stay here," she said, gesturing to the ugly red paint that warned her to go. "And I've been away from work long enough."

"Why didn't you tell me you'd broken up with Wertinger?" he asked, moving closer to her in the doorway. His eyes bored down into hers and she couldn't tell if he was angry or...something else.

Diana blinked and recovered. "I didn't realize I had to check with you first," she replied tartly.

"Well," he said, his voice slowing to a dangerous pace, "I guess I'd like to know if I'm sleeping with a woman who's going home to her fiancé or not. The idea of sharing doesn't appeal to me. I'm sure you can understand why."

Diana's heart was pounding like a tom-tom, and she was finding it difficult to read him. His brown eyes had gone cool and remote, just as they'd been the day he realized she'd changed the locks on him. She put on her lawyer hat and removed herself and her emotion from the situation, placing her closing arguments out on the line. "Let me clarify for you, then, Ethan. I have indeed ended things with Jonathan, so you're off the hook for sleeping with a cheating woman. Although the fact that you thought you were does give me pause—"

"What was I supposed to think?" he asked, again in that dangerous voice.

"As you might recall, I was a *little* distracted and distraught last night. I'm sorry that it wasn't top of mind. And also, you're not *sleeping* with me. We *slept together*, and it was mind-blowing, I'll give you that, Ethan. But it's past tense. Right?"

"Right," he said. His eyes raked over her as he at last stepped aside to let her go into the house. They were cold and flat.

Diana started to walk by him, but as she brushed past, she felt him exhale deeply. Then suddenly, his arms closed around her and with one fluid movement, he flattened her back against the edge of the doorway. His mouth settled over hers with a surprising fierceness, his lips forming to hers in the same way they'd done the night before—but with an edge. The kiss was warm and hot and slick and intense and Diana couldn't keep from succumbing to the renewed flare of desire that swarmed up and over her body. Ethan's mouth was firm and soft, coaxing and demanding, and his tongue licked her insides in a way that had her fairly collapsing into the wall.

Strong arms pinned her against the door, fitting her between muscular thighs and the ridges of the doorjamb. Solidness, strength, heat and wildness covered her, and she allowed herself to feel the range of emotion to her every last nerve ending. She wanted him as much here, now, with this dangerous edge, as she had last night when he first touched her.

Then, suddenly, he released her and stepped back. He looked down at her with eyes that were flat and emotionless, even as he reached out to touch her cheek in a light caress. "Safe travels, Diana. Good luck back in Boston. I hope you're happy there."

And with one last, long look, he spun and walked away—off the porch, heading home.

She almost called him back. Even now, as she finally reached Boston, Diana remembered how she'd had to curl her fingers into the edge of the door to keep from going after him. She'd bit on her lip to keep her mouth closed.

The subject, she reminded herself. *You are the subject.*

She'd had enough hurt and pain in the last month and a half. Why expose herself to more?

Why indeed.

But more than once during her drive, she'd lifted her fingers to brush over her cheek just as he'd done. And remembered how kind and efficient he'd been during her migraines, how solid and sure he'd acted when all of the vandalism had occurred. And she thought about the way his face eased and his demeanor changed after their first frank conversation, when she apologized to him for thinking he was a shyster and they talked for a long time in her kitchen. And how he'd teased her about her nicknames for Valerie, enjoying her being undignified—even including her bold use of the F-word.

Ethan Tannock was a good man. He just wasn't the man for *her*.

Drawing in a deep breath, Diana went up the sidewalk to their townhouse—*Jonathan's* townhouse—and she could hear his voice through the open windows. Her heart lodged in her throat. What if Valerie the Surgery Slut was there with him again?

But she didn't hear any other voices and so she slipped in the front door as quietly as possible.

"I'm working on it." She could hear his voice coming from the den, where his office was. He sounded stressed, tense, more strung out than she'd ever heard him before, and he was coming closer. "Yes. Yes, I just need more t—" He stopped when he came out of the office and saw her standing there.

Diana balked at the expression on his face. He looked gray, almost sick, and his skin was damp with perspiration. His hair, already wispy and thin, was flyaway and uncombed. He was wearing an untucked shirt, half-buttoned, and workout pants—an uncharacteristic uniform for the proper physician. "I'll be in touch," he said quickly into his cell phone and disconnected. "Diana, what are you doing here?"

"I'm here to get my things," she said. "Are you all right? You don't look very good."

"I've been sick," he said a little sharply. "Food poisoning. This is the first time I've gotten out of bed in two days, and it was to deal with this," he added, gesturing with his phone. "Antoni is at it again."

"Oh," she said. And realized that not only did she not care about the latest problem with the partners in his practice, but that she didn't have to listen to him talk about it and *pretend* to be interested. Ever. Again.

"I didn't expect you until tomorrow," he said. "Is everything all right? Did you change your mind?" he added, hope lighting his face as he stepped toward her. "Please tell me you changed your mind."

"No," she said, putting her suitcase down. "I haven't changed my mind, Jonathan. I'm going to pack up a few things and get out of your way."

"There's no need to do that, Diana. It's late and there's an extra bed. Why don't you just stay here tonight? I promise, I won't impose my presence on you," he added. "You can take a few days to get your things packed and ready to go."

That sounded reasonable. Very reasonable, and Diana nodded gratefully. "Thank you. I appreciate that. I'll just go out and get the rest of my things." Maybe this wasn't going to be as difficult as she'd imagined.

Once outside, she walked around to the back of her car to retrieve her shopping bags from the trunk, and then remembered her all-important laptop, her lifeline to her work, her world...the one she hadn't touched in days. *Not until I went to Portland and put it in the car*, she remembered with a sudden burst of clarity.

Diana stopped, there in the middle of the street, shopping bags dangling from both arms, and realized she'd put the laptop case in her car before heading for Portland the night of the vandalism and second break-in. That was odd—odd that she'd bring the computer on an evening out. And odder still, she reflected, that she'd felt compelled to put the Tarot cards in the computer case before doing so...along with Belinda's journal. Possibly saving them from being stolen or vandalized in the break-in?

She broke out in a cold sweat as she stood on the quiet Saturday evening street. Diana remembered feeling a strange, strong need to bring the computer with her. It was almost as if she'd known... or that someone was telling her what to do.

She shivered and carried the laptop case into the house, setting it on the kitchen table where she usually worked.

Diana took her time arranging her things in the guestroom, unwilling to have to interact with Jonathan more than necessary. She'd find a place as soon as possible, and in the mean time, she'd spend as much time at the office as she could.

It was almost dark by the time she left her room in search of something for a late dinner. Diana walked into the kitchen, but the sight that greeted her made her stop short.

Jonathan had the countertop television on, but he wasn't paying any attention to it. Instead, he had opened a familiar mahogany box and spread the black silk to pull Aunt Belinda's Tarot cards from its depths. He was flipping through them, tossing them into careless piles onto the table in front of him.

Irrational rage swept through Diana at the sight, tinting her vision with red.

"What are you doing?" she demanded. She pulled the cards out of his hands, scooping up the ones off the table in a second hasty motion.

"I was just looking at these cards." Jonathan stared up at her. He appeared to be feeling better, for the odd cast to his skin had faded.

"Those are Aunt Belinda's—they're mine now—and they shouldn't be touched by anyone but the user. Unless you're having a reading done." Her breath was coming in quick shallow gasps, and even as she berated him, Diana realized she was overreacting. But the sight of his hands on the cards made her *so angry*.

Jonathan's expression didn't change, but his voice became sharp. "What's the matter with you? They're just cards."

"I know that," she snapped, carefully straightening them into a neat pile. She picked up the box. "What were you doing, digging through my computer bag anyway?"

"I was looking for a pen and I found them in the case." He stood and brushed past her, his bewildered expression giving way to irritation. "I'm going to bed. Good night."

Diana stared after him for a moment, then she walked into the living and sank onto the sofa, still holding the mahogany box in one hand and the oversized deck of cards in the other. The sudden force of anger had blinded her to reason, and now, as it faded, she was shaken. *What was that all about?*

She looked down at the cards. She held them face down in her hand, and for a moment, she was tempted to turn the whole deck over and see what the bottom card was. Diana set the box carefully on the table in front of her, still holding the cards. Clutching them.

She felt a trembling begin in the base of her spine, shivering up to her tense shoulders and down her arms. She saw the hand that held the cards begin to shake as queasiness roiled in her stomach.

Drawing in a deep breath, she forced herself to relax.

Then, in a sort of daze, Diana opened her mind to the swirl of images and thoughts from Damariscotta, and Boston, and everyone she'd seen and spoken to in the last month. And then she cleared her thoughts, closed her eyes, took a deep breath, and looked down.

She rested the deck on the table, cut it, and stared at the card she was to turn over.

She swallowed heavily, the nausea becoming more intense, the tom-toms of a migraine starting in the base of her skull.

She turned the card over.

The High Priestess.

Her steadiness wavered. Again. Yes, again. She drew in a deep breath, reminding herself what it meant.

Accessing the unconsciousness...opening the doors to the unknown...seeking what is concealed.

She nodded, swallowing back the lump in her throat. *Okay.* Now what? The pounding became harder, sharper, more violent.

She cut the deck again, closed her eyes, and selected a card. Opened her eyes.

Death.

A sudden rush of terror surprised her at the sight of the black-armored Death on his horse. Irrational, deep, and cold, the fear swept over her, leaving her shaking and ill. All at once, darkness tried to suffocate her, and she struggled to breathe, to shake off the powerful emotion.

"No," she said, and shoved the cards roughly into their black silk covering. "No."

Half-blind with pain and smothered by shadows, she slammed the top back onto the box and shoved it back into her computer bag next to the journal, hands shaking, stomach roiling, head pounding.

She staggered to the bathroom, making it just in time to be violently ill into the toilet. Her head throbbed and felt as if it were being squeezed in a vise as darkness cloaked her vision. Tears came as she held onto the cold porcelain, then at last she collapsed on the floor in misery and pain.

Diana wasn't certain how many hours later she dragged herself off the bathroom floor, but it was very dark and quiet in the house. Her skin was clammy and her muscles trembled, and the remnants of the migraine—or whatever it had been—still throbbed in the back of her skull.

Either Jonathan hadn't heard her getting sick, or he didn't care—and either way, she was grateful for the fact that he hadn't come around trying to be solicitous. The only person she wanted comfort from was Ethan.

And that thought had her gritty eyes popping open wide with shock and fear. That was not a good thing to be thinking *at all*.

Trying to banish the frightening thought, she climbed between the sheets of the guest bed, weak and shaky, and tried to fall asleep. But whenever she closed her eyes, those horrible dark images pressed down, smothering and stifling her, hot and heavy. She tossed and turned, trying to stay awake and then giving in, succumbing to sleep. But each time, the nightmares grew darker and more insistent, wrapping her in what seemed to be long, snakelike tendrils of evil, thick heavy ropes of horror, and she clawed her way back to wakefulness.

Through it all the black-armored Death rode slowly and steadily through her nocturnal images. His flag snapped dully in a nonexistent wind, ominous in its incessant rhythm. Like the sound of an army approaching, or that of a death knell. *Thwack, snap, thud...thud...Di-an-a...Di-an-a....*

"Diana?"

Her eyes peeled open and she saw that the world was light once again. Someone was pounding on her door. Jonathan.

She couldn't answer; her brain was still fogged, smothered by the dreams. She looked at the clock. Two. In the afternoon?

"Diana," Jonathan said again, and this time he cracked the door.

"What?" she croaked.

"I'm—leaving for awhile. Thought you might want to know." His gaze traveled the room lighting on her suitcases. "I hope you're still here when I get back," he added, looking at her hopefully.

She didn't respond with more than a little wave. Her hand trembled noticeably and her head still thudded. Mercifully, the door closed and moments later, she heard Jonathan leave the house.

Only then did she feel able to pull herself from the bed on shaky legs and make her way to the kitchen. Coffee didn't appeal, but she had juice and then went to retrieve her cell phone from its pocket in her purse.

No missed calls. No texts.

Not that she'd expected any from anyone. Ethan didn't even have her cell phone number...did he? Not that he'd call her.

Why would he call her? She was nothing more than a summer fling who also happened to be a *subject*. The nausea returned in full force and she directed herself back into the kitchen to find something on which to nibble, realizing she hadn't eaten since yesterday on the road.

With a few crackers in hand, Diana sat herself firmly down at the kitchen table with her laptop and the intention of working. Tomorrow was Monday, and she'd be back in the office bright and early, ready to get back to her normal life.

No more thoughts about Tarot cards, no more worries about someone breaking into her house, and certainly no more daydreaming about a handsome, dog-loving parapsychologist.

Two weeks after her return from Damariscotta, Diana was in her office trying to concentrate on a brief when her assistant poked her head around the door. "Got a minute? It's the Merkovitz case," Mickey said.

A twinge of unease shivered over her. She'd been avoiding spending any time on the case, justifying it by the fact that she had months before the hearing. But she couldn't ignore it and its difficult client forever. "Of course. Come in."

Mickey, who was, as always, dressed at the height of trend, clomped in on her chunky-heeled shoes and proffered her boss a stack of manila folders as she took a seat.

She was as close to a best friend as Diana had had in a long while—next to Jonathan. They were the same age but their lives leading up to their current positions were completely different.

Raised in the North End among the Italian Catholics, Mickey had married at age seventeen immediately out of high school, bore her first child at eighteen, her second at twenty, her third at twenty-one, and got her tubes tied shortly thereafter over the vehement protests of her mother Salem. Now, her children were in school—the youngest was eleven—and she'd decided to pursue the career she'd never had a chance to start before. Her husband, Dominic, had been surprisingly supportive. Mickey maintained it was because she was such an awful cook, and that with her at work, his mother could cook for them.

Regardless of how or why she'd come into this position, the fact was she was the best assistant, confidant, and friend Diana had ever had working for her...even though Mickey tended to be a bit too outspoken.

"What's the update?" Diana said from her seat on the other side of the mahogany desk.

"Don't think I haven't noticed how you've been avoiding this case. And Merkovitz's calls," Mickey said, tossing a cloud of frizzy blond hair behind her shoulder.

Diana bit her lip. She couldn't hide much from Mickey. "That obvious, huh?"

"Not that I blame you—the guy's still the biggest dickwad I've ever met, and that's saying a lot, coming from the North End. And having five brothers."

"Your brothers aren't that big of jerks," Diana protested, remembering many a dinner overrun by the big, loud, Italian-Catholic family. Except maybe Leo, who'd once stuck his hand up her shirt after too many glasses of Chianti.

"No, but they have a lot of friends who are."

Both of them chuckled and then Diana returned her attention to the matter at hand. "So tell me the latest. You met with the CNA and the nurse?"

"Right. They were in the surgery that Merkovitz allegedly screwed up—Jenkson is the patient's name. They were only willing to talk off the record, but I'm sure they'll be subpoenaed. They both stated, independently, that they were certain he was intoxicated during the surgery. Slurred words, a bit of a stumble, shaking hands—the whole nine yards. But they didn't smell anything on him, so …."

"Damn," Diana breathed, placing her hand softly, firmly on the desk. What had always been a prickling annoyance about the previous case, one that she'd forced herself to ignore, expanded into full-blown comprehension. "I knew it." Anger and disbelief warred inside. He'd lied to her. She'd even asked him point-blank if he'd been under the influence of any drugs or intoxicants, and he'd lied.

No, she'd allowed him to lie to her.

Diana rested her head in her hand, feeling as if blinders and shutters were falling away. Now all she saw was cold, empty realization. "I suspected as much in the last case. I *knew* something was wrong. And I got him off then—dammit. And someone *died*."

She sat there for a moment, furious with herself and with Roger Merkovitz, and stunned that she could have been so blind—or allowed herself to be. This was what gave attorneys a bad reputation.

"What are you going to do?" Mickey asked after a long moment.

Standing, Diana shoved her chair away from the desk and it rolled back into the credenza. Her heart was pounding, her world in flux...but she knew what she had to do. "I'm going to call him and tell him I can't represent him in this case."

"You're his attorney—you have to defend him even if he's guilty. And you don't *know* that he was at fault in the previous case. You could get disbarred for saying otherwise," Mickey said. Her expression was serious, but not condemning. There was no judgment in the woman who'd worked closely with her on the previous case. She knew just as much as Diana did.

"I won't be his attorney any longer."

"He won't like that. He's our biggest client."

Diana's stomach pitched. "It doesn't matter. I can't do this. I have to have some integrity." She looked at her friend. For some reason, an image of the High Priestess flickered into her mind. "Even if I can't pay the bills." Her heart was pounding, her palms going slick. But she'd made her decision. She was listening to her instincts.

"*Word*," Mickey said, softly vehement. "I'm a hundred percent supportive. It'll work out." She stood and started to leave, then paused, her hand on the door. "Jonathan's not going to be very happy." Her steady gaze was both challenging and filled with question.

"It doesn't matter what Jonathan thinks," Diana said shortly. She'd moved out more than two weeks ago, but hadn't mentioned anything to Mickey. Although, clearly, her assistant suspected something was up—particularly since several bouquets of flowers had arrived at the office in the last few weeks. All from Jonathan.

"It doesn't?" pressed her friend. Her eyes had narrowed and were looking at her sharply. "Anything you want to tell me? Li-ike...the fact that you moved out?"

Diana sighed. "Fine. I moved out. I told him it was over."

"Hot damn, woman! I knew it!"

Diana blinked and looked at her. "You sound very pleased."

"You know I was never that crazy about him. There's just something...*off* about him. Something that bugs me. And of course the fact that he's a cheating asshole doesn't help."

Diana didn't even ask how Mickey knew about Jonathan's indiscretion. She just gave her friend a look and said, "Get Merkovitz on the phone so I can end this."

—⁂—

Late in the afternoon three days later, the intercom on Diana's desk blared, interrupting a meeting with Mickey.

"Diana, Jonathan's on line three for you," said Corey, the receptionist. "He says it's urgent and he's been trying to get your on your cell."

Damn. Yes, she'd been avoiding him. She sighed and capitulated. "I'll take it." Diana picked up the phone, and looked up just in time to see Mickey's eyes roll. She shook her head and pushed the button for line three. "Diana Iverson," she said in a businesslike tone.

Jonathan didn't even greet her. "I just got off the phone with Roger Merkovitz and he was so irate I could hardly understand what he was saying. It sounded like he said you'd dumped him."

Faintly surprised that he wasn't calling about all of texts he'd sent, and the notes with the flowers, she replied calmly, "That's correct. I had to drop his case. As you can imagine, he wasn't pleased."

"You did?" Jonathan's voice rose to a volume she'd never heard before. "Why would you do such a stupid thing? What's going on?"

Diana pulled the receiver away from her ear and stared at it. "I had to drop his case," she repeated, falling back on her calm, emotionless persona that served as a thick shield in such situations. "I'm sorry if I've upset you." Her voice remained steady and cool, but inside, she was shocked and bewildered. Jonathan had never raised his voice in this manner—she knew he had a temper, but it had never yet, in the last year, been directed at her.

"*Why?*" As if realizing his irrationality, Jonathan calmed his tones. "Diana, do you know what this will do to you? To your reputation? Merkovitz will have it in shreds. You won't be able to practice law in this town—"

"Stop it, Jonathan," she interrupted. "Roger Merkovitz does not make or break my career or my practice. And if I make the decision to drop a case, it's my decision, not yours. I'm sorry you're friends with him, but I can't represent the man. And might I remind you that we're no longer a couple anyway, so it really shouldn't reflect poorly on you—if that's what you're worried about."

"But why?"

Diana gripped the phone tighter. "Ask him. I was very up-front about my reasons. If he wants you to know, he can tell you himself. Now, I really have to get back to work. Good-bye."

Ethan had been back in Princeton for more than three weeks. He didn't mind being on campus so much, but he'd come to prefer Damariscotta. There weren't any young fresh-faced, manipulative students trying to trick him into bed up there, nor the undercurrents of gossip related to Jenny and Bruce—but nor were there many other prospects for a man who'd been sleeping alone for much too long. Much as he loved his cabin tucked away in the woods, he was lonely.

He'd left for New Jersey the Monday after Diana rushed back to Boston, looking for a change of scenery and to take care of some business regarding his latest co-published journal article. Aside from that, he didn't want to have to be answering any questions from Helen Galliday or avoiding Joe Cap's meaningful looks about Diana Iverson.

He got back to his office after a long lunch with some of his friends and found the voice mail light blinking on his desk phone. And then he heard a soft buzzing sound, and realized he'd left his cell phone in his jacket pocket, and his jacket slung over his chair.

Someone was trying to get in touch with him. A faint, derisive, ridiculous hope that it was Diana, begging to see him again, was quashed when he pushed the buttons to access his office voicemail and Helen Galliday's sharp, unmistakable voice pierced his ears over the phone lines.

"Ethan? Ethan Tannock, is that you? …. I tell you, I don't like these confounded machines, you know …. Are you there?... Young man, I don't know where you've been off to for the past few weeks, but there's trouble brewin' up here and you need to do something about it! …. Can you hear me? …. The autopsy's come back an—"

Something cut her off at that point, but the indomitable Helen was not about to be stopped, for the second message was the same strident voice. "...Ethan?...Ethan, this blazin' voicemail of yours is abominable! Why can't you answer your phone yourself? It turned off on me last time!...And I was tellin' you somethin' important!... You best get back here right away...They're saying Belinda was murdered! Murdered in her bed!...D'you hear me?...I was going to say that in the last message but that infernal machine turned off... you come home right now!" And that second message had been terminated by the unmistakable sound of a phone receiver being slammed into its cradle.

The third and final message was short and to the point: "Where the hell are you? Call me."

It was Joe Cap.

Boston's on the way back here from Princeton, Joe had said. *Cady's having a great time here with me and Penny. You can stop off and give Diana the news. It's better that she get it in person, Ethan.*

Yeah, right. And since when was Ethan a member of law enforcement, and required to deliver such bad news? But here he was, against his better judgment, standing in the hallway in a high-rise in Boston's financial district. It was just before five o'clock, later than he'd anticipated thanks to Friday afternoon traffic, but here he was. He knew she'd be there: a dedicated, workaholic lawyer like her wouldn't be turning off the lights until she'd hit her 70-plus-hour a week billable time.

Diana's office suite was separated from the hall by a large, mahogany door and a discreet gold-lettered sign: *Diana M. Iverson—Medical Malpractice*. There was a narrow band of window running along one side of the door, and Ethan could see an efficient-looking receptionist busily answering phones. Of course—Diana would suffer nothing less than efficiency.

He still couldn't believe he'd agreed to help Joe. When Diana had driven away in her shiny gold Lexus, he told himself he'd be happy to never see her again. Manipulative, secretive, frosty Diana, who'd shut him down with a cool, lawyerly argument right on the front porch of Belinda's house.

But now, here he was, and he was already regretting it. He supposed he could just leave without seeing her, and tell Joe that he'd not been able to connect with her...then he stopped. Why should it bother him so much to talk to her? And he owed it to Belinda.

That was the real reason he was there, he told himself. And that was the last twist of Joe's knife that had convinced him to agree.

He'd purposely chosen to come late in the day, and not to make an appointment. Since he had no desire to be there himself, he didn't want to give her any choice in the matter either.

Strangely nervous, he opened the heavy door and the young woman looked up with a pleasant smile. She was wearing a headset obviously attached to the phone, for she was talking with someone, and she nodded in greeting at him, holding up a pink-manicured finger to let him know she'd be right with him. Corey Geisoff, read her nameplate. She was seated at a desk behind a high counter that almost hid her face, but was of the right height for someone to stand at and rest one's briefcase or planner atop it.

While he waited for Corey to assist him, Ethan scanned the small waiting area, noting two black leather armchairs separated by a small mahogany table and a matching loveseat. A telephone, a calla lily, and several daily newspapers were within easy reach of anyone waiting to meet with Diana or her coworkers. Several old maps of Boston decorated the walls, and other than that, the area was comfortably plain.

By the time he'd finished assessing the room, Corey had finished her phone call. Just as she looked up at him, a whirlwind of blond, neon green, and jangling silver bracelets shot around the corner from the back of the suite. "Corey—oh, excuse me!"

The streak stopped short and Ethan smiled at the bundle of energy topped by an incredible mass of frizzy blond hair.

"No problem," he said as he flashed a charming grin, knowing he had to get them on his side if he was going to get in to see Diana without a fight. The woman returned his smile, slapping a stack of manila envelopes onto the counter. "Go ahead," he offered, "I'm in no hurry."

She was wearing a suit of neon green, silver bangled earrings and bracelet, and chunky white shoes. Despite her state of activity—which equated, Ethan thought, to that of a tornado—she was the picture of trendy professionalism and efficiency. "Thanks," she said, and he saw the hints of crow's feet at her eyes and the lines in her cheeks and realized she was not the young, recent college graduate he'd assumed. She turned to Corey and gestured to the stack of envelopes. "Can you get these couriered over to the court a-sap? And let me know if Gerald Deets calls back—Diana wants to talk with him."

"Absolutely," Corey replied, taking the envelopes and then turning her attention back to Ethan. "I'm sorry for the delay, sir, what can I do for you?"

"I'm here to see Diana."

The receptionist smiled regretfully. "I'm sorry, but Ms. Iverson is tied up at the moment. Was she expecting you?"

"No, she's not expecting me." Ethan lounged against the high counter. "Is she here? I'll wait for her."

The older woman in the neon green suit had been listening to the conversation and now she stepped in. "I'm Diana's assistant, Mickey. Is there something I can help you with?"

"Unfortunately, no. It's Diana that I need to see."

"She is here, but she's in a meeting. I'm not sure how long she'll be—would you like to make an appointment to come back?"

"That's all right," he replied, just as pleasantly. "I'll wait." He gave them both his most charming grin and walked casually over to the rounded leather armchairs.

"You're certainly welcome to wait until she's free. In the meantime, could I get you anything? Coffee? Soda? Water?" she offered, her eyes scanning him with candid—*very* candid—interest.

"No thanks. I'll be fine."

Mickey started to go, then paused, looking at him again. "Can I let her know who's waiting?"

Again, his grin was meant to disarm. "I'd rather it be a surprise, but thanks."

—⁂—

Ethan was only halfway through today's *Boston Globe* when he heard her voice. It was low and sounded stressed, but he recognized it right away. He looked up in time to see Diana come around the corner and pause to talk seriously with Mickey.

"...called as well. I'm sure Merkovitz is involved in all of this."

She didn't see him at that angle, so he had a chance to observe her at his leisure. She was wearing a slim, short-skirted gray suit and black heels that showed off her shapely legs, and she carried a shiny, gold-plated pen that she flicked nervously against her palm as she spoke. Her hair was more tamed than he'd ever seen it—the thick, dark waves smoothed into a black helmet that cupped her chin and neck. She looked different…but not in a bad way. His lungs felt as if they'd constricted and he was shamefully aware that his heart thudded harder.

Mickey, as though realizing they could be overheard, directed her boss's attention toward Ethan. "He's waiting over there."

"Hello—" Diana turned to face him and the greeting froze in mid-air. "Ethan."

He had to give her credit—she couldn't have been more surprised, yet she handled the shock with cool aplomb. "Hi, Diana," he said, rising to his feet.

"I—have you been waiting long? I'm sorry about that, but we seem to be in crisis mode at the moment." Her words were pleasant, but her face bore a tension and worry that concerned him. If this was what she was like in her work, he pitied her for having a job that wore on her so heavily.

"I haven't been waiting more than fifteen minutes. I'm sorry to drop in without an appointment," he made certain his words didn't sound too sincere, then continued, "but I was on my way home from Princeton and needed to talk with you. Actually, Joe Cap wanted me to stop by and talk to you."

"Oh." The simplicity of her response indicated how confused and stressed she was. "It's about—that. Why don't you come on back."

Ethan followed her, getting his pulse under control as he watched the sway of her hips as she started down the hall into the depths of the suite. Mickey followed, once again offering him something to drink.

"Coffee," he replied this time. "Black, please."

"I'll have some too," Diana told her assistant.

Her space was a large, corner office with a stately mahogany desk, large potted plants, a well-filled bookcase, and two walls of windows that looked into nowhere but the next buildings. Diana took a seat at her desk, which, although organized, was not clear of papers and folders, and gestured to him to take a seat.

He chose one of the barrel chairs that faced her desk—that piece of furniture that she probably used to intimidate when the situation warranted it, or, in this case, more likely, to separate herself from her guest. There was silence for a moment and he looked her over easily, carefully, noticing that she seemed tense and tired. He took a moment to admire the curve of her mouth drawn tensely down, realizing that, yes, he still wanted her—and he didn't care that she might have used him to betray her commitment to another man, didn't care that she might have done so in revenge or to assuage her ego—he just *wanted*. Damn it. He'd hoped whatever attraction he'd felt would have faded over the last month.

Diana looked up as Mickey opened the door and brought their drinks, then nodded her thanks at her assistant. She was obviously bursting with curiosity, for she asked, "Did you need me to sit in?"

"No, thanks. Ethan is here to speak with me—about Aunt Belinda's death, I assume?" She directed this last part toward him, and he nodded once. "Hold my calls, please."

"All right." Mickey gave him one last appraising glance, and with a sudden understanding in her eyes and a faint smirk curving her fuchsia lips, left the room.

As the door closed, Diana spoke. "Well, Ethan, I don't need to comment on what a surprise this is, as I'm sure you know it already. Have you joined Captain Tettmueller's staff, or is it just curiosity that brings you here?" Her words were soft, unaccusing, but cool and steady.

"I'm doing this as a favor to him—and to your aunt's memory." He noted with a perverse satisfaction that her face tightened at his words. *Chalk one up for me*, he thought to himself, determined to have and to keep the upper hand in this unwanted interview. Although with the way his mouth kept wanting to go dry, he wasn't sure how easy that was going to be. All of a sudden, he was like a geeky teenager trying to talk to the head cheerleader. Did she have to look so coolly beautiful, even in the uniform of her profession?

"Why didn't Joe just call me himself?" She picked up that gold-plated pen and started flicking it again. "Ethan, I really don't have time for this—whatever it is. I—*oh*." Comprehension crossed her face and her eyes flashed to his. "It's about the autopsy."

Ethan's reserve melted at her apprehensive expression, at the sudden fear in her eyes. Joe had been right to ask that he do this in person. "I'm afraid it is. And I'm afraid the news isn't good."

"Was I right?" she whispered. Her face had gone pale, almost gray, and her eyes lost their blue, turning dull and colorless.

"She was asphyxiated," he said, holding her gaze. "Joe got the results yesterday."

Diana was silent, and as the quiet stretched, he found he was having to force himself to remain seated. Not to go over to her.

"I'm sorry," he said at last, offering comfort the only way he felt he could. "For you as much as for me. I loved your aunt. She was a great friend and more than a little bit of a mother. And to know that someone did that …." Rage prickled through him. Joe had promised he was doing everything he could, investigating the break-ins, the vandalism, and now a murder. But it wasn't fast enough. It wasn't *enough*.

"Thank you for coming here to tell me," she said at last. She hadn't moved except to rest her pen neatly on the desk blotter.

He shifted in his chair, then rose to walk to one of the windows. He looked down onto the gray line of a street, studded with toy cars and dotted with people, and to keep his thoughts calm. But there were things that had to be said. "Diana, have you thought about the fact that you could be in danger as well?" He took a step away from the window, toward her, as she sat stiffly in her chair.

She rose. "That's ridiculous. Whatever the person wanted they've either found by now, or determined it didn't exist. Aside from that, they've got what they wanted—me away from the house. Problem solved, I'm out of the picture."

Ethan shook his head. "No, Diana, problem not solved. They could think you have the item."

"I'm here in Boston," she said. "I'm not even in Damariscotta. Whoever it is couldn't think I'd be a danger *here* to whatever their problem is back *there*."

"Diana, you can't know what this person is thinking. I'm not trying to frighten you, but you should be aware of the possibility that *you* are at risk. This isn't simple vandalism and breaking and entering. Your aunt was murdered." He searched her eyes with his, noticing that they were almost the same level with his, due to her heels. "What does your instinct tell you?"

She stared at him without speaking, her face etched with weariness, then turned to look out the window. "I pulled a card from the Tarot deck. I...was sitting there one night, and for the first time, I actually concentrated and drew a card." She expelled a shuddering breath, touched her face with fingers that trembled. "It was The High Priestess again. She is showing up so often and seems to be adamant that I...open my mind. So, to answer your question: my instinct tells me that I should be worried." She looked as if she was about to say something else, but she stopped abruptly.

Her breathing had become rough and when she turned back to look at him, he was shocked by the haunted expression in her eyes. "What is it?" he asked.

She looked away, out into the distance, somewhere far away. "Something happened...I wanted to call you …."

He mercilessly shoved away a spark of hope and remained silent, waiting as she groped for the words. This was not the same woman who'd given him such a cool set-down the morning after they'd made love. This was one filled with anguish and confusion. Part of him wanted to gather her into his arms and help her work through it—all of this. But the other part forced himself to take an emotional step back. This was work...an addendum to his research. It couldn't be anything more.

All at once, she blinked and her face changed. The reserve was back, accompanied by a distant cast to her eyes. It was as if a door closed, or curtains shuttered her face.

Just as well, Ethan decided. And he put on his scientist hat. "When you looked at the card, or later, when you thought about it, did anything pop into your mind? Was there anything else there?"

She swallowed audibly. "Nothing that meant anything. I thought about all of the newspapers that Aunt Belinda had in her den, and about the quilting group. I...thought about Jonathan... and ...." She stopped, her voice trailing off and she turned again to look out the window. "If...*if*...Aunt Belinda was right, and I do have some kind of...psychic ability, wouldn't it be telling me *something*—who this is, or what they want?" Diana's voice had risen a bit.

With effort, he kept himself detached and replied, "If it's true, you've been suppressing the ability for years. You aren't used to interpreting the feelings or thoughts that may accompany precognitive abilities. It's not always—in fact, rarely is it—a clear vision or picture, like in a crystal ball. At least, that's how it was for your aunt. If indeed you really are opening your mind, it's a bit rusty, and it'll take time for you to learn to interpret and trust your instincts. As I said once before, Diana, cards don't read the future or tell us how to live our lives. People do. If they can learn to understand their instincts."

She stared back out the window, and just as she turned, the intercom buzzed.

"Diana, I'm sorry to interrupt, but it's Jonathan. He says he needs to speak with you. He's insistent and is threatening to show up here if you don't take the call."

She hesitated for a moment, her face going from surprise to apprehension. Avoiding Ethan's gaze, she replied reluctantly, "I suppose I'd better. Send it in."

Ethan walked back to the window, up to the ceiling-to-floor glass, and stood against it, almost touching it, and listened unashamedly to the one-sided conversation.

"Yes..." she murmured, obviously trying to keep her voice down. "We've been getting calls all week .... Jonathan, I don't— No. I'm not going to change my mind .... . I don't expect you to .... You can tell him that. Good-bye."

He waited until he heard the receiver placed on its cradle before he turned. She sat at the desk, staring down at her unmoving hands, as if oblivious to his presence. He saw that she was breathing heavily, slowly, as though trying to regain some control.

"Diana?"

She jerked, and raised her face to look at him. "Was there anything else?"

Her countenance had the life of a clay mask, her eyes like dull ebony pits. His insides dropped like a pile of stones. "Jesus, what is it?" he asked, coming to her, taking her cold hands.

She shuddered once, then withdrew her fingers, looked away. "He's ruining me."

"Jonathan?" Ethan was incredulous. Fury swept over him. "Over what? Over...us?" The words slipped out before he could catch them.

She stared at him in surprise, then her lips moved. "No, oh no, over nothing that trivial." Her voice strengthened, gathering bitterness and sarcasm. "No, and it's not my former fiancé who's ruining me...it's a colleague of his. Someone whose case I had to drop."

"You dropped a case?"

She nodded. "I couldn't defend a person who wasn't innocent, and I told him so. I guess perhaps I...don't have a true understanding of the law...a true belief in it. Everyone is entitled to representation, even the basest of murderers...I just found that I can't argue for someone who doesn't take his profession seriously, or cautiously." She was speaking, but not looking at him. He thought perhaps she wasn't looking at anything.

She drew in a deep breath, then let it out. It wavered. "Jonathan warned me that this man could make or break me. I guess he's decided to break me."

ELEVEN

LATER, DIANA WOULDN'T BE ABLE to recount just how she ended up with Ethan at the house she was subleasing...but she did, and, at the time, she was distressingly grateful for that fact.

"Nice place," he said, opening the door and gesturing her in as if it were his own place. "You're not expecting Jonathan, I presume?"

"No," she said, looking at him sharply. "I don't see him anymore."

"But you take his calls even after you told your people not to disturb you," he reminded her. "Even after you said to hold all your calls. Interesting." The tone in his voice was flat, almost accusatory.

She turned away, but not before she had the image of Ethan, standing tall and dark and strong in the foyer of her temporary home. He was taking in the details, just as she had done when she visited him. Her insides fluttered at the memory of his log cabin and what had transpired there, and she felt warm and weak all at once. This was not good. She did not want to succumb to the temptation of Ethan Tannock again, giving him more material for his work.

Pride—the only defense she had—kept her from telling him what she'd seen in his office. After all, if she admitted she'd seen those notes, admitted the hurt and the betrayal she felt, he'd know just where she stood. How vulnerable she was. How she'd begun to feel for him.

But the longer she was with him, the weaker her resolve seemed to become. And so she said, "Ethan, I really appreciate you seeing me home, but—"

He stepped in further and stood right by the open door to her bedroom. He gestured toward the kitchen. "Are you hungry? I'm starving. Do you want to order something in, or are you in the mood to cook?" He glanced into the bedroom, where the large four-poster bed sat, neat and made up, just as she'd left it this morning. Beyond, there was the door to the master bath, and across the hall was the second bedroom, or den. "Nice place. Is it yours or Wertinger's?"

"Neither," she said. "I needed a place to stay after I moved out, so I'm subleasing it from the parents of a colleague. They're in Alaska for the summer."

That made him stop and look at her more intently. "You did end things with him."

"I told you I did," she replied.

His face relaxed a bit. "Good. At least I don't have to worry about him showing up here. Now, what should we do about something to eat? It's nearly seven."

"Ethan," Diana began...and then she stopped. What would be the harm in having dinner with him? She didn't really want to be alone, anyway, while her business was collapsing around her. And with the news about Aunt Belinda. "Dinner," she said. "That's it. And then you have to leave."

"If that's the way you want it."

"That's the way I want it," she replied firmly, noticing the way his eyes wandered back to the open bedroom door behind her. A flush threatened to rush up and over her chest and throat. "What happened before was...like I said, it was nice. But—"

"Nice?" he repeated. "I don't think that was the word you used before. Mind-blowing comes to mind."

She kept her expression bland, her voice even. "Mind-blowing? Is that what I said? I'd forgotten."

"You've forgotten?" His voice became smooth and silky, and dark challenge came into his eyes.

Suddenly, she was afraid...and more alive than she'd ever felt. Her skin prickled and her chest squeezed and she felt light-headed, trapped by his eyes like a doe in a pair of headlights.

Her mouth turned to cotton as he closed his fingers around one of her narrow wrists, drawing it behind him so that she was forced to step up to him, just a hairs-breadth away from his solidness. Diana's breath caught and she couldn't breathe for a moment as she struggled to regain her senses.

"Perhaps I should remind you how good it was," he murmured, his voice thick, his eyes hooding as he continued to look down at her. "How...mind-blowing. Toe-curling."

"Ethan ...." She meant to stop him, but her voice sounded like it was begging, as it came out breathy and husky. She pushed at him, in her last vestige of sensibility, and he deftly caught her fingers, transferring them to join the others in the bondage of his left hand.

He traced a light forefinger over her jaw and chin, down the length of her neck and along the unbuttoned neckline of her blouse. She struggled to breathe, and her chest rose as if to meet the tip of his finger. His hand slid further, just brushing into the warmth of her cleavage, and back over the swell of the top of one breast. Her skin leapt and danced beneath his touch, and she had to close her eyes for a moment to remind herself where she was. Who *he* was.

"Ethan," she said in a voice that was meant to be strong, but wavered. She tried again to step away, to free her wrists, but he kept her imprisoned. "Don't...."

He stilled, and there was only the rasping, rhythmic sound of their breathing for a long moment; then suddenly he released her hands and stepped away. "I haven't forgotten about it, Diana, and neither have you."

Then, as if annoyed with himself, he spun and walked into the kitchen. She heard him open the refrigerator, and rummage around in there.

"Make yourself at home," she muttered, trying to instill a bit of humor into the tense moment. Then she went into her bedroom to change out of her suit.

By the time Diana reappeared from the bedroom, Ethan had managed to gain control of himself and his rashness, and was seated on the living room sofa, drinking a glass of wine. There hadn't been any beer in the refrigerator so he'd resorted to a Pouilly-Fuissé.

He should have left, he told himself when Diana walked hesitantly into the room...but there were a few things he wanted to talk with her about. He had his hormones under control now, but there had been a moment there, where he could see a glimpse of her bedroom from the hallway, that he'd almost tossed her on the bed to really tear up the sheets. Probably'd be the first time they'd really be mussed up, he thought to himself with a complacent grin. *Unless she's been sleeping with someone else now that she dumped the douchebag doctor.*

His grin disappeared and anger sliced through him at the thought. Then he forced himself to do a mental shrug. *She did it with you, why wouldn't she do it with someone else?*

He looked up and realized she was still standing in the doorway, watching him as though she feared he would leap across the room at her. The vulnerable look on her face struck him, blasting some sense into his sex-crazed brain, as he remembered all that was going on in her life right now.

His irritation with her evaporated.

He stood, facing her, and said, "If you want me to leave, I will. But I'd like to stay and...be here for awhile. I know you're going through a lot, and it might help to have someone to listen if you want to talk. That's all." He spread his hands, holding the wine glass out over the coffee table.

She was silent, measuring him with her eyes as if to see what trick he intended this time. But Ethan's motives were, probably for the first time since he'd met her, purely unselfish in that he wanted nothing from her: not to observe her, not to judge her, not to sleep with her.

"Thank you," she said at last. She didn't directly accept his offer, but instead, said, "Would you like something to drink other than wine? No beer, but I have Scotch and gin."

"Thank God." He set the wine glass down on the table and gave her a genuine smile. "Scotch would be appreciated."

"There's a good pizza place around the corner that delivers, and also a Thai place up the street, if you're still hungry." She seemed to be trying to smooth the awkwardness between them, and he was glad to let her. He believed she didn't want to be alone anymore than he thought she did—even though she might not admit it.

They ate on a small patio in the back of the brownstone, sharing a pizza and antipasto salad. Diana drank red wine, and instead of the offered whiskey, Ethan had dashed to the store for a six-pack of beer, which he drank right from the bottle.

She'd told him as much as she dared about the Merkovitz situation, and how Jonathan's dire prediction was coming true: that the orthopedic surgeon, who wielded an inordinate amount of influence in Boston's medical community, was obviously blackballing her name so that her clients would withdraw. Today when he called her office, Jonathan had told her if she'd reconsider, he was certain he could get Merkovitz to stop sabotaging her...but she would not.

Now, they sat in companionable silence as the orange ball of the sun finished dipping behind the rooflines of the houses in the distance. It was still early—just past nine o'clock—but Diana wondered whether Ethan planned to drive back to Damariscotta that night, or to take a room somewhere in the area. No matter what happened, he wasn't staying there, she promised herself.

"So, Diana," his smooth voice rumbled, interrupting her thoughts, "have you given anymore thought to who might have had a reason to murder Belinda?"

She stiffened as the reality of it all came back. "I've tried not to think about it too hard, but I know I should." She looked at him in the lowering light. "You probably have as good an idea—

or better—as I do." She said it without rancor, just regret, that it should be true.

His smile flashed for a moment, then he sobered. "I don't know. Let's talk about motive, first. The classic motives are money, passion, revenge, and fear. I'd say money is the most obvious in this situation, since Bee was loaded."

Diana nodded. "She didn't live like she was as wealthy as she was, though—did the people in town know?"

"Did they know? Does Helen Galliday live in Damariscotta? Hell, yeah, they knew." He finished off his beer, and Diana caught herself being distracted by the long, sinewy cords in his neck as he tilted his head back. "So who would gain by Belinda's death?"

"I would."

He nodded. "I know. You'd be the most obvious suspect, in a classic case, especially since you only got back in contact with her a year ago. How did that happen, by the way, if you thought she was dead?"

She looked at him, wondering if he was making an implication, or if he was just curious. "It was odd, but I got a letter from her— out of the blue. I suppose she must have either kept track of me, or found a way to track me down. Or maybe she saw something in the paper about me and a case I was working on."

Ethan was nodding. "I do remember that. She was very excited to have located you."

Diana felt the old guilt creep up, followed by the continuing anger toward her mother for keeping her apart from her great-aunt. "I called her right away, but I never got a chance to see her." *I never* made *the chance to see her.*

"So, other than you, who else would benefit from her death?"

"The only other beneficiary is the town animal shelter—I guess that would be Doug Horner, wouldn't it?" She looked at him for a moment, then a thought struck her. "It was at his office that my tires were slashed...and he was at lunch when we went to the quilt shop. It could have been him who broke into the house."

"Hm. Yes, he's a possibility." He didn't sound convinced. Ethan was quiet for a long moment, drumming his long fingers on the tile-topped table in front of him. "Diana, what would happen to Belinda's money if anything happened to you?"

"I don't have any family, so I guess—" She stopped. "Jonathan." She said it aloud without thinking as her stomach curled in upon itself tightly, hurting her. "It would have been Jonathan, if we'd gotten married."

"But you didn't," Ethan said softly. "You aren't."

"No. But …." Her arms prickled. Could that be why he was so insistent that they work things out? Then she shook her head violently. "Absolutely not, Ethan. That's absurd. He doesn't even need the money—he has a thriving practice. And aside from that, he seems to have accepted that it's over."

He just looked at her. "It's usually the one closest to the victim …."

"But I'm not the victim!" she returned, her eyes burning with tears. *No, not this…not this on top of everything else.*

Then, she remembered, and light-headed relief swept over her. "It can't be Jonathan—he has an alibi."

"An alibi?"

"Yes. Several of them, in fact. He was at a conference on the day the tires were slashed, I know that for sure, because it was in North Carolina and he had to speak. And, he called me from his office on my cell—Caller ID—after the first break-in. That night, that night I came home and someone was in my house."

"And you thought it was me." His voice was flat. "Well, I guess that leaves out Jonathan."

"Yes, I did think it was you. You'd been in there uninvited once before—what was I to think?"

"Someone was searching for something," Ethan said, ignoring her question. "Money, perhaps—if it's someone who thought they were going to inherit but didn't."

"That could make you a suspect." Diana looked at him closely, no longer believing it, but playing devil's advocate. "After all, you did enter the house at least once without being invited."

"Yeah, right. And I slashed your tires while we were at the quilt shop. And I murdered Belinda while I was in Princeton.

Fat chance." His voice was easy, as if he, too, knew she was just making an argument. He had an almost-smile on his lips.

How far they'd come from suspicion and judgment to casual discussion. No accusations.

The sun was gone, and the last light faded from the sky. The far-off rumbling of traffic reminded Diana that she was in Boston, not in Maine, looking into someone else's back yard, not over Lake Damariscotta...and all of a sudden, she missed it. She missed the peace and the quiet and the slow hum of living...not the day-to-day race to work.

She smelled that someone was barbequing—it was nearly ten, but that wasn't an uncommon time for the workaholic professionals who lived in the Back Bay to eat a Friday night meal—and it smelled artificial, like the gas grill on which it was cooked.

"Diana." Ethan's voice came to her, bringing her back to the tiny porch where they sat. "So you have no other family? You have no other relatives?"

"No. My father died when I was very young, and Mother never remarried or had any other children. Aunt Bee and Uncle Tracer were the only family I ever knew. Until I met Tommy and Bella. I guess they're family now." She stood abruptly, batting her hand in the air. "Bugs are getting bad."

Despite the fact that he hadn't seen one mosquito or even a no-see-um, he stood, helping to gather their dishes.

In the kitchen, he looked at her, allowing his emotions—the attraction, the need—to leak forward into his consciousness. He'd been trying to keep them at bay all evening, focusing on their conversation and not the way he felt, being here with her in a casual, informal, domestic sort of way. So comfortable. So *right*.

But now desire pushed inside him, struggling to have its way. A vision of Diana, sprawled among the mussed sheets of the four-poster mahogany bed that was just down the hall, formed, caught, and would not be dislodged.

And, almost as though she'd been waiting for it—maybe she had, maybe all she'd wanted was for the suspense to end as much as he did—she turned away from the counter and faced him. Their gazes caught across the kitchen, and her mouth opened in a soft little **O**.

In two strides, he was there next to her, his hands curving under and around her bent elbows, pulling her body to his. Where it fitted. Where it *belonged*.

He felt rather than heard her small gasp of pleasure and protest, and ignored the insistent pressure of her hands molded to his chest as he lowered his mouth to hers.

"No," she whispered, even as she raised her chin to bare the softness of her neck to his lips. "God, Ethan, don't tempt …." Desperation swathed her voice, and he heard the unmistakable soft sigh of pleasure that faded into a groan when he finally captured her lips with his.

"Oh, yes," he murmured, and a scorching heat flashed through him when she moved, pressing her hips into his, welcoming the swell of his pounding erection against her belly. "Jesus, Diana."

He lost all but three points of coherent thought: the direction of the bedroom, the swell of breasts against him and the warm juncture of her thighs parting as he hoisted her against him.

Moments later, they were on the bed—he had no recollection of getting there—and he'd pinned her wrists into the feather pillows with one hand while the other tore off her clothes. He had no memory of what she was wearing, nor how he got it off, he just knew the taste of her mouth, sweet with wine and Diana, and the trembling of her body as he touched her.

Ethan was heavy and warm and solid, and Diana arched into him, reveling in the feel of strength and his pleasing, masculine scent. His mouth kissed and coaxed, slid and sucked, demanding her response, and all the while she kissed him back, she fought back the despair of knowing she would regret this moment of abject pleasure. But she needed it—Lord, she needed it. She needed him.

When he closed his mouth over one breast, Diana jolted in surprise from the change of smooth, sensual kissing to deep, driving passion. He sucked, pulled, hard, as though trying to take everything from her, trying to gain her satisfaction there, and she shuddered and trembled as pleasure rolled through her. It was good...so good.

Ethan's breath came heavy and fast, fanning heat over her skin, and he released her wrists, pulling up and away to yank off his shirt. Diana couldn't just lie there—she had to touch him, to slide her splayed hands through the hair on his chest, over the smooth sinews of his shoulders and along his ribs. His hair, as thick and dark as her own, curled wildly in all directions, giving him a darkly angelic look as he stared down at her with deep, burning eyes. The sight of his mouth, his glistening lower lip, firm and sensual, sent that driving lust through her again and she reached for his belt.

He groaned with relief when she yanked open the zipper and pulled him free, to hold his heavy erection in her hands, to stroke the throbbing length of him and to close her fingers around it.

And then, before she could catch her breath, he caught her hands again, taking them from their torture, and kicked off the rest of his clothes with a fierce, determined look on his face. She pulled free and slid her arms around him as he came up to kiss her, opening her legs and easing him in...slowly, tortuously, endlessly slowly, keeping him from slamming into her as she knew he needed to do.

It was exquisite torment, teasing him, teasing her, as she guided him, holding him back with her hand, sliding in...then out, then in a bit more, until they were both breathing like they'd just broken the surface of water. She wanted to scream with frustration and smile with control.

He trembled—his arms, his legs, his shuddering mouth as he tried to taste her everywhere at once. "Diana," he murmured, desperation coloring his voice as his fingers slid between them. He found her hot and ready, and he brought her to the edge, teasing her just as she'd been teasing him.

And then, knowing she was ready for it all, she moved her hand, and with a shift of her hips he filled her. Completely.

She cried out, sobbing, shaking, climaxing. He followed, groaning her name in release.

And then...they slept.

———⚬———

"Toe-curling."

The soft murmur in her ear awakened Diana and for a moment, just a moment, she allowed herself to bask. Ethan was next to her, warm and solid, his body textured with rough hair and soft skin and firm muscle. Oh, and naked.

Completely naked.

She couldn't help a smile as he nuzzled her neck, softly and lightly, gentling her awake. "Mm-hm. I'd say that was toe-curling, mind-blowing sex," he said, his words hot against her skin. His hand slid around to cup her breast, lightly stroking her responsive nipple as she felt herself begin to tighten and swell elsewhere.

It surprised her how readily her body answered to his touch, how quickly she became hot and damp. And when he eased himself closer, fitting together with her, Diana pushed away lingering sleepiness and opened her eyes to enjoy.

Some time later, the sun blazed brightly through the window and she woke once again. This time, with wakefulness came uncertainty and regret. Hesitation and distance.

As if sensing this, even though she hadn't moved or spoken, Ethan opened his eyes and all at once they were gaze-locked. Close, so close, she couldn't hide what was surely in her expression.

"Regrets already?" he asked, his voice mild but his body easing back. His eyes dipped into wariness and he didn't move to touch her.

She drew in a breath to deny it—but what would be the purpose? Everything in her life was in an upheaval. She might as well own up to another disruption. Another shaft of pain. "I didn't expect you to stay. I didn't expect to ever see you again," she managed and shifted away, her body sliding into the cooler area of the bed.

"Same here," he said, his voice low and quiet. "I didn't even want to come here, but Joe Cap guilted me into it."

"Oh." Diana couldn't help the cold vise that closed over her heart. Nothing like a blast of honesty.

"I haven't been able to stop thinking about you. Even though you left Damariscotta so abruptly, as if you were ashamed or, well, regretful about what happened. Or you felt guilty, because of Wertinger." He looked down at her hand, splayed on the bed between them as she held herself half upright. "That's why I didn't want to come. Not because I didn't want to see you, but because I knew you didn't want to see me."

He flung back the sheets and bedcovers with a quick, smooth motion and was out of the bed before she could respond. He stalked into the bathroom and closed the door behind him, leaving Diana with a pounding heart and the impression of a very nice set of legs topped by a very fine ass—as Mickey would say.

Moments later, he came back out and their eyes met across the room. "I guess I should be going," he said. His face was blank. Empty. He'd pulled on his shorts.

Something shifted in her chest and Diana curled her fingers around the bedclothes. *It's now or never.* "I saw the papers," she said. "In your office."

He stilled, confusion coming over his face. "Papers?"

"The ones, the notes about me. So I know that this is just... well, it doesn't really mean anything," she fumbled, spreading her hand to include the rumpled bed and the whole evening. "It's just a side benefit," she said, smiling crookedly, "of your research. And that's okay. I'm just coming out of a relationship, and I don't want—"

"Wait, wait, *wait,*" he said, suddenly moving. He was back at the edge of the bed, standing there with his thighs bumping the mattress. "You saw my notes, about you?"

"Yes. The morning after...the storm. They were on the floor in your office, they'd blown all over in the wind," she added defensively. "I wasn't snooping around, but I couldn't help but see...'the subject.' Me being the subject. So...I knew. I understand."

Comprehension dawned in his eyes. "Is that why you got so... cold? Why you left so quickly?"

"Well, partly," she said, unwilling to completely lay herself bare. "I wasn't interested—I mean, I live here, and you're in Jersey, and there wasn't really any point ...."

"Is that why you left? Because you thought you were a research project to me?" This time, his voice was sharp and cold.

Diana nodded, unsure why he seemed so angry. "I'd just broken up with Jonathan—something I realized was long overdue—and I wasn't about to let myself get hurt again. Surely *you* can understand that," she added with a bit of flintiness in her own voice.

"I can completely understand that," he said, his voice softening. "But, Diana, you need to know...I'm falling in love with you."

Her throat went dry with shock and emotion. "What?" was all she could say.

"You're not just a research project to me. Yes, I was making notes and observing, but it was an excuse to be around you. To spend time with you, knowing you were already involved with someone else. It was the only way I could justify...how I felt about you." He was on the bed now, sitting next to her, reaching to lay his capable, tanned hand over her narrow, pale one.

She looked up at him, her heart slamming in her chest as she tried to comprehend—to *believe*—what he was saying to her. It was impossible to accept. It didn't make sense. Why her? Why would he want *her*?

"I...but we live so far away," she said lamely. Knowing it didn't make sense—but the whole situation didn't make sense. She wasn't his type. "From each other."

Ethan shrugged, his eyes still on her. "That's not a deal-breaker." But that wariness was back and she could see that he was beginning to retreat.

She didn't know what to say. Did he really mean it? "I didn't expect...it never occurred to me that you could...feel that way. About me."

"Well, maybe you could at least tell me if you'd want to see me again," he said. "That's a start."

"I definitely want to see you again," she said, her palms damp and her insides fluttering. Joy began to fill her. "Definitely. For certain."

He smiled, and she felt as if something warm and liquid rushed over her body. And then he eased onto the bed next to her and that warm, liquidy feeling became pleasure and contentment.

TWELVE

I SAW HIM TOO!" exclaimed Pauline Whitten, fluttering blood-red fingernails at her throat. She was at the quilt shop because it was a Wednesday and didn't interfere with her Thursday Scrabble games. "And I thought, I thought to myself, he looked just like a murderer—with those beady eyes and slouching shoulders."

Diana choked discreetly behind her cup of tea and settled it into its hand-painted saucer. She reached for a scone, trying not to let the giggle escape from between her lips.

Despite—or maybe because of—the trials and problems with her law firm, it was good to be back in Damariscotta.

"I called Chief Tettmueller right away and reported him." Helen Galliday barreled on with her own description, her voice overriding that of Pauline's. "I told him I saw that man take three boxes of matches from the Green Oaks Grille and a handful of toothpicks, and if that ain't the sign of a vandalizing-murderer, why I don't know my own grandson!" She snapped her head in a vehement nod and dumped three lumps of sugar into her own teacup.

Diana had only been back in Damariscotta since yesterday morning, and already she'd been invited—or, rather, summoned—to tea twice, lunch once, and was being strong-armed into joining the quilting ladies for dinner that evening. They seemed to be intent on keeping her occupied while at the same time doing their own detective work and finding Aunt Belinda's murderer—not to mention blocking quilts and selling them to the slowing stream of summer tourists.

If it weren't so horrible a situation, Diana would have found it even more amusing. As it was, she chalked it up to motherly concern—at least, in everyone except Helen Galliday—and went with the assumption that Joe Cap was working on the case even harder than the gaggle of ladies.

However, in the grand scheme of things, Diana decided it was better for them to expend their energy staking out innocent tourists and identifying "suspects" rather than sticking their collective noses into her personal life. The very first question she'd been asked yesterday at tea was about Jonathan, and when she confessed that they were no longer together, a frightening, calculating gleam settled in Helen Galliday's eyes. The subsequent inquisition included enough implications about Ethan that Diana was bound and determined not to let the ladies know that she and Ethan were already...whatever they were.

More than three weeks ago, in early August, he'd come to Boston to tell her the results of the autopsy. Since then, they'd seen each other twice: once they'd met in New York, a fairly central location, and once he'd come back to Boston.

And the weekends had been filled with relaxation, conversation, and, of course, great sex. Really, *really* great sex. Her stomach became all fluttery just thinking about it.

"Are you feeling all right, Diana?" asked Rose Bettinger suddenly. "You look a little flushed. Could be coming down with something. "

Diana blinked and realized all eyes had settled on her—including Helen Galliday's all-knowing, all-seeing ones. "I'm feeling fine," she said. "I got a little bit of sun yesterday. So what did Chief Tettmueller say when you called and reported your suspicions?"

Helen took a long slurp from her tea before replying. "He took down the information and told me he'd check up on that man—but in the meantime, he says, 'you ladies keep your eyes peeled for other suspicious-looking strangers in town.' I told him I'd be happy to take on some of the investigation myself—interviewing B&B hosts, and restaurant owners to see if they knew anything... but that Chief Tettmueller says it's better for me to be discreet because that way I won't tip them off that I'm working with the Department on the case."

"*Ha*," Martha Woden cackled, "he just said that to you so's you don't bother him anymore." She took a ladylike sip of her own brew and looked smugly at Helen. Having one-upped her friend at last, she smiled brightly at Diana and offered her another sugar cookie.

Diana heard the faint tinkle of the bell hung over the door of the shop, and moments later, Betsy came to the back, a sparkle in her eyes and an unusual flush to her cheeks. "Dr. Reardon is here," she announced, gesturing for the gentleman in question to precede her into the back room.

Helen struggled to her feet and grabbed the ever-present cane to aid in hasty steps to his side. "Well, come in, now Doctor. It's too bad that Pauline here was so quick to tidy up, else there'd been some tea left for you." She shot a withering look at her friend, who was in the process of removing the cups from the table by now.

"Now, Dr. Reardon, don't fret," Pauline said in her motherly way. "We can put on another pot of tea, unless you'd rather have coffee?"

"Why thank you," he replied easily, settling into one of the chairs. "Coffee, if it wouldn't be any trouble, would be great. Hello Diana. Welcome back to Damariscotta."

"Hello, Marc. How are you? How's business going as the summer's winding down? Pretty soon all the tourists will be gone."

"Quite well, actually." He reached for a scone, pulling back his pressed shirt sleeve so that the cuff wouldn't brush the plate. "The tourist season certainly helps business—poison ivy, swimmer's itch, sprained ankles—you know, the minor things that have to be treated on one's vacation. And I'm the one always paged when there's an emergency—the EMTs are twenty miles away. But I confess, I won't be sorry to see things slow up a bit in September.

But, I should be asking: how are you? I heard that Belinda's death was not as it seemed."

Diana nodded, not at all surprised he knew.   After all, everyone must know by now. "Yes, that's true. Joe Tettmueller is investigating."

"No more...er, incidents up at the house?" he asked.

She shook her head. "No. Everything's been quiet. The contractor finished repainting the siding where all the spray paint was, and the broken windows, and I came up to check out the job." And to see Ethan again—but he was back in Princeton for another three days, and she thought it was best if their visits didn't exactly overlap. Helen Galliday was much too clever to let something like that pass as coincidence.

She turned, wanting to change the subject, and took another of the delightfully fattening blueberry scones. "These are incredible, Betsy. You'll have to share your recipe with me."

"The secret is Maine blueberries, picked right off the bushes and popped in the batter," Betsy told her with a smile. "Your aunt has quite a nice-sized patch up there to the house. They're just finishing their season, so next year, I'll show you the tricks."

Conversation scattered from that point to stories of other recipes and Maine traditions, and soon after, Diana took the opportunity to slip from the table. She had the urge to take another look at that Crazy Quilt and see the last block her aunt had been working on.

Rose Bettinger left the others and joined her at the quilting table. "The other day, we found those old notes of your aunt's I told you about. She was writing them just before she...well, when she was working on the last block for the Crazy Quilt. I don't know what Helen did with them, but I'll ask. They weren't much besides a couple names. Margie something was one of them. And Cameron. But I'm sure you'd like to see them. And, anyway, I wanted to show you—see here, I finished blocking Bee's last piece and added it right in. Just last week, it was."

Diana had seen it just before Rose pointed it out to her. She maneuvered the large blanket so the piece was in front of her, and she squinted down at the block. Once again she recognized a pair of small fish in one corner, and brushed her fingertip over it. The snake entwined in the tree caught her attention then, and Diana scrutinized the intricate black stitches, suddenly unconvinced that it was indeed a snake in a tree. She touched that image too, and closed her eyes for a moment, and felt as if there was something just at the edge of her mind...something she should know.

A shiver scuttled down her spine. What was it about this small, six-by-six-inch piece of handiwork that stuck in her mind like a hook? Diana opened her eyes and looked again at the sun and moon and stars appliquéd and embroidered throughout the block. She knew there was something her subconscious was trying to tell her. Staring at it, she allowed her eyesight to blur as she tried to open her mind to the secrets there.

"Beautiful handiwork," Marc's smooth voice wafted near her ear. He stood very near behind her, gazing over her shoulder. "What's so interesting about this piece?"

Startled out of her reverie, Diana took a sidestep away, turning slightly to look up at him. "Nothing in particular," she said. "It was the last piece my aunt was working on before she died, and I thought...I thought it was interesting. It's such a conglomeration of things, it doesn't seem to have any rhyme or reason."

Marc looked down at the quilt, staring at the section she still held between her fingers. "Your aunt was psychic, or so she said. You don't think she meant anything by those symbols on this quilt, did she?"

Diana shrugged, surprised that he would put her own thoughts into words so easily. "I don't know what she would have had on her mind that could come out in this piece of material. After all, she had a journal—if there was something bothering her, she would most likely have written about it rather than done some cryptic symbolism in a piece of quilt."

Marc sighed. "I suppose. But it was such a romantic idea, you know." He beamed down at her and, to her surprise, brushed a manicured fingernail lightly along her cheek. "Damariscotta has been quite boring since you left, Ms. Iverson."

"I thought you said you'd been quite busy," Diana stammered, taken off-guard by his pointed comment. Since their conversation at his barbeque, she assumed he'd lost any interest he might have had in her. Either that, or the quilting ladies had made certain he knew she and Jonathan were over. Oh. They must have arranged for Marc to stop by today while she was there.

"I have been...as far as work is concerned. But on the other hand, my social life has been quite dull. I—"

"What are you two chatting about so cozily over here?" screeched Helen, pushing her way to their sides. "I saw your two heads together, as if you're plotting something without including the rest of us." Her eyes gleamed with a pleased light, and that clinched it for Diana. The old bat was definitely trying to match-make her with Marc. Well, at least that took the pressure off her trying to hide her involvement with Ethan.

"We were just chatting about all the hours of handiwork you ladies have put into this quilt," Marc lied smoothly, stepping a bit further away from Diana. "When do you think it will be done?"

His question, as it was likely intended to do so, sent Helen off on a different tangent about the trials and tribulations of arthritic fingers and cataracted eyes working on such minute stitchery. Soon, the other ladies were crowded around as well, adding their own complaints masqueraded as anecdotes.

This left Diana the opportunity to once more contemplate Aunt Belinda's last bit of quilting work. She couldn't help but remember her dreams from last night—so different from the smothering, darkling ones she'd first had upon arriving in Damariscotta. In fact, she hadn't had the dream of being smothered since receiving the results of the autopsy report. Since confirming that her dream was, in fact, real.

But last night, Diana had nocturnal visions of a quilt. She'd seen it quite clearly—wrapping around her arms and legs, smothering her and then being pulled away. And there was a snake in a tree, hissing at her, and a fish flopping helplessly at her feet...and then there were Tarot cards, scattered on the ground, blowing into her face from a big wind...and the tattered pages of an old book.

Even as she stared down at the fabric block, she couldn't peel through the murky memories and draw out whatever it was her subconscious was trying to tell her. Instead, the familiar tom-tom of an encroaching migraine began to throb in her temples and at the back of her skull.

Just what she needed to have happen here, in the midst of these busybodies.

As if honed in on their guest's very existence, Rose Bettinger asked, "Are you feeling all right, Diana? You're looking pale now."

"I'm starting to develop a terrible headache," Diana told her, "and I've found the best way to handle it is to lie down in the dark after popping a few aspirin."

"A migraine?" Marc asked, looking at her with concern.

"Likely. I have a history of them." She scanned the group, seeing Helen's pointed face sharpen as her excuses were made, and Martha Woden leaning over to Pauline, who was whispering in her ear—no doubt repeating the entire conversation for the hard-of-hearing woman.

"Let me give you a ride home," said Marc. "Migraines can be debilitating, and you don't want to be behind the wheel if that happens."

"No, thank you—I don't have far to go, and it's just beginning. I'll have plenty of time to get home and lie down."

"Are you certain?" asked Marc, suddenly behind her. "My office is closer. You could lie down there in a dark room until it passes. And I might have something stronger than what you're used to taking."

Diana picked up her pocketbook and forced a smile onto him. "Thank you for your concern, but this doesn't seem to be anything more debilitating than a regular, need-to-rest, throbbing headache. But I do appreciate your help."

"I'd feel better if you'd stop in for an exam," Marc insisted. "Some time. Any time—I'll fit you in. There are many new drugs on the market that might help."

She agreed to do so and made her escape, as she'd come to think of it, then got behind the wheel of her Lexus to drive back to Aunt Belinda's house. Popping two pills and slugging them down with a big coffee—a habit she had yet to fully break, even here in Damariscotta—she drove off through the small town to the winding, country roads that would take her home, hoping she would get to the house before the flashes of light and shadow obscured her eyesight. Her cell phone dinged and chimed, announcing text messages and voice mails that had obviously been saved up until she was in range of a tower, but she couldn't check them now.

Diana drove up the drive to the clapboard house in the nick of time, and had to fairly feel her way through the front door. The pills had kept the nausea at bay, but her head pounded and her vision was becoming increasingly shattered. The settee in the den was the closest horizontal place to rest, and she sank onto it gratefully.

Sometime later, she was awakened by something soft kneading her belly. Opening her eyes cautiously, she found herself face to face with Motto, who'd obviously decided that Diana's midriff was a good place to take a nap.

The migraine was gone, and Diana sat up gingerly, taking care not to displace the aloof feline. Doc Horner had been kind enough to keep the cats while their new mistress was in Boston, but since she'd returned, both Motto and Arty had seemed pleased to see her. At least, they'd actually made appearances when she fed them, and once Motto had actually come when Diana called.

Just then she realized someone was knocking at the front door. *Can't be Ethan.* He'd just walk in, she thought with a rush of affection and a secret smile. And besides...he wasn't due back to Damariscotta for another few days.

It could be Marc, checking up on her, she thought with a bump of irritation.

When she tried to pick up Motto to carry him with her to answer the knocking, the cat would have none of it and jumped out of her arms. As Diana came out of the den, she saw the murky impression of a man's figure through the frosted glass of the door and stopped in shock.

It looked like Jonathan. It couldn't be Jonathan.

Why would he be here in Damariscotta? And in the middle of the week?

But it was Jonathan. Diana couldn't have been more surprised when she flung open the door and found him standing on Aunt Belinda's porch. "Hi, Jonathan...what are you doing here?"

His face was weary and strained, his eyes bloodshot. There were deep grooves in his cheeks and around the nose. He looked terrible. "I tried to call you. Text you. You've been ignoring me."

Diana couldn't deny that. "So you came up from Boston to Maine because I wasn't taking your calls?" A flash of nervousness rushed through her. Was he stalking her? Erm, yes, a man who drove five hours to see a woman who was ignoring him could certainly be considered stalking her. Her insides shifted in alarm.

"I need you, Di," he said. "I needed to see you. I want you back. And I thought I'd better bring this to you." He produced a manila envelope.

She took it, aware that her body was thrumming with apprehension and anticipation, but her nervousness eased. "A letter...from Aunt Belinda?" How could a dead woman send a letter?

"I found this behind the desk in the den. I was cleaning out... after you left. It must have gotten mixed up with some junk mail, and then slid down behind the desk."

"It's postmarked the day after she died," Diana said, staring at it. The hair over her entire body seemed to be standing on end, and her nerve endings sizzled.

"I noticed that. She must have mailed it on Sunday, because she died that night," Jonathan pointed out.

"I can't believe it. But you didn't have to drive this all the way up here, Jonathan."

"I just thought you'd want it right away, since it is the last thing you have from your aunt—except for her money, of course." Jonathan's voice held a twinge of something unlikable woven in it. "And...I wanted to see you. Won't you let me come in?" He started toward the door, but she didn't move out of his way. "So we can talk?"

"Jonathan, I told you. It's over. There's no chance of us getting back together. I'm seeing someone else," she added.

He stepped back as if stung. "You're—you are?" His expression turned hard. "You don't need to lie about it, Diana."

"I'm not lying," she replied, wondering why it was so unbelievable to him that she'd found someone else. Just because she hadn't dated in years before meeting Jonathan didn't mean she was unattractive to men. It *didn't*.

"But...what about us?" he asked. "We were going to get married. I want to marry you, Diana. Please let me come in." He put his hand on the door and she felt him pushing on it.

"Jonathan," she said firmly, a little frisson of nervousness jittering through her, "you need to leave. Thank you for bringing me this letter, but you need to leave *now*."

"Diana, you're being ridiculous." Jonathan's voice was short and abrupt. "Why don't we go in and talk about this. You're a wealthy woman now, you know, and that makes you easy prey for a man. I already loved you and wanted to marry you before your aunt died," he said. "I love you, not your money."

Despite the discomfort his words caused, she was firm. "You aren't listening to me. I don't want you to—"

Her words were cut off by his sharp voice. "Diana, I didn't come all the way up here to drive back to Boston tonight. Now, please. I'm your fiancé and I have a right to be here if I want to be." He gave the door a little push and the force caused her to stagger a bit.

She gave a surprised cry. "You aren't my fiancé, and I'm telling you to leave. Now." Already, she was calculating which was closer: Uncle Tracer's rifle or the pepper spray in her purse. Just in case.

Just then, Diana caught a movement from the woods at the edge of the property. The next thing she knew, a streak of black bolted from the tall grass and bounded across the lawn. And all at once, Cady was there, on the porch, growl-barking at Jonathan.

She didn't look pleased.

Diana's heart gave a delicious little thump and she looked over, expecting Ethan to come striding out of the woods that divided their properties. But it wasn't Ethan. It was Joe Cap who came ambling into view, as if he had all the time in the world.

"Hello Cady," Diana said, crouching to greet the black lab. She did it before she realized she was actually face to face with the massive beast, close enough to those big wicked teeth that she could be grabbed by the throat with them. But Diana was so glad to see Cady that she hardly flinched when the big pink tongue swiped her across the cheek.

Once having properly greeted Diana, the dog was back on duty, sneering up at Jonathan, who'd backed away as soon as the lab clattered onto the porch. "Who's this?" he managed to say over Cady's barking. "Nice doggie."

"Hiya there Diana," said Joe Cap as he approached. His gaze went from Diana to Jonathan and back again, curious and observant. "Nice to see you back in town. Everything okay here?"

"Everything's just fine," she said, absently patting the lab on her head. "Jonathan delivered something for me, and he was just leaving."

To her relief, Jonathan took the cue and turned away. "Goodbye, Diana," he said, walking off the porch to his car.

She and Joe watched as he got in and drove away, then she said, "Any news?"

"Nope," he replied. "Sorry to interrupt," he added, glancing at her, then at the empty drive down which Jonathan had just disappeared, and then to Cady. "I took her over to Ethan's place to check up on it and she got away from me."

"You didn't interrupt," she told him, looking down at the manila envelope. A spike of nerves and excitement mixed with fear had her sounding distracted. She had to read this letter, and she wanted to read it without any further delay. "I don't mean to be rude, but I've got to take care of this," she said, flapping the envelope at him. "It's...important." Her insides were all aflutter.

"Sure," Joe said with a slow smile. "No problem. See ya at the Grille." He beckoned for Cady, who seemed uncertain about whether to stay or go. But in the end, the lab left the porch when she saw a squirrel, electing to chase it across the yard.

Diana closed the door and leaned against it, listening as Joe called Cady to follow him back into the woods. The whole incident left her upset and a little queasy. What had Jonathan been thinking? Was he really that desperate to get her back? And how convenient was it that he'd found this last letter from Aunt Belinda.

The envelope felt strangely warm and solid, much more so than its appearance and weight would permit, and Diana held it for a moment, closing her eyes, pulling it to her chest, and breathing deeply, as though she could smell the scent of Aunt Bee's lilac powder. A tear stung one eye, then suddenly, they came in torrents, unstoppable and exhausting, as Diana made her way to her favorite settee in the den.

She cried for things she knew about—for the loss of her aunt, for the years they could have had, but didn't. For the way Belinda had died, alone and helpless under someone's heavy hand, evil and malignant. She cried for the disintegration of her law practice, for the blood, sweat, and energy she'd put into it, believing that no one could take it away from her if she worked hard enough...and the way it was eroding because of one selfish, angry man.

It was a long time later when Diana opened her swollen eyes and looked around. She sat up carefully, suppressing a groan and wincing at the pounding in her head from such hard tears. Now. Now that she had all of that out of her system, she must read Aunt Belinda's last words to her.

She slid a finger under the flap and tore the envelope open.

Inside was a neatly-clipped newspaper article from the *Seattle Times* and a letter from her aunt. Diana put the article aside and unfolded the letter.

Dearest Diana—

I hope this finds you well. I am fine, but missing you, and, knowing that you are so busy that it is difficult to get away, I still hope that you will be able to come up here this summer sometime and visit with me to make up for our lost years.

I have a wonderful neighbor whom I'd like you to meet—he has been an enormous help to me around the house, and with other things that you may not yet understand. I think he might be someone you would enjoy getting to know.

I've enclosed this newspaper article because I'd like you to do some research for me and find out more about this situation of assisted suicide. I have been having some odd readings in the cards lately, and feel as though something is about to happen. If I could find out more about the people in this article, perhaps it would help. I continue to dream about it and have visions during my readings about those people who succumbed to the temptation to kill themselves.

If you learn anything at all, no matter how insignificant, please let me know so that I can put myself out of this misery!

I am sorry this note is so short. I just want to get this in the mail to you. There's something compelling me to even drive to the post office on a Sunday afternoon in order to post it. It's something that I need to do.

Take care of yourself, and I hope to see you soon. Your loving aunt Belinda.

Diana's throat tightened, its dryness painful when she swallowed, and she knew she would have cried again if she had any more fluid in her body. Instead, she could only blink sandpaper-dry eyes and gently set the letter aside, once again suppressing the ache of guilt.

She reached for the newspaper clipping.

API, Salem—Oregon's recently-approved assisted suicide statute has been exercised more than five times in the last two months, reports State Attorney General David Anthony. "There have been five deaths identified as assisted suicide by the families of the victims, or by pre-recorded videotapes taken at the scene in which the victim succumbed to the carbon monoxide poisoning used to kill them."

In each case, Anthony states, the attending physician has testified to the extent of the patient's illness, stating that it was a case of terminal illness. Doctor Cameron Darr, one of the physicians who advised and assisted at three of the suicides, spoke in defense of his patients' wishes when the family of one contested the victim's health status. "Marjorie Gaunt had just been diagnosed with bone cancer, she was terminal, and she chose to spare her family the long, drawn-out illness that would have ensued, and would absolutely have resulted in her death. She simply chose to die at a time and place, and in an environment, that suited her."

Marjorie Gaunt's family, residents of Beverly Hills, CA, and well-known for their chain of Amaretto's restaurants along the West Coast, charge that since she had just been diagnosed, Dr. Darr should have taken time to treat her before recommending that she move ahead with her plans for suicide.

"Ms. Gaunt was ill, and she did not want to experience further pain. She knew she was terminal, and she made her decision. I merely assisted her in attaining a graceful way to end her life," responds Dr. Darr.

Ms. Gaunt's son, Bradley Gaunt, has told the press that he intends to open an extensive investigation into the situation of his mother's death and, if necessary, will sue the State of Oregon to suspend Dr. Darr's medical license until the case has been resolved.

Other similar cases have been filed in states such as Michigan, where an assisted suicide statute has not been approved, but retired pathologist Jack Kevorkian has been a champion of assisted suicide. In 1999, Dr. Kevorkian was convicted of assisting a patient to commit suicide in the State of Michigan.

Diana frowned and checked the date on the article. It was more than seven years old, and the images included a picture of Marjorie Gaunt, and one of the state's Attorney General. The woman was elderly, and she was flanked by her son and daughter, the caption explained.

If Aunt Belinda held onto an article that was so outdated it was probably related to one of her psychic visions. But what did she want from Diana?

She reached for the letter, which she'd left on the table next to the chair, and reread it. Aunt Belinda had been insistent that she was bothered by (having visions and dreams was how she phrased it) people who chose to commit suicide, and she wanted Diana to do research on the people in the article. That was easy enough, but it didn't seem pressing.

After staring at the letter—holding it in her hands, as if to feel any remainder of Aunt Belinda's presence, she pulled to her feet. It was time to stop feeling sorry for herself and find out who killed her aunt, and why. She was certain, in the deepest part of her, that this letter and article had something to do with it. Aunt Belinda had sensed that something was going to happen. She just hadn't known it was her own murder.

Time to do a little research. Diana pulled out her laptop and plugged it in, waiting for it to power on. She was feeling around in the large, outside pocket for a pen when she touched the tattered binding of Aunt Belinda's journal. Starting in realization, she pulled out the book, followed by the Tarot cards that were still wrapped carefully in their mahogany box.

She hadn't looked at the Tarot cards in weeks, and she'd forgotten about the journal. All at once, she remembered the image from her dream of the old, tattered book. That looked *just* like the one in her hands. A little prickle skimmed over her, raising the hair on her arms.

I guess it's time to read a bit more of Aunt Belinda's journal. Diana flipped toward the back of the book, hoping that the last entries would give her some clues as to what was bothering her aunt when she died...and if perhaps it had anything to do with someone trying to burn her house down.

The last entry, written Sunday night—the night of her death—gave little information but a discourse on the status of her flower garden and a discussion of the quilting ladies' evening out at the Green Oaks Grille the night before. Only the last paragraph caught Diana's interest: *"I have a doctor's appointment tomorrow and expect to have the results of those tests back before I go. I'm sure it will be good news, and then I can find out what is going on. I hope that Diana gets back with me soon. Perhaps I'll call her about that little Diana-gram I sent her."*

Diana-gram. Diana gave a melancholy smile at the terminology, and sobered at the realization that Aunt Bee had expected to be given a clean bill of health at the doctor's office. How frightening that she should die by someone's hand the very night before.

Diana flipped a few pages back in the journal, skimming the entries and finding nothing of interest other than one page of rants and raves about Helen Galliday and her meddlesome ways. Apparently, Helen had tried to set Aunt Belinda up with the postman and it backfired when she found out that he hated cats.

As she glanced up from the journal, her gaze fell on the bright screen of her laptop. Diana gently put the book aside and turned her attention to finding something out about Marjorie Gaunt—a woman who wanted to die.

The keys clicked and the computer hummed as she browsed through the reams of information on the Internet, trying to find something of interest. It took awhile, but she finally found another article about Marjorie Gaunt.

API, Salem—SERIAL KILLER! ANGEL OF MERCY! Those were the opposing sentiments raised today by picketers outside the capital building in Salem. The case of Marjorie Gaunt is receiving widespread attention from parties including the American Civil Liberties Union, who supports the right to assisted suicide, and the AARP, who expresses severe concern that the elderly will be taken advantage of if this statute continues to remain in force.

The case of Marjorie Gaunt involves Dr. Cameron Darr, an oncologist who recently came under fire for a more recent assisted suicide. Gaunt's family alleges she wasn't ill enough to be diagnosed as terminal and that Dr. Darr urged her to kill herself prematurely.

Dr. Darr, who has assisted in more than five suicides in the last six months, including that of Mrs. Enid Oregon, former wife of the World Toy Emporium magnate, was unavailable for comment.

Marcus Sperka, attorney for the Gaunt family, anticipates that they will obtain enough evidence to take this case to trial by the end of the summer.

Diana took note of the name Enid Oregon—another woman who sought her own demise. She noticed that date on this article was only four months after the previous one. The picture of Marjorie Gaunt was the same, but there was another photo captioned "Cameron Darr." Diana peered at the controversial physician, who had a grainy, black-and-white countenance due to the quality of newspaper print and the limitations of her PC. He had dark hair and a full moustache, but there was something about his eyes that caught her attention. The way he looked at the camera—it was a candid shot, taken, perhaps, outside of a courtroom or at a press conference—gave her a shiver.

"I don't think I'd take *his* word for the fact that I was dying," Diana murmured aloud, reaching for another bite of the limp sandwich.

She searched a bit longer online, but found nothing new about Marjorie Gaunt. Perhaps the case had never gone to trial, or maybe the Gaunt family couldn't find the evidence it was looking for to convict Darr.

Diana closed the lid of the laptop. Weariness pulled at her, and she knew her mind was too tired to function further tonight, but then her attention fell upon the mahogany box.

She hadn't even opened it since the awful experience at Jonathan's condo, when she'd been destroyed by pain and illness. But tonight, she was drawn to the cards and she moved toward their little wooden chest as if in a dream.

She had to do it. Though exhausted beyond belief, Diana took a deep breath, steadying herself. *Aunt Belinda, if you're here... help me.*

Now was the time, she thought to herself. If she was ever going to believe that she had some kind of ability, this would have to be it. Diana closed her eyes and gingerly shuffled the oversized deck of cards, remembering what Ethan had once told her. "Open your mind, and let the images of the cards lead you on a trip through your subconscious. The pictures are only there to open doors in your mind. They mean whatever you want them to mean."

As she shuffled, a card flipped from beneath her fingers and fell to the floor. It landed face-down, and Diana stared at it for a moment, her body going hot and cold and weak all at once.

She drew in a deep breath, closed her eyes...and decided to leave it there for a while. She'd continue with her plan to deliberately choose from the deck and turn that card over only when she was finished.

Moving the errant card out of the way, she set the neatened deck on the floor. Although she wasn't sure what she was doing, Diana went with her instinct. Heart pounding, she cut the deck once to the left, and then stopped, staring at the stack of cards. A tingling in her fingers crawled up her arms and sparked in her stomach, and she knew this was the right thing to do. She didn't feel ill. She felt energized.

With a deep breath and a quick prayer, Diana reached for the deck and turned up three cards in rapid succession, laying them out in front of her.

The first card she had seen before: *Two of Swords*. It depicted a blindfolded woman holding two long swords crossed in front of her, as if to block someone or something. Diana remembered that it implied avoidance or the obstruction of emotion.

The tingling became stronger and her heart galloped in her chest as she realized that was how she'd been, how she'd previously responded to the possibility of another level to her knowledge for a very long time. *This card*, she thought in a burst of self-revelation, *shows how I was before I came to Damariscotta*.

Her heart slowed its breakneck pace to a calmer one as she looked at the second card. It was an image of a chalice overflowing with water, held by a large hand belonging to an unseen entity. A dove swept down into the cup. The caption on the card read *Ace of Cups*.

Diana knew from the times she had looked through the book on the Tarot that the suit of cups implied emotion or intuition, perhaps even love or affection. The ace of any suit was the epitome of that suit, embodying the essence of that symbol and exhibiting it in its truest, fullest form.

If the first card is the way I was, Diana thought to herself, *then perhaps this suggests how I am now. Past, present, and future.*

She looked at the card again and felt fullness. Her cup was overflowing, she was attuned, sharp, and vulnerable to her feelings at this time. Emotions had bubbled within her—warred within her—at a heightened level for the past few weeks. Her feelings for Ethan, the fear of why she'd been a target for vandalism and the break-ins, the confusion and fear over her aunt's murder, the depression from the implosion of her career...and now, the opening of her mind to accept the abilities that Belinda had understood so well.

All of these emotions swarmed over her, swamping her so that she felt exhausted and exuberant at the same time. Confused and mixed up, frightened and exhilarated by love. These forces were foreign to Diana in their strength—to she who had always prided herself on her stability and unemotional detachment to people, places, and events.

She took a deep breath, suddenly at such peace with herself that calm settled over her. *Now, the third card. The future, perhaps.*

This, too, was a card she did not recognize but could glean some meaning from its caption. *King of Wands,* it read. Diana didn't know much about the suit of wands, except that it implied creativity, energy, and action. The wands were equated with the element of fire, which was a forceful, bold entity. The king himself sat on an ornate throne, holding a wand as a staff.

Diana stared at the card, trying to equate the persona of the king with something that could happen or be a part of her future. The king could symbolize a person—one who exhibited those energetic, forceful characteristics...or it could mean she would attain or experience an atmosphere of drama or daring...or, even, that she herself was symbolized by the energetic persona of the king.

She shook her head, still looking at the King of Wands, wondering what it could mean.

After a long moment, she came back to herself, back to the floor where she sat cross-legged. Her eyes lit on the fourth card, the one that had fallen from the deck while she was shuffling.

With a deep breath, she reached for it. Flipped it over. And saw *Death*.

Now, she shivered as a blast of cold air rushed over her, and that same black wave of terror she'd felt at Jonathan's threatened to encompass her.

No, not again. No...

She fought, focused on the Ace of Cups, turning her mind sharply, firmly from the image of Death. *I won't succumb this time.* She focused, meditated, prayed, hypnotized herself with the picture of the overflowing Cup, curling her fingers around solid objects: the edge of the piecrust table, the cushion of the settee.

And all at once, Motto appeared, jumping up onto the sofa next to her. He butted against her leg and side with his warm, furry body. Then he looked at her with blue eyes and sat next to her, large and warm and *alive*, twitching his tail as she came back to herself.

Smiling, victorious, she gathered the feline into her arms. And he let her.

—⚡—

Diana woke in the middle of the night, sitting bolt upright in her bed.

Cameron Darr.

Marc Reardon.

Cameron Darr was Marc Reardon.

The names were merely rearrangements of the letters—anagrams. *Dianagrams!* Of course. How could she have missed such an obvious thing?

Scrambling out of bed, Diana fumbled for the lamp and turned it on. She sat on the edge of the mattress, breathing as if she'd been running and running.

Queasiness grew in the pit of her stomach. Aunt Belinda had known what she was doing when she sent her that article. But was it true—was Marc really Cameron Darr? And if he was, what was he doing in Damariscotta, using a different name?

The possible explanations were obvious: he had changed his identity and disappeared to escape the lawsuit, or had just moved away to start anew after being accused of murdering Marjorie Gaunt. Diana knew how much damage even a minor malpractice lawsuit could do to a physician's practice—she wouldn't blame him if he'd decided to relocate and start over again. Many doctors had been forced to do so.

Now, the question was whether the fact that Marc Reardon was probably Cameron Darr had anything to do with Aunt Belinda's murder. To what lengths would he—or anyone—go to keep a changed identity a secret?

Diana thought the answer wasn't too difficult: if he'd changed identities illegally, he'd probably go to any length. If not, then the two facts were probably not related. So far as she knew from the cursory research she'd done, Cameron Darr had only been accused of assisting Marjorie Gaunt in a premature death—and she'd found nothing that indicated he'd been brought to trial. So, then, perhaps he'd just settled the case, then moved across the country to escape the bad publicity.

But why was Belinda seeing two doctors?

That thought came from nowhere. Diana turned it over in her mind for a moment. She needed to find out the name of the physician in Portland, and then perhaps she'd know the answer. Of course, she could ask Marc if he'd referred Belinda...but for some reason, she didn't like that option.

I'll look in the phone book tomorrow and see if I can find the doctor's name.

She crawled back into bed, pulling the light goose down comforter over her in protection against the chill Maine night. Diana turned out the light and willed herself to sleep.

—⁓—

Diana was up and dressed by seven o'clock—an unusual feat for her while in Damariscotta. Her dreams had been filled with warped images of snakes climbing trees, and newspaper clippings...along with a grinning, half-illuminated Marc and an angry Jonathan standing on her porch. Aunt Belinda had made an appearance, beckoning with her wrinkled hand toward some unfamiliar room, and, of course, the Tarot cards had fluttered onto the scene, lightly batting at her arms and face.

As she flipped through the Portland area phone book looking for the phone number for Aunt Bee's Portland doctor, Diana found the answer to another question.

She drew in her breath sharply. The name of Aunt Bee's physician was Clancy Harbaugh...and he had a small, block advertisement on the page with a symbol that could be mistaken for a snake climbing a tree if it were clumsily embroidered on a quilt block. It was a caduceus—the symbol for the medical profession—and she stared at it, kicking herself for not recognizing it from Aunt Belinda's amateur stitches.

She thought again about the quilt block that had bothered her. Now she knew that at least part of it had to do with a physician...and as she mulled over the rest of the images, she guessed that the Pisces symbol was an indication of someone's birthday—perhaps Marc Reardon/Cameron Darr's. The stars and moon meant nothing to her; but it was possible, Diana realized, that they indicated some astrological sign. At any rate, she felt she knew enough to make a phone call to Clancy Harbaugh, and then, perhaps to pay a visit to Marc to see what she could learn on the sly. Maybe there'd be something in his office—a diploma, for example, that would help her identify him. Or something that indicated he'd lived in Oregon. Then, if she thought things were making sense, she'd head directly to Joe Cap's office and tell him her suspicions.

And she'd call Ethan when she was in town and had service on her cell phone.

When she called Dr. Harbaugh, she explained who she was and used her reputation as a malpractice attorney to gain access to the physician himself. Within five minutes of conversation with him, she learned that Aunt Belinda had not been referred by Marc Reardon, and that she'd come to the doctor in Portland for a second opinion on a diagnosis. *And* that her Aunt Belinda had been in perfect health.

Diana's heart bumped in her chest as she allowed the receiver to slip back into its cradle. Marc Reardon had misdiagnosed her aunt. And Aunt Belinda had known it.

Diana walked briskly along Main Street. She clutched her handbag to her body, trying to contain her nerves. *It's just a doctor's appointment*, she told herself firmly. Marc had told her to stop by to see him about her migraines, and she'd decided to take him up on it in hopes that she'd have the chance to peek at Aunt Belinda's medical records, and perhaps find something else that could confirm her suspicions. Then, she could go to the police.

She passed the ladies' quilt shop on her way to Marc's little cottage office, and almost stopped in to let them know where she was going...just in case. But the sign on the door said 'Closed' and she was forced to walk on by.

A block further down, she turned onto the short, neat sidewalk that led up to the office. When she opened the door to go in, she saw a pleasant-looking receptionist on the other side of a desk and Diana relaxed. She didn't have anything to be nervous about.

"Hi, I have a noon appointment with Dr. Reardon," she told the woman.

"Ah, yes, Diana Iverson, Belinda's niece? Dr. Reardon told me to make sure I fit you in if you called, even during the lunch hour if necessary." She smiled to reveal two chipmunk-sized teeth with a quarter-inch space between them. "Dr. Reardon asked that you fill out these new patient forms, and he'll be with you as soon as possible."

Diana took the clipboard and perched on one of the wicker chairs in the waiting room to complete the paperwork. She was just finishing when the receptionist came out from behind the desk, carrying her purse. When Diana looked up at her inquiringly, the woman explained, "Got to run out for lunch today, dearie. But don't you worry—Dr. Reardon is almost finished with his last patient. Patty's in there with him and she'll come out for you when he's done."

"Patty's the nurse?" Diana asked, feeling a bit nervous.

"Oh, yes," called the receptionist as she bustled out the door.

Diana gave a small sigh of relief, then silently berated herself for her nerves. What was going to happen to her in a doctor's office in the middle of town?

With the receptionist gone, though, this was as good a time as any to try to take a look at her aunt's medical records. Diana rose slowly from her chair, and, carrying the clipboard, slipped through the door to the back room. If anyone came in, she'd say she made a mistake on the forms and was looking for a new one. That, she thought, was as good an excuse as any—and if anyone caught her, it would likely be Patty.

It took only a quick moment to ascertain that Belinda Lawry's medical records were not filed with the rest of Dr. Reardon's patients. No sooner had Diana learned this than she heard approaching footsteps and she hurried back into the waiting area. She was just in time to be found examining the quilt that hung on the wall when the door opened.

"Diana!" Marc's smooth voice caused her to start and turn. "I'm so glad you decided to take me up on my offer. Come on back."

"Hello," she smiled. "Thank you for seeing me on such short notice—and on your lunch hour, too."

"Not a problem—never a problem for Belinda's niece. We'll be in the last examining room on the left. I'll be there in just one moment."

Diana looked in vain for signs of the nurse Patty but could hear no one else in the office. She went into the examining room a bit reluctantly and found that she was too nervous to sit on the table. Instead, she looked out the window and tried to relax.

The click of the door opening behind caused her to whirl. "I'm sorry, Diana, but it's going to be just the two of us. My nurse has gone to lunch already." He shut the door behind him without turning.

When Diana looked at him, she knew he knew. The flare of understanding must have shown in her eyes, for Marc's austere face cracked into a chill smile.

"Ah, you've figured it out, then." He stepped closer to her and Diana tried to move out of his way, frantically looking for something with which to fend him off. The countertops were cleared of anything she might use as a weapon.

Marc chuckled. "Come now, Diana, you don't think I'm that foolish, do you?" With a swift movement, he snared her arm and yanked her so hard that she stumbled and hit her head against the storage cabinet.

"What are you doing?" she managed to gasp as he imprisoned both of her arms behind her, pulling up on her elbows with such violence that she cried out in surprised pain.

A cloth-covered hand groped at her face and she struggled to kick backward at him, to avert her nose and mouth from the sick, sweet scent of the drug, to shrug out of his grip.

"Couldn't you have left well enough alone?" he said breathlessly as he struggled to subdue her. "Wasn't the money from your aunt enough?"

"Why are you doing this?" she asked desperately, knowing she was losing the battle. The cloth found her nose and mouth and his fingers pinched into her face as he held her immobile.

"I have no choice," he said in that cultured voice. "You would upset my apple cart too much to let this pass."

The scent was sweet and cloying, clogging her nostrils and drying the inside of her mouth. Diana gave one last futile twist even as she felt her body weaken, succumbing to the numbing sleep forced upon her. Everything went dimmer, then dark, then black.

THIRTEEN

DIANA BECAME AWARE OF VOICES and felt herself being lifted and moved. Jolted, none-too-gently, and then all at once she was falling.

She managed to peel her eyes open as she landed on the edge of a sofa, then weakly rolled off onto the floor. As she struck ground, she noticed the rug with a shock of recognition and lifted her throbbing head to look around.

Aunt Belinda's den. She'd been dumped carelessly onto the settee on which she'd spent so many hours.

"Well, look who's returned to the living," said a familiar voice.

Diana looked up to see Marc Reardon smiling down at her with a thin-lipped, supercilious expression. The room tilted and spun, and her muscles felt like jelly, but she dragged herself up, using the settee as a brace. He watched in amusement as she crawled with agonizing slowness onto the narrow sofa, and sat, clutching its arm.

"What …" she tried to speak, but her mouth was so dry she couldn't even swallow. What had he drugged her with? And how long ago had it been? From what she could see, daylight still streamed in through the windows of the den.

"What am I doing? What am I going to do with you? What are we doing here? Which very unimaginative question shall I start with?" he said mockingly. "I thought you might have been able to do better than that. Perhaps something like…how did I connect with my partner in crime?"

Diana shook her head in confusion, but any coherent thought she might have had was caught in the cobwebs of the drug. Then she heard noises from the kitchen.

She and Reardon weren't alone. But who was with him? Something icy slipped down her spine and her heart began to pound. Who was it?

She must have formed the question with her lips, for Reardon's eyebrows shot up in disbelief. "Do you mean to say, you haven't figured it out? I thought for certain …." He smiled with genuine humor. "You aren't as smart as I thought you were, Diana darling. You obviously figured me somehow—it was written all over your face when you walked into my office today. I'm not sure how you ever got to be so good at hiding your thoughts in court—for I understand that you are, indeed, quite an excellent attorney. It's a shame I didn't know you back in Oregon, or it might never have come to this. I don't really care for Maine, you see," he said, settling conversationally on the edge of the settee next to her. "I much prefer the cosmopolitan cities and the lifestyle they offer. But here I am, stuck in this tiny little shit-town because Marjorie Gaunt's son got too damn suspicious and I had to disappear."

Diana could hear a low voice from the kitchen; it sounded as if someone was speaking urgently on a telephone. She couldn't even tell the gender of the speaker, let alone discern the words. "Who is it?" she managed to croak out, glancing in that direction.

"Oh, let's not do that quite yet, shall we?" Reardon said with a smile. "Let's talk about other things first. I'd like you to fully understand my position and where I was before I met up with my partner. That will make it all the more delicious when you see who it is, darling Diana."

She glanced around, looking for a chance to escape, but she knew her legs wouldn't hold her. And even if they did, he'd catch her before she got far. And so she swallowed again, hard, trying to think, trying to clear her mind. But her thoughts buzzed like a swarm of flies, confused and random, and in the end all she could do was listen as the megalomaniac continued to speak.

"I made quite a lot of money back in Oregon," he was saying. "Getting rich ladies to pay me loads of money to help them into a dignified, painless death—all before they lost their hair and memory and succumbed to the intense pain I told them would be inevitable. I didn't want them to suffer like that, the poor darlings. Most of them weren't even terminal, but they believed me and allowed me to help them end their lives on their own terms, in their own ways. And then Marjorie's son got suspicious, and I had the DA and then the Attorney General looking at all of my records...and so I knew it was time to disappear. Not that I'd done anything wrong—they couldn't really pin anything on me. After all, it was suicide. I just provided the tools. And the motivation." He smiled calmly.

"I'd intended to go to Costa Rica," he continued, "but I wasn't able to get a good enough fake passport for Marc Reardon. And so here I am. On the opposite coast in a little po-dunk town, and hating every minute of it."

He smoothed the starched shirt he wore, adjusting his monogrammed cuffs and frowned. "I began to get bored with General Practice about two months after I got here and decided it would be best if I could find a way to leave the country as I'd originally intended. But there's not a lot of money to be had here in Damariscotta, except from a few wealthy individuals. And so I began to diagnose a few cancer cases and one terrible aneurysm that was ready to pop at any moment. And then I got to know your aunt. She had a lot of money. She was elderly. If she had a heart attack, no one would think anything of it—especially if I had already been treating her for heart disease. All I had to do was charm her into changing her will. And that shouldn't be hard, since her closest relative was a career woman in Boston who had neglected her for years. Or I could somehow attach myself to said relative."

The rumbling voice from the kitchen had ceased speaking, and now Diana heard footsteps coming from that direction. Her stomach curdled with fear and apprehension as Reardon caught her gaze and gave her an arch smile.

"My partner is about to assuage your curiosity, darling," he said.

But she wasn't listening, for he'd already walked into the den.

Diana couldn't breathe. Her vision flashed dark, then bright, and then she went numb. Hardly aware of her fingers digging into the settee's upholstery, she felt her entire world falling away, caving in around her.

"Or," Reardon was saying with a smile, "I could find the man the heiress was going to marry."

"Jonathan," Diana managed to whisper.

He stood over her, wearing an expression she'd never seen before. It was calm and yet laced with chagrin at the same time. Almost as if he were embarrassed or ashamed to be here—but not enough to change his mind.

"Christ, Reardon, this isn't a damned movie recap," Jonathan said, running a hand through his hair. "This is business and we don't have a lot of time for chatting. Let's finish this up so I can get back to Boston. I'm supposed to be in New York and my office keeps calling me. Damned cell phones don't work up here."

"What are you doing here?" Diana managed to say, anger and pain forcing the words out clearly. "Are you really involved with this, Jonathan?"

His smile was weak but his eyes cold. "I needed the money, Diana. I thought after we were married I'd have access to whatever I needed—or, if worst came to worst, something could happen to you so I'd inherit. I didn't really want it to go that way, but I don't have any more time. No more choice. If I don't pay the money, or at least prove I have access to it in three days, I'm dead."

Diana shook her head hard and seemed to dislodge some of the remnants of fog. "Money? To who?"

"Gambling," Reardon interrupted. "Your fiancé has a terrible gambling habit. He's in deep, past his elegant ears, and he's borrowed so much that there isn't any more to borrow. Now his benefactors are getting impatient, and they need funds. What? You didn't know he gambled?"

She shook her head blankly, simply unable to assimilate what was happening. Impossible. It just couldn't be. "But...how did you—"

"How did we meet up? That's the amazing, serendipitous part about it," Reardon said congenially. "It was at a convention, about a year ago. In Vegas, of course," he added, glancing at Jonathan, who had the grace to look away. "He was commiserating about his bad luck at the blackjack table, and I happened to be listening. One thing led to another and I mentioned I hated living in Damariscotta, and he recognized the name of the town. Apparently, you'd just recently met but hadn't started to date, or somehow he knew about your connection here. From that initial conversation, we managed to put everything together—even to get your aunt in touch with you again, just by accident. All by accident." He smiled, so very pleased with himself. "And of course, with a large inheritance on the horizon, your friend Jonathan became very motivated to get you locked in with a wedding ring."

Diana actually curled her fingers into a fist and would have punched him in his supercilious face if Jonathan hadn't been looking out the window and made a sudden noise of alarm.

"What is it?" Reardon asked, and Diana stiffened, ready to use the distraction as an opportunity to escape.

But she'd barely had the thought when Jonathan moved suddenly, out of view of the window, and all at once there was a silver gun pointing at her. A *gun!* "It's your new boyfriend. What's his name—Tannock. He's just pulling up the driveway."

Diana's heart leaped—he was two days early!—and then at the same time, it plummeted, leaving her cold and shaken. Oh, God, what if he walked into the house? Which was just what he would do. He'd walk right into this.

No, Ethan, no ....

She tried to think of a way to warn him, but the other two had moved into action. The gun didn't waver from its focus on her, and Jonathan's expression told her he wasn't feeling ashamed at all at the moment. "Don't make a sound. Don't move."

"I know how to get him out of here," Reardon was saying. "He's not going to want to see her with anyone else—everyone in town knows his first wife screwed him over."

"I can't be seen here," Jonathan said sharply. "And your car is out there because I drove here in hers." He turned a tight smile on Diana. "You'd better do exactly as I say, or your boyfriend's going to be the next casualty."

She heard the slam of a car door as Jonathan dragged her out of the den, ignoring her stumbling feet and weak knees, into Belinda's bedroom. He shoved her toward the bed and she fell onto it. "Make it good, Diana. Put a little effort into it for once. Or I'll put one of these into your boyfriend's head."

She was shaking and still weak from the drug, but she watched as Jonathan slipped behind the long curtains across the room. She could see the barrel of the gun between the curtain and the wall, aimed right at the open bedroom door. He'd have a perfect shot at Ethan.

Reardon had unbuttoned his shirt and slid onto the bed next to her just as she heard Ethan calling from the front. "Diana?"

He'd wonder about Marc Reardon's car being parked out there next to hers. And he'd walk in.

And then she couldn't think of anything else as Reardon yanked her shirt open. Buttons scattered and the next thing she knew, her bra was unfastened and he was pulling her on top of him in a straddle position.

"Make it look good, darling," he murmured, sliding a hand up and over her shoulder while another held her firmly at the hips. "Lean down and kiss me like the little slut you are."

"Diana?" Ethan's voice was closer, sharper, and then she heard the front door open...and close. Footsteps. "Diana!"

She was cold and shaking, and she looked over at Jonathan. He caught her eyes from behind the curtains and she saw the cold determination in his face. Swallowing hard, she placed her hand on Reardon's bare chest and as those steps came closer, she closed her eyes and bent forward.

"Don't worry," Reardon murmured, "I'm just as revolted as you are." Nevertheless, a warm hand slid down over her breast and gave her nipple a sharp tweak. She gasped in surprise and pain and then his eyes became slits. "Make it good, Diana."

She swallowed back the rush of nausea and revulsion and moved closer, forcing her mouth to touch his. He kissed her back, his lips dry and smooth and she nearly gagged, but didn't move away.

The footsteps stopped abruptly. She heard a sound in the doorway—something guttural and low and agonized, and she couldn't control herself. She jolted upright, turning to look. Reardon released her, but it was too late.

Ethan was gone.

The front door slammed, the house shaking in its wake.

She heard the squealing, grinding of a key turned too far in the truck's engine, then the terrible pealing sound as Ethan sped away down the stone drive.

And then Diana was left alone with two murderers.

—⁄⁄⁄—

Ethan felt nothing.

He slowed the crazy careening of his truck to one of a normal speed and drove up to his cabin. He kept his mind blank. He couldn't feel his fingers or his legs.

Hell. Cady wasn't even here to greet him, to comfort him. She was still with Joe Cap.

Ethan had come to see his other lady first thing on his arrival. And look what changing his loyalties had gotten him. Look what the thought of surprising her had done.

He slammed the door of the truck a little harder than necessary and let himself into the cabin. Closed the exterior door with a bit too much force.

He walked into the living room, into the kitchen, yanked out the bottle of Scotch he kept on hand, and poured himself a nice healthy drink. And then he stared down into the golden liquid, realized his hands were shaking and he felt like puking, and whipped the glass across the room.

It shattered against the fireplace with a short, vehement sound.

How the hell could this happen to me again? *What the hell have I ever done to deserve this?*

God, Diana. How could he have been so wrong about her?

When he found out about Jenny, he'd drunk himself into a stupor for a few nights. He'd been enraged. He'd been sleepless. Then he'd gone on a revenge bender, hitting the bars and taking a different woman home each time.

But this time, he felt nothing. Hollow, empty, numb.

He wasn't going to fall apart this time. He was going to be cool with it. He was going to handle it.

The phone rang and he couldn't bring himself to answer it. He stood, arms hanging loosely at his sides, listening as the ringer bleeped and then his answering machine came on.

"Ethan. Got your text. Don't worry about picking up Cady tonight. We'll keep her until you get here. Have fun." Joe Cap's voice had a bit of a sly tone to it and Ethan suddenly wanted to fling the answering machine across the room.

But he was good. He was cool. He could handle this.

The answering machine disconnected with a short beep and he walked aimlessly into the living room. Picked up the remote control with shaking fingers. Turned it on. Swallowed the ball of concrete that settled in his throat. Fought back the desire to puke.

The phone rang again.

Ethan turned off the TV. Dropped the remote. And listened to the rings, his greeting once more, and then Joe Cap's voice came on. "Me again. Wanted you to know there was an incident yesterday at Diana's house. Her boyfr—her ex-boyfriend was there and it didn't look very cozy. She seemed upset. I made sure he left. Just thought you should know."

Yeah. She was probably really upset that Wertinger might see her with Reardon.

A sudden thought seized Ethan. An ugly, uncomfortable one.

If she was seeing Reardon, everyone in town would know.

They'd all know Ethan had been screwed over again. Cuckolded. What a stupid word. Cuckolded.

Hell. Even Joe would know. God. And Helen Galliday. Aw, Christ.

And the last thing Ethan wanted was pity.

Which meant he couldn't hide here and sulk. He had to go out and act like nothing happened. Like it had been a mutual thing. Like he didn't give a flying fuck.

He rubbed his eyes, unwilling to acknowledge that the dampness there was related to grief and pain. Nope. Ethan Tannock had no reason for tears.

FOURTEEN

I T TOOK EVERY OUNCE OF FORTITUDE Ethan possessed to walk into the Grille. It was after eight on a Thursday evening, but late enough in the tourism season that it wasn't overly crowded—a fact for which he was immensely grateful. But that, of course, meant not only would it be filled with regulars, it would also be easier to notice anyone else who might come in— Diana and Reardon, for example.

He felt ill at the thought of seeing them here together, but he told himself to buck up. As was his habit, he strolled to the bar and taking a seat at the counter he waited for a bustling Mirabella to notice him. She was wearing aqua and orange today, and her hair was back to a spun gold bouffant. She slid a couple plates in front of customers at the other end of the bar then pivoted and saw him.

"Ethan, honey, what's wrong?" She was at his end of the counter in a millisecond.

He blinked and forced an easy smile. "Nothing's wrong, Bella. Everything's great. Just got in from Princeton and knew I had to come here right away to get fed." He patted his stomach and tried to look hungry.

"Don't lie to me, young man," she said flatly. "I've never seen you look like this. Did someone die?" she asked, her voice going soft and empathetic.

Did someone die? Pretty much. But he just shook his head, suddenly not trusting himself to speak. Christ. What a mess.

Bella seemed to understand and she didn't say another word as she snagged a heavy mug and pulled the lever to fill it with Blue Moon. Setting it in front of him, she turned to holler back into the kitchen, "Tommy! Get your buns out here!"

Ethan took a drink and his stomach rebelled, so he made it a short sip and put the glass down. *Just great. I can't get plastered either.*

Just as Tommy came out of the back, wiping his meaty hands on a stained white apron, the door to the restaurant opened and the quilting ladies flooded in. *Oh Christ. What next?*

Ethan tried to look unobtrusive, but Tommy and Bella were standing on the other side of the counter (she was telling him about Ethan looking like hell—as if he weren't sitting there, looking like hell) and of course Helen Galliday wasn't about to let a conversation go uninterrupted.

She stomped over, her cane working furiously, shouting as she came. "Ethan Tannock! You're back two days early," she said in accusation. "What are you doing here?"

"I came to eat," he managed to say. "What do you think?"

Helen wagged her head in clear irritation. "That's a pile of bunk if I ever heard one. Look at you, you look like you're gonna hork all over the place if'n anyone put something edible in front of you. Martha! Rose!" she screeched across the room. "What're you waitin' for? Get over here! We've got problems. I tol' you we had problems. And where the blazes is Pauline when I need her? Playing her danged Scrabble game, I allow," Helen complained.

Ethan would have found her use of the slang term amusing if he hadn't actually *felt* like horking. As it was, he could do nothing but try to smile and brush off the questions from Tommy and Bella as the other ladies gathered around him in a cloud of rosewater and polyester.

What was it again that he liked about Damariscotta? It sure as hell wasn't the privacy.

"Where's Diana?" asked blind old Martha Woden, peering around the restaurant as if the woman might materialize at any moment.

Something must have shown in his face, for Bella's hand slammed down over his on the counter. "Where's Diana?" she asked, looking sharply at him.

Damn. He'd never seen the resemblance between her and his middle school English teacher, but he did now. "Why would I know?" he replied, eyeing the tall Blue Moon with a combination of trepidation and desire.

"What d'you mean, why would you know?" Helen latched onto that like a teen-ager with a *Penthouse* centerfold. Her beady eyes were right there, boring into Ethan's. As the other ladies moved in closer, he felt as if he'd been cornered by a herd of feral cats. "You and she've been bonking each other for more'n a month now, ain't you? Don't tell me you've done something stupid and got her all mad at you."

So much for playing it cool. "I just saw her," he said flatly. His voice was way rough. "With Marc Reardon."

"She was talking to Dr. Reardon?" Martha asked querulously, peering at him from behind her glasses. "About her headaches?"

"I don't think they were talking," Bella said grimly. She hadn't released Ethan's hand and now she patted it comfortingly. "Drink up, hon. There's another one waitin' for you when you're ready." Then she spun to Tommy. "Damn good thing I never caught you with your hand down Felicia Nooney's shirt, baby, or you'd be regretting the loss of me to this very day."

"You know damn well I never had my hand down her shirt. I was too afraid of you." But Tommy's booming laugh sounded hollow and he slapped his wife on the ass. "Gotta get back in the kitchen. Send him in to me if he needs to talk to a man," he added with a bracing look at Ethan.

"What do you mean you saw her with Dr. Reardon?" Helen shouted into his ear. "Doing what?" Her mouth had tightened into a small, wrinkled **O** and for once, her cane wasn't moving.

"I saw her. With. Reardon. *With* him," Ethan added for emphasis. "And they weren't talking. At all." He blocked the image of a half-dressed Diana straddling the lean, handsome doctor, her hand on his bare chest, him murmuring something up into her ear. *Don't fucking go there.*

"That's impossible," Helen screeched. "Are you saying they were—*bonking*?"

"Shut up, Helen," Bella snapped, looking as angry as Ethan had ever seen her. "Can't you tell he's miserable? For once, just keep your thoughts—"

"Now listen here, missy," Helen said, her eyes flashing as she thrust her chin belligerently at Mirabella. "You just be quiet for one minute and let me say something—"

"You've said quite enough already," Bella fumed. "Now if you don't go sit over at your table and leave off Ethan here, I'm going to—"

"But isn't Dr. Reardon *gay*?" Martha said in a stage whisper.

Ethan spun to look at her as Helen cried in triumph, "That's just what I was trying to tell you, if you hadn't been flapping your jaws! Marc Reardon is as gay as the Maine winter is cold. There's no way on this side of the grass he was doing what you thought he was doing. He wouldn't touch Diana. You, maybe," she added with an arch look at Ethan, "but not a woman. Something else is going on here," she said, shaking an arthritic finger at him. "I've suspected him all along. And we've gotta do something. Or I think your Diana is gonna be in some kind of trouble."

And her cane started moving again. "Give me the phone, Mirabella," she ordered, and held out her claw-like hand. "I got an idea."

—⁓—

Bound with ace bandages to a chair in Aunt Bee's kitchen, Diana already knew she was in trouble. It was the way Jonathan kept looking at her, with an expression that made her go even colder than she already was.

She'd managed to pull her ruined shirt back on when they forced her out of the bedroom—"This place gives me the creeps," Jonathan had said, looking around the room—and into the kitchen. But her blouse had no buttons and it sagged open as she sat with her wrists tied to the arms of the chair, and her ankles fixed to its legs.

"What do you want from me?" she asked. "What are you going to do?"

"Ah, are we back to this inane interrogation again?" Reardon asked. "I'll give you three guesses, and the first two don't count." He smiled, adjusting the cuffs of the shirt he'd rebuttoned.

"Stop with the games," Jonathan snapped. "I assume you read the letter from your aunt," he said, looking at her. "What did it say? Did it mention me?"

"Do you mean you didn't read it yourself?" Diana retorted. "You kept it long enough."

"Ah, she's got some spirit back," Reardon said with approval. "That's good. That'll keep things a little more interesting." Just then a soft buzzing sound made him clap his hand to his waist. He pulled his beeper free and looked at it. "Damn. An emergency. Not good timing. Or...maybe it is," he said, with a quick glance at Jonathan. "I'll have an alibi and you're not supposed to be here in town. You can take care of this all while I'm gone, after it gets too dark for anyone to see the smoke. This *is* good." He reached for the ugly black phone and dialed a number.

Diana opened her mouth to scream but saw the gun in Jonathan's hand again. "I suggest you remain silent for the time being."

Moments later, Reardon hung up the phone, looking annoyed. "Chest pains presenting up at the Grille. Probably indigestion, with the greasy food they serve there. I hope to hell it's Helen Galliday," he added with a sneer. "I'll give her a hand and make sure it's fatal. I was going to diagnose her with ALS, but this would be better." He laughed. "I'll make an appearance and be back later, when it's dark. Maybe you can get her to tell you where Belinda's journal is. Or anything else incriminating."

"If you'd found it the *multiple* times you searched before, we wouldn't have to burn the damn place down," Jonathan said.

Reardon left, whistling jauntily, and Jonathan turned to Diana. "Well," he said, sitting at the table across from her. His eyes traveled down over her gaping shirt. "This is a little awkward."

She bit out a short, sharp laugh. "Really? Is that all you have to say?"

"I didn't intend for things to happen this way," he said, real sincerity in his voice. "But at this point, I have no choice."

"You keep saying that, but you always have a choice, Jonathan," she said, trying not to sound too desperate. But she was. Desperate. What was going to happen when it was dark? Was there any way to reason with him? He wasn't a killer; she knew it. He was just...misguided. Frightened.

"No, I'm afraid I don't. The mob's going to kill me, and Merkovitz is tight with them, too. Your dumping his case made things very difficult for me. Either way, I have neither the desire to die nor to spend the rest of my life in prison for first-degree murder."

"You killed Aunt Belinda?" she whispered. "I thought...I assumed it was Marc."

"I came up for a little visit under the guise of getting to know my fiancée's closest relative and planning a surprise visit for you, and after a nice cup of tea, I sneaked back later that night and introduced her to a cloth with chloroform and a pillow. She didn't fight...much." He gave a little shudder. "Being back in that room today wasn't the best experience, but what's done is done." He shrugged. "I'm really sorry that you're going to have to go as well, Diana."

She shook her head, fear causing nausea to burn the back of her throat. "Let me go, Jonathan. That'll help you get a plea deal. I'll talk to the D.A. This was all Reardon's idea, his plan, his direction—you were frightened and in danger and you felt you had no choice but to comply. He was blackmailing you, I'm sure. And—"

"That's a nice idea, but, no, that's not how it's going to go. Even a plea deal, even if I give them Cameron Darr, will put me in prison for years. It's first-degree murder. No, I've got a better idea. Thanks to Reardon's quick thinking, and your boyfriend's eyewitness report, when they find your burned body next to Marc Reardon, it'll look like an electrical fire caught two trysting lovers off-guard in the middle of the night. Then I won't have to worry about Reardon rolling over on me and getting his own deal. And... when they figure out that Reardon is Cameron Darr, and that you dumped me for him, it'll be clear that the two of you helped your aunt to an early death. And why."

Diana was shaking her head. "It'll never work. You're crazy, Jonathan." Her heart was pounding out of control now.

He was smiling and shook his head. "There was nothing in the letter from your aunt that incriminated me? That was a miscalculation on my part. I was concerned—well, she was a psychic. I thought maybe she'd put some sort of message in there, in whatever she was calling a Diana-gram, that told you to beware of me or something. I saw her post the letter after I left her house for the tea. And of course, I did read it when it first arrived at home."

"So it was Reardon who was breaking in? Who cut my tires and graffitied the house? He was looking for Aunt Bee's journal. For her notes about what she'd learned."

"Yes, of course. I couldn't do that from Boston."

"But you're not even going to get Aunt Belinda's money now, Jonathan," she said, unable to keep the desperation from her voice. "It'll all be for naught."

"Oh, that's not true. I have it all worked out. When we got engaged, you made a will naming me your heir. And even though you're with Reardon now, you haven't gotten around to changing it."

"But I didn't …." Her voice trailed off as she saw the truth in his eyes. "But no one will believe …."

He was shaking his head. "Silly, Diana. Of course I had it notarized and witnessed. It helps," he added with a sly smile, "having a notary in the office. One who leaves her seal in a locked drawer every night. In a desk to which all the partners have a key."

She swallowed and tried pulling at the bandages holding her arms in place. "So you're going to double-cross Marc when he comes back here? How are you going to do that?"

Jonathan's smile was bland. "Don't worry your pretty head about it. If he's not back before dark, I'll take care of him later. You, my dear, and the contents of this house, are the priority." Now his glance turned speculative and she felt his attention skim back over her half-covered torso again. "We do have some time to kill until the sun goes down. What do you think—for old times' sake, hmm, Diana?" He reached and slipped his hand under her shirt.

She flinched and jolted, trying to move away from his questing, pinching, stroking fingers. Nausea roiled and surged inside her. "Don't," she cried, twisting in her chair.

Then all at once he swore sharply and pulled away, bending down to look at the floor. "Damn cat," he said furiously, kicking under the table.

A streak of white zipped out of the room and when Jonathan's hand returned to view, she saw that there was blood on it. Quite a bit of blood. He wiped his hand off and turned back to Diana. "Now, where were we?" He stood, his hands on the sides of the chair, and bent toward her. She was helpless to do anything but struggle against her bonds as he slipped his hands down over her breasts. Despair had her heart pounding and her skin going clammy with revulsion.

"Sonofabitch!" he exclaimed, jerking away once more. "What the—" He looked around furiously. "Damn cats. I'm going to—" He kicked again with such violence that he nearly lost his balance.

This time, it was Arty who sauntered out from beneath the table. He definitely sauntered, rather than streaked, and as Jonathan lunged at him, the feline leaped quickly and easily onto the kitchen table. When Jonathan went to knock the beast off, Arty hissed and swiped at him with a paw.

"Dammit," he swore. Four bright red streaks colored the back of his hand. "I ought to blow your head off you little shit." He'd barely got the words out when he hopped back with another cry of pain. Motto darted from beneath the table and launched himself onto the kitchen counter.

He sat there next to the telephone, and Arty remained on the table, and they stared at Jonathan with unblinking eyes. "Stop that," he said to them. "You're giving me the creeps."

But of course, they didn't move. They just stared.

Every time Jonathan made a move toward her, or once when he tried to drag her out of the room, one or both of the cats jumped at him. They were much too agile and speedy for him to catch, and their claws and teeth were sharp. And when they weren't attacking him, they sat and watched. And watched.

If Diana wasn't so worried about what would come next, she would have laughed.

As it was, she tried not to think about what the setting sun would bring. It was low, and casting long shadows across the lawn.

—⁂—

Ethan and Joe Cap were behind the double swinging doors of the Grille's kitchen, waiting for Marc Reardon to make his appearance. But their attention was refocused when Pauline Whitten burst into the restaurant.

"I've got it!" she cried, waving a scrap of paper. Her fire-engine red manicure added much-needed color to the wood-toned decor, and her long, pudgy legs moved with surprising speed, carrying her over to the quilting ladies. "I figured it out!"

"Hush up, Pauline," Helen ordered from her position slumped in one of the booths. She jabbed the cane at her friend. "I'm having a heart attack."

"We're waiting for Dr. Reardon to get here and save her," explained Martha.

"What?" Pauline said, looking down at Helen. "You don't look like you're having—"

"Of course I'm not. My blasted ticker's stronger'n a mule. But that quack's going to be here any minute now. Something's up with Diana, and Bee, and—"

"Yes, I know that. I've got it all figured out. I don't have a 1500 Scrabble ranking for nothing," she boasted. "If I'd seen Bee's notes before, I would have known immediately, *weeks ago*. It's an anagram! Marc Reardon is *Cameron Darr*. And Cameron Darr is—"

"*I* know who Cameron Darr—*ohhhhh!*" Helen moaned suddenly and gestured toward the restaurant door as she slumped back dramatically. "Arrghhhh ...."

Dr. Reardon rushed in, looking, Ethan thought, much more formal and official than he had the last time he saw him. He ground his teeth, hoping to bloody hell that Helen was right about all of this. As soon as he had the chance, he was going to be putting his hands around Marc Reardon's neck and squeezing a lot of red into the bastard's face—whether Joe allowed it or not.

Helen gave another groan that sounded obviously fake to Ethan, but Reardon didn't seem to notice or care. He bustled over to the elderly lady, medical bag in hand, and pushed everyone out of the way.

"Please, move away. She needs air," he ordered, leaning forward as he put his stethoscope around his neck. "This is terrible, Mrs. Galliday."

Ethan bunched up his muscles, ready to launch from behind the swinging doors of the kitchen, but Joe's fingers around his arm held him back. "Wait," he hissed.

"Yes it is terrible, Dr. Reardon," shrieked Helen, popping into an upright position with the alacrity of a kid on Christmas morning. "Or should I say...*Cameron Darr!*" she added dramatically, her cane swinging into view.

As Ethan and Joe watched in horrified amusement, she whipped it up and thwacked Reardon soundly on the back, then with surprising speed, she came back around and whacked him again on top of his head. "Who is wanted for" —*thwack!*— "murder in Oregon. And" —*smack!*— "breaking into Belinda's house and *murdering* my *friend!*" This last was punctuated by the sharpest, hardest, blow yet, and even Ethan winced.

Reardon was on the floor by now, having been driven there by Helen Galliday and her lethal cane. He held up his arms to cover his head and face, taking the brunt of her violence in the shoulders and hands, all the while shouting, "Call her off! Get this old bat off me! She's insane! Where's the damned police?"

"And there's our cue," said Joe, stepping out of the kitchen a half-step behind Ethan.

"Hurry up, you fools!" Helen shouted, thwacking and smacking with hair-raising enthusiasm. "I can't hold him off much longer."

"All right, now, Mrs. Galliday," Joe said, gently pushing her aside. "You'd better step away for a minute here, or we might have another problem on our hands."

"You insane *bitch*," Reardon was saying as he wiped a trickle of blood away from his mouth and struggled to his feet. "What the hell are you doing, standing there, Tettmueller? Arrest this termagant. She *attacked* me!"

Helen copped her soft old-lady face and said querulously, "I'm so sorry, Captain Tettmueller, but I must have tripped. These old eyes don't see too good anymore. Hope I didn't hurt the fella with my cane."

"It was terrible," Rose Bettinger said earnestly, "how she just tripped and fell right on top of him. What a horrible accident!"

"And then they got all tangled up with her cane," added Pauline Whitten with genteel malice. "Poor Dr. Reardon. Or should I say, Dr. Darr?"

"I don't know what you're talking about," Reardon said, brushing off his clothing. Blood streamed from his nose. "And I didn't murder anyone."

"Where's Diana?" Ethan said, grabbing the physician by his collar. "I don't know what was going on at her house today, when I saw you—"

"I thought it was rather obvious," he replied with a smirk. "I had my hands fu—"

Ethan didn't remember exactly what happened—it was a blur—but the next thing he knew, Tommy and Joe were pulling him off a much bloodier Marc Reardon, who, true to form, was cowering in a corner, gasping for breath.

"That's enough there, cowboy," Tommy said, holding onto Ethan.

Ethan's hand throbbed and he suspected he might have broken something, but that didn't deter him from wanting to take another shot. Or two.

Joe Cap stepped forward, pocketing a small device he'd been perusing—presumably to get the details on the warrant for Cameron Darr. "Marc Reardon, also known as Cameron Darr, you are under arrest for the murder of Marjorie Gaunt, Belinda Lawry, for vandalism, breaking and entering, assault and—"

"It wasn't me! I didn't touch Belinda Lawry," Reardon said, stepping back. "You can't pin that one on me—I have an alibi that night."

"Then who did it?" Ethan said from between clenched teeth. He grabbed Reardon's shirt, himself suddenly, amazingly free from Tommy's grip.

"Wertinger. It was Wertinger. And he's up at the house with her right now—ready to send it up in smoke as soon as it gets dark. You might be too late."

FIFTEEN

FOR THE SECOND TIME that day, Ethan drove pell-mell along Belinda's driveway. This time, however, he was speeding *toward* the house, not away from it. And this time, Cady's head was hanging out the window in delight. *God, please let me get there in time.*

It was too dark to see much and Ethan prayed he wouldn't hit a deer as he roared along the narrow, gravel drive. But as he drew closer, he smelled smoke. His heart began to race, adrenaline spiking through his body.

Before he even reached the clearing, he saw the orange blaze in the windows that would have been Belinda's den. Diana's Lexus stood in the drive and Ethan felt his heart leaping into his throat. *Jesus, God, Diana.*

He tore out of the truck, leaving the keys in the ignition, and ran toward the house, calling—screaming—her name. Cady was on his tail, barking frantically in her high-pitched tone of alarm.

He dashed around to the bedroom window and tried to peer in, but he couldn't see anything. The window was too high for him to reach from the ground. At least there were no flames inside that room yet. Cady was still charging in circles around and around the burning home, running toward the woods and back again, barking non-stop.

Ethan tore around to the back entrance, where the fire seemed to be less furious. He turned on the water and ripped off his t-shirt, then held it under the hose until it was soaking. Cady ran up to him, barking and whining with the same desperation he felt, but he ordered her away. He had to go in.

Wrapping the dripping shirt around his head, with the sleeves dangling to be held over his nose, he smashed the hose into one of the windows of the kitchen. The glass shattered and heavy black smoke billowed out, catching him in the face. He stumbled backward in surprise, but forced himself back to the window. He was able to reach in and unlock the deadbolt, pulling the door open.

Again, black smoke burst through the new opening, and he coughed, paralyzed by its venom. He pulled the wet t-shirt over his mouth and nose, and bending low, staggered into the house. *Diana.*

It was a nightmare inside. A blanket of hot, heavy smoke darkened the room, enveloping him instantly. Though he could see no flames, Ethan felt the heat searing into his bare skin. Keeping the wet shirt over his nose and mouth, he strained to see, to hear, something. Anything.

He couldn't call out, for the smoke was too heavy, and it smothered any sound but the insistent blaze. Ethan took two steps and realized he couldn't go further—it was dark, and close, and incredibly hot.

With a sob of frustration, he turned and panicked when he couldn't see the doorway. He could see nothing but dark and orange-red shadows. Then, suddenly, to his right he could see the faintest outline of...something *glowing*.

Not orange-hot, or red with flame, but a soft greenish-white glow. Bobbing in the air.

All at once a chill rushed over him and he felt a great force of wind. The hair rose all over his body and suddenly, Ethan didn't feel the heat, or the smothering heavy smoke. *Belinda.*

It was Belinda.

He edged toward the greenish-white blob and it moved away, and he stepped closer, realizing he was to follow. He was otherwise blind in the darkness, desperate, and still breathing the ash-laden air. He took careful steps, following the cool light, and the next thing he knew, he was stumbling out of the house.

Alone.

He drew great, gulping breaths of fresh night air. His lungs seared when he drew in, and his skin was dripping sweat, but he had no time to regain composure. Diana was still in there. Cady was there, too, barking and whining and nudging him roughly.

Why had Belinda led him out? He needed to find Diana! Frustration and fear drove Ethan back around to the bedroom window. As he stood outside, pounding on the window looking for something to break the glass with, he heard the sound of sirens.

"Hurry!" he cried, his voice raw and desperate, ignoring Cady's increasingly frantic sounds. Finally finding a rock big enough to break the window, he heaved it through, hoping that it would awaken Diana.

The sirens were closer, and he could feel the ground trembling from the weight of the trucks. Ethan was frantically removing splinters of glass from the window when two trucks burst into the clearing, lights and sirens flashing.

Running toward the vehicles, as if doing so would get them out of them faster, he shouted hoarsely, "She's still in there! She's sleeping in there!" A fit of coughing overtook him and he felt as if he were going to hack up a lung.

Then he could do nothing else as the firemen suited up in their heavy gear. Cady still bounded around to and from the woods, barking like a maniac, bumping into him, even jumping up on him. What the hell? Was there a deer or something in—

Oh, Christ.

"Cady!" Ethan shouted, calling the lab back after she'd dashed into the thick darkness. His voice was raw, but his dog heard and streaked from the woods back into the yard. "Let's go," he said, gesturing to the woods.

Just as he started into the darkness, another set of headlights roared up the drive and he recognized them as Joe Cap's F10. Ethan hesitated. Then, prudence being the better part of valor, he ran over to his friend, still coughing from the exertion.

"He's in the woods. Follow Cady," he said, grabbing Joe by the arm.

Overjoyed that her master had finally gotten a clue, Cady tore into the darkness leaving Ethan and Joe, along with one of his cops, to follow on their less agile bipedal legs. As they made their way deeper into the woods, Ethan heard a stifled scream.

Diana!

"Get'em, Cady!" he shouted hoarsely. "Get'em!"

There were sounds of crashing in the brush and excited, ferocious barking, and then suddenly a gunshot. Ethan's heart stopped even as he propelled himself through the darkness, praying, praying it wasn't either of the ladies he loved.

The insane barking kept on, giving Ethan both hope and trepidation, and at last he burst into a small clearing. The full moon and array of stars lit the area nearly as clear as day. There was an old structure about the size of a single-car garage that even in the moonlight appeared ramshackle, and from what he could see, Jonathan Wertinger's shiny black BMW had been parked inside.

And standing next to it, backed up against the sagging wall, was Jonathan Wertinger, treed by the ferocious Cady. The lab snarled and growled at him, and Wertinger wasn't going anywhere.

Ethan saw all that in an instant, and a moment later saw a figure on the ground nearby. "Diana!" he cried, rushing toward her, confident that Cady had things well in hand. His heart was choking him so that he could hardly speak, and when he knelt next to her and she reached for him he nearly burst into tears.

"Ethan," she murmured. "Thank God you're here. I'm so sorry. I'm so, so sorry. It wasn't what you thought. I wasn't—"

"Christ, Diana, did you really think—of course I know you weren't—" His voice gave out and he gathered her up close to him, heedless of the soot and ash that smeared all over her. "I was so stupid—I knew you better than that. I don't know how I couldn't have known something was wrong. Are you all right? Are you hurt? I heard a shot."

"I'm fine, I'm fine Ethan. He missed. He tried to shoot *Cady* and he missed, thank God." She clung tighter to him. "He was going to shoot you," she said, her face in his chest. "He was going to shoot you if I didn't—I didn't want anything to happen to you. I love you. I love you."

He held her close, dimly noticing the activity going on around them: Joe had extricated Wertinger from Cady, and now that her work was done, the lab galloped over to join him and Diana. To his surprise and delight, she opened her arms for the dog, hugging him and burying her face in the soft black fur. And when Cady began to wash the salty tears away from both of their faces, Diana merely laughed and allowed it.

And then all at once Ethan heard a rustling in the bushes and Helen Galliday erupted into the clearing, her cronies trailing behind. She made a bee-line for Wertinger, who stood handcuffed next to Joe.

"You! You fiend!" Helen screeched. Before Joe Cap could stop her, she thwacked the prisoner across the calves with her cane as hard as she could, then slumped to one side, leaning on it as though she would collapse at any moment.

Martha Woden followed her, peering around from behind coke-bottle glasses, flanked by Rose and Pauline and trailed by two paramedics. "And him!" She peered up into Wertinger's face. "You beast!"

"Now, ladies, you can back off now," Joe was saying. "We're taking him into town. Ethan, what the hell were you doing, going into a burning building?"

This drew everyone's attention to him and Diana. He'd helped her to her feet and now stood, holding her against him just to feel the warmth of her body and smell her hair.

"You went into a burning building? Are you *insane?*" Diana demanded, pulling away to look up at him.

"I did, and if it weren't for Belinda, I'd have been stuck in there," he said, looking around at the elderly lady's friends.

"What?" Diana was looking up at him, her eyes gleaming in the moonlight. "Aunt Belinda helped you too?"

He explained about the glowing greenish light, then said, "Too?"

Diana nodded. "Aunt Bee was there. When Jonathan tried to put me in the bedroom—he was going to make it look like I died in my sleep during the fire—he couldn't even go into the room. It was frigidly cold, and there was this horrible, blasting rush of wind. That's what I felt, but I think he sensed something even worse, because he ended up taking me out of the house before he set the fire. I guess he thought he'd find another way to— uh—" Her voice cracked. "Anyway, I guess Aunt Bee wasn't going to let him commit another murder in that same room. Thank goodness."

"Let me look at you," Pauline Whitten demanded, suddenly pulling them apart. "What's wrong with your hand, Ethan?"

Ethan looked down and noticed that he was cradling his hand to his chest, and that his fingers were bent awkwardly. He grinned. "You ought to see the other guy."

"All right, all right, save the sappy stuff for later." Helen pushed her way into the crowd, implementing her cane with less violence than usual. "You're bleedin' all over creation, here, and I forgot to go to the powder room before we left the Grille, so let's get out of these woods and get back to civilization."

Despite the fact that Ethan wanted more than anything to gather up Diana and take her away somewhere safe, he stopped right there, realizing what Helen had done for them this day. No one was more surprised than Helen when he pulled the old bat into his arms and bestowed the biggest, wettest kiss on her cheek that he could give. "You old crone, you saved the day with your plan, and that cane of yours!"

For the first time in her life, Helen Galliday seemed to be at a loss for words: she actually stood there for a moment looking as if she were about to cry. Then, shaking off the surprise, she pulled away from him. "Off with you, now, you old boy! You got yourself a woman there—don't you be comin' 'round me and makin' her all jealous!"

He smiled and said, "But you and Cady will always be my favorites."

EPILOGUE

Three days later

DIANA BROUGHT THE TAROT cards with her to the ruins of Aunt Belinda's house, walking over from Ethan's cabin on a bright morning. She'd left him sleeping, for he'd inhaled too much smoke, and had had surgery to set his hand. He was recovering well, but she wanted to do this alone.

She came through the woods along the trail Ethan often walked and into the clearing to see the half-blackened white clapboard still looming in its place. It was no longer smoldering, but smoke was still heavy on the air. The den windows were empty and black, and there were other places where shattered glass glittered sunlight off its shards, but other than that, the home appeared as it always had.

She was taking her time. She was on-edge, eager, sensitized, *ready* for this...but she took her time walking across the sunny yard, holding the mahogany box.

Oh, Aunt Bee! She sighed sadly, internally, as she stepped up onto the porch and opened the door. *Perhaps now you can rest easy, and, perhaps, I, too can as well.*

Inside, the shell of the house allowed the lake's breeze to whistle through and caress the corners of each room with a freedom open windows had never allowed. Diana felt like she was standing in the ruin of an old castle, on a high cliff overlooking the sea, ceiling open to the blue sky. Smoke still permeated the rooms, and a dusting of gray ash covered everything.

If it hadn't been for Aunt Bee, she would have been nothing more than a bit of gray ash herself. A little pleasant shiver filtered over her shoulders, just like it had the day she'd sensed her aunt's presence in the kitchen. *Thank you for everything, Aunt Bee.*

Diana would never forget that moment of terror as Jonathan used his gun to force her toward the bedroom. He'd already created a massive pile of papers in the den and pulled the curtains down, making the old fabric an easy trail for the flames to follow into other areas of the house. He didn't use an obvious accelerant, for fear arson would be suspected.

She hadn't cared as he explained all of this to her—she was trying to find a way to get free. Losing hope, she'd tried to think of some way to distract him so she could dodge past him and run out of the house. The cats had disappeared after lurking about and protecting her for so long—perhaps it was self-preservation because they sensed the impending fire—and now it was just Diana and Jonathan.

But as they came to the bedroom where Jonathan had killed Aunt Belinda, his steps became slower and he hesitated. When he tried to force her through the entrance into the room, a cold gust of wind blasted from inside, ruffling her hair. She smelled the old comfortable scent of her aunt, and closed her eyes, silently pleading for help.

Jonathan's face had turned stark with terror, and he seemed hypnotized by some vision in the room beyond. Diana couldn't see anything except for a foggy mist in there, but she didn't care. It was her chance to escape. She turned, shoving past Jonathan and tore down the hall, racing for the front door on wobbly legs.

But no sooner had she reached it, fumbling with the knob to yank it open to freedom, than Jonathan slammed his full body into her. She hit her head against the wall, then her temple hit the knob as she fell to the floor. After that, he changed his plans and kept her with him under gunpoint. He even made her drop the lighted match onto the pile of papers in the den, then made her stand and watch at the edge of the clearing as the house went up in flames.

It was only when the beam of headlights cut the darkness that Jonathan jammed the gun more harshly into her side and forced her into the deep woods where his car was hidden. She'd become a hostage instead of a sacrifice.

But when Cady appeared in the night like a feral black streak, Diana had never been so glad to see the ferocious animal. Jonathan had clocked her on the side of the head with the gun as he swung wildly at the dog, knocking Diana to the ground where Ethan found her.

She would never forget how her life had been saved by two cats, a black lab, and a ghost.

Now, she sat on the floor in the middle of the ruined den. Most of the hardwood strips had been pulled up, and little of the rubble had been cleared away. Diana wore denim shorts and a t-shirt, with bare legs and sandals, but the ruined room called to her to sit there.

As she settled on the floor, she smiled wryly, thinking that only two months ago she'd scoffed at the thought of psychics and Tarot cards. And now, here she was, opening her mind as the High Priestess had insisted she do.

With a calm breath and trembling fingers, she removed the lid of the mahogany box and pulled away the black silk.

That was how Ethan found her: sitting in the midst of a fire-blackened room, under the late August sun, Tarot cards clutched in her hands. Her thick hair tousled around her face like it did after he made love to her, sleek and curvy like the rest of her body.

Jesus.

The sight of her hit him like the figurative lightning bolt, freezing him there for a moment just so he could look at her upturned face, eyes lidded against the sun, long slim fingers holding the cards. He couldn't breathe. The sight of such beauty and serenity made his throat hurt and his heart bang insistently against his ribcage, as though it was trying to tell him something.

She hadn't heard him, for she was engrossed in her thoughts, and he waited, unwilling to bring her back too abruptly from wherever she was. He could look at her forever.

Just then, Diana opened her eyes and looked directly at him.

He felt like he would drown in that blue gaze, felt the heat as it radiated from her shiny dark hair. "Diana...how are you feeling?"

"I feel wonderful, Ethan. Absolutely wonderful. At peace with myself." Her words were cloaked with peace and he felt his heart swell. "I didn't want to wake you," she said with a smile. "You were finally sleeping without that awful ragged breathing. But I'm glad you're here."

How could he ever have thought he loved Jenny? Nothing was as strong as the love he felt for Diana right now—and yesterday, and even weeks ago when he'd first kissed her...and the way he would feel tomorrow, next year, and at the end of his life.

"You look so beautiful sitting here. I was almost afraid to interrupt."

She smiled and reached up touch his hand, his love for her echoing back in the touch of her fingertips. "Ethan. I am so lucky to have found you." She gave a short, bitter laugh. "I used to think I was lucky to have found Jonathan. What a fool I was."

Then the sharpness was gone again as though she couldn't bear to ruin the moment, and her fingers stroked his jaw. "I would be a fool to walk away from this. From you. Can I stay in your place while Aunt Bee's house is rebuilt?" she asked with an impish grin.

"Diana, love, you can stay *forever*." His voice dropped. "Will you stay forever?"

She nodded, looking up at him with dancing eyes, and he pulled her to her feet for the softest, tenderest, most important kiss of his life. When they moved away to look at each other again, he saw that she was clutching a Tarot card.

"What's this?" he asked, teasing in his voice. "Are you reading cards now?"

She offered it to him, and he looked down to see the figure of a man sitting on an ornate throne, holding a wand as a staff.

"It's my future," she said. "It was the third card I drew for myself in a past, present, future spread—a few weeks ago. I didn't realize it at the time, but it's you."

King of Wands.

He looked at her, his heart swelling, and reached for the cards. "Draw one for me."

Holding his gaze, she cut the deck, once, twice, thrice. Then, without looking, she chose a card and pulled it up so he could see it.

Ace of Cups.

His cup runneth over.

More romantic suspense with a twist of the supernatural…

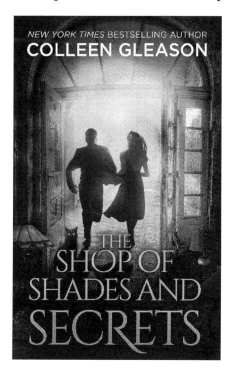

The Shop of Shades and Secrets
featuring Ethan's sister Fiona Murphy

When Fiona Murphy inherits a small antiques shop from an old man she met only once, she's filled with surprise, confusion and delight—and a little bit of terror at having a new responsibility in a life she prefers to be free and easy.

As she takes over ownership of the quaint shop, odd things begin to happen. Lights come on and off by themselves, even when they are unplugged…and there is a chilly breeze accompanied by the scent of roses even when the windows are closed.

H. Gideon Nath, III, is the stiff and oh-so-proper attorney who helps settle Fiona's inheritance, and despite her flightiness and fascination with all things New Age, he finds himself attracted to her against his better judgment.

After she finds an unpleasant surprise in one of the shop's closets, scares off an intruder in the store, and uses her skill at palmistry to read Gideon's future--of which she seems to be a part--Fiona begins to realize that her free and easy life is about to change...whether she wants it to or not.

Coming in 2016:

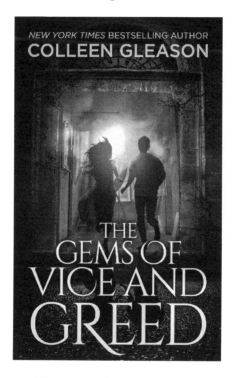

The Gems of Vice and Greed
featuring Leslie van Dorn from
The Shop of Shades and Secrets

Colleen Gleason is an award-winning, *New York Times* and *USA Today* bestselling author who's written more than two dozen novels. Her books have been translated into more than seven languages, and she writes in a variety of genres, including steampunk, paranormal romance, and action adventure.

She loves to hear from readers, and can be found on the web at:
http://www.colleengleason.com
http://www.facebook.com/colleen.gleason.author

Sign up for her newsletter for updates, information, and contests!
http://cgbks.com/news

Made in the USA
Charleston, SC
29 March 2016